Praise for *Thursday's Children*

"You'll ache for Frieda as she tears open old wounds and cheer when she finally shows signs of healing from her lacerations."

—*Kirkus Reviews* (starred review)

"This visceral read tackles a sensitive subject with empathy, anger, and grace. A skillfully woven plot and deftly drawn characters complement the central mystery, which engages and satisfies while developing the series arc." —*Publishers Weekly* (starred review)

"Complex psychological suspense at its best." —*Booklist* (starred review)

"Fierce, fascinating, and full of insight, Frieda Klein is irresistible."

—Val McDermid, bestselling author of *Splinter the Silence*

Praise for *Waiting for Wednesday*

"There's enough backstory for this third Frieda Klein mystery to stand alone, but the greatest pleasure is in following the series from the beginning to see the evolution of Klein, a detective of the mind, who endures a rough patch here but makes it through the darkness. Another compelling entry in this complex, suspenseful series." —*Booklist* (starred review)

"Demanding the reader's full attention, this richly detailed and intricate thriller weaves the story of Frieda's life, past and present, into a compelling and suspenseful story. Fans of Elizabeth George will appreciate French's attention to subtlety and detail." —*Library Journal* (starred review)

"Not only is the plot of this story intricately woven by this husband and wife team of writers, but the ending is one that will leave you gasping for breath!" —*Suspense Magazine*

Praise for *Tuesday's Gone*

"A fiercely intelligent, multilayered thriller." —*Kirkus Reviews*

"Seamlessly mixes a foreboding tone and deliberate pacing with deft plot twists that should leave readers pleasantly chilled to the bone."
—*Publishers Weekly*

"Starts as a grim psychological thriller in the vein of Dennis Lehane's darker novels and turns into a fascinating puzzle in which character analysis holds sway. Highly recommended for fans of psychological suspense who enjoy a complex protagonist." —*Library Journal* (starred review)

"The plotting is fast-paced with surprises galore, and characters literally come to life on the pages. . . . When readers are through, they will find themselves waiting impatiently for *Wednesday* to arrive!"
—*Suspense Magazine*

"If you are looking for wickedly inventive crime fiction, you need look no further than the writing team of Nicci Gerrard and Sean French. . . . Unless you are into tension, paranoia, and burning the midnight oil to finish a book, don't embark on reading *Tuesday's Gone* after suppertime!"
—*BookPage*

"*Tuesday's Gone* is one of those great, great books in the mystery genre wherein the more you know, the less you know—peel back one stratum and you cannot shovel fast enough to get into the next, which reveals anything but what you expected. French takes the novel on a number of unexpected twists and turns, not the least of which relates back to *Blue Monday*, which, as it turns out, didn't quite end on its last page." —Bookreporter.com

Praise for *Blue Monday*

"Fast-paced and spooky . . . it leaves readers with the promise of intriguing tales to come."
—*People* (starred review)

"A neat puzzle with a satisfying resolution and a terrific twist at the end."
—*The New York Times Book Review*

"[A] superb psychological thriller . . . With its brooding atmosphere, sustained suspense, last-minute plot twist, and memorable cast of characters, this series debut will leave readers eager to discover what color *Tuesday* will be."
—*Publishers Weekly* (starred review)

"With its smart plot, crisp prose, and a stunning final twist, this is psychological suspense at its best. Absolutely riveting."
—*Booklist* (starred review)

"This is psychological suspense done right. The authors pace themselves and build the tension slowly while carefully developing each of the players. For fans of Tana French's and Lisa Gardner's moody, dark, twisty thrillers."
—*Library Journal*

"Complex and flawed, Frieda Klein is a refreshingly human protagonist, an intriguing debut for a truly unique character."
—Tami Hoag, bestselling author of *Down the Darkest Road*

"A searing psychological thriller in the rich vein of Kate Atkinson and Laura Lippman, *Blue Monday* is powerful and gripping—a page-turner with heart and soul. Psychotherapist Frieda Klein is an enormously appealing new series hero."
—Joseph Finder, bestselling author of *Buried Secrets*

"Unrelenting . . . Unnerving . . . Unforgettable. Psychological dynamite."
—Alan Bradley, bestselling author of *The Sweetness at the Bottom of the Pie*

PENGUIN BOOKS

FRIDAY ON MY MIND

Nicci French is the pseudonym of the internationally bestselling writing partnership of suspense writers Nicci Gerrard and Sean French. They are married and live in Suffolk and London, England.

ALSO BY NICCI FRENCH

Friday
on My Mind

A FRIEDA KLEIN MYSTERY

NICCI FRENCH

PENGUIN BOOKS

PENGUIN BOOKS

An imprint of Penguin Random House LLC
375 Hudson Street
New York, New York 10014
penguin.com

A Pamela Dorman/Penguin Book

First published in Great Britain by Michael Joseph, an imprint of Penguin Books Ltd, 2015
First published in Penguin Books (USA) 2016

Map of Earl's Sluice by Maps Illustrated

LIBRARY OF CONGRESS CATALOGING-IN-PUBLICATION DATA
Names: French, Nicci, author.
Title: Friday on my mind : a Frieda Klein mystery / Nicci French.
Description: New York : Penguin Books, 2016. | Series: A Frieda Klein mystery ; 5
Identifiers: LCCN 2016013489 (print) | LCCN 2016019733 (ebook) |
ISBN 9780143127222 (softcover) | ISBN 9780698184756 (ebook)
Subjects: LCSH: Women psychotherapists—Fiction. | Murder—Investigation—Fiction. |
London (England)—Fiction. | BISAC: FICTION / Mystery & Detective / General. | FICTION /
Mystery & Detective / Police Procedural. | GSAFD: Suspense fiction. | Mystery fiction.
Classification: LCC PR6056.R456 F75 2016 (print) | LCC PR6056.R456
(ebook) | DDC 823/.914—dc23

Printed in the United States of America
1   3   5   7   9   10   8   6   4   2

Set in Granjon
Designed by Alice Sorensen

To Kersti and Philip

Friday
on My Mind

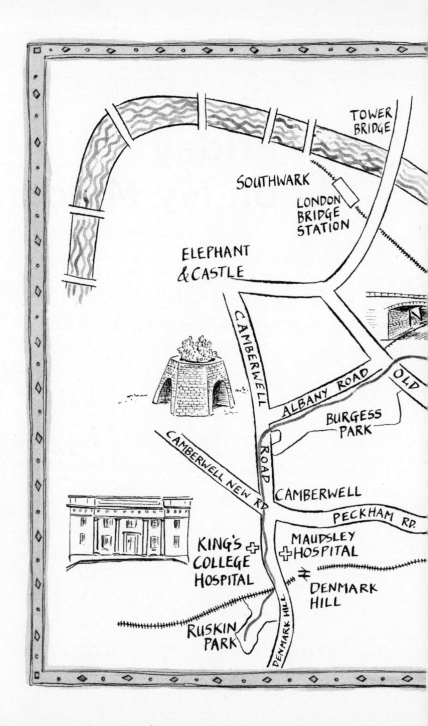

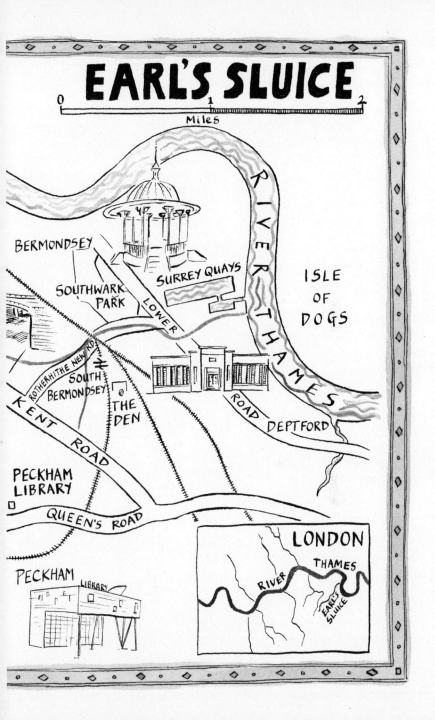

Kitty was five years old and she was cross. The queue for the Crown Jewels had been long and they weren't so special anyway. The queue for Madame Tussauds had been longer, and she didn't even recognize most of the waxworks, and she couldn't see them properly with all the crowds. And it had been drizzling. And she hated the Underground. When she stood on the platform and heard the rumble of an approaching train, it felt like something terrible coming out of the darkness.

But when they got on the boat she became a little less cross. The river was so big that it felt almost like the ocean, heaving with the currents and the tide. A plastic bottle floated past.

"Where's it going?" said Kitty.

"To the sea," said her mum. "All the way to the sea."

"The Thames Barrier will stop it," said her dad.

"No, it won't," said her mum. "It's not a real barrier."

As the boat pulled away from the Embankment, Kitty ran from one side of the boat to the other. If she was seeing something interesting on one bank of the river, that meant she was missing what was interesting on the other or in front.

"Calm down, Kitty," said her mum. "Why don't you write a list in your book of everything you see?"

So Kitty got out her new notebook, the one with the elephant on the cover. And her new pen. She opened the notebook at a fresh page and wrote a number one and drew a heart-shaped circle around it. She looked about her. "What's that big thing?"

"Which big thing?"

"That one."

"The Eye."

So that was number one.

The boat was almost empty. It was a Friday and it had only just stopped raining. Kitty's parents drank coffee and Kitty, whose school was closed for a training day and who had been looking forward to this trip for weeks, frowned over her notebook while a voice on the loudspeaker said that the River Thames was a pageant of history. It was from here, said the voice, that Francis Drake had set off to circle the globe. And it was here that he returned with a ship full of treasure and became Sir Francis Drake.

Kitty was so busy that she was almost irritated when her dad sat down beside her.

"We've stopped," he said, "so we can look at the Thames and at London Bridge."

"I know," said Kitty.

"Do you know 'London Bridge Is Falling Down'?"

"We done that at school."

"*Did* it."

Kitty ignored this and carried on writing.

"So what have you seen?"

Kitty finished the word she was writing, the tip of her tongue protruding from the side of her mouth. Then she held up the notebook. "Five things," she said.

"What five things?"

"A bird."

Her dad laughed. She frowned at him. "What?"

"No, that's very good. A bird. What else?"

"A boat."

"What? This boat?"

"No." She rolled her eyes. "Another boat."

"Good."

"A tree."

"Where?"

"It's gone." She looked back at her notebook. "A car."

"Yes, there are lots of cars driving along by the river. That's very good, Kitty. Is that all?"

"And a whale."

Her dad looked at the notebook. "'Whale' has an *h* in it. W-H-A-L-E. But this is a river. It doesn't have whales in it."

"I saw it."

"When?"

"Now."

"Where?"

Kitty pointed. Her dad stood up and walked to the side of the boat. And then the day that was already exciting got more and more exciting. Her dad shouted something and then he turned to Kitty and shouted even louder. He told her to stay exactly where she was and not to move a single step. Then he ran along the deck and down the steps, and the man who was talking on the loudspeaker stopped and then said things in a loud voice that sounded completely different. Other people started running around on the deck and looking over the side and shouting and a fat woman began to cry.

The loudspeaker said that people should move away from the side but they didn't. Kitty's mum came and sat next to her and talked to her about what they were going to do afterward and about the summer holidays, which weren't long off now; they were going camping. Then Kitty heard the loud noise of an engine and she got up and saw a huge motorboat heading along the river and getting closer and closer until it stopped and she felt the waves from it move their own boat up and down so that she almost fell over. Kitty's mum got up and stood with everyone else at the railings. Kitty could see only their backs and the backs of their heads. It was like being at Madame Tussauds, where her dad had had to put her up on his shoulders.

This time she could go to the edge of the group and look through the railings. She could read the writing on the side of the boat: "Police." That would be number six on her list. Two men were climbing down on a little ledge at the back of the boat. One of them had big yellow clothes on and gloves that looked like they were made out of rubber and he actually got into the water. Then men used ropes and they started to pull the thing out of the water. There were groaning sounds from the people on the boat and some of them moved away from the railings and Kitty got an even better view. Other people were holding their phones up. The thing looked strange, all blown up and blotchy and milky-colored, but she knew what it was. The men wrapped it in a big black bag and zipped it up.

The two boats moved together and one of the men climbed from the other boat onto the lower deck of this boat. The other man, the one in the big yellow clothes, stayed on the other boat. He was fixing a rope and tying a knot. When he had finished he stood up, and he looked at Kitty at exactly the same moment that she was waving at him. He smiled and gave a wave and she waved back.

Nothing was happening now, so she went and sat down again. She wrote a number six and circled it and wrote "Police." Then she looked at number five. Carefully, letter by letter, she crossed out "Whale" until it was entirely obliterated. With great concentration she wrote: "M-A-N."

2

Detective Chief Inspector Sarah Hussein and Detective Constable Glen Bryant climbed out of the car. Hussein fished her mobile from her pocket, and Bryant took a packet of cigarettes and a pink plastic lighter from his. He was tall and burly with cropped hair, big hands and feet and broad shoulders, like a rugby player; he was sweating. Beside him, Hussein looked small, cool, compact.

"Something's come up and I'll be back late," said Hussein into the phone. "I know. I'm sorry. You can give the girls pasta. Or there are pizzas in the freezer. I don't know what time I'll be home. They shouldn't wait up. Nor should you. Nick, I've got to go. Sorry."

A man was approaching them. His face was flushed and his hair was rough and untidy. He seemed more like a trawlerman than a policeman.

"Hello." He held out a hand to Bryant, who looked sheepish but took it. "I'm Detective Constable O'Neill. Marine Policing Unit. You must be DCI Hussein."

"Actually . . ." began Bryant.

"This is Detective Constable Bryant," said Hussein coolly. "I'm DCI Hussein."

"Oh. Sorry. I thought—"

"Don't worry, I'm used to it."

Hussein looked along the river to her right at Tower Bridge and to her left at Canary Wharf and across at the smart new riverside flats of Rotherhithe. "Nice position."

"You should see it in November," O'Neill said.

"I'm surprised it hasn't been sold off for flats. Riverfront property like this."

"We'd still need somewhere to put our boats."

DC O'Neill gestured at what looked like a large square tent made out of blue plastic sheets. Hussein pulled a face. "Really?"

"It's where we put them for a quick check. So we can decide whether to call you guys." O'Neill pulled the sheet aside and showed her through. Inside the sheets, two figures in plastic caps and shoes and white gowns were moving softly around the body. "Sometimes we're not sure. But this one has had his throat cut."

Bryant took a deep, audible breath and O'Neill looked round with a smile. "You think this is bad? You should see them when they've been in the water for a month or two. Sometimes you can't tell what sex they are. Even with their clothes off."

The body was lying in a large shallow metal basin. It looked swollen, as if it had been inflated with a pump. The flesh was unnaturally pale but also blotchy, marbled and bruised on the face and hands. It was still dressed in a dark shirt, gray trousers, robust leather shoes—almost more boots than shoes. Hussein noticed the laces were still double-knotted, and she couldn't help thinking of him stooping and tying them, pulling them tight.

She made herself examine the face. There were remnants of the nose, little more than exposed cartilage. All the features seemed blurred, corroded, but the slashed neck was plain to see. "It looks violent," she said finally.

Bryant made a small noise of assent beside her. He had his handkerchief out and was pretending to blow his nose.

"It doesn't mean anything," said O'Neill. "Apart from the throat. The river really knocks them about, the birds get at them. And then in summer things happen more quickly."

"Where was he found?"

"Up near HMS *Belfast*, by London Bridge. But that doesn't mean anything either. He could have gone into the river anywhere from Richmond to Woolwich."

"Any idea how long he's been in the water?"

O'Neill cocked his head to one side as if he were doing some mental arithmetic. "He was floating. So we're looking at a week. No more than ten days, the way he is."

"That's not much help."

"It's a good way of getting rid of a body," said O'Neill. "Much better than burying it."

"Was there anything in his pockets?"

"No wallet, no phone, no keys, not even a handkerchief. No watch."

"So you've got nothing?"

"You mean *you*'ve got nothing. He's your baby now. But, yeah, there is something. Look at his wrist."

Hussein pulled on her plastic gloves and bent across the corpse. There was a faint sweet smell she didn't want to think about. Around the left wrist there was a plastic band. She lifted it gently. "It's the sort of thing you get in hospital."

"That's what we thought. And it looks like it's got his name on it."

She leaned right down close. The writing was faint, barely legible. She had to spell it out for herself, letter by letter. "Klein," she said. "Dr. F. Klein."

They waited for the van to arrive, gazing out over the river glinting in the late-afternoon sun. The rain had cleared and the sky was a pale blue, streaked with rose-colored clouds.

"I wish it hadn't happened on a Friday," said Bryant.

"That's the way of things."

"It's my favorite day, usually. It's like an extra bit of the weekend."

Hussein snapped her gloves off. She was thinking about the arrangements she would have to cancel, her daughters' crestfallen faces, Nick's resentment. He would try to hide it, which would make it worse. At the same time she was running through the list of tasks that lay ahead, sorting them into priorities. It was always like this at the start of a case.

"I'll go with the van to the morgue. You find out who this Dr. Klein is and what hospital that tag comes from, if it is a hospital. You've got a photo of it."

Bryant lifted up his phone.

According to the plastic bracelet, Dr. Klein's date of birth was November 18 but they couldn't make out the year. There were two letters and a series of barely legible digits underneath the name, alongside what looked like a bar code.

"Missing People," said Hussein. "Male, middle-aged, reported between five days and two weeks ago."

"I'll call you if I find anything."

"Call me anyway."

"I meant that, of course."

The plastic ID came from the King Edward Hospital, in Hampstead. Bryant called and was put through a series of departments until he ended up with an assistant in the executive medical director's office. He was told very firmly that he would have to come in person with his request before they gave out personal information about staff or patients.

So he drove there, up the hill in thick rush-hour traffic, hot and impatient. It could almost have been quicker to walk: he should buy a scooter, he thought, or a motorbike. In the medical director's office, a thin woman in a red suit carefully checked his ID and he repeated what it was he wanted, showing her the image on his phone.

"I thought it must be someone who works here."

The woman looked unimpressed. "Those wristbands are for patients, not for staff."

"Yes, of course. Sorry."

"The staff wear laminated passes."

"I'm more interested in this one."

He was asked to wait. The minute hand on the large clock on the wall jerked forward. He felt sweaty and soiled, and kept picturing the bloated, waterlogged thing that had once been a man. The woman returned, holding a printout.

"The patient was admitted here three years ago," she said. "As an emergency." She looked down at the paper. "Lacerations. Stab wounds. Nasty."

"Three years ago?" Bryant frowned and spoke almost to himself. "Why would he still be wearing his hospital ID?"

"It wasn't a he. The patient was a woman. Dr. Frieda Klein."

"Do you have an address?"

"Address, phone number."

Bryant felt a small twitch of memory. "Why does that name ring a bell?"

"I don't have a clue. Shall I call her?"

"Yes. Ask her to come to the morgue."

"To identify the body? I hope she's up for that."

Hussein stood outside the forensics suite eating a bag of crisps and watched Frieda Klein following the officer down the windowless corridor. She was probably the same age as Hussein herself, but taller, and dressed in gray linen trousers and a high-necked white T-shirt. Her nearly black hair was piled on top of her head. She walked swiftly and lightly, but Hussein noticed there was a slight drag to her gait, like that of a wounded dancer. As she got closer, she saw that the woman's face, devoid of makeup, was pale. Her eyes were very dark, and Hussein felt that she was not just being looked at but scrutinized.

"Dr. Frieda Klein."

"Yes."

As Hussein introduced herself and Bryant, she tried to assess the woman's mood. She remembered what Bryant had said after he had spoken to her: *Dr. Klein didn't seem that surprised.*

"You might find this distressing."

The woman nodded. "He had my name on his wrist?" she asked.

"Yes."

The morgue was harshly lit and silent and very cold. There was the familiar smell, rancid and antiseptic, that caught in the back of the throat.

They stopped in front of the slab. The shape was covered with a white sheet.

"Ready?"

She nodded once more. The morgue attendant stepped forward and drew back the sheet. Hussein didn't look at the body, but at Frieda Klein's face. Her expression didn't alter, not even a tightening of the jaw. She stared intently and leaned closer, unblinking. Her eyes traveled down to the gaping wound at the neck. "I don't know," she said at last. "I can't tell."

"Perhaps it would help to see the clothes that he was found in."

They were on a shelf, folded into transparent plastic bags. One by one, Hussein lifted them down for inspection. A sodden dark shirt. Gray trousers. Those heavy leather shoes, whose laces were blue and double-knotted. Hussein heard a tiny intake of breath beside her. For an instant, the expression on Frieda Klein's face had altered, like a landscape that had darkened and chilled. She curled one hand slightly, as if she were about to lift it to touch the bag that contained the shoes. She turned back toward the terrible body and stood quite upright, staring down.

"I know who this is," she said. Her voice was soft and calm. "This is Sandy. Alexander Holland. I know him by his shoes."

"You're quite sure?" asked Hussein.

"I know him by his shoes," Frieda Klein repeated.

"Dr. Klein, are you all right?"

"I am, thank you."

"Have you any idea why he was wearing your old hospital ID round his wrist?"

She looked at Hussein and then back at the corpse. "We used to be in a relationship. A long time ago."

"But not now."

"Not now."

"I see," said Hussein, neutrally. "I'm grateful to you. This can't be easy. Obviously, we'll need all the details you can give us about Mr. Holland. And your details too, so we can contact you again."

Freida Klein gave a slight tip of her head. Hussein had the impression she was making the greatest effort to keep herself under control.

"He was murdered?"

"As you see, his throat has been cut."

"Yes."

When she left, after they had taken her details, Hussein turned to Bryant. "There's something odd about her."

Bryant was hungry and he was in need of a smoke. He stood on the balls of his feet, then subsided again. "She was calm. I'll give her that."

"Her reaction when she saw the shoes—it was strange."

"In what way?"

"I don't know. We need to keep an eye on her, though."

3

When Alexander Holland's sister opened the door, Hussein noticed several things at the same time. That Elizabeth Rasson was getting ready to go out: she was wearing a lovely blue dress but no shoes and she had a flustered air, as if she'd been interrupted. That there was a child crying somewhere in the house, and a man's voice soothing it. That she was tall, dark-haired, rather striking in an angular kind of way. And that Bryant, standing just behind her, was stiffly upright, like a soldier on parade. She felt that he was holding his breath, waiting for her to say the words that would change this woman's life.

"Elizabeth Rasson?"

"What is it? It's really not a good time. We're on our way out." She glanced beyond them, down the street, letting out an exasperated sigh.

"I'm Detective Chief Inspector Sarah Hussein. This is my colleague Detective Constable Bryant." And they both held out their IDs.

Moments like this always got Hussein between the shoulder blades and in the thickening of the throat. However calm she felt and prepared she was, it never became automatic, just part of the job, to look into a person's face and tell them that someone they loved was dead. She had come here straight from this woman's brother, lying swollen and decomposing on the slab.

"Police?" the woman said. Her eyes narrowed. "What's this about?"

"You're the sister of Alexander Holland?"

"Sandy? Yes. What's happened to him?"

"Can we come in?"

"Why? Is he in trouble?"

Say it plainly, clearly, with no room left for doubt: that's what they had all been told during training, many years ago now. That was what she did, each time, looking into the person's eyes and telling them without a quaver that someone they had known, perhaps loved, had died.

"I'm very sorry to tell you that your brother is dead, Mrs. Rasson."

Suddenly Elizabeth Rasson looked bewildered. Her face screwed up in an expression that was almost comic, cartoonish.

"I'm very sorry for your loss," Hussein said gently.

"I don't understand. It's not possible."

Behind them, a young woman came running along the pavement and in through the gate to the front garden. Her ponytail was crooked and her round cheeks flushed.

"I'm sorry, Lizzie," she gasped. "The bus. Friday evening. I got here as quickly as I could."

Hussein gestured sharply at Bryant, who stepped forward and took her by the arm, steering her away from the front door.

"We were supposed to be going out," said Lizzie Rasson. Her voice was dull. "To dinner with friends."

"Can I come in for a minute?"

"Dead, you say? Sandy?"

Hussein led her into the living room.

"Will you sit down?"

But Lizzie Rasson remained standing in the middle of the room. Her attractive face had taken on a bony, vacant look. Upstairs the child's screaming got louder and higher, piercing enough to break glass; Hussein could picture the furious red face.

"How did he die? He was healthy. He went running most days."

"Your brother's body was found in the Thames earlier today."

"In the Thames? Sandy drowned? But he was a good swimmer. Why was he in the river anyway?"

Hussein paused. "His throat was cut."

Suddenly the crying stopped. The room filled with silence. Lizzie Rasson looked around her as if she were searching for something; her blank gaze drifted across furniture, books, family photographs. Then she shook her head. "No," she said assertively. "Absolutely not."

"I know this is a terrible shock, but there are questions we need to ask you."

"His throat?"

"Yes."

Lizzie Rasson sat down heavily in one of the armchairs, her long legs splayed. She looked suddenly clumsy. "How do you know it's him? It could be someone else."

"He has been identified."

"Identified by whom?"

"Dr. Frieda Klein."

Hussein was watching Lizzie Rasson's face as she spoke. She saw the involuntary flinch, the tightening of the mouth.

"Frieda. Poor Sandy," she said, but softly, as if to herself. "Poor, poor Sandy."

They heard footsteps running down the stairs and a solid, open-faced man with reddish hair came into the room.

"You'll be glad to know he's asleep at last. Was that Shona at the door?" he said, then saw Hussein, saw his wife's stricken face, stopped in his tracks.

"Sandy's dead." Saying the words seemed to make them true for the first time. Lizzie Rasson lifted a hand to her face, held it against her mouth, then her cheek. "She says his throat was cut."

"Oh, my God," said her husband. He put a hand against the wall as if to steady himself. "He was killed? Sandy?"

"That's what she says."

He crossed the room and squatted beside the chair in which she was sprawled, lifting both her slim hands in his large, broad-knuckled ones and holding them tightly. "Are they certain?"

She gave a strangled, angry sob. "Frieda identified him."

"Frieda," he said. "Jesus, Lizzie."

His arm was round her shoulders now and her blue dress was crumpled. Tears were gathering in her eyes and starting to roll down her cheeks.

"I know." She gave a gulp, swiped her wrist under her nose.

He turned to Hussein at last. "You don't need to believe everything that woman tells you," he said. His pleasant face had hardened. "Why did she identify him, anyway?"

Bryant entered the room and stood beside Hussein; by smell, she knew he had smoked a cigarette before coming back in again. He hated things like this.

"I'm sorry," said Hussein. "But there are questions we need to ask you, and the sooner we do so the better for the investigation."

She looked at the couple. It wasn't clear if they understood what was being said to them. Bryant had taken out his notebook.

"First of all, can you confirm your brother's full name, date of birth and current address—and can you tell us the last time that you saw him?"

By the time they left the Rassons' house, the sky was dark although the air was still soft and warm against their skin.

"What do we know?" asked Hussein, climbing into the car.

Bryant took a large bite from the sandwich he'd bought. Tuna mayonnaise, thought Hussein—that was what he always had, that or chicken and pesto.

"We know," she continued, not waiting for him to answer, "that Alexander Holland was forty-two years old, that he was an academic at King George's and his subject was neurology. He came back from the U.S. a couple of years ago after a brief stint there. He lived in a flat off the Caledonian Road."

She held up the key that Lizzie Rasson had given them.

"That he lives alone. That he has no regular partner, as far as his sister knows. That she last saw him eleven days ago, on Monday, June the ninth, when he seemed much as usual. That his throat was cut left to right, so it's likely we're looking for a right-hander, and he was found floating in the Thames. No indication of where the body entered the water. That he has been dead a week minimum, so that gives us a window of possibility, from June the tenth, or even late on the ninth, to Friday, June the thirteenth."

"Unlucky for some," put in Bryant.

Hussein ignored this. "That he was found on Friday, June the twentieth. That, according to his sister, he has many friends and no enemies. The last of which cannot be true."

She held out her hand and Bryant handed her his sandwich. She took a bite from it and gave it back. Her phone vibrated in her pocket but she didn't take it out: the call was probably one of her daughters and would make her feel guilty and distracted.

"Anything else?" she went on.

"They don't like Frieda Klein much."

4

"Oh, well," said Bryant.

"You sound disappointed," said Hussein.

Hussein and Bryant were standing in Sandy Holland's flat, their feet bagged, their hands gloved.

"I thought there might be blood," said Bryant. "Signs of a struggle. But there's nothing. It looks like he just left of his own accord."

Hussein shook her head. "If you kill someone in their own home, you probably leave them there. Getting the body out is just too much of a risk."

"You don't think the murderer could have killed him here and cleaned the place up?"

"It's possible," said Hussein, but she sounded doubtful. "Forensics will tell us anyway. It looks pristine to me."

The two of them walked around the flat briskly. It was on the two top floors. There was a living room with two big windows and a narrow kitchen leading off it, a small study and, upstairs, a bedroom with a roof terrace that looked out over rooftops and cranes.

There were shelves of books in every room. Bryant took out a large one, opened it and pulled a face.

"Do you think he'd read all of these? I can barely understand a single word."

Hussein was about to reply when her phone rang. She answered and Bryant watched her as her expression changed from irritation to surprise to a kind of alarm.

"Yes," she said. "Yes. I'll be there."

She rang off and stood for a moment, lost in thought. She seemed to have forgotten where she was.

"Bad news?" said Bryant.

"I don't know," said Hussein slowly. "It's about the woman who identified the body: Frieda Klein. She popped up on the system. Two weeks ago she reported someone missing."

"Alexander Holland?"

"No, a man called Miles Thornton. Sophie followed it up and the next thing she knew there was a call from the commissioner's office."

"You mean Crawford? What about?"

"About the case. About Frieda Klein. He wants to see me. Straight away."

"Are we in trouble?"

Hussein seemed puzzled. "How can we be? We haven't done anything yet."

"Do you want me to come along?"

"No, you need to stay here."

"Where do I start? What am I searching for?"

Hussein thought for a moment. "I was looking for a phone or a computer or a wallet, but I didn't find anything. Could you have another go?"

"Sure."

"And there is a pile of mail by the front door. That should tell us when he was last here. And try to talk to the tenant in the other flat, find out when they last saw him."

"All right."

"Forensics should be here soon. I know they don't like being told what to do, but there are a couple of dressing gowns on the bedroom door. And there are condoms in the bedside table. They should check the sheets."

"I'll nudge them."

DC Sophie Byrne went with Hussein in the car and guided her through some of the printouts as they drove along by St. James's Park. Hussein felt like one of those people you saw going into an exam still desperately trying to do the revision they should have done earlier. She'd never been one of those people. It made her uncomfortable. She liked being prepared.

She was expected. A uniformed officer escorted her through security and into a lift, then up to a floor that needed a card to access it. There, she was introduced to a receptionist who took her through into the commissioner's office; her first impression was of a blaze of light and that she hadn't realized how high up she was. She felt a childish urge to run to the window and enjoy the view over the park.

Looking at Crawford, she was struck by several impressions at the same time. His smiling florid face. His uniform. The size of his desk. And its emptiness, except for a single file. Didn't he have papers to sign? Or was he too important even for that?

"Detective Chief Inspector Hussein," said Crawford, as if he were savoring each word individually. "It's taken too long for us to meet."

"Well . . ." Hussein began, then couldn't think of anything to add.

"We're proud to have a senior officer from your community."

"Thank you, sir."

"Where do you come from, Sarah? Originally."

"Birmingham, sir."

There was a pause. Hussein looked out of the window. The sun was shining. She suddenly felt how nice it would be to be out there, walking in the park on a summer evening, rather than here.

"This case," said Crawford. "Alexander Holland. Tell me about it." He waved her into a chair in front of his desk.

She told him about the discovery of the body and its state, and about his flat.

"And you met Frieda Klein?"

"Briefly."

"What do you think about her?"

"She was the one who identified the body. Holland had her hospital identification tag on his wrist."

"That sounds a bit odd."

"They'd been a couple."

"I mean, I've heard of wearing someone's ring but . . ."

"I'd planned to talk to her again."

"What do you actually know about her?"

"Just what one of my DCs told me on the way over. The name rang a bell but I couldn't place it. I gather she was the therapist who was involved in getting that Faraday boy back a few years ago and with that murder down in Deptford. There was that other one. The tabloids called it 'The Croydon House of Horrors.' That was her too."

"You shouldn't believe everything you read in the papers."

"I'm just going by what was in the police files. Wasn't she involved?"

Crawford gave a sort of snort. "There's involved and involved," he said.

"I don't understand."

"You know how it is," he said. "When we get a result suddenly everybody wants to jump on the bandwagon. And the papers love it, the idea of a bloody therapist coming in here and telling us how to do our job."

"The only thing I read about her in the papers, she was being blamed for something. I can't remember what it was."

"You don't know the half of it," said Crawford darkly.

There was another pause.

"I'm sorry," said Hussein, who was feeling irritated now. "I'm probably being slow, but I'm not clear what you're telling me."

Crawford leaned forward and, with the tips of the fingers of his right hand, pushed the file across the desk. "That's the other file on Frieda Klein," he said. "That's *my* file. You can take it away with you." He stood up and walked to the window. "But I'll give you the short version." He looked around, and when Hussein saw his face, it was as if someone had turned a dial to make him angrier. "I'll tell you, Sarah . . . Is it all right if I call you Sarah?"

"Of course, sir."

"When someone called me and said that a body had been found and that Frieda Klein was involved, I told myself that this time I was going to find out who was in charge and I was going to warn them in advance. You've already met Klein and you probably saw her as some quiet, studious doctor type . . ."

"I didn't really—"

"But she isn't. You say you read about her in the papers." He stepped forward and rapped on the desk. "I'll tell you what wasn't in the papers. Did you know that she killed a woman?"

"Killed?"

"Stabbed her to death. Cut her throat."

"Was she charged?"

"No, it was considered to be self-defense. Klein didn't even admit to *that*. She said it was done by Dean Reeve, the kidnapper in the Faraday case."

Hussein frowned. "Dean Reeve? But he died. He hanged himself before the police could get him."

"Exactly. But this is Frieda Klein we're talking about. She operates under different rules from the rest of us. She has this bee in her bonnet that Dean Reeve is still alive and it was his identical twin who died. Ridiculous, of course. Also, everyone talks about Klein getting that Faraday boy back and the girl. They don't mention the other woman Klein got involved and didn't get rescued."

"How did Klein get her involved?"

"What?" Crawford seemed at a loss for a moment. "I can't remember the details. It's all in the files. She's been arrested for assault as well. She got into a brawl in a West End restaurant a few years ago."

"Was she convicted?"

"Charges were not pressed," said Crawford, "for reasons that were never clear to me." He tapped the file. "But it's all in here."

"Is she still on the payroll?"

"God, no. I saw to that. The last I heard she was up in Suffolk crying rape, hurling accusations around, and the man she accused also ended up being murdered. That's what I'm trying to tell you, Sarah. Wherever this woman goes, trouble follows and people get killed. The only blessing about the last sorry business is that she was up in Suffolk, annoying the police there, rather than down here annoying us."

"Rape?" said Hussein. "Was she a victim or investigating a rape or what?"

"A bit of both, as far as I could gather. It ended up with two people being murdered, as it generally seems to when Dr. Klein is involved."

Hussein reached out her hand toward the file and took it. "I'm sorry," she said. "I want to be clear about this. What is it that we're talking about here? Are you claiming that this woman is delusional or are you accusing her of something systematic or do you have certain suspicions or . . . well, what?"

"You'll be wanting to talk to people, I'm sure, in the course of the investigation. I'm going to put you in touch with a psychological expert that we really do employ, Hal Bradshaw. He shared my reservations about her performance, had something of a run-in with her and his house ended up being burned to the ground. About which, I have to say, he has been remarkably forgiving."

"Are you suggesting that Frieda Klein is an arsonist as well?"

Crawford spread his hands in a gesture of helpless innocence. "I'm suggesting nothing," he said. "I'm a simple policeman. I just follow where the evidence leads me, and in this case the evidence suggests that where Frieda Klein goes a trail of chaos follows. What her precise role in this happens to be has always been difficult to pin down. As you will probably discover, Frieda Klein also has some strange associates. How these things happen, I don't pretend to know, but they happen, and they continue to happen."

"But when she did work with the force," said Hussein, "to the extent that she did, who did she deal with?"

"You see, she's crafty as well. She worked with one of my DCIs, Malcolm Karlsson. He just fell under her spell and she made use of that."

"'Fell under her spell'? Was there some kind of relationship?"

Crawford pulled a face. "I'm not saying there was and I'm not saying there wasn't. I don't know anything about it and I wouldn't like to speculate. All I'll say is that Mal Karlsson lost his sense of perspective. But you'll want to talk to him yourself. Be warned in advance, though, that he's not entirely reliable where Frieda Klein is concerned."

Hussein looked down at the file. "It's possible that Frieda Klein doesn't have anything to do with this."

Crawford walked round the desk and helped Hussein out of the chair. "And it's possible," he said, "that you can get into a shark pool and that the shark won't eat you. But it's better to be in a cage."

Hussein smiled at the extravagance of the image. "She's just a witness," she said.

"Forewarned is forearmed," said Crawford. "And if she gives you any trouble, remember, I'm right behind you."

5

"What have we got?" Hussein looked at the men and women grouped around her in the incident room.

What have we got? The words she always used during the first hours or days of a case, when they were assembling the corners and straight lines of the investigation, before starting on the jumble of pieces that built up the picture.

"Shall I begin?" Bryant said. "Our victim is Alexander Holland. He's a"—he glanced down at the printed sheet in front of him—"a professor of cognitive science at King George's College, London."

"What's that mean?" asked Chris Fortune. He was new on the team; she noticed that he jiggled one knee continually and chewed gum with vigor. Probably trying to give up smoking.

"That he's cleverer than we are. Or *was* cleverer. The university term ended on June the sixth for the long summer vacation, which explains why no one there was concerned about his absence. Although the records show that a woman"—he glanced down at his notebook—"a Dr. Ellison apparently rang the police to say he seemed to have disappeared. It's unclear why she was worried. It had only been a few days and what she meant was that he hadn't been in touch with her."

"Dr. Ellison?"

"Yes."

"Go on."

"He's fairly new to the job. It was created specially for him. He came back from the States, where he had been working for a couple of years, eighteen months ago."

"Why?" asked Hussein.

"Why what?"

"Why did he come back?"

"I don't know."

"Go on."

"He was forty-two. Previously married to a Maria Lockhart but divorced eight years ago."

"Where's she now?"

"She lives in New Zealand with her new husband. And, no, she hasn't paid a visit to London recently to kill her ex. He doesn't have any children. Parents both dead. He has one sister. We've talked to her."

Hussein thought of the distraught woman in her blue dress, wringing her hands together, shaking her head from side to side in bewilderment. "Is he in a relationship?"

"Not that we know of."

"Sophie." Hussein nodded at the young woman, who sat up straighter, looking nervous. "Tell us what's been found in his flat."

She listened intently as Sophie Byrne talked. Alexander Holland had not been in his flat long, but something of the man emerged from where he had lived: he had liked cooking—the pots and pans were expensive and obviously used, and there were lots of ingredients neatly stored in the cupboards, as well as recipe books. He had also, it seemed, liked drinking. There was a large number of empty wine bottles in the recycling bin under the stairs and a healthy supply of full ones in the kitchen, as well as a couple of bottles of whisky. He had been sporty, judging from the tennis and squash rackets and the running clothes, and the several pairs of trainers. He was a bit of a dandy: expensive shirts and jackets hung in the wardrobe. He had liked art—or, at least, there were paintings on the walls, and also two drawings in his bedroom. He was sexually active. There were condoms in the drawer by the bed.

"*Probably* sexually active," said Hussein.

There were two dressing gowns hanging from the hook, one for a man and a smaller one for a woman—and the woman's had been worn by several different people. There was a supply of toothbrushes in the bathroom cabinet, alongside paracetamol and mouthwash. He read a lot, mostly books to do with his work.

"What's noticeable," said Sophie, "is what's not there. No passport. No wallet. No computer. No phone."

"Keys?"

"One set of keys in a bowl near the front door. And then some keys that don't belong to the flat."

"His sister's, perhaps?"

"We're checking."

"Any correspondence?"

"No—but it was probably on his computer, which is also gone."

"We should presumably be able to get it from his server. Or perhaps he has a computer in his office at the university. Get onto that, will you, Chris?"

"Sure." Chris gave an extra vigorous chew on his gum.

"There was a notebook on his desk," said Sophie Byrne. "But it was mostly lists of things to do, things to buy. There was also what looked like a schedule written down, dates and times with asterisks by them. It was headed 'WH.'"

"WH?"

"Yes."

"OK. What about phone calls, Glen? Any joy?"

"Ah." Bryant looked pleased, cleared his throat, picked up a sheaf of printouts stapled together. "His mobile's missing, as you know. But we've got a record of the calls that were made, going back six months to the beginning of the year."

"And?"

"Over a third of all calls were made to the same number."

"And whose number was that?" asked Hussein, already guessing the answer.

"Frieda Klein's."

"Are you going to call a press conference?" Bryant asked Hussein after the meeting.

"Tomorrow."

"Shall we bring her in?"

"Dr. Klein? Not yet. There's a couple of people I think I need to talk to first."

Then she remembered something else that had been like a small niggle in her brain.

"When Frieda Klein's name first came up on the system, it was because she had reported someone missing. Miles Thornton. Can you look into that?"

"Come in, come in," he said, holding out his hand and grasping hers with a wrenching firmness.

Hal Bradshaw had bare feet and artfully unkempt hair, glasses whose frames were long, thin rectangles that made it hard to see the whole of his eyes. Perhaps that was the point. He led her into his study, a bright, book-lined room with several framed certificates above the desk, a photograph of himself shaking the hand of a prominent politician and a long sofa to which he gestured. She took a seat at one end and he sat rather near to her. He smelled of sandalwood.

"Thank you for agreeing to see me, Dr. Bradshaw. Especially on a Sunday."

"Professor, actually. Recent thing." He smiled self-deprecatingly. "I've been expecting you."

She was slightly perplexed. "I know. I rang you to make the appointment."

"No, I mean as soon as I heard about her finding the body of her friend. Her ex-friend."

"Can I ask how you know about that?"

Bradshaw gave a modest shrug. "It's part of the arrangement."

"With the police?"

"Indeed," he said. "They keep me in the loop. The commissioner himself called me on this one."

"In fact, Dr. Klein didn't actually find Alexander Holland. She was the one who identified him."

"Yes, yes," he said, as if she were corroborating what he had said. "Can I offer you some tea, by the way? Or coffee?"

"No, thank you. I'm here because Commissioner Crawford suggested it would be useful to get some background information about Dr. Klein."

The expression on Bradshaw's handsome face was thoughtfully sad. "I'll do what I can."

"I've read the file that the commissioner gave to me. Can we perhaps begin with the case of Dean Reeve?"

"Dean Reeve is dead."

"Yes, I know, but—"

"But Frieda Klein is convinced that he is still alive. And"—he leaned toward Hussein—"*out to get her.*"

"Do you know why she thinks that?"

"I've written a book about the very thing."

"Perhaps you could summarize your argument."

"People like her—clever, articulate, neurotic, highly self-conscious and self-protective—can develop a personality trait that we call *narcissistic delusion.*"

"You mean she makes things up?"

"A person like Frieda Klein needs to feel at the center of the world and she is incapable of acknowledging failure, of taking responsibility. In the case of Dean Reeve, you may or may not know that he murdered a student directly as a consequence of her interference."

"I've read that a woman called Kathy Ripon was supposedly killed by Dean Reeve."

"She has compensated for that by deluding herself into believing he is still alive and out to get her. Thus she makes herself into the target and the victim, the hero of the story if you like, rather than dwelling upon the consequences of her own actions."

"She saved Matthew Faraday, didn't she?"

"She likes to insert herself into investigations and then take credit. It's not uncommon. It's another symptom, in a way. And you know about that poor young woman, Beth Kersey, whom she killed?"

"I read that Beth Kersey was psychotic and that it was self-defense."

"Yes. But that's not what Frieda Klein says, is it? She says that she *didn't* kill Beth Kersey, in self-defense or otherwise. Dean Reeve did. Are you beginning to see a pattern?"

"I see what you're suggesting. But perhaps she was telling the truth," said Hussein.

Bradshaw raised his eyebrows. "Sarah," he said. "Can I call you Sarah?" Just like the commissioner, thought Hussein irritably, and didn't bother to answer. "So, Sarah, she probably believes that she is telling the truth. Her version of the truth. I am a charitable man and I like to think I'm quite perceptive." He paused, but Hussein didn't feel the need to add anything. "Even if I have good reason to believe that she actually set fire to my house."

"You have no real proof of that."

"I know what I know."

"Why would she do that?"

"Perhaps I am what she wants to be. I've attained a respect she resents."

"She burned your house down out of jealousy?"

"It's a theory."

"What are you saying, Dr. Bradshaw?"

"Professor. I'm saying be careful. Be very careful. She can be persuasive. And she has surrounded herself with people who prop up her sense of importance. You'll probably meet some of them. But she's not just an unreliable witness. She's dangerous. A year and a half ago, she was crying rape and two people died. And you know she was arrested for attacking that therapist—another rival, perhaps? Mm?"

"She wasn't charged."

"It is my belief that her behavior is escalating. I wasn't surprised when I heard about her lover being found dead."

"What are you implying?"

"I just want you to know what you're dealing with, Sarah."

"A violent arsonist and fantasist who may have killed several people, you mean? I'll watch my step."

Bradshaw frowned, as if he were suspicious of Hussein's tone. "Whose side are you on here?"

"I didn't know it was a question of sides."

"The commissioner might not like it if you ignored his warnings."

Hussein thought of Commissioner Crawford's florid face. She remembered Frieda Klein's dark eyes and her stillness, the almost imperceptible flicker that had crossed her face when she stood beside the body.

"Thank you for your time," she said, rising to her feet.

At the door, Bradshaw put his hand on her arm. "Are you going to see Malcolm Karlsson?"

"Perhaps."

"Of course, he's someone who has collaborated with Klein."

"You make that sound like a bad thing."

"Colluded with her."

"That sounds even worse."

"You can judge for yourself."

"What can I say?" said Detective Chief Inspector Karlsson. "She has been a valued colleague and she's a friend."

"Did you also know Alexander Holland?"

"Sandy." Karlsson spoke soberly, but kept his glance fixed on her. "Yes."

"You may or may not be aware that he has been killed."

Karlsson was visibly shocked. He looked away for a moment, collecting himself. Then he started asking questions and Hussein had to go through the explanation, the discovery of the body, its state, the plastic tag on the wrist bearing Frieda's name and Frieda's visit to the morgue. He sat forward in his chair, listening intently.

"Can you tell me something about his relationship to Dr. Klein?" she asked.

"Not really."

"I thought you were friends."

"Frieda is a very private person. She doesn't talk about things like that. They split up well over a year ago, that's all I can tell you."

"Who ended it?"

"You'll have to ask Frieda."

"Have you seen him since then?"

Karlsson hesitated. "A couple of times," he said reluctantly. "Briefly."

"Was he upset at the ending of the relationship?"

"Again, you'll have to ask Frieda. I can't comment."

"I'm sorry," said Hussein. "I don't think that's a proper answer."

"I mean that I don't really know. It's not the kind of thing that Frieda would ever talk about to me."

"Commissioner Crawford seems to think that Dr. Klein is at best unreliable, at worst dangerously unstable."

"Oh, that."

"He is your boss."

"Yes. You'll just have to judge for yourself."

"I intend to. And Dr. Bradshaw—" She stopped and grinned to herself. "Sorry, *Professor* Bradshaw put it even more strongly."

"You've been busy."

"There's nothing you can tell me that might help?"

"No."

She turned to leave, then stopped. "Do you have any idea what the initials 'WH' might stand for?"

Karlsson thought for a moment. "They might stand for the Warehouse," he said.

"What is that?"

"It's a therapy clinic."

"Is Dr. Klein connected to it?"

"She works there sometimes. And she's on the board."

"Thank you."

An officer called Yvette Long showed her out, glowering, as if Hussein had said something to offend her.

Bryant called her as she was leaving. "That person Dr. Klein reported missing."

"Yes?"

"Miles Thornton. He was a patient of hers."

"Was?"

"He was her patient on and off—more off than on recently, because he was sectioned for a few weeks. He was psychotic and deemed to be a danger to himself and others. Now he seems to have disappeared. Or, at least, he hasn't been seen recently. His family aren't overly worried: they say he often goes AWOL."

"But Dr. Klein reported him missing."

There was a slight pause. Hussein could imagine Bryant chewing the edge of his thumb, thinking. "Why is this relevant?" he asked at last.

"It probably isn't. But don't you think it's a bit odd how she's surrounded by distress and violence? Bradshaw would say that's just evidence of her narcissistic delusion."

"What?"

"Never mind. There are too many doctors and professors in this case."

6

The Warehouse wasn't Bryant's idea of a medical institution. With its stripped pine, metal, plate glass, it looked more like an arts center, somewhere you'd be led through on a school outing. And the woman he'd spoken to on the phone the day before, Paz Alvarez, didn't look like a manager. Dark-eyed, flamboyantly dressed, she was like a flamenco dancer or a fortune-teller. Bryant had told her that he wanted to talk about Frieda Klein and she was clearly suspicious. Reuben McGill was seeing a patient. He would have to wait.

Bryant waited in Paz's office. When she talked on the phone, she seemed a different person, laughing, cajoling, ordering. Then she would hang up, look round, and her expression would darken. Bryant tried to make conversation. Did she know Frieda Klein? Of course. Had she known her long? A few years. Did she see her often? When she came into the clinic. Was that often? A shrug.

He gave up and looked around her office. There was a rug on the wall, small sculptures and metal ornaments on every surface. A man appeared in the doorway and looked at Paz, who nodded toward Bryant. Bryant stood up.

"Dr. McGill?"

"Come through."

Bryant followed McGill along a corridor and into a room that was simple and stark, with just an abstract print on the wall and two wooden chairs facing each other.

"I thought there'd be a couch," said Bryant.

McGill didn't smile, just gestured for him to sit in one of the chairs and sat himself in the other. McGill didn't look like Bryant's idea of a senior doctor either. He was wearing walking boots, gray canvas trousers, a faded blue shirt. His thick, graying hair was swept back off his forehead.

When people met police officers they were usually nervous or agitated. They could sometimes be confrontational. McGill said nothing and looked just a little bored.

"We're investigating the murder of Alexander Holland," Bryant began.

"I knew him as Sandy," said McGill. "It sounds wrong hearing him called Alexander. I can't believe that this has happened. It's a terrible thing, especially for Frieda."

"You knew him?" Bryant continued.

"Yes, of course. I met him several years ago."

"Through Frieda Klein?"

"That's right. They were in a relationship, though that ended some time ago now."

"We're looking into people who knew him well. Like Dr. Klein."

"I'm confused. Can't you talk to her directly?"

"My boss is talking to her this afternoon. But your name came up."

"In what way?"

"Frieda Klein is an analyst. But you were *her* analyst. How does that work?"

McGill looked amused in a way that Bryant didn't like.

"Work? It meant that she had sessions with me a few times a week. But this was all many years ago."

"I don't know anything about this," said Bryant. "Is it usual to be analyzed by someone who's your friend?"

McGill made an impatient gesture. "If you're training to be a therapist, you first have to be in therapy yourself."

"Why?"

McGill's grim expression lightened slightly. "That's a good question," he said. "Probably the main reason is that by the time you've had your own therapy, you've spent so much time and so much money, you'll be a good, obedient therapist and you won't ask awkward questions about the old masters or the efficacy of what we do. It's also useful to deal with some of your own issues so they don't get in the way when you start seeing patients." He frowned again. "We became friends later. I was her analyst, then I recruited her and then we became friends."

"And through her you met Alexander Holland."

"Yes."

"They were a couple."

"Yes."

"And then they broke up."

"Yes."

"Do you know why?"

McGill crossed his arms. Bryant felt he was being pushed away.

"You must have friends."

"I've got a few."

"When their relationships break up, do you really know why?"

"Usually. Maybe one of them had an affair or they argued too much or one of them got bored."

"Well, I don't know why they broke up."

"Do you know who initiated it?"

McGill unfolded his arms. "Why do you need to know all this? You seem to be asking me about Frieda rather than Sandy."

"Holland was murdered. We want to know what was happening in his life."

"Frieda ended it."

"Do you know why?"

"She's her own woman. Maybe she felt trapped. I have no idea."

"How did he take it?"

"What do you think? He wasn't happy."

"How did he show that?"

McGill shrugged. "By not being happy. By complaining. By trying to get her to change her mind."

"Was he threatening? Or violent?"

"Not that I'm aware of."

"Did you talk to him after it ended?"

"Once or twice."

"Why?"

"He may have seen me as a way of getting to Frieda."

"What was his demeanor?"

"Demeanor?" McGill smiled. "That's a word only policemen and lawyers use. We've all been there. It's the most hopeless thing in the world, trying to persuade someone to love you again."

Bryant pulled a photocopy from his file and pushed it across the table. "What do you make of that?"

McGill stared at the sheet of paper that showed the column of dates and times that Sandy had written down under the initials "WH." "Nothing."

"It's a reasonable assumption that 'WH' means the Warehouse." McGill didn't respond. "If so, can you think of what these dates and times refer to?"

"No."

"For instance, they wouldn't be the dates and times that Dr. Klein works here?"

"I'll have to check that."

"Thank you," said Bryant.

"It would be easier if you simply asked Frieda."

"We'll do that as well." He glanced down at his notebook, reminding himself. "One more thing. Does the name Miles Thornton mean anything to you?"

"Yes." McGill was visibly wary. "He is a patient here. Or was."

"He's been reported missing."

"Yes."

"Why?"

"Because he hasn't turned up for his usual sessions."

"His sessions with Dr. Klein?"

"Yes."

"Why is that particularly worrying? Presumably lots of patients miss their sessions."

"What has this got to do with Sandy's death?"

Bryant, who didn't know the answer to that, waited impassively.

"Miles Thornton is a particularly troubled young man. Perhaps we should never have taken him here—a hospital might have been more appropriate. He was in a psychiatric ward of a hospital for a bit and when he was released he felt we—Frieda in particular—had betrayed him. He could be violent, even psychotic at times. So when he disappeared"—he gave another of his shrugs—"well, it was obviously worrying. It was our duty to report him missing."

"I see." Bryant stood up. "Let me know about that list, will you? I'll leave it with you. Is there anyone else here I can talk to?"

"You've met Paz. And there's Jack Dargan, who was Frieda's trainee. He works here now. But they'll just say the same as me."

Now it was Bryant's turn to look disapproving.

Jack Dargan was a brightly dressed young man. Bryant liked to be invisible: on or off duty, he wore clothes that were dark, muted and interchangeable. But the man who came into the room wore a thinly woven yellow cardigan over a royal blue T-shirt and baggy trousers that looked like pajamas. Perhaps this was what therapists put on to see their patients. His hair was colorful as well, a tawny orange with a kind of wave running through it that he emphasized by pushing his hand into it whenever he was asked a question. There was a perpetual restlessness about him that made it hard for Bryant to concentrate fully on what he was saying—but it was clear that he was saying *no*. No, he didn't know any details about Frieda Klein's breakup with Alexander Holland; no, he had not met him after Frieda had ended things, except for a couple of brief glimpses (here, his eyes slid away from Bryant's); and no, he had nothing to add to Reuben McGill's statement about Miles Thornton.

"Did Alexander Holland come to the Warehouse much?"

Jack put his knuckles into his mouth and squinted. "No."

"You never saw him behaving angrily or violently?"

"Violently? No, I never saw anything like that."

"Or angrily?"

"I can't believe this has happened," Jack said.

"Was he angry?"

"I don't know. He was disappointed, the way people are when relationships go wrong. We've all been there."

"How disappointed?"

"He'd lost Frieda."

"There's nothing you can tell me that may be helpful to our investigation? And this isn't just someone dropping litter, remember. A man you used to know has been killed."

"I realize that. I'm terribly sorry and shocked about that. But, no, I can't think of anything that would be helpful. You'll just have to ask Frieda."

It was what they all said: *ask Frieda*.

"This must be difficult for you," said Hussein.

Frieda was pouring tea and didn't seem to hear. She put a coaster on the table in front of the detective and put a mug of tea on it. Then she took a sip from her own mug. "In what way?"

"Alexander Holland was someone you cared about and—"

"Can you call him Sandy? I never knew him as Alexander. It makes him sound like a stranger."

"Of course. Sandy was someone you cared about and he's been murdered."

"One thing I've discovered," said Frieda, "is that when something happens, people want to become a part of it. If someone has a tragedy, then other people want to grab some of it for themselves, as if it happened to them as well. This wasn't my tragedy. It was Sandy's and his family's tragedy. Can we take it as read that I'm deeply shocked by what's happened?"

"That sounds a bit cold."

"I'm sorry, but I've never been good at crying for the cameras." She paused for a moment, then added, "I know that I probably appear cold to you. But, as you know, people react very differently to distress and anger. They tend to make me withdraw into myself and appear harsh."

"All right. Thank you."

"I was explaining, not apologizing."

"They said you were difficult," said Hussein, who felt nettled and wrong-footed.

"Who's 'they'?"

"Commissioner Crawford. He told me about his experiences working with you. And Professor Bradshaw."

Hussein was surprised by Frieda's response. She didn't seem angry or discomfited. Just curious.

"How did that come about?"

"Your name's on our computer. And Crawford thought he should brief me about you."

"That explains things." Frieda smiled thinly. "This. You being here."

"It explains nothing. Alexander—" She stopped herself. "Sandy Holland has been found murdered. He had your hospital identification tag on his wrist. You were in a relationship with him. Of course I need to investigate you. Of course I need to ask you questions."

"So ask a question."

"Had you been in contact with the deceased?"

"I hadn't seen him properly for months."

There was a pause. "Would you like to elaborate on that?"

"In what sense?"

"You said, 'seen him properly.' I said 'contact.' And I'm not at all clear what you mean by 'properly.'"

"I've glimpsed him."

"Glimpsed?"

"Yes."

"That's all?"

"Yes."

"You mean he just happened to be passing and you saw him out of the window? Out of a bus? Walking by on the other side of the street? At the house of a mutual acquaintance?"

"I saw him a few times near where I sometimes work."

"The Warehouse."

"That's right. I go there twice or three times a week."

"But you didn't talk to him."

"No. Or, at least, no more than a word or so."

"When was the last time that you saw him?"

"A couple of weeks ago, perhaps. I can't remember precisely."

"A couple of weeks? The first week of June."

"I suppose so."

"You can't remember the exact date?"

"Not off the top of my head."

"His sister last saw him on Monday, June the ninth. Was it after that?"

Frieda considered. "I usually work at the Warehouse on Tuesdays and I think it might have been the Tuesday of that week."

"No later?"

"I don't think so. I'm almost sure not."

"So that would be Tuesday, June the tenth. A Dr. Ellison apparently rang the police to say he seemed to have disappeared. No one took her concerns very seriously. That was on June the sixteenth, six days after. Did you *glimpse* him any time between when you saw him at the Warehouse on June the tenth and then?"

"No."

"You're sure?"

"I am sure."

"Any other forms of contact?"

"Sandy called me on the phone occasionally."

"Occasionally?"

"Sometimes."

"You know that we've seen his phone records?"

"He wanted to stay in touch."

"You mean he wanted to get back together with you?"

Frieda paused, hesitant. "I was always very clear that it was over."

"Was he angry about that?"

When Frieda replied, it was with a forced calmness: "I cared for Sandy a great deal. I still do. I only wished him well."

"It sounds like there's a 'but' coming."

"But these things are always painfully difficult. You hear about break-ups that are civilized, with no hard feelings on either side. I've never seen one."

There was a ring at the front door. Frieda got up and answered it. Hussein heard voices, and when Frieda came back, she was accompanied by a man. He was large and imposing. Frieda's living room suddenly seemed smaller. He wore heavy, dusty boots, jeans and a gray-ribbed woolen sweater, in spite of the heat. His hair was dark brown and unkempt and his cheeks were stubbly.

"This is a friend of mine," said Frieda. "Josef Morozov. This is Detective Chief Inspector Hussein. She's here to talk about Sandy."

Josef held out his large hand, and as she shook it, Hussein felt it was rough, worn, stained. "Was very bad." He looked at Hussein with suspicion.

"Sit down," said Frieda to Josef. "We'll be done soon."

"Not *that* soon," said Hussein tartly.

Josef sat on a chair to one side, just out of Hussein's eyeline. She felt certain that Frieda had invited him to be present while she was being interviewed. It made her feel as if she were being checked on, and anger rose in her. She looked round at Josef, who was regarding her with utter impassivity.

"Did *you* know Mr. Holland, Mr. Morozov?"

"Three years," he said. "Four years. Frieda's friend is my friend." And he gave her a nod, as if he were warning her.

"Do you live here?" she asked.

"Here in England?"

"Here in this house."

"No."

She turned back to face Frieda. "About a third of all his calls were to you," she said.

"Is that a question?"

"You might like to comment."

"I don't know what to say."

"We found objects connected with you in his flat."

"What sort of objects?"

"Photographs, for example."

"When you've spent years together, there are going to be remnants."

"Are there remnants of Mr. Holland here?"

"Probably."

"Like what?"

"I don't know. I can't think of any just now."

"You sound defensive."

"What would I be defending myself from?"

"You know what I don't understand? If I had been close to someone and they had been found horribly murdered, and I'd been the one who identified the body and then the police had wanted to talk to me about it, I would be racking my brains and trying to come up with anything, anything at all, that could help them. I would produce any information that could be helpful. I'd probably try to help so much that it would almost be annoying."

"You're saying that you want my help?"

"From what I hear, that's what you do. I was told that when you get interested in a case, nothing will stop you from getting involved."

"I don't think that's quite all you heard. I assume you're quoting Commissioner Crawford here and that he didn't mean it as a compliment. But if you want my help, I'll do anything I can. Of course I will."

"I don't want your help," said Hussein. "I want you to do your duty as a citizen."

Now Frieda looked at Hussein with a sharpness in her dark eyes that was new. Her face was paler, her jaw clenched slightly. "All right," said Frieda, in a softer voice, so that Hussein had to lean forward to hear it. "This might not be the help you're wanting, but I believe I know who murdered Sandy."

"And who is that?"

"A man called Dean Reeve." Frieda paused for a moment, as if waiting for a response. "I'm not a detective, but when someone identifies a suspect in a murder case, I at least expect you to get out a notebook and write the name down. Otherwise it might not appear on the record and I want this on the record."

"I don't need to write it down. I've read your file."

"I'm surprised I've got a file. It's not as if I've been convicted of anything."

"Well, if you take information from here and there and print it out and gather it together, it becomes a file. And one of the things that emerge in this file is your repeated accusations against Dean Reeve for various murders and attacks. The problem being that Dean Reeve died five years ago."

"If you've read the file, you'll also know that I don't accept that he's dead."

"I saw that."

"Dean Reeve is still alive and he is a very dangerous man. He has some warped notion of looking after me, or perhaps of controlling me. If he believed that Sandy was pestering me, he could easily have killed him. He would do it with pleasure." She closed her eyes for a moment, then opened them again and gazed at Hussein, waiting for her response.

"I have heard what you say," said Hussein eventually.

"All I ask," said Frieda, "is that you look at this file of mine with your own eyes, not Crawford's or Bradshaw's."

Hussein stood up. "All right," she said. "I will. But I expect you to be straight with me as well."

"Straight with you? Why wouldn't I be?"

"I told you. I've read your file."

7

The couple who lived in the flat under Alexander Holland's hadn't known him very well but he'd been a pleasant, friendly, unobtrusive neighbor. He'd had visitors but they were never loud; several women had come to see him but they weren't aware of any particular one. They often saw him early in the morning when he went for a run. His assistant at the university, Terry Keaton, a round-faced youngish woman with blond hair cut in a fringe, hadn't seen him since the summer holidays began. She had liked him a lot and was obviously distraught. She didn't know of any tensions either at work or in his personal life— but he kept himself to himself, although he was always friendly and respectful. She hadn't come across Frieda Klein. His oldest friend, Daniel Lieberman, whom he had been at primary school with, said that he had last seen him on Sunday, June the eighth, twelve days before his body had been found. They had played squash and then gone for a couple of drinks; he had been fine. Yes, Lieberman had met Frieda Klein a few times. He confirmed that his friend had been upset at the separation—and added that he had returned from the States to be with her, which had made it doubly traumatic when they broke up. When Sophie Byrne asked him what he had made of Dr. Klein, Lieberman had pulled a face. "You wouldn't want to be on the wrong side of her. But Sandy adored her."

His colleagues were shocked and mystified. His sister was full of grief and a pent-up rage against Frieda Klein for whom he'd given up his prestigious job in America and who had shortly after ended their relationship. His doctor confirmed he had been in good health as far as he knew. He had money in the bank.

One woman came forward when she heard about his death, saying she had met him in a bar at the end of May, on Friday the thirtieth. She had gone back with him and they had had several more drinks before they spent the night together. She hadn't seen him again; he obviously hadn't been interested in anything beyond a one-night stand.

On June 11, nine days before his body was found, he had taken two hundred pounds from a cash machine. He had bought groceries at the Turkish shop on Caledonian Road. He had sent two texts to Frieda Klein and rung her once that same day—and also talked to his sister and to a friend in the States late in the evening. The pub at the end of his road thought he might have gone in there for a drink around then. The mail hadn't been opened since then. It was likely, therefore, that he had been murdered on June 12 or 13.

"Is that what we've got?" asked Hussein.

It wasn't quite. That afternoon, a woman called Diane Foxton had walked into Altham police station, saying she needed to speak to an officer about Alexander Holland. Hussein went to talk to her. The woman was obviously having chemotherapy: she had lost her hair and had mauve patches under her eyes; she was painfully thin.

"I didn't know whether I should come—I thought it was probably nothing—but my husband persuaded me. So here I am." She made a gesture with her skeletal hands.

"It's about Alexander Holland?"

"Yes."

"Did you know him?"

"Oh, not at all. But when I saw his face on the TV, I recognized him."

"Where from?"

"I only saw him the once, but I wasn't going to forget it. I was walking home and he was suddenly there."

"There?"

"Yes. He came tumbling onto the pavement, so he almost sent me flying. He was shouting. Properly shouting. His face was so angry it made me scared. I thought he was going to do something violent. He had a half-filled bin bag in his hand and he flung it at her. A few things fell out onto the pavement, a T-shirt and a book, and he bent down and picked them up and threw them at her as well. He looked half mad."

"Her, you say? He was shouting at a woman?"

"Yes."

"And it was her he threw the bag at?"

"Yes. I assumed he was returning things to her or something."

"Was she with him on the pavement?"

"Not with him but at the door, which is a few yards from the road, and—"

"Hold on, Mrs. Foxton. Can you tell me exactly where it was? What door?"

"I thought I said. That medical place in Primrose Hill."

"Do you mean the Warehouse?"

"I don't know the name. It's on Wareham Gardens."

"That's the one. And the date?"

"It was a week ago last Tuesday—I was on my way home from the doctor's. Around three thirty."

Hussein made a mental calculation: June 10. Ten days before Alexander Holland had been discovered floating in the Thames with his throat cut; at the most, three days before he died. And the same day that Frieda admitted to having "glimpsed" him.

"What did the woman look like?"

"I didn't really look at her. Pale-skinned. Dark hair, I think. Not blond, anyway."

"Any idea of her age?"

"Not really. Not very young but not old either. Mid-thirties or forty, perhaps."

"Was she responding?"

"No. I don't think she said much, if anything. Someone else came and joined her. A man. He looked as though he might get involved but she stopped him."

"How?"

"Just put a hand on his arm or something. I'm not sure. I was more concerned with the man on the pavement. He was that far away from me." She held her hands apart to show Hussein. "I couldn't get past him."

"Then what happened?"

"The man kicked at a rubbish bin and strode away and she picked up the bag, put the book and T-shirt back into it, and tied it up. She seemed quite calm. Calmer than I would have been. Then she went back inside. That was it. So nothing actually happened. I just thought—well, I thought it might be helpful. Maybe I'm wasting your time."

"You're not wasting our time. We're grateful to you, Mrs. Foxton."

"It gives me a shivery feeling, remembering his face. So angry. And then to know he's been murdered. I'd have been less surprised if he'd been the one doing the murdering."

The next time that Hussein met Frieda Klein, the Tuesday after the body had been found, it was at the police station, and a solicitor, Hopkins, was present. Hussein sat on one side of the table and they sat opposite her. Nobody wanted tea or coffee; there was no small talk.

Hussein had met Tanya Hopkins once before. She was a middle-aged woman, plump, with graying hair and a face bare of makeup. She wore soft, rumpled clothes with flat shoes and there was a maternal air about her—but her gray eyes were shrewd and when they got down to business she was incisive.

"I have several questions," said Hussein.

Frieda Klein nodded and rested her hands on the table in front of her. She didn't seem nervous and she kept her dark eyes on Hussein's face, but there was a subdued air about her.

"It is very clear that Alexander Holland was still obsessed with you. Would you like to tell me something about that obsession?"

Hopkins leaned over to Klein and murmured something that Hussein couldn't make out. Klein didn't reply but just gave her a curious smile.

"It's all right," she said to Hussein. "Sandy and I broke up about eighteen months ago."

"You broke up with him."

"Yes. He found it hard to accept that something that was once so important to both of us was over. I wouldn't call that an obsession."

"He was wearing your old hospital tag on his wrist."

Frieda's face was serious. "People can be strange," she said.

"Indeed. I understand that he came back from America in order to be with you."

"Yes."

"And that he was very supportive of you when you found yourself involved in a case that stirred painful memories for you."

"You can call it by its proper name. When I was a teenager I was raped. I went back to my hometown to find out who had done that. Yes, he was very supportive."

"And yet you ended it."

There was a pause. Hussein waited. Frieda said, "I'm sorry. I didn't think that was a question. Yes, I ended it. You cannot stay with someone simply out of gratitude."

"Was he extremely angry?"

"He was upset."

"Angry?"

"Sometimes being upset takes the form of anger."

"Eighteen months later, he was still angry?"

"He was still upset."

"Did you ever encourage him to think there was a chance?"

"No." Her voice was clipped. "I did not."

"You never got back together with him?"

"No."

"Yet he rang you or texted you almost every day, sometimes several times a day."

Frieda had been speaking in a quick, precise tone. Now she paused and when she spoke it was almost in a sigh. "It was painful."

"For you or for him?"

"For both of us, of course. But probably more for him."

The door opened and Bryant came in, shutting it quietly behind him. He nodded at Frieda, introduced himself to Tanya Hopkins and pulled a chair to the table. Hussein waited until he was sitting before she spoke again.

"Did you talk to him when he called?"

"Not very often. At first I did, but not recently. I thought it would be . . ." She frowned. "Counterproductive," she said at last.

"When you did talk, what were the conversations like?"

"I don't understand the question."

"It's quite simple. Did he plead with you, shout at you, insult you?"

"Sandy was a proud man."

"That's not an answer."

"You're making him sound"—she slightly lifted a hand from the table, then let it drop—"disordered."

"Was he disordered?"

"He was in a dark place in his life. So he probably did all those things. Usually I didn't answer his call. I let it go to voice mail."

Hussein pulled the photocopy of the dates and times that had been found at the dead man's flat. "Do you recognize this?"

Frieda looked at it. "That's when I'm scheduled to be at the Warehouse," she said in a low voice.

"So he knew your movements?"

"He must have done."

"You told me at our last interview that it had been a long time since you had actually met him but that you had—what was the word?—yes, *glimpsed* him a couple of weeks before he was found dead. On Tuesday, June the tenth. Treat that as a question," she added when Frieda just looked at her with her unnerving dark eyes.

"Yes, that's right."

"I want to know more about this last encounter with him. What was his mood?"

Before Frieda could speak there was a knocking at the door. Hussein looked around angrily. She nodded at Bryant, who got up and opened it. He could be heard speaking to someone outside, then he returned. A man came in with him. He was dressed in a dark suit, with a sober dark blue tie. He had rumpled gray hair and tortoiseshell glasses and he gazed about the room blinking like an owl. He was carrying a brown file under his arm.

"I wondered if I could sit in," he said.

"This isn't a public event," said Hussein.

"I know, I know." He fumbled in an inside pocket and took out a small white card, which he handed to her. As Hussein examined it, he looked around, as if he were uncertain of where he was.

"You're not from the Met?" said Hussein.

"No," said the man.

"I don't quite understand who you are."

"There's a number you can call, if you want," he said amiably.

"I certainly do want. Here, Glen." She handed the card over to Bryant. "Go and check this out, will you?" She looked at the stranger. "We'll wait until DC Bryant returns before we continue."

"Of course. Terribly sorry to be a nuisance."

Bryant went out of the room and Hussein waited, clenching and unclenching her fists on the desk. Frieda Klein sat still and upright opposite her. When Bryant returned a few minutes later, he had an expression of comic bewilderment on his broad face, but he nodded at Hussein and whispered a few words in her ear.

Hussein's mouth tightened with anger. "It looks like your friends are bigger than my friends," she said.

"I'll try not to be in the way."

He didn't sit down. He walked to the far corner of the room and leaned against the wall, crossing his arms and holding the file against his chest. His expression was impassive.

"Don't worry," he said to the room at large. "Ignore me. I'm not part of the inquiry."

"You'd better not be." Hussein turned to Frieda. "Where were we?"

Frieda didn't answer at once, but turned toward the man leaning against the wall, with a vague smile on his face. "I would prefer you to stand where I can see you, please."

"Fair enough." The man moved farther into the room, so that he was to one side of Frieda. "Better?"

Frieda nodded, then turned her gaze back to Hussein. "You were asking whether I remembered Sandy coming to the Warehouse," she said. "And the answer is, yes, I do remember."

"And behaving in a violent manner?"

"I don't think I would call it that."

"Shouting, throwing a bin bag at you, kicking the dustbin. What would you call it?"

"Agitated."

"All right. Let's call it agitated. Why did you not see fit to tell me about this *glimpse* of your former partner?"

"I didn't think it relevant."

"You do realize that this was one of the last known sightings of him before he disappeared? You can safely assume that he didn't have long to live. A day or two at the most."

Frieda stared at her; her face was like a mask and her eyes glittered.

"For eighteen months Alexander Holland has been harassing you, and then he is murdered. What have you got to say to that?"

"That's not a serious question," said Hopkins.

"All right. I'm interested in how you seem to be surrounded by a network of violence and trauma. We've already talked about your previous history—"

"Stop," said Hopkins. "If you have specific questions relating to the crime, Dr. Klein can answer them."

"Can you tell me something about Miles Thornton?"

Frieda Klein frowned and leaned forward slightly. "Miles? Has he been found?"

"No." Bryant spoke for the first time. "But you reported him missing, and I understand that he was also behaving violently toward you."

Tanya Hopkins started to speak but Frieda turned toward her. "It's all right," she said. "I know that you want to protect me from myself, but I want to answer these questions. Yes, I reported Miles missing. Yes, he could be violent and chaotic in his behavior and was sometimes psychotic."

"So," said Hussein, "now we have not one but two violent men turning on you in the past few weeks. One of whom has gone missing and one of whom has been killed."

"That's enough." Tanya Hopkins rose and looked down at Frieda, expecting her to do the same.

"It probably is nearly enough," she agreed, staying put. "But I want to say that Miles is an unstable young man who might be a danger to others, but above all to himself. That's why I reported him missing. I'm sorry he hasn't been found or returned." For the first time, she seemed to relax, speaking without her cool formality. "As a matter of fact, it was him I was expecting to find in the morgue."

"Miles Thornton?" Hussein remembered the quiver that had passed over Frieda Klein's face.

"Yes. Not Sandy."

"I see."

"He felt I had betrayed him when I was involved in having him sectioned some months ago. In a way, of course, I had. And, of course, in a way I had betrayed Sandy as well. He must have thought me heartlessly cruel. Sometimes I think that of myself."

Tanya Hopkins sat down heavily again. "I don't think we need to continue this particular line."

"Dr. Klein, would you give us permission to search your house?"

"My house?" A look of distress momentarily tightened her face. "What for?" Hussein waited impassively. "No, I don't think so. If you want to go through all my private possessions, I think you should get a search warrant."

"Very well."

"Now we really are going." Tanya Hopkins rose for a second time and Frieda Klein also stood. She gazed first at Hussein and then at Bryant.

"You're looking in the wrong direction," she said. "And all the time you're doing that, the man who actually killed Sandy is allowed to get away with it."

"You mean Dean Reeve."

"Yes. I mean Dean Reeve. You seem to be a woman who wouldn't accept other people's versions of the truth. Follow up on what I've said."

"Dr. Klein—"

"I know that patient tone of voice. Please don't 'Dr. Klein' me. You've already decided that I'm deluded."

"You're worse than deluded. You're obstructive."

"You mean about the search warrant? All right." She shrugged wearily. "Search my house. Where do I sign?"

"Sometimes," said Tanya Hopkins, taking her by the elbow and pulling her toward the door, "a client can be their own worst enemy. We are now leaving."

"Dr. Klein?"

Frieda, Hussein and Tanya Hopkins all looked round. It was the man leaning against the wall.

"Yes?" said Frieda.

"Can I ask a question?" he said.

"Who are you?" Frieda asked. "I have no idea why you're here."

The man blinked again. "I'm so sorry," he said. "I didn't introduce myself. My name's Levin. Walter Levin."

"I mean, who *are* you?"

"I'm nothing to do with the investigation. I'm on temporary assignment from the Home Office. It's a bit difficult to explain."

"Any questions need to go through me," said Tanya Hopkins.

"It's not about this case." Levin straightened himself. "I've been reading your file." He beamed. "Fascinating stuff. Absolutely fascinating. Gosh. About the case of that girl you helped find. In the house in Croydon."

"Please." Hussein was exasperated. "We're in the middle of an investigation."

"It's all right." Frieda looked at him properly for the first time, taking in his smiling face and his sharp eyes. "What do you want to know?"

"I was curious," he said. "It wasn't clear from the case file what aroused your suspicion in the first place."

Frieda thought for a moment. It all felt so long ago, as if it had happened to someone else.

"A patient came to see me. He turned out to be a fake. It was part of a newspaper story. But he told me a story about cutting his father's hair as a child. That sounded strange and there was something real about it. I wanted to discover where that story came from. That's all."

"Golly," said Levin vaguely.

"Is that what you came to ask?" said Hussein. "About a two-year-old investigation?"

"No. I wanted to see Dr. Klein in person," said Levin. "So fascinating, you know."

"What for?" said Hussein. "What are you doing here, aside from being fascinated?"

Levin didn't answer. He just looked at Frieda with an expression of puzzlement. "I'm awfully sorry about all this," he said.

"I'm sorry too," said Frieda.

8

Hussein had been involved in many searches and she had become familiar with the different ways that suspects behaved. Sometimes they were
angry, sometimes upset, even traumatized. Rummaging through drawers
in front of them could feel like a constant, insistent, repeated violation.
Sometimes the suspect accompanied her around the property, telling her
about it, as if she were a prospective buyer.

Frieda Klein was different. As the officers moved around her house,
through to the kitchen, upstairs, opening cupboards and drawers, she
just sat in her living room, playing through a chess game on the little
table with an air of deep concentration that surely must have been fake.
Hussein looked at her. Was she in shock, or angry, or in denial, or stubborn, or sulking? Once Klein looked up and caught her eye, and Hussein felt that she was looking right through her.

There was a thumping sound, someone coming down the stairs two
at a time. Bryant came into the room and placed something on the
table. Hussein saw that it was a leather wallet.

"We found that upstairs," said Bryant. "It was in a clothes drawer.
At the bottom, wrapped in a T-shirt. I'll give you one guess who it
belonged to."

Hussein looked at Klein. She couldn't see any hint of shock or surprise or concern. "Is it yours?"

"No."

"Do you know whose is it?"

"No."

"Then why do you have it? And why do you keep it hidden?"

"I've never seen it before."

"How did it get there?"

"I don't know."

"Shall we look inside?" continued Hussein. She thought that she should be feeling triumph.

Frieda looked at her with her dark eyes burning and didn't say anything.

Hussein snapped on her rubber gloves and Bryant handed her the wallet. He was grinning broadly. She opened it up.

"No money," she said. "No credit cards. But several membership cards." She pulled one out and held it up so that Frieda could see. "The British Library," she said. "Dr. Alexander Holland, expiry date March 2015." And another. "The Tate, expires November 2014. This is not an old wallet." She looked at Frieda. "You don't seem very surprised. How did it get here, Dr. Klein?"

"I don't know. But I can guess."

"Guess then."

"It was planted, of course."

"Of course."

"By Dean Reeve."

Glen Bryant gave a loud snort. Hussein laid the wallet on the table. "I think you'll need to talk to your lawyer again."

Tanya Hopkins looked puzzled when Frieda arrived for their Thursday morning meeting with a middle-aged man in a suit and dismayed when she introduced him as Detective Chief Inspector Malcolm Karlsson.

"I don't understand," said Hopkins.

"I'm here as a friend," said Karlsson. "To give advice."

"I thought that was *my* job."

"It's not a competition."

Hopkins was clearly dubious. "If DCI Hussein knew that a colleague was attending a meeting with a suspect and her lawyer . . ."

"This is my day off. I'm simply meeting a friend."

Hopkins turned to Frieda, who had walked over to the window and was staring out. Hopkins's office overlooked the canal basin in Islington. Children in bright yellow life jackets were paddling in two canoes.

"Are you involved in the investigation in any way?" Hopkins asked.

"No."

"Have you had any privileged access?"

"No."

"I'm Frieda's lawyer, not yours. If I *were* yours, I'd drag you out of this room by the scruff of your neck."

"So I've been warned."

The three of them sat down on chairs around a low glass coffee table. Hopkins opened a pad of paper. She took out a pen and removed the cap. "We have been instructed to report to Altham police station tomorrow at ten. It's all but certain that they'll charge you with Alexander Holland's murder."

She looked around as if she were expecting a response but there was none. Karlsson was staring at the floor. Frieda seemed to be thinking hard but she didn't speak.

"You'll be granted bail," said Hopkins. "But you'll have to surrender your passport. There'll be certain conditions attached, but they shouldn't be a problem. So, now we need to think of our strategy."

"Our strategy?" said Frieda.

"I've got a barrister in mind. Jennifer Sidney would be a perfect fit."

"She did the Somersham trial," said Karlsson with a grim smile.

"Is there something funny?" asked Frieda.

"Not exactly funny. But if she can get Andrew Somersham off, she can get anyone off."

"It was the right verdict," said Hopkins. "On the evidence."

"That's one way of putting it."

"Well, we want the right verdict as well."

"Why have a lawyer at all?" said Frieda.

"What?"

"If I'm charged . . ."

"You're going to be charged."

"All right, when I'm charged, I would just like to go into court and tell my story, truthfully, and then they choose to believe me or not believe me."

Hopkins laid her pen down softly. Karlsson saw that she had gone quite pale. "Frieda," she said quietly. "This isn't a time for grandstanding or giving a philosophy lecture. This is an adversarial system. The Crown has to make a case against you. All you have to do is to rebut the specific accusations they make. You don't have to prove that you're innocent, you don't have to win a prize for virtue. You have to not be definitely guilty. That's the way the system works."

Frieda started to speak but Hopkins held up her hand. "Stop," she said. "So far, I've had to stand by while you've sabotaged your own case. If you want to carry on doing that, you can get yourself another lawyer or no lawyer at all. But, first, hear me out."

Frieda nodded her acquiescence and Hopkins continued: "The basic strategy is obvious. It all comes down to the wallet. There's a whole lot of other prejudicial evidence—or so-called evidence—but they can't use it. Just so long as you stay disciplined."

"What do you mean by that?"

"You mustn't mention your Dean Reeve theory."

"Why?"

"If you even mention his name, they can bring up everything. Your involvement in the death of Beth Kersey, the death of Ewan Shaw, the arson attack on Hal Bradshaw's house, your various arrests for assault."

"And?"

"*And?*" said Hopkins. "It's my belief that if those incidents are put before a jury you are overwhelmingly likely to be convicted and you will spend the next fifteen to twenty years in prison. But, as I said, there is no reason for them to be introduced. No, it all comes down to the wallet. Now, isn't it possible that the last time you met Mr. Holland, he left his wallet by mistake?"

"No," said Frieda.

There was a pause.

"Frieda," said Karlsson. "I'm not sure if you quite appreciate how serious this is."

"They found the wallet hidden in a drawer," said Frieda. "If Sandy could have left it there—with his cash and credit cards removed—I would have said."

"I was never happy about that search. Did they warn you of your rights before asking you about the wallet?"

"No."

"Excellent."

"Sandy didn't leave it there," said Frieda. "He hasn't been there for a year. A year and a half. All the cards in it were current."

There was another silence. A longer one. Karlsson and Hopkins exchanged glances. When Karlsson spoke, he sounded tentative, almost scared.

"There's an obvious question, Frieda. But I'm not sure I want to ask it."

"Careful," said Hopkins.

"As I said, I don't know how it got there." Frieda turned her eyes on the two of them. "Though I can guess."

"Please," said Tanya Hopkins sharply. "Let's concentrate on what we know rather than follow your theories. That last time you met Sandy. That row at the clinic. He drops the wallet, you pick it up. You take it home, meaning to give it back to him."

Frieda shook her head. "I'm not going to tell you something that simply isn't true."

Hopkins frowned. She looked discontented. "It's not possible that there was a later meeting between you that you haven't told us about?"

"No."

"You meant you *did* meet him or you *didn't*?"

"I didn't. The last time I saw him was on that Tuesday, outside the Warehouse."

"What I haven't enjoyed about this case is that I keep discovering things you haven't told me and they're always bad things."

"You talked about strategies," said Frieda. "What other ones are there?"

"If you're reluctant to mount a defense, I suspect we could offer to plead guilty to manslaughter. I've got some psychologists who could come and testify on your behalf."

Karlsson glanced nervously at Frieda. For the first time she looked genuinely startled. "What would they say?" she asked.

Hopkins picked up her pen and tapped it thoughtfully on the table top.

"You're a victim of rape," she said. "You were the object of an attack that almost killed you. And there are witnesses that Holland made violent threats against you."

"They weren't threats . . ."

"I think I can virtually guarantee that you would receive a suspended sentence."

"So all I have to do is to confess to murdering Sandy," said Frieda. "And I get away with it."

"It's not getting away with it," said Hopkins. "You'll be on license for the rest of your life. You'll have a serious criminal conviction. But it may be better than the alternative."

"You make it sound tempting," said Frieda.

"I'm just trying to lay out your options."

Frieda looked at Karlsson, who was shifting uncomfortably in his chair. "What do you think?"

"I've asked around," he said. "Hussein's good. She's clever and she's thorough. She's built a strong case. I want to warn you, I've seen this strategy from the other side. You challenge this bit of evidence, that bit of procedure, bit by bit, you get it all thrown out." He turned toward Hopkins. "You've probably thought of claiming that the police planted the wallet."

"I've thought about it," said Hopkins.

"Careful," said Karlsson. "It's the nuclear option. You don't know whose case it'll blow up."

"*They* didn't plant it," said Frieda.

"Were you there when they found it?" said Hopkins.

"Not in the exact room."

"Really? That might work. If the worst comes to the worst."

"The good thing about all these options is that they work just the same whether I did it or I didn't."

Hopkins was in the middle of a complicated doodle of cubes and cones; she paused and lifted her head. "If I weren't so sweet-tempered, I might give you a lecture about the importance of a system that gives the accused the benefit of the doubt and doesn't compel her to give evidence against herself or to reveal irrelevant personal information." She gave a smile. "But I am. So I won't." She stood up. "We'll meet at nine thirty tomorrow. There's a café on the canal, just a few hundred yards from the station—it's called the Waterhole. Come there. Then we'll go into the station together and you will not say anything at all, apart from what you have agreed, in advance, with me."

She held out her hand and Frieda shook it.

"I know this has been difficult," said Hopkins. "But I'm confident that we can achieve a resolution that we'll all be satisfied with."

"I'm sorry," said Frieda.

"What do you mean?"

"I don't think I've been a good client. But I want to thank you for what you've done."

"Let's not be premature."

"That's my point," said Frieda. "I want to be clear that, whatever happens, I'm grateful."

Karlsson and Frieda walked down the stairs. Outside on the pavement they looked at each other warily.

"So what just happened in there?" said Karlsson.

Frieda stepped forward and gave him a brief hug, then stepped back.

"What was that?" he said, with a nervous smile.

"There was only one thing in there that really meant anything," she said.

"What?"

"That *you* were there."

"But I didn't do anything."

"Yes, you did. You came. You broke the rules in a flagrant and unprofessional manner."

"Yes, I thought you'd appreciate that."

"Seriously. If it got out, I don't know what would happen to you. It was an act of kindness and friendship and I'll never forget it."

"That sounds a bit final."

"Well, you know, you should treat every moment as if it's your last."

Karlsson's eyes narrowed in suspicion. "You're all right?"

"I'm going to walk home, alone, along the canal. How could I not be all right?"

Karlsson stood and watched her go, straight-backed, hands in pockets, and he shivered, as if the weather had suddenly changed.

9

Frieda Klein had a single session that afternoon, with Joe Franklin whom she had been seeing for years. She had only to see the set of his face as he entered through the door, the shape of his shoulders, the heaviness of his footfall, to know his mood. Today he was quiet and sad, but not despairing. He talked in a soft, slow voice about the things he had lost to his depression. He told her about the dog he had had when he was a child, a brindled mongrel with beseeching eyes.

Before he left, Frieda said, "I may not be able to see you for some time."

"Not see me? For how long?"

"I don't know."

"But—"

"I know that it will be painful for you, and if I could avoid it I would. But I'm going to give you a name. She's someone I know, and I trust her. I want you to call her tomorrow. I'll speak to her in advance. And I want you to see her instead of me until I return."

"When? When will you return? Why are you going?"

"Something's happened." She looked at him steadily. "I can't explain now, Joe. But you will be in good hands. We've done well together, you and I. You've made progress. You are going to be all right."

"Am I?"

"Yes. Remember to call that number. And take care."

She held out her hand. Normally she never made physical contact with her patients, and Joe took it in a kind of bafflement and held it for a moment. "I don't want you to go," he said.

Frieda spent the rest of that afternoon phoning patients, canceling them and arranging for cover. To each, she said the same thing: that her absence would be indefinite. To each she recommended alternative therapists, and she called these colleagues to entrust her patients to their care, until she returned.

Only when she was satisfied that she had left no one uncovered did she go home, walking through the backstreets. She stopped outside the café owned by her friends. She went to it almost every day, but today it was closed and forlorn looking. A couple of minutes later she was back in the little cobbled mews where her narrow house stood squeezed between the lockups on its left, the council flats on its right. She turned the key in the lock and pushed open the door, stepping into the cool hallway with the same relief she always felt. But now she saw her house—the living room with its chess table and the fire she lit each day in winter, the bathroom with the magnificent bath her friend Josef had installed without her permission and with a large amount of chaos, the small study under the roof where she sat and thought and made pencil and charcoal drawings—with fresh eyes. She didn't know when she would see it again.

She made herself a pot of tea and sat with it, the tortoiseshell cat she had unwillingly inherited on her lap, thinking, making a list in her head. There was so much she had to do. For a start, someone would have to feed the cat and look after her plants. That was simple. She picked up the phone and punched in the number.

"Frieda, is me. All good?" He was from Ukraine, and although he had lived in London several years now, his accent was still thick.

"There's something I need to ask you."

"Ask anything." She could picture him laying his large hand over his heart as he spoke.

"Tomorrow morning I have an appointment with the police. They are going to charge me with Sandy's murder."

There was a silence, then a loud bellow of protest. She couldn't quite make out what he was saying, but certainly threats of violence and pledges of protection were in there.

"No, Josef, that's not—"

"I come now. This moment. With Reuben. And with Stefan too,

yes?" Stefan was his Russian friend, who was large and strong and of dubious occupation. "We sort it out."

"No, Josef. I do need your help, but not like that."

"Then tell."

"I need someone to look after the cat and—"

"The cat! Frieda. You joke."

"No. And water the plants. And," she continued, over his yelps, "there is one more thing I want to ask you."

She went through her list: first of all, she wrote a long, careful e-mail to her niece Chloë, whom she had kept a close eye on over the years since Chloë's father—Frieda's estranged brother David—had left Olivia. Chloë had been a troubled child, a reckless and needy teenager, but was now twenty and had dropped out of studying medicine and was planning instead to be a carpenter and joiner. She then wrote a much shorter but equally careful e-mail to Olivia, whom she didn't want to talk to: Olivia would become hysterical, then probably drunk and would want to rush round and weep. She was about to call Reuben but he beat her to it, having been told by Josef what was going on. To her surprise, Reuben was calm. He offered to come to the police station with her the next morning but she told him her solicitor wanted to meet her beforehand. He said he would come round at once, to be with her, but she said that she needed to be alone that evening and he didn't press her. He was steady, consoling, and she was reminded of what a good supervisor he had been to her, all those years ago.

After she had put the phone down she sat for several minutes, deep in thought. No one—not her solicitor, not Karlsson, not Reuben or Josef—had asked her if she had killed Sandy. Did they believe that she had, believe that she hadn't, not wanted to know or not dared to ask? Or perhaps it was irrelevant: they were standing by her whatever she had or hadn't done, unconditionally. She stared blindly into the empty fireplace, as if she could find an answer there.

There was one more person she had to tell, and a phone call or e-mail wouldn't do. Her heart felt heavy.

• • •

Ethan's nanny, Christine, answered the door. Frieda had met her several times before but only briefly. She was tall and vigorous, with strong arms. Her hair was always tied back, then held in place by multiple grips; she seemed very businesslike and strode around the house with an air of purpose. Frieda got the impression that Sasha was intimidated by her and she wondered what Ethan made of her.

"Yes?" said Christine, as if she'd never set eyes on Frieda before. "Sasha's not back yet."

"I must be a bit early, then."

"No. She's late. Again."

"I'm sure she'll be here soon. You can leave if you want and I'll look after Ethan."

"That would be good."

"It must be harder for Sasha now that it's just her," Frieda said.

"Tell me about it."

She opened the door wider and Frieda followed her into the kitchen. Ethan was strapped into his chair. He had bright spots on his cheeks and a mutinous look about him that Frieda recognized.

"Hello, Ethan. It's you and me now."

"Frieda," he said. He had an oddly husky voice for a toddler.

Christine stared from him to the mess on the floor, where his bowl and cup lay upturned. "You're a bad boy," she said in her cool voice, not angry but implacable.

"I can take it from here," said Frieda. "And you should be careful about calling someone bad."

"You're not the one who has to clear up the mess."

"I am now. You go home."

Christine left, then Frieda went across to Ethan and kissed him on his sweaty brow, untied him and lifted him onto the floor. He put his sticky hand into hers. He had Frank's dark eyes and hair, Sasha's pale skin and her slenderness; Frank's determination and Sasha's sweetness. Frieda had met him when he was less than a day old, a crumpled, scrawny little thing with a face like an anxious old man's, changed his nappy (something she'd never done for anyone else's baby), looked after him when Sasha was too sick and sad to do so, taken him for walks and read to him. He was still a mystery to her.

"What are we going to do before Sasha gets home?"

Before Ethan had time to say anything, she heard the door bang open. "I'm so sorry," Sasha called. "The bus was late."

Frieda went to the door. Her friend's hair was dishevelled and her face flushed. "Hello, Sasha."

"Oh, God, Frieda. I got here as quickly as I could."

"It's fine. You're just a few minutes late."

Sasha bent down and lifted Ethan into her arms, but he squirmed impatiently and she put him down. He dropped to his hands and knees and disappeared under the table, which was his favorite place to be. He would stay there for hours, if left to himself, with the tablecloth hanging down to make a kind of enclosure and his miniature wooden animals, which he moved around and talked to in a low, urgent whisper.

"Where's Christine?"

"I sent her home."

"Was she all right?"

"Fine," said Frieda. "Rather brusque."

"I'm a bit scared of her when she's cross."

"That doesn't sound like a very healthy working relationship."

"No," said Sasha forlornly. "Since Frank left, I always seem to be half an hour late for everything. No wonder she gets impatient."

"Let's have some tea. There's something I need to tell you."

Sasha filled the kettle and dropped tea bags into the teapot. Frieda, watching her, was struck by how very beautiful her friend was and how fragile she seemed. They had first met after Sasha had come to see her as a client, in the wake of a disastrous affair with her previous therapist, but later Sasha had helped her professionally, and they had gradually become friends. When Sasha had met Frank, she had been luminously happy for a while, but after Ethan had been born she had suffered from catastrophic post-natal depression and hadn't quite returned to an even keel since.

"Frank's coming in half an hour or so. Thursday's his evening with Ethan."

"I don't know if I'll still be here."

"You'll probably want to keep out of his way, after last time."

Frank was Ethan's father, Sasha's ex, and had for a while been Frieda's friend. But that was before his relationship with Sasha had started to go wrong. For a while, Frieda had stood on the sidelines and watched as her friend had become increasingly dejected and defeated—reminding her of how she had been when they had first met: Sasha had come to her as a vulnerable client. At last, she had told Sasha that she did not have to stay with someone who made her feel worthless; that although it might not feel like it at the moment, she always had a choice. She could choose to stay or choose to leave.

"I don't mind meeting him," said Frieda. "But there mustn't be any kind of scene in front of Ethan."

"Of course not." Sasha put a mug of tea in front of Frieda and sat down opposite her. "What was it you needed to tell me?"

As Frieda told her, she didn't seem to understand the words. Her thin face was distraught. Her eyes seemed enormous.

"How can they think such a thing?"

"I can see why," said Frieda. "His wallet hidden in my drawer, for instance."

"How did that happen?"

Frieda shrugged. "Let's not go through all of that again," she said. "The point is, I'm to go to the police station tomorrow morning and I am assured by my solicitor, who seems to know what she's talking about, that I will be charged."

"Then what will happen?"

"I'm not sure."

"I don't know what to say."

"You don't have to say anything."

"I do." Her eyes brimmed with tears. "You're my friend, my dearest friend, and you've stood by me through thick and thin."

"We've stood by each other."

"You've stood by me," repeated Sasha, "from the moment we met, when you punched my creep of a therapist in the face and ended up in a police cell, to now, when you've helped me through my breakup with

Frank. I don't know how I would have coped with all of that, and being a single mother, without you."

"You would have coped."

"I don't think so. I can't just let this happen. Tell me what I can do now. Tell me how I can help you."

"You can be all right, you and Ethan."

"Frieda, you make everything sound so solemn."

Frieda smiled. "It is quite solemn," she said. "I'm about to be charged with the murder of a man I once loved."

"But you won't go to court—you won't be found guilty! They'll let you go."

"Maybe."

"Your lawyer—"

"My lawyer seems very competent. But there's only so much she can do."

"I can't believe this is happening."

"It is rather strange. Like a dream," said Frieda. "Like the kind of story that happens to other people."

"How can you be so calm?"

"Am I calm? I suppose I am."

"I'll do anything, anything at all. Just say the word."

"There is no word. I wish there was. I'm rather tired."

Sasha took the chair beside her, grasped her hand and held it. "At any rate, tell me," she said at last.

Frieda looked at her curiously. "What?"

"You know."

"You mean, did I kill Sandy?"

Sasha nodded. "I would understand if you had. It wouldn't make me feel differently toward you. But I'd like to think you could tell me."

"I could tell you," said Frieda. There was a pause. Ethan shuffled under the table; they heard the small clicks of objects being laid down on the tiles.

"Go on," said Sasha.

"There's not much I want to say, except for a long time now, I have felt that Sandy should never have met me. His life would have been much

happier without me in it. I was to blame for his unhappiness and I hold myself responsible for his death."

"Well, we should talk about all of that," said Sasha. "But you haven't given me an answer, you know."

Frieda smiled at her. "You're the only person who's actually dared ask."

Suddenly Sasha's face was very pale. "I'm sorry," she said. "I feel—" And she stopped.

"What do you feel?"

There was a loud series of knocks on the front door, followed almost immediately by another.

"That's Frank," said Sasha, standing up. "He always knocks like that—impatiently, as if I'm keeping him waiting." But she spoke tolerantly.

She went to let him in and Frieda put her head under the tablecloth. "Frank's here," she said.

Ethan looked up. His face was very close to hers and she could see herself reflected in his deep brown eyes. "Come in my cave," he said. "It's safe."

At twenty-five past nine the following morning, Friday, June 27, one week after Sandy had been found in the Thames with his throat cut, Tanya Hopkins arrived at the Waterhole café and secured a free table looking out over the canal. It was a beautiful June day, clean and fresh, with the last softness of morning in the air. People walked, ran, biked past the window. Ducks bobbed among the drifts of litter in the glinting brown water.

Tanya Hopkins ordered herself a cappuccino and a pastry. She checked her phone for messages but there was nothing important. She drank the coffee and tore off pieces of pastry. She opened her notebook and put it in front of her on the table. She looked at her phone once more. It was twenty minutes to ten. She pressed Frieda's number and listened to the ringtone. The call went to voice mail and she left a curt message.

She wrote the date on the top of the page of her notebook and underlined it, finished her cappuccino and thought about ordering another. But, no, she would wait until Frieda arrived. She shaded the letters, then

crosshatched them, and then she crossed them out in impatient black lines.

When she looked at her phone again, it was past a quarter to ten. In fifteen minutes, they were meant to be at the police station. She called Frieda's number once again but this time left no message. Her irritation had turned to a heavy anger that sat like a stone in her stomach.

At five to ten, she paid and went outside, looking up and down the towpath for her client. She walked up the steps and gazed around. She phoned one last time, without expectation. She waited until three minutes past ten and then she went into to the station and announced herself. She was shown into DCI Hussein's room.

"Something must have happened to hold Frieda up," she said in a pleasant voice. "We're going to have to rearrange her appointment."

Hussein looked at her across her desk. She was very still and her face was grim. "So," she said at last. "You're not serious?"

10

Commissioner Crawford pointed a quivering finger at the chair and Karlsson sat down.

"Do you know why you're here?"

"I can guess."

"Oh, spare me your playacting. Of course you know. Your Frieda Klein has absconded. Disappeared. Buggered off. Gone."

Karlsson didn't move. Not a muscle of his face changed. He stared across the large desk into the commissioner's face, which was so red it was practically steaming. He could see the tidemarks of anger in his neck, above his shirt collar. "Did you know? I said, *Did you know?*"

"I knew that she had gone."

"No." He banged his fist on his desk so his empty cup shifted and the pens rolled. "I mean, did you know she was planning to go?"

"No. I didn't."

"I know that she has talked to you."

"As a friend."

"A friend." The sneer in Crawford's voice made Karlsson stiffen; his mouth tightened. "We all know about you and Dr. Klein."

"I talked to her as a friend."

"With her solicitor. You were there with her fucking solicitor. Jesus. You are in such shit here, Mal. Up to your neck."

"Frieda Klein is a colleague, as well as a friend. We're supposed to look after our own."

"Ex-colleague."

"I know you've had your differences—"

"Stop it, Mal. This friend, this colleague, has murdered a man and now she's run off before we can charge her."

"I'm sure there's an explanation." The dull ache behind Karlsson's eyes had spread and now occupied his entire skull. He thought of Frieda the previous day, how she had hugged him, although they had never touched each other except for a hand on the shoulder, and how she had thanked him. He realized now that she had been saying good-bye, and he heard his words to Crawford through the thud of pain. "I trust her," he said.

"Get out of here. If I ever find out that you've helped her, in any way, I'll have your head."

On his way out he met a gray-haired man, with tortoiseshell glasses, holding a file. "It's Malcolm Karlsson, isn't it?"

"Yes. Can I help you?"

The man looked thoughtful, as if he were genuinely trying to think of a way in which Karlsson might be able to help him.

"No, no. Not at the moment."

"I'm sorry, who are you?"

"Oh, don't mind me. Just visiting."

Hussein looked across the table at Reuben. Reuben wasn't looking back at her. They were sitting in the conference room at the Warehouse. One whole wall was glass and it had a view that took newcomers by surprise, looking southward right across the city. On a clear day—and today was a very clear day—you could see the Surrey hills, twenty miles away. After a full minute, Reuben turned to face the detective. "I've got a patient in a few minutes," he said. "So if you've got any questions to ask, you'd better ask them."

"Do you know about the offense of perverting the course of justice?"

"I know it's something you're not meant to do."

"It carries a maximum sentence of life imprisonment."

"So I'm convinced that it's serious."

"Did you know that a warrant has now been issued for Frieda Klein's arrest?"

"No."

Hussein paused. She looked at Reuben's face carefully. She wanted to see his reaction to what she was about to say. "Do you know that she has absconded?"

"Absconded? What do you mean?"

"She was due to report to the police station this morning, along with her lawyer. She didn't appear."

"There's probably been a mistake. Or an accident."

"She went to her bank this morning and withdrew just over seven thousand pounds in cash."

Reuben didn't reply. He rubbed his face with his hands, as if he were waking himself up.

"You seem to be taking this very calmly," said Hussein.

"I was thinking, that's all."

"I'll tell you what you need to think about. If you've helped Dr. Klein in any way, if you discussed this with her, then you have perverted the course of justice and you have committed a criminal offense. If you've done anything, if you suspect anything, then you need to tell me now."

Reuben touched the surface of the table very softly with his fingertips.

"Do you really think she killed Sandy?" he asked.

"It doesn't matter what I think. We built a compelling case and the CPS elected to prosecute." She leaned forward across the table. "This won't work, you know. This isn't the nineteenth century. It's not even the 1990s. Someone like Frieda Klein can't just disappear. What she has done is not just against the law, it's insane. When she's caught—and she will be—it's going to be very bad for her and it's also going to be bad for anyone connected with her. Do you understand?"

"Yes, I do."

"Good. Do you know where she is?"

"No."

"Or might be?"

"No."

"Did you know she was planning to abscond?"

"No."

"Who else would Dr. Klein turn to?"

"I don't know. She's a very independent woman."

"When I met her, there was a man with her, a foreigner."

"You mean Josef?"

"Yes, that was his name. Who is he?"

"A friend of Frieda's. A builder. He's from Ukraine."

"Why would someone like that be a friend of Frieda Klein?"

"Is that an insult to Ukrainians or to builders?"

"How can I reach him?"

Reuben thought for a moment, then took out his phone, checked it and wrote the number on a piece of paper. He pushed the piece of paper across the table.

"Who else might help her?"

"Am I meant to name names so that you can go around and threaten them?"

"You're meant to obey the law. Does she have any close relatives?"

Reuben shook his head. "One brother lives abroad, another out of London, near Cambridge. She wouldn't turn to him and he wouldn't help her if she did." Reuben checked his phone again. He reached back for the piece of paper and wrote a name and number. "She's got a sister-in-law she sees quite a bit of. Olivia Klein. You can waste some time talking to her."

Hussein took the piece of paper and stood up. "You were her therapist," she said. "I thought people told their therapists everything."

Reuben gave a short laugh. "I was her therapist years ago and even then she told me only what she wanted to tell me."

"I know you don't care what I think," said Hussein. "But a man has been murdered and your Frieda Klein has gone off on some self-indulgent meltdown. She's wrecking a murder inquiry, breaking the law, and for what?"

Reuben stood up. "You're right," he said. "I don't care what you think."

Olivia Klein also lived in Islington, farther east but still less than a mile from Sandy's flat. When she opened the door and Hussein identified herself, her eyes filled with tears. When Hussein mentioned Sandy's name she started to sob and Hussein had to lead her into the living room, propping her up and then settling her down on the sofa. She went through to

the kitchen and found a box of tissues. Olivia pulled them out in handfuls, wiping her face and blowing her nose.

"I can't tell you what Frieda's done for me over the years. She's saved
me. Completely saved me. When David left, I was just completely . . . I
mean totally . . ."

Her words turned back into sobs. "And then my daughter, Chloë,
went through a terrible time, she was a complete bloody tearaway, and
Frieda helped her with her schoolwork and talked to her. She even put
her up for a while, which deserves some kind of a damehood."

"I suppose she needed a father."

"She needed a fucking mother as well. I wasn't any good to her.
With Sandy, I really thought she'd finally found someone and then it
went wrong and then this. It's so . . ."

Her face disappeared into her tissues once more.

"Mrs. Klein . . ."

"I don't know anything. I didn't really know Sandy well and I haven't
en't seen him for a year. Two years. A long time anyway."

"It's not that."

"Then what is it?"

Hussein was almost reluctant to begin because she knew what was
going to happen. But it didn't. When she described Frieda's disappearance, Olivia just seemed so shocked that Hussein didn't know if she
was taking it in. She looked like a child, with a blotchy pale face, who
had cried and cried so much that there were no tears left.

"Why?" said Olivia, in a small voice that was hardly more than a
whisper. "Why would she do that?"

"I was hoping you could tell me."

"How could I know? I've never known why Frieda does things,
even after she's done them."

"She's done this"—Hussein said each word slowly and clearly so that
there was no mistake—"because she knew she was about to be charged
with a very serious crime."

"But you can't think that she did it. It's not possible."

"We need to be very clear," said Hussein. "If you know anything

about this, if you've helped Frieda in any way, then you need to tell me. That's very important."

"What, me?" said Olivia, suddenly speaking loudly. "I don't even know how to work the DVD player now that Chloë's at college. Every time I want to watch something, I have to phone Chloë up and she talks me through it and I still don't remember. You think Frieda would turn to me to arrange an escape? I'm a drowning woman. When you look at me, you're looking at a woman who's literally drowning. Sometimes Frieda has rescued me and pulled me to the shore and then I've fallen in again. But I can tell you that if Frieda had turned to me, then I would have done anything for her that I could."

"It would actually have been a crime."

"I don't care. But she wouldn't turn to me because she's got too much bloody sense."

The house in Belsize Park looked like it was being demolished from the inside. There were four Dumpsters lined up along the road. Old planks and plasterboard and cables were being carried out of the front door. Meanwhile scaffolding was being unloaded from a van and assembled around the façade. Hussein had to be issued a hard hat, and Josef summoned from somewhere deep inside. Hussein had become used to the strange reactions of people when they had to deal with the police, but when Josef appeared in the doorway and noticed her he just gave a slow smile of recognition, as if he had been expecting her. She followed him into the house and he led her right through and into the large, long back garden.

"It seems like a big job," she said.

He looked up at the rear façade of the house as if he were seeing it for the first time. "Is big."

"Looks like they're taking it apart."

"Gutting. Yes."

"Expensive."

Josef shrugged. "You spend fifteen, twenty million on house, then two or three more is little."

"Not for me."

"Me also."

"We're looking for Frieda. Do you know where she is?"

"No."

She waited for him to elaborate, to protest, but he simply stopped as if he had said all that needed to be said.

"When I met you with Dr. Klein, I felt like you were there as some kind of backup."

"Friend. Only friend."

"I read the police file on Dr. Klein. Your name appears in it."

Josef seemed to smile at the memory. "Yes. Funny thing."

"You were badly hurt."

"No, no. It was small thing." He made a gesture on his arm and a puffing sound.

"You know that Dr. Klein is now a fugitive?"

"Fugitive?"

"On the run. We want to arrest her."

"Arrest?" He looked startled. "Is bad."

"It's bad. It's very serious."

"I must work now."

"You're Ukrainian?"

"Yes."

"If you know anything at all about Frieda Klein's whereabouts, or if you've helped her in any way, you've committed a crime. If so, you will be convicted and you will be deported. Understand? Sent back to Ukraine."

"This is . . ." He searched for the word. "Threat?"

"It's a fact."

"I'm sorry. I must work."

Hussein took a card and handed it to Josef. He looked at it with apparent interest.

"If you hear anything, anything at all," she said.

When Hussein was gone, Josef stood in the garden for several minutes. When he went back inside, he found Gavin, the site manager. Then

walked out of the front door, along the avenue, and turned right on Haverstock Hill. He walked down the hill until he reached the hardware store. The large, shaven-headed man behind the counter nodded at him. Since the job had started, he'd been in there every day. The delivery was ready. Josef took out his phone and checked the time.

"Back in half hour," he said.

He came out of the shop and crossed the road into Chalk Farm station. He took a train south, just one stop to Camden Town. He exited the train just as the doors were closing. He looked around. There was almost nobody on the platform, except for a party of teenagers, probably heading for the market. He came out of the station and walked north up Kentish Town Road. He reached the steps off to the left and walked down to the canal. He could see the market ahead of him but he turned left away from it, under the bridge. As he walked along, he saw the occasional runner. A cyclist rang a bell behind him and he stepped aside. Ahead, he saw a canal boat chugging toward him, an old, gray-bearded man steering it from the stern. Josef stood and waited for the boat to pass him. The brightly colored curlicued decorations made him smile. The man waved at him and he waved back. Ahead of him, he saw a familiar silhouette, standing under a bridge.

As he approached, Frieda turned round. Josef took a piece of paper from his pocket and handed it to her. She unfolded it. "Is he a friend?"

Josef nodded.

Frieda put the paper into her pocket. "Thank you," she said.

"I come with you to see him."

"No. You won't know where I am. You won't know how to get hold of me."

"But, Frieda—"

"You must have nothing to hide and nothing to lie about." She looked into his woebegone face and relented. "If I need you, I promise I will find you. But you must not try to find me. Do you hear?"

"I hear. Not like, but hear."

"And you give me your word."

He placed his hand over his heart and made his small bow. "I give my word," he said.

"Have they been to see you?"

"The woman. Yes."

"I'm sorry. You know, Josef, I'm not good at saying these things . . ."

Josef held up his hands to stop her. "One day we laugh about this."

Frieda just shook her head and turned away.

11

Frieda walked along the canal and bought a pay-as-you-go phone from a little shop on Caledonian Road. She made the call, then took the Overground through the East End, crossing and recrossing the canal, looking into back gardens, breakers' yards, warehouses, allotments. Then the train plunged underground and after a few minutes reemerged into the light in a different country: South London. Frieda got out at Peckham Rye and needed the map to steer her through residential streets, past a school and underarch repair shops until she reached the housing estate. Each large building had a name: Bunyan, Blake, and then—the one she was looking for—Morris.

A man was standing on the pavement talking on his phone. He looked as if he should have been on a touchline somewhere. He was dressed in trainers, tracksuit bottoms, a yellow football shirt with the name of a utility company across the chest and a black windcheater. He was tall, with long hair tied back in a ponytail, revealing earrings in both ears. One eyebrow was also pierced. He might have had a mustache and a goatee or he might just not have shaved for a few days. He noticed Frieda and held up his free hand in a gesture that greeted her, apologized, told her to wait. He was making complicated arrangements about a delivery. When he had finished he stowed away his phone.

"By the time you tell them, it's quicker to do it all yourself."

The accent was a mixture of South London and Eastern Europe. He held out his hand and Frieda shook it.

"This way," he said, and led her in through the gateway to the courtyard separating Blake from Morris.

"Friend of Josef?" the man said. Frieda nodded. "Lev."

"Frieda. Are you from Ukraine as well?"

"Ukraine?" Lev's face broke into a smile. "I am from Russia. But we are like brother and brother."

"Yes. I've been reading about it in the papers."

Lev glanced at Frieda with a frown, as if he suspected he was being made fun of, and Frieda suddenly felt that making any kind of fun of him might be a bad idea. Lev led her up a stairwell, one flight, then another, and up to the third level. He walked along the terrace. Flat after flat was bricked up with large, blue-gray cinder blocks.

"They really don't want people to get in," said Frieda.

Lev stopped and put his hands on the rail, looking out across the space toward Blake House, like a concerned owner. "They are pushing the people out," he said, "then the bricks."

"What's happening to the place?"

"The far house is empty. Next year they knock down and build. In two years, three years, this house too."

He continued along the terrace and stopped in front of a door that had been whitewashed but with only a single coat so that the dark paint underneath showed through. Lev produced a key ring with two keys and a small plastic figurine of a naked lady dangling from it. He detached one of the keys and looked at it. "I give you the key," he said. "And you give me . . ." He stopped to think for a moment. "Three hundred."

Frieda took a small wad of twenties from her pocket and counted out fifteen. She handed them to Lev, who put them in his pocket without checking them.

"For the . . ." He waved a hand, searching for the word.

"The expenses?" supplied Frieda.

"Some things to pay, yes."

He unlocked the door. "Welcome," he said and stood aside to let her in.

Frieda stepped into the little hallway. There was a smell of damp and piss and something else, a rotting sweet smell. It looked as if the flat had been abandoned quickly. Whatever had been hanging on the wall seemed to have been pulled away, leaving cracked and pitted plaster. She turned a wall switch on and off. Good. There was light at least. She put down her holdall and walked around from one room to another.

There was a sofa and a table in a living room, a single bed in a back room and nothing at all in the bathroom or kitchen. No table or chair, no pot or pan.

"Do you own this?" asked Frieda.

Lev grimaced. "Look after," he said.

"And if someone comes and asks me what I'm doing here?"

"Nobody come probably."

"If someone asks, do I mention your name?"

"No names." Lev bent over a portable electric heater in the corner of the living room. He looked up. "When you go out, do not have this switch on," he said. "Is maybe problem. And maybe not when asleep as well."

"OK."

"You here just three weeks, four weeks?"

"I guess. Who else lives here?"

"Only you."

"I mean in the rest of the building."

"All kinds. Syria now. Romania. Always the Somalis. They come and they go. Except one very old woman, very old. English from long ago."

"Is there anything I need to know?"

Lev looked thoughtful.

"Lock the door always from inside. They sometimes play the music very loud. The ear muffs is good, not the complaining."

He held out his hand and shook Frieda's.

"When I'm done, what do I do with the key?"

He made a contemptuous gesture. "Thrown in the bin."

"And if there's a problem, how do I reach you?"

He zipped up his jacket. "If there is a problem, the best is to go away to another place."

"Shouldn't I have your number?"

"For what?"

Frieda really couldn't think of any reason why. "What about the next rent payment?"

"There is not rent."

"Well, thank you, for all of this."

He shrugged. "No, no, this was a thank-you to my friend Josef."

Frieda didn't want to think of what Josef might have done for Lev to have earned a favor like this. She hoped it was only some cheap building work.

"So," he continued, "good-bye to you." He walked to the front door. "And now I think of it, maybe not to use the heater any time. Is not so good. And this is summer, so no need." And he left and Frieda was alone.

She paced the flat. She stopped in the living room and looked at a corner where the wallpaper was coming away. The whole place felt abandoned, desolate, forgotten. It was perfect.

First things first. She took a notepad and pen from her shoulder bag and made a list. Then she left the flat, locking the door after her, and went down the three flights of stairs, through the courtyard and back onto the street. She retraced her footsteps and soon was on the high street. The sky was a flat blue, making everything look slightly garish.

She went into a pound shop, which was crammed with all manner of apparently random objects. There was an entire section devoted to Tupperware, another to water pistols. Paper plates, bath toys, streamers, several fishing rods, mop heads, bath foam, photo frames and patterned cups; plastic flowers, toilet brushes and sink plungers; kitchenware of all kinds. Frieda selected a pack of paper plates, another of plastic forks and knives, washing-up liquid, lavatory paper, a white mug and a small tumbler, a miniature kettle in lurid pink.

She didn't intend to spend much time in her new home and there was no fridge or cooker, but in the small supermarket a few hundred yards up the road she bought ground coffee, tea bags, a small carton of milk, a box of matches and a bag of tea lights.

Laden now, she carried everything back to the flat and laid it out on the table. She took a bottle of whisky from the holdall and put it out as well. She had brought very little with her—just a few basic clothes, a book of academic essays about psychotherapeutic practice and an anthology of poetry, toiletries, a drawing pad and some soft-leaded pencils.

She filled the kettle with water that spat unevenly from the tap and plugged it into one of the sockets. Once she had made herself a mug of tea, she sat on the sofa, avoiding the suspicious stain at one end, and looked around her. The sun shone through the dirty window and lay in blades across the bare floor. So this was freedom, she thought; she had cut all her ties and cast herself off.

Fifteen minutes later, back on the high street, she went into what was labeled a "camping" shop: row upon row of extraordinarily cheap tents, wellington boots, 99-pence T-shirts, footballs, children's fishing nets, zip-up fleeces and waterproof jackets. She found what she was looking for in the dimly lit back of the shop—a sleeping bag for ten pounds.

She had seen the Primark when she came out of the Underground station. She had never been in one before, although Chloë used to buy half her wardrobe there, triumphantly flourishing her haul of sandals and leggings and stretchy dresses that barely covered her backside. She entered the shop now, blinking in the fluorescent dazzle that made everything seem like an overlit stage set, and was momentarily startled by the overwhelming abundance of things—shelves and racks and bins of clothes. A mirror blocked her way and she stopped to look at herself. A woman in austere clothes, pale face bare of makeup, hair pulled severely back: she wouldn't do at all.

Half an hour later she left with a red skirt, a flowery dress, patterned leggings, a natty striped blazer, flip-flops with a little flower between the toes, three T-shirts in bright colors, two of which had logos on them that she didn't even bother to read, and a shoulder bag with studs and tassels. She didn't like any of the clothes and she particularly hated the bag, but perhaps that was the point: they were clothes that represented a self she was not, a role that she must step into.

There was still one more thing she had to do.

"How do you want it?"

"Short."

"How short? A bob, perhaps? With a choppy fringe?"

"No. Just short." She glanced around her and pointed a finger at a picture. "Like that, perhaps."

"The urchin look?"

"Whatever."

The girl standing at her shoulder examined her critically in the big mirror. Frieda hated sitting in the hairdresser's, in the bright lights, seeing the endless duplications of her face. She lay back, her neck on the dented rim of the sink, and closed her eyes. Tepid water sluiced over her hair and trickled down her neck. The girl's fingers were on her scalp, too intimate. Frieda could smell the tobacco smoke on her, and the sweet perfume overlying that. When she sat up again, she kept her eyes closed. She felt the blades of the scissors snickering their way through her hair and cold against her neck, and imagined the locks lying in damp clumps on the floor. She had not had short hair since she was a young girl, and rarely had it professionally cut—Sasha or Chloë or Olivia just trimmed it every so often. She thought of them now, each in their separate lives. Everything seemed very far away: the world on the other side of the river, the streets she walked at night, her little house in the mews, her red armchair in the consulting room, her old and known self.

She opened her eyes and a woman stared back at her. Short dark hair whose tiny tendrils framed a face that seemed thinner and perhaps younger; large dark eyes. Strained, alert, unfamiliar. Herself and not herself; Frieda who was no longer Frieda. As she left the salon and stepped out onto the unknown street, she took the thickly framed spectacles she had bought from her bag and put them on. They were plain glass, yet the world looked quite different to her.

She crossed the road to a mini-supermarket. In the stationery section she found a small notebook with a picture of a horse on the cover and a small box of pens. She bought them and walked farther along the road, past a betting shop and a showroom with secondhand office furniture. On the corner was a shop with a large, bright orange sign: "Shabba Travel Ltd. Cheap Tickets Worldwide. Money Transfer. Internet Café." Taped to the window was a printout of the current conversion rate for the taka. She stepped inside. Frieda hadn't realized that travel agents still existed, but this didn't look like any travel agent she remembered. There were no posters on the walls, no brochures. And it didn't look like a café either.

There was an array of tables, each with its own computer terminal. On the left side of the room there was a laminated counter, behind which was a wall of box files and a man talking on the phone. He was sweating, even though the day was cool, and his blue T-shirt was tight on him, as if it were two sizes too small. When he noticed Frieda, he looked at her suspiciously.

"Can I use one of these?" she said.

"It's fifty p for fifteen minutes," he said. "One twenty for an hour." She put two coins onto the counter. "Which one do I use?"

He just waved vaguely at the room and continued talking. Only one table was occupied. Two young men were sitting at one of the terminals, one of them tapping at a keyboard, the other leaning across him, offering him loud advice. She sat at a terminal at the back, and turned the screen so that it faced away from everyone except her. She went straight to Google and typed in her own name. She looked down the list that appeared and felt a sudden tremor. The first item she saw was "Frieda Klein obituary." It didn't seem like a good omen. She clicked on a link that really did refer to her and saw the familiar photograph of her that the newspapers had used before:

COP DOC LINKED TO MURDER
INVESTIGATION GOES ON THE RUN

POLICE APPEAL FOR WITNESSES AS
FRIEDA KLEIN GOES ON RUN

Frieda had hoped that a psychotherapist failing to appear for a police interview might be a fairly minor news story, but she was wrong. The story appeared on site after site, always with the same photograph. One link was to a local TV news report. She clicked through and saw a blond female newscaster mentioning her name. As she felt around the edge of the terminal to lower the volume, she suddenly caught her breath. The newscaster cut to DCI Hussein standing on the pavement at the entrance to the police station. Frieda's photograph appeared once more and a number for members of the public to call. Then the report changed to footage of a royal visit to a London primary school. Frieda just stared for a few seconds at a group of very small children performing a folk dance in their playground. She got up.

"You need to switch it off."

"What?"

She looked around. The man had finished his phone call and was leaning on the counter. Frieda switched the terminal off.

"There's no refunds," he said.

Frieda walked out onto the pavement. Which way should she go? Since it didn't matter at all, she found it strangely hard to decide. She turned right and walked along the road, then right again along a residential street until she came to a small park. At one end was a children's playground, but the rest was just rhododendron bushes and grass. She went and sat on a bench away from the playground. For a time she found it difficult to organize her thoughts. They felt more like images from a dream than anything coherent. She closed her eyes and saw Sandy, as in a montage, in fragments. Sandy with his slow smile, Sandy lying in bed and watching her while she dressed, driving in the car with her beside him, that last awful walk down to the Thames when she had broken with him. And then the way he had been after, stuck in his anger and distress. Suddenly she felt an urge to hand herself in. It would take only a phone call. Let someone else deal with all of this.

She was shocked by a strange sensation on the fingers of her right hand, warm and wet. She opened her eyes. It was a tongue. A dog was licking at her fingers. It was a Staffordshire bull terrier with a studded metal collar, like a dog in a cartoon. She gently stroked its snout and it sniffed at her. She wondered whether this was wise. Weren't they fighting dogs? Didn't they bite you and then not let go even if you were dead?

"You like dogs?"

The owner looked much like the dog. His round fat head was shaved except for a little neat mustache and goatee.

"I like cats," she said.

"He likes cats too," he said, with an ominous laugh. "Come on, Bailey." He hit the dog halfheartedly with the lead and Bailey slunk away.

Frieda saw a man wheeling a shopping trolley right through the middle of the park. It was piled with stuffed bin bags and rolled blankets. Then Frieda didn't see anything at all because she was thinking about Dean Reeve. The thought of him nagged away at her and wouldn't let her go. It was like a sharp stone lodged inside her shoe, hurting with every step.

Dean Reeve: she had met him five years ago and then, as far as the police were concerned, as far as the world was concerned, he had died. He had killed himself. But Frieda knew that he wasn't dead and ever since he had haunted her. He was like a figure in her dreams, watching her, watching over her. Once upon a time a young woman had tried to kill Frieda. She had stabbed her and stabbed her. But when the police arrived, the woman was dead, her throat cut. The police believed Frieda had done it in self-defense, but she knew it was Dean Reeve. Hal Bradshaw had taunted Frieda, tried to destroy her, and his house had been burned down. People believed that Frieda had instigated it somehow, but she knew it was Dean Reeve. And a man had committed a terrible crime against Frieda when she was just a girl. Frieda had tracked him down, found him. The law could do nothing against him, but he had been found dead, brutally killed. Frieda knew that Dean Reeve had done it. She had broken up with Sandy. There had been cross words, bad feelings, and now Sandy was dead. It had to have been Dean Reeve. It just had to.

Frieda got up and started to walk out of the park. There was only one way to begin. She walked to the station and caught the train going north of the river. She changed at Shadwell onto the Docklands Light Railway and headed east. She was retracing a journey she had taken before, but it felt different. Looking out of the window at the back gardens, the allotments, the junk yards, the piles of tires, she felt as though she were in a foreign city, as if she didn't belong.

Frieda got out at Beckton. She knew the way. Dean Reeve had disappeared. His only brother was dead. But Dean Reeve had a mother, June. She lived in the River View Nursing Home and Frieda had visited her there. As she walked into the front entrance, the smell of floor cleaner and disinfectant vividly brought back a memory of that shriveled old woman, the woman who had done terrible things with Dean. Frieda walked up to the front desk. There was nobody there. She rang a bell and a gaunt, harassed woman in a nurse's uniform emerged from an inner office. Frieda forced a smile.

"Hello," she said. "My aunt's here. June Reeve. I wonder if you could tell me where she is."

The woman seemed puzzled. "Yes," she said. "Yes. And your name is?"

"Jane. Jane Reeve."

"Her niece, you say?"

Frieda met her gaze; her face, with its new glasses and haircut, felt naked. "That's right."

"I'll just check." Frowning, the woman disappeared back into the office.

Frieda looked at the front desk: there was a phone and a computer on it. The sort of computer you would check for patient information. So where had the woman gone? Something was wrong. The woman knew who she was. She turned at a sound behind her: a man was pushing a trolley along.

"I've got something for June Reeve," she said.

The man stopped.

"Didn't she die?" he said. "I think she died. The manager's going to the funeral in three days' time, at the crem down the road. I'm sure that's what she said. Hang on, I'll—"

"That's all right," said Frieda.

It took a great effort. Inside her head, a voice was screaming at her to run, to get out of there as quickly as possible. She turned and walked at a normal pace outside onto the street. It felt like slow motion, as if she were in a nightmare, walking in wet sand. She cursed herself for her carelessness. Karlsson knew about her and June Reeve. He had even been to this very place with Frieda. She wasn't just up against Hussein, she was even perhaps up against Karlsson, and he knew her. He knew her as well as anyone. She turned a corner and then another corner. She didn't dare make for the Docklands Light Railway. They might guess she'd head there. She needed to walk away in a completely different direction.

As she walked, she thought. June Reeve was dead but there was still the funeral: on Monday at the local crematorium, the man had said. Would Dean go to that? Perhaps. And would the police?

She saw a bus pulling up at a stop and jumped on it without even checking the destination. She went upstairs and sat at the front, where she could see the street. It seemed unreal, like a film she was watching. She knew that she would go to June Reeve's funeral, because she could think of no other way in which she could find Dean. This frail thread was all she had to lead her to the man who had killed Sandy.

Frieda had not realized how tired she was until she sat down with a tumbler of whisky as the summer sky darkened in the window frame. She had eaten a poached egg on toast at a little café down the road, looking out at the flow of people passing on the street outside. Now she thought about what she should do tomorrow, which seemed an appalling blank. She remembered that when she was a student one of her professors had once said: "If you can't solve a problem, then find a problem you *can* solve." A name came into her mind and she held it there.

Miles Thornton.

12

Frieda woke to the sound of pipes banging and a man shouting in a language she didn't recognize. She lay for a few moments, looking up at the ceiling, which was cracked and stained. In her own little house, the cat would be walking from room to room, where everything was clean, neat, ordered. Her bed was made, waiting for when she would return.

It was still early, but she rose and swiftly washed in cold water, then dressed in her bright new skirt and top, her head feeling oddly light after her haircut. As she went down the flights of stairs, a young woman sitting hunched in a corner of the stairwell, smoking, lifted her head and stared at her, but incuriously. In the courtyard a bristle-haired boy with jug ears was cycling round and round, singing to himself. Otherwise, the place felt deserted; under the white sky, it was like a ghost town.

Frieda had a mug of bitter coffee in the café she had eaten in the previous evening, then set out for the Underground station. On the train, she thumbed through the pages of a *Metro* that was on the next seat and found a photograph of herself and a brief story. All around her, people were reading the same paper. She put on her fake glasses.

She knew the road that Miles Thornton lived on in Kensal Green, and she remembered that he had once talked about living with three others above a shop that sold office furniture. It wasn't hard to find. She knew that he had violently fallen out with his flatmates; one of them had moved out rather than live with him as he entered his period of most florid psychosis. The other two had sometimes locked him out of his own home and, on a couple of occasions, reported him to the police. But it had been Frieda who had finally had him sectioned, believing he was a danger both to himself and to others, and it was Frieda who he felt had betrayed him above all others. He had called her a cold-hearted bitch, a monster, a cunt. She remembered his face as he shouted at her, wrenched almost beyond recognition, his mouth wide and wet and his eyes brilliant with hatred. But she remembered him, too, as he was on calmer days, when he was terrified by himself.

She rang the bell, and when a voice crackled on the intercom, she announced herself.

"This is Anne Martin. I'm from social services and it's about Miles Thornton. Could I have a quick word?"

The person at the other end said something unintelligible and she was buzzed in. Her new sandals clacked on the boards as she went up the narrow stairs. A young man was standing at the open door of the flat, wearing smart trousers and a shirt but barefoot. He was holding a mug of coffee.

"Hello," Frieda said, holding out a hand. "Anne Martin."

"Duncan Mortimer," he said. "Hi."

"Could I come in? This won't take long."

She didn't wait to see if he would ask for identification, but walked past him into the flat. She should probably have bought a briefcase yesterday. She pulled her notebook from her bag.

"Would you like some coffee?"

"No, thank you. I won't take up your time." She could hear a tap running down the hall, then a door slammed.

"You said this was about Miles?"

"Yes. Just a routine follow-up."

"Poor sod." He took a gulp of coffee. "Tell me. Have you seen him yourself?"

"Seen him? You mean, before?"

"I feel gutted about what's happened and just want to know if he's OK."

"Of course, we all do. That's why I'm here."

"But will he be all right?"

Frieda looked at him; she felt that they were having different conversations. "That's impossible to say, until we find him."

"Find him?"

"You did know that Miles has been missing for several weeks?"

"What?" She started to speak, but he interrupted her. "Don't you know?"

"Know what?"

"Haven't the police told you?"

"I don't understand."

"He's come back."

"Miles has come back?"

"Yeah. He turned up yesterday. I thought that was why you were here."

"Oh," said Frieda. She pushed her glasses back up her nose and tried to keep her expression neutral. "Well, that's good news."

The young man's laugh was harsh and unsteady. "You think so? He's in a complete fucking mess."

"Psychotic?"

"That's the least of it. He's off his head, as far as I can make out. And he's badly injured. Well, that's the polite way of putting it. I spoke to his poor mum. She said he looked as if he'd been tortured."

The room suddenly seemed smaller and colder.

"What does that mean?" Frieda asked.

"It's all I know. She was weeping so hard I didn't like to ask her for details. I wanted to go and see him but he probably doesn't want to see me. We didn't part on very good terms."

"Do you know where he is?"

"He's in that psychiatric hospital south of the river. Hang on, I wrote down the name."

"It's all right. I know the one you mean."

"If you see him, tell him I said hi. Tell him I said get well soon."

"I will."

After she'd gone to an internet café to look up the time that June Reeve's funeral would take place the day after tomorrow—it was eleven fifteen at the East London Crematorium—Frieda bought a cinnamon pastry from a bakery on the high street, then went into a quiet square to eat it and to think. She sat on a wooden bench; the sun was warm on her exposed neck and bare legs; a pigeon pecked at the grass a few feet away. She ate the pastry very slowly, feeling its stodgy sweetness comfort her. Tortured. What did that mean? Who would have done such a thing? The question was like an ill wind blowing through her, making her feel chilly in spite of the summer heat. Because she thought she knew the answer.

She opened her *A-Z*, found herself on the map and saw she was near Peckham Rye Park. She would go there and she would decide what to do next; she would make herself a plan, a grid for the hours ahead. Frieda was a woman who ordered her days. Even when she was relaxing, she did so purposefully, setting aside time for friends, or for making her drawings in her little garret room. Now the day seemed large and shapeless. She sat in the ornamental garden, in the flat summer green of the park. For a while, she concentrated upon the fact of Miles Thornton's reappearance, and his torture. But it was like a foggy darkness that she couldn't grasp and she let it slide back into her mind. She would retrieve it later.

Normally she would be in her consulting room now, sitting in her red armchair, watching the face of a patient opposite her and listening to their words or their silence. She'd let them go and there was no way of knowing whether they were all right or not. Her mind turned to Josef and his mournful brown eyes, to Reuben, to her niece Chloë, who had always known that when she was in trouble or need—as she often was—she could turn to Frieda. Not anymore.

Then she let herself think of Sasha and Ethan, and her heart constricted painfully. Of everyone she had left behind, it was they who worried her the most. Chloë was often chaotic, but she was also angry and resilient. Sasha, on the other hand, never fought her own corner. She was vulnerable and needy, especially now that she was a single mother with a demanding job, a small child, an angry ex and a nanny who, as far as Frieda could tell, was self-righteously unsympathetic. And Ethan couldn't stand up for himself. However much he retreated under the table to his own small place of safety, in the real world he had a crumbling mother, a wounded and angry father, and a hard-voiced nanny who called him a "bad boy."

She consulted her *A-Z* once more, then made up her mind. Ten minutes later she was on the train that went from Peckham Rye to Dalston Junction. From there she walked to the bus station and took the 243 toward Wood Green. She was the only person on it, apart from a small, sad-looking woman with a bedraggled miniature dog at her feet. Neither of them paid any attention to her. She got off at Stoke Newington and went into a small health-food café where she bought a vegetable wrap and a bottle of water. Then she walked toward Sasha's house. It took an effort not to glance round continually. She kept a steady pace as she passed the door, looking sideways but seeing nothing. The curtains upstairs were closed, the shutters downstairs half open. There was no sign that anyone was in. She walked to the top of the road and leaned against a plane tree. She wasn't hungry but ate some of her wrap, watching to see if anyone came or went. Sasha would be at work for a few more hours, but Ethan and Christine would surely turn up.

At two o'clock, she left her post and walked the short distance to Clissold Park. She had been there many times before, with Sasha and Ethan, sometimes Frank as well—and a few times with Sandy. They had taken Ethan in his buggy when he was a small baby and shown him the ducks, the deer. For a moment, she almost felt Sandy beside her now, looking at her, listening, throwing back his head in laughter, taking her hand in his. But, no, he was dead—murdered—and she was alone. How had they come to this?

She stood by the enclosure where the deer were kept and put her face to the fencing, and then she saw them on the other side, half hidden by trees. Ethan first, his face red and blotchy, and there was Christine beside him, holding his hand and pulling him. He was crying; now she could hear him, though she couldn't make out the words and perhaps there were no words, just a sobbing wretchedness. Christine was tugging him, her face set hard. She wasn't responding at all to his distress, simply dragging him along as if he were a heavy object that needed to be moved to a different place. Ethan stumbled and she kept on walking at her brisk, steady pace while he hung from her. "Mummy, Mummy, Mummy," he was saying, and reaching behind him, pulling to go back in the direction they had come from, his face screwed up and blubbery with tears.

Frieda stood quite still and watched them as they disappeared round the bend in the path and Ethan's sobs died away. Her fists were clenched; her heart was clenched. It took all her strength not to run after them and wrench the child from the woman's grip. But she did not. She turned and walked down the path they had come from. She noticed items scattered in front of her and, bending down, discovered they were some of Ethan's miniature wooden animals—the ones he took with him under the table into his imaginary world. That was what he had been trying to get back to. She picked them up one by one, carefully checking that she had not missed any and brushing off the dirt.

Frieda walked for several hours that afternoon, missing her familiar comfortable shoes. She walked down to the canal, past all the houseboats, some of which were large and freshly painted and others that looked like floating slums, then all the way to Islington, coming up at the tunnel and descending again until she came to the Caledonian Road. She walked past Sandy's old flat, though she knew she shouldn't, and let herself imagine walking to her own house. She went instead to the little nature reserve by King's Cross, where she sat for a while looking at the barge that had been turned into an herb garden and hearing the shouts of the schoolchildren who were being taken round by a volunteer.

Then, when it was early evening and the sun was dipping lower in the sky, she walked back to Stoke Newington and stood once more at the top of Sasha's road. She knew that Sasha would come back from work from the opposite direction and, sure enough, just past six, she saw her friend making her slow way toward her house. Even from a distance, she appeared thin and her shoulders had a familiar droop. When she got to the door, she dropped her key and knelt down to retrieve it from the dirt. When she stood up again, she didn't immediately open the door. It was as if she were fortifying herself for an ordeal. At last she went inside.

Four minutes later, Christine marched out, crisp and neat and vigorous. Lights went on upstairs. Frieda waited for a few moments, then went to Sasha's door. She had bought some envelopes earlier and put the wooden animals into one, writing Ethan's name in large block capitals. She pushed it through the mailbox and, before she weakened, she walked swiftly away.

Margaret Farrell. She looked at her dates and did the arithmetic. She'd lived to be ninety, or maybe eighty-nine.

The coffin was deposited at the front and a woman in a dark suit stood up and walked to the lectern. She didn't look like a priest, and she wasn't. The woman described Margaret Farrell as a teacher, feminist, humanist, wife and mother, not necessarily in that order, and there was some laughter and snuffling around her. As people followed each other, delivering tributes, singing, playing a violin, it sounded like a good life. Certainly a far better life than June Reeve had led. Frieda felt a little ashamed at being there under false pretenses. She suspected the police might be there, too, looking at people arriving at June Reeve's funeral, but they wouldn't think of checking the departures from the funeral before. At least, she hoped not.

Frieda heard snatches of poems and music that Margaret Farrell had loved but mainly she was thinking her own thoughts. She knew that Dean had visited his mother in the nursing home once or twice. Might he come to the funeral? It would be the last chance. The two names, Dean Reeve and Miles Thornton, were joined together in a tune she hated but couldn't get out of her head.

The mourners stood up again and started to file out to a scratchy old jazz recording. As Frieda waited for the family members to move past, an old woman turned to her: "How did you know Maggie?"

"Through reputation, mainly," said Frieda.

As they left the chapel, the official was there again, steering them away from the main entrance toward side doors that stood open, leading to the Garden of Remembrance. It reminded Frieda of the elaborate ways that therapists design their consulting rooms so that the arriving patient doesn't bump into the departing one. The proprietors of the crematorium didn't want one group of mourners to collide and remind each other that the chapel was just being rented, like a hotel room or a public tennis court.

The wreaths had been laid out on a patch of lawn that was as smooth as a carpet. People gathered around them and read the labels. Frieda was able to move to a group that was to one side, from where she could

13

Frieda went back to Primark. She needed clothes she could wear to a funeral. She looked through the racks, trying to find something that was dark and didn't have a slogan blazoned across the front. She found some dark gray slacks and a brown pullover. They would do, though Chloë would have wrinkled her nose at the gray/brown combination. She went into a chemist's and bought a cheap pair of sunglasses.

June Reeve's funeral was due to begin at eleven fifteen the following day. The East London Crematorium was farther out, toward Ilford, and Frieda set off early, taking the tube and then a bus, and she arrived just before ten. She walked through the large iron gates that led up to a building that might have been a Victorian library or a private school, with its façade of pillars and classical doorways. There was a large crowd for the funeral before June Reeve's, a hundred people or more, in dark suits and dresses. They stood in groups, hovering, waiting to be allowed inside. Like all large funerals, it was partly a somber occasion and partly a family reunion. Frieda saw women greeting each other, hugging and smiling, then realizing where they were and looking somber. The doors were opened and the mourners started to make their way inside. Frieda attached herself to a group on the edge who didn't seem like family or close friends.

They walked into a large entrance hall. The Victorian building had been boldly modernized, with plate glass and steel between the pillars. An official steered the group to the right, into the East Chapel. It was like a church interior in stripped pine, from which religious symbols had been tactfully removed. Frieda sat in a pew at the back and to one side. She was so lost in her thoughts that it came as a surprise when she had to stand up as she heard a creak behind her and a coffin was carried down the aisle. Frieda picked up the leaflet in front of her.

see the front of the building. The hearse was just pulling away and immediately another hearse drew up in the special bay in front of the portico. Slowly Frieda edged sideways, so that she could get a full view. The scene was completely different from the one an hour earlier. As the undertakers slid the coffin from the hearse and hoisted it to their shoulders, there was nobody there at all. Frieda moved a few feet forward and bent down to look at a very small bunch of wildflowers that looked as if it had been picked by hand. Attached to it was a piece of paper with a child's drawing of a girl with a princess's crown under a smiling sun and the words: *from sally*.

Frieda glanced round. Not nobody. A large woman was standing on the steps. Probably a nurse. And two young men, both in jeans and dark jackets. Plainclothes policemen. That was all. The woman walked inside. The two men stayed outside. Frieda felt a nudge and gave a start. Had she been careless? She stood up and was faced by a woman of about her own age.

"We're driving over to the house," said the woman. "We've got space in the car. Can we give you a lift?"

"That would be great," said Frieda.

As they walked down the drive, the woman talked about how Margaret Farrell had been her headmistress, thirty years before, and what she'd been like. Frieda rather wished she'd known her. When they reached the high road, Frieda said that she'd suddenly remembered that someone else had promised her a lift and the woman said it didn't matter and Frieda felt rather bad about the whole thing.

An hour and a half later, Frieda stood in the entrance hall of the Jeffrey Psychiatric Hospital. She examined the large map of the building. It showed the toilets and the various food outlets, coffee shops and gift shops. But Frieda was looking at the staircases and the fire exits. It was like a party game. Find your way in and find your way out. She had visited the hospital from time to time, and she'd even been based there for a few weeks when she was a student, but she had never paid it that sort of attention. Now she stared and stared at the map, getting a sense of the building as if it were a body, seeing how it fitted together. She had already found out where Miles was and that the visiting time was later in the day.

She walked along the corridor and up three flights of stairs. As she emerged onto the corridor, she saw a man and a woman walking toward her, deep in conversation. She knew him. Sam Goulding. She'd referred a patient to him and they'd met to discuss her. But that had been a couple of years ago. He wouldn't be expecting to see her and he was distracted. She looked to one side. But as they passed, she noticed a movement and he said, "Hey." She kept walking and didn't respond. He hadn't said her name and she wasn't even sure it had been addressed to her. But still. She looked at her watch. It was eight minutes to one. If he remembered her, if he knew what had happened to her, he'd still have to make a phone call. Someone would have to make the connection. Even so. She looked at her watch again. Ten past one: whatever happened, at the latest she would have until ten past one and then she would go.

She turned right, reached Wakefield Ward and went up to the nurses' station. A nurse was fiddling with a paper jam in a fax machine. She looked up.

"I rang earlier," said Frieda. "I'm Miles Thornton's cousin."

"Visiting hours start at three," said the nurse.

"I explained that on the phone. I've just come down on the train. They said it would be all right. I'll only be five minutes. You can check if you like."

The nurse gave a tug at the paper. It was thoroughly stuck. "He's down there on the left," she said. "Bed two."

"Thanks so much."

Frieda looked at her watch. Four minutes to one. The ward was more like a network of corridors. In the first bed, a very old man was sitting up, staring straight in front of him. As Frieda walked past, his eyes didn't even flicker. The next bed, bed two, looked unoccupied, as if it had been left unmade. There was just a bundle of hair on the pillow that showed Thornton was there, unconscious or asleep. She knelt on the floor by his head. Three weeks earlier this face had been distorted with anger and resentment. Now it was swollen and discolored, half swallowed by the pillow. Tentatively, Frieda put out a hand and touched his cheek.

"Miles," she said. "It's me. Frieda. Frieda Klein."

He gave a sort of groan and his head shifted slightly.

"Miles. You've got to wake up. I need to talk to you."

His eyes opened and he looked at her, blinking. He raised his right hand toward her as if to shield himself. It was heavily bandaged. She took it in her hands as gently as she could. He gave another groan. Her touch seemed to be painful.

"I've been looking for you," she said.

"Drink."

There was a jug of water on the table by his bed and a plastic cup. She half filled the cup and held it to his lips. He had to prop himself up to drink from it. She replaced the cup. She looked at her watch. One o'clock. She could see the front desk from where she was.

"Where were you?" she said.

"Voice in dark," he said.

"What voice? What did it say?"

"Telling me. He was cross."

She had heard this before. When he first came to see her, he was experiencing anxiety, but in the next sessions he had begun to talk about the voices he heard, about how angry they were with him, and Frieda had decided that talking therapy wasn't going to be sufficient.

"Was it the same voice as before?"

"No. Not that. You're wrong."

"How do you mean?"

"Didn't just talk. Punish. Said punish."

"I'm sorry," said Frieda. She was starting to think that this wasn't going to amount to anything. It reminded her painfully of when the sessions had started to go awry.

"No. Not that. Really punish."

He started to fumble at the bandage on his hand.

"No, don't," said Frieda.

"He came back every few minutes. Every few minutes. Took me to punish me. Then he'd come back every few minutes, day and night."

Frieda looked at her watch again. Four minutes past one. It was nearly time to go. "What do you mean come back?"

"Tied me up. Come back to hurt me more."

Tears were running out of the corners of Thornton's eyes. He pulled at the bandages. Frieda saw that he was in a state of terrible distress but he was still clearer than when she had last seen him. More lucid. More coherent.

"Did my fingers," he said.

He pulled the last of the bandage off. The tops of the fingers of his right hand were nothing more than remnants. There were no finger-nails and the upper joints were mangled and shapeless, as if they'd been flayed.

"Oh, God," she said softly. "Where were you, Miles? Where?"

"Far away." It was barely more than a whisper; a creak of sound. "Far, far away. Trussed up like a carcass for the journey. Bumping, bumping along, everything dark. Just a long road and then more dark. Nobody to hear me. Nobody came. So many days. Days and nights and nights and days. I couldn't count anymore."

"You mean you went on a long journey?"

"He took me to the sea."

"Who, Miles? Who took you and did these terrible things to you? You have to tell me."

"I could hear the sea all the time. Even when I was crying I heard the waves. They wouldn't stop, on and on. He wouldn't stop. Never left me, never went away, never let me sleep. There was a clock on the wall and I watched it. Never away for more than twenty minutes. On and on. Then let me go. He said tell her."

"Tell who?"

Frieda heard a sound. Two men had come into the ward, one in a suit, one in some sort of uniform. Security. Suddenly it felt like she'd left things too late.

"You," said Thornton. "Frieda Klein. He said tell her. It's for Frieda Klein."

The two men were talking to a nurse.

"Tell her it's for Frieda Klein."

"I see," she said. And she did see.

She had to go. She stood up and started to walk in the opposite direction from which she'd come. She heard a voice behind her. She mustn't look round and she mustn't run. She remembered the map. There was another exit from this ward. She reached the door. It was closed and there was a sign: "Fire escape only. This door is alarmed." She tried to remember the map. Was there another exit farther down the ward? She couldn't risk it. Someone was shouting her name. She pushed the door open and immediately there was an electronic pulsing alarm. She ran down the stone stairs. The noise was so loud that it hurt. One floor down, she pushed a door open and stepped almost into the arms of a man in a uniform.

"There's a woman in the ward above," Frieda said. "She's causing a disturbance."

The man ran past her into the stairwell. Frieda counted to five, then followed him back into the stairwell and went down rather than up. She counted the floors. On the ground floor, she saw the sign to the main entrance and went in the opposite direction, toward the day clinic, which had its own exit and its own car park that led onto a different road. Within five minutes she was outside and away from the hospital, but she continued walking, taking a series of turns into different residential streets, until she was absolutely sure she wasn't being followed.

She saw a bench and sat down. She needed to because her head was spinning and her legs shook. She felt as if she might faint. But she forced herself to calm down and to think clearly about what she had just heard.

Torture: to turn someone into an instrument, an object; to take away their humanity; to humiliate and wound them until all they are is pain, and then nothing. She thought of Miles Thornton's wild, animal face and his creaking voice and his mangled stumps of fingers. She knew who had done that and she knew why he had done that, and for a few minutes she sat there and felt so sick and full of helpless anger and confusion that the world in front of her blurred.

Then she got out her notebook and pen and made a table of dates:

- *Tuesday, 10 June: last sighting of Sandy.*
- *Monday, 16 June: Dr. Ellison (who is she?) reported her concerns about his absence to the police.*
- *Friday, 20 June: Sandy's body found in the Thames.*

She looked at the dates, then added some more.

- *April–May: Miles Thornton sectioned; own responsibility for this.*
- *27 May: Miles Thornton out of hospital and comes to WH, violent and upset. Loudly angry; felt betrayed by me. Returned several times.*
- *3 June: Miles Thornton did not turn up for session.*
- *3 June onward: Miles Thornton not answering calls, e-mails, etc.*
- *Monday, 9 June (right date?): reported Miles missing.*
- *27 June (approx?): Miles Thornton returns, badly injured.*

Frieda stared for a moment at what she had written. There was one more thing to complete the picture:

- *Wednesday, 25 June: June Reeve dies.* She knew that from the funeral notice.
- *Monday, 30 June: June Reeve's funeral.*

She had been wrong all along, terribly wrong. Dean Reeve had abducted Miles, taken him a long distance to somewhere by the sea, and tortured him, of that she was quite certain. And she knew, too, that Miles had been missing since the beginning of June, when Sandy had still been alive. Dean had held him captive until two or three days ago, repeatedly abused him in her name, as a punishment that she was intended to know about: he had sent Miles back with a message. She guessed that Dean had stopped when he had because he had heard that his mother had died and he needed to come back, if not for the funeral, then at least to pay his respects. He had loved his mother, in his own perverse manner.

However hard she tried to make a different story from the dates in front of her, she could not. Dean Reeve had tortured Miles Thornton. But he couldn't have killed Sandy.

14

Frieda sat in her depressing room with a tumbler of whisky, watching the sky turn from blue to pale gray, pale gray to darker gray, then to a bright darkness, scattered with stars. She had bought flowers from the market stall down the road, but their fresh colors only emphasized the dingy aspects of her surroundings, the stained, damp walls and threadbare carpets.

She thought about what she had: nothing.

She had left her home, left her friends, left her job, left her safety and her known world; she had run from the police, ruined her reputation, destroyed her future, lost everything she had built up over the years. For what? For nothing.

She had done all of this because she had believed that Dean had killed Sandy, the man she had once loved more than she had ever loved anyone, and who had been murdered. She had been so sure that she had never even considered the possibility she might be wrong.

She had been wrong, and now she did not know what she should do. Perhaps the only thing left was to give herself up. She let herself imagine it: Hussein's calm and steely face, Commissioner Crawford's triumph, Karlsson's distress. At the thought of her friend, she pressed her glass to her forehead and held it there, closing her eyes. She would be charged, she would be found guilty—especially after going on the run. She would go to jail. For a moment, the thought of being in prison was almost restful.

Then she thought of Sandy. She remembered him as she had first known him, buoyant with love and happiness, and she remembered him as he had been in the last eighteen months, soured and jangled by his wretchedness and anger. Someone had killed him and that person was still out there. If she gave herself up, that person would always be out there. She was not going to let that happen. She set down her whisky and, going over to the window, she stared out at the night sky. She waited there, feeling her resolution harden.

She retrieved her notebook from her bag. She had to start with Sandy. What did she know about him? Who were his friends, his colleagues, his drinking buddies, his affairs and his one-night stands? Who had loved him, hated him, been treated badly by him, felt jealous of or rivalrous with him? She wrote his name at the top of the paper and drew little leaves and flowers curling out of the block letters, as if she were bringing him back to life once more. Then she jotted down every solid fact she could remember, every friend she knew or he had mentioned.

She started with his work. She wrote down the names of people she knew or knew of: Calvin Lock, the professor of neuroscience, who had worked closely with Sandy before he'd gone to America; Lucy Hall, his assistant at that time; Aidan Dunston and his wife Siri, whom they had had dinner with a few times. Who else? She searched through her memories. There was that geneticist in New York, Clara someone-or-other. Surely she wasn't relevant here. And what was the name of his assistant at King George's, whom she hadn't met but had spoken to on the phone? Terry Keaton.

She turned to his family, but Sandy had almost no one. His parents were dead and she couldn't remember him mentioning aunts or uncles or cousins. There was his sister, Lizzie, and his brother-in-law, Tom; their son, Oliver. What was the name of their nanny? She couldn't remember and, anyway, perhaps she'd left by now. After all, she and Sandy had separated eighteen months ago—a lot could happen in eighteen months.

There was Sandy's ex-wife, Maria, who lived in New Zealand. Sandy had spoken of her occasionally. As far as she knew, they had had no contact with each other for years. Since Maria, and before Frieda, there had been a violinist called Gina, whose last name she didn't know, and an Italian economist, Luisa. Sandy had not talked about either of them much.

Friends: there was Dan Lieberman from primary school, with whom he played squash regularly. There was Josh Tebbit. Janie Frank and her partner, Angela. The Foremans. Who else?

She stared at the list, her brow wrinkling. It didn't seem much for someone she had known intimately for many years, and inevitably there had been nothing after they had parted: she had no idea of the shape of his life since then. Sandy had often resented the way that Frieda guarded her independence so fiercely. It had taken months before she had allowed him to stay the night at her house. She had been wary about introducing him to her friends, and had kept aspects of her life secret from him. She had told him of her father's suicide years after they first met, and only confided that she had been raped as a teenager when that episode in her past came back to haunt her present: it was the revelation that had brought Sandy home from America, giving up his job there. But now she saw that she knew very little about him. She knew his tastes; knew what he loved to cook, to eat, what wines he liked. She knew what books he'd read, what his politics were, what his views were on the NHS or organized religion or the placebo effect and antidepressants. She recognized his expressions, understood what made him angry, jealous, glad or wretched. She could *read* him, yet at the same time she knew almost nothing of the ordinary daily details of his life.

Another fact came into her mind, so obvious she had almost let it become invisible: whoever had killed Sandy had known about her. They had let themselves into her house—how?—and planted his wallet there. They had set out to frame her.

She stood up once more and stared into the patch of night sky the little smeared window gave her. Another name came into her mind and settled there. Dr. Ellison. The woman who, Hussein had said, had reported Sandy missing. Who was she? It was at least something to go on, a way to begin, and she pulled on her new unfavorite jacket and went out.

There were several other people at the internet café, all bowed over their computer screens. The room was silent, save for the occasional bleep and hum of the machines, and the light was a sour dim yellow, which made Frieda's head ache slightly.

First of all she Googled "Dr. Ellison." Even when she was only looking for women, there were lots of them, all over the world. She added "UK" and the names dwindled, but there were still too many to be helpful. She pondered, then went to the King George's website; there was no way to do a search on a Dr. Ellison, so she started scrolling through the names of staff in each separate department, beginning with the sciences. Nothing in Neuroscience or Neurobiology, Biomedicine, Genetics, Physics or Molecular Biophysics, Chemistry, Environmental Science, Engineering . . . But suddenly, amid the blur of names, she saw a Dr. Veronica Ellison, who was a fellow in the Psychology department. She clicked on her name and a face came onto the screen, a woman who was probably about Frieda's age, blond, smiling, eyebrows slightly raised as if in surprised inquiry. There was an e-mail address but Frieda didn't want to e-mail her, so she wrote down the number of the department in her notebook. She would call tomorrow. Although it was the summer vacation, someone would be there to answer calls and would at least pass a message on to Veronica Ellison.

On her way back to her rooms, she met the woman she had seen before smoking on the stairs. She raised her head. She had a bruise under her left eye and a split lip. She nodded at Frieda.

Frieda stopped. "I saw you before."

The woman smiled—a smile that was knowing and rueful and oddly jaunty. "Who are you anyway?" she asked.

Frieda sat beside her on the steps. "I'm Carla."

"What are you doing in a shithole like this?"

"Passing through."

"That's what we like to think."

"Your face looks sore."

The woman touched it lightly with the tips of her fingers. "That's nothing. But I could do with a drink."

"I have some whisky in my room."

"That'll do."

Frieda stood up and the woman held out her hand, like a child, to be helped up, then didn't let go of Frieda's at once.

"Carla, you say?"

"Yes."

"I'm Hana." She smiled crookedly again. "Just passing through."

The next morning, just before nine, Frieda walked into the deserted courtyard and called the number for the Psychology department at King George's, and when a woman finally answered, sounding harassed, explained that she needed to contact Dr. Veronica Ellison.

"She's just come in to pick up some books."

Frieda was momentarily taken aback. "Could I speak to her, then?"

"One moment."

Frieda waited several minutes, then a husky, slightly breathless voice said: "Hello? This is Dr. Ellison. How can I help you?"

"My name is Carla," said Frieda, trying to think of a convincing second name. She looked around and saw the name of the building over the gate. "Carla Morris. I am—I was—a friend of Sandy's. I was hoping I could talk to you."

"About Sandy?"

"I lost touch with him and then I heard about his death. I wanted to talk to someone who knew him."

"Why me?"

"A friend mentioned you," said Frieda. "He said you'd been worried about him."

"Well, yes. I was." The woman sounded uncertain.

"I thought perhaps you could tell me what happened."

"Were you and Sandy . . . ?" Her voice trailed off.

"He was just a friend, many years ago. But for a while we were close. Now I need to understand what happened."

"I don't know. I'm going on holiday tomorrow morning."

"Just fifteen minutes of your time, and I could come to wherever was convenient for you."

"All right." Now that she had made up her mind, her voice was brisker. "Come at midday to the garden center just off Balls Pond Road.

It's called Three Corners. I've no idea why. I have to pick up some plants before I go."

"I'll be there."

"Carla, you say?"

"Carla Morris."

"I'll be with the climbing roses."

Frieda had nearly three hours. And the garden center was about ten minutes' walk from Sasha's house. She was anxious about Sasha, and about Ethan. The last sight she had had of him, being pulled along by his implacable nanny, his mouth open in a howl and his dark eyes wet with tears, kept returning to her.

Thirty-five minutes later she was standing in the same position near Sasha's house as she had been two days before. She knew that Sasha often left for work late, and she thought perhaps she would see her. But there was no sign of her leaving and there was no sign of Christine or of Ethan either. Probably she had arrived too late and no one was there.

Even as she was thinking this, the front door flew open and Sasha emerged, in a sleeveless blue work dress. But she was holding Ethan by the hand and talking into her mobile phone. Frieda could see she was disheveled and, even from this distance, there was an air of agitation about her. She watched as Ethan skipped and twisted at his mother's side. Sasha put her phone into her pocket and stopped walking. She put a hand to her throat in a gesture of distress that was familiar to Frieda, then took out the phone once more and made another call. Ethan tugged at her hand.

Frieda put her dark glasses on, buttoned up her bright jacket and walked down the street after them. Now she could hear Sasha talking. "No," she was saying, and, "I'm sorry. I don't know who else to ask."

"Sasha," said Frieda.

Sasha swung round. She stared, her eyes huge in her pale, thin face. Frieda took off her dark glasses.

"Your hair's all gone," said Ethan.

"Frieda! Oh, God. What are you doing here? I thought—the police came, you know."

"I wanted to make sure you were all right."

"I'm trying."

"Where's Christine?"

"She sent me a text this morning saying she doesn't want to be a nanny for a single mother. She says it's more trouble than it's worth."

"Good."

"Good? I'm going to lose my job, Frieda, and then what will I do?"

"Go to work right now. I'll take care of Ethan. If that's OK with you, Ethan."

Ethan nodded and slid his hand into hers.

"I don't understand anything," said Sasha. "And your clothes are weird. Why have you cut off all your lovely hair?"

"Give me your key and go to work before they miss you. We can talk later. Tell no one."

"But, Frieda . . ."

"No one. Now go."

"Can we play animals?" said Ethan, once they were alone together.

"Later. First we're going to a garden center, to see the roses."

He didn't seem impressed.

15

Almost immediately Frieda asked herself, with a kind of horror, what she had done. Absconding, fleeing from the police, leaving all her friends, living among strangers, cut off from her own life: that was one thing. But this felt much worse. She was walking along the pavement with a two-year-old boy who didn't belong to her. His father had left him and his mother was almost in a state of collapse. Yet there he was, his warm little hand in hers, entirely trusting. She could be taking him away from his home never to return and there would be nothing he could do about it. And he was so fragile. He could fall over. He could run into something. He could run out into the road. She tightened her grip as a bus passed and she felt the wind blowing against them in waves.

"Ow," Ethan said, and she loosened her grip, just a little.

He was small and helpless and there were about another twelve or thirteen years before he would be able to look after himself. She thought of her niece, Chloë. Make that fifteen or sixteen years. How did any child manage to get through to adulthood?

"What's that?" said Frieda, pointing.

"Bus," said Ethan.

"What color is it?"

"*Red*," he said, in an assertive, contemptuous tone, as if the question were insultingly easy.

"We're going to play a game," said Frieda. She wasn't exactly sure if two-and-a-bit-year-olds knew how to play games, but she had to try something. "You're going to call me 'Carla.'" There was no answer. She wasn't even sure if he had heard her. "Ethan, can you call me Carla?" His attention was entirely fixed on a man who was walking toward them leading—or being led by—four dogs, each of a different breed and a different size. Frieda waited until they had passed.

"Carla," she said. "Can you say that? Go on."

"Carla," said Ethan.

"That's really clever. My name is Carla."

But Ethan seemed already bored by the idea, so Frieda pointed out a bicycle to him and a bird and a car, and quite soon she was running out of objects, so she was relieved when she saw the green archway ahead at the entrance of the Three Corners Garden Center. She had never noticed it before. It was set slightly back from the road, next to a large shop selling bathroom fittings. The entrance was a narrow driveway but, behind, it opened up on both sides into a mews area that, a hundred and fifty years earlier, must have been stables.

"What we're going to do," said Frieda, "is find the best flower that we can and we're going to bring it back as a present for your mummy. Is that a good idea?" Ethan nodded. Frieda looked around and saw, with some alarm, a section of ornamental trees and climbing flowers. "A little flower," she added. "A really little one." Then she knelt down so that her face was at the same height as Ethan's and whispered to him in what she hoped was a playfully conspiratorial tone, "What's my special name? My name in our special game?"

Ethan frowned in intense concentration but said nothing.

"Carla," said Frieda. "Carla."

"Carla," he said.

She stood up, put on her glasses. Where were the roses? She walked across to a dreadlocked, tattooed, multipierced girl, who was wielding a hose along a line of pots. Ethan looked up at her in fascination. She pointed to the far side, where the space was bounded by a high wall. Frieda and Ethan went across; she saw nobody, so they moved slowly along the rows of roses. They were named after characters from English history and TV celebrities and old novels and stately homes and current members of the royal family.

"Carla?" said a voice.

Veronica Ellison was a striking woman: her blond hair was pulled back off her face, and she was wearing royal blue leggings, wedge trainers and a loose white T-shirt. She looked summery and fresh. She was regarding Frieda with an appraising expression that Frieda found disconcerting. She suddenly realized that she hadn't thought through how she was actually going to do this. The woman hadn't sought her out. There was no reason why she would want to talk to a stranger about Sandy, even if she had anything significant to say.

"Dr. Ellison?"

Veronica Ellison smiled at Ethan. "Is this your son?"

"He's called Ethan," Frieda said. "I look after him."

"Not much fun for him here," said Ellison. "Has Carla brought you to this boring gardening center, Ethan?"

Ethan looked up at her sternly.

"Frieda," he said.

"What?"

"He's at a funny age," said Frieda. There was a pause. It was entirely up to her to make this work, she thought. "It's very good of you to see me," she said. "I needed to talk to someone who knew Sandy. I'll only be a few minutes."

Veronica paused, obviously wondering whether she had the time for this. "All right," she said. "There's a little café here. Shall we grab a coffee?" She looked at Ethan. "And they do very nice ice cream."

Ethan didn't answer. He was shifting his weight from one foot to the other, then back again.

"Does someone need the toilet?" said Veronica.

"What?"

"I mean Ethan," said Veronica. "I've got a three-year-old nephew. I recognize the signs. There's a toilet in the café."

"I was just about to take him," said Frieda, feeling like the most incompetent nanny in London. She wondered about the chances of her getting Ethan back to Sasha alive and basically uninjured. She took him into the ladies' toilet and went through the complicated process of unfastening his dungarees and hoisting him onto the bowl, then redressing him and getting him to wash his hands. Back in the café, Veronica had ordered two coffees and a bowl of ice cream with two scoops: strawberry and chocolate. She had taken over, Frieda saw. That was good. She arranged a cushion on the bench so that Ethan could sit and help himself. Within a few seconds, the ice cream was partly in his mouth and partly around his face. Veronica contemplated him.

"When I see a child, like Ethan, I partly want one of my own and I partly think it would just be too much of a burden."

"It has its compensations."

"You must think so, looking after other people's children for a living. Do you find that satisfying?"

"It's what I do," said Frieda. She thought about her consulting room, the people who came there with their troubles, and here she was, a fake nanny with a false name, wearing tacky, alien clothes and feeling her way into an appropriate manner. "Children keep you seeing the world differently," she added. "That's what makes it interesting, constantly surprising."

"I can see that. But it must be hard work."

"I like hard work. I need purpose—everyone does," said Frieda, firmly, knowing at the same instant that she sounded too like her old self.

A gleam of interest appeared in Veronica's eyes; she sipped at her coffee and looked at Frieda. "I don't quite understand you, Carla."

Frieda was worried that Ethan might correct her again but although his eyes widened suspiciously, his mouth was too full of ice cream. "Why?"

"You seem to have your hands full but then you somehow track me down. What for? What do you want from me exactly?"

Frieda took a breath. This was it. "I knew Sandy. He was kind to me at a difficult time of my life. For a while we were friends of a sort and then we lost touch with each other. Then I read in the paper about what happened to him. I felt . . . I felt I needed to talk to someone else who knew, who'd known him at the end."

"Why?"

"The Sandy I knew was calm and happy and in control. I couldn't believe something like that could happen to him."

"I was just his colleague," said Veronica. "I was working on a project with him."

"What sort of project?"

"It's technical," she said dismissively. "You wouldn't understand."

"But do you recognize the Sandy I described?"

Veronica visibly hesitated. She was clearly deciding whether she could really commit herself to this. "What were your words? Calm? Happy?"

"And in control. Someone who knew his place in the world."

"He helped you, you say."

"Yes." Frieda paused, but seeing that Veronica was waiting for her to elaborate, she said: "He helped me by allowing me to be myself."

As was happening so often now, she had a sudden vivid flash of Sandy as he had once been, brimful of confidence and love. She saw the smile he turned on her. It was perhaps more painful to remember him happy than to recall him grim, angry and wretched. It almost took her breath away, the memory of what they had once had.

Veronica shook her head. "I liked him a great deal," she said. "He was kind. I saw that in him. He was the cleverest person I ever worked with. But he . . ." She took a deep breath. "Things were complicated."

There was a silence broken only by Ethan's slurping and the scraping of his spoon in the bowl. Frieda wondered whether to take the risk and decided she had to. "Were you . . . ?" she began.

"Were *you*?" said Veronica, with a smile.

"No," said Frieda. "It wasn't the right time."

"It wasn't the right time for me either," said Veronica. "But we had a brief . . . Well, I don't know what the word for it is. Something. I wish I'd known the Sandy you were describing. The one I met was more complicated. He could be cruel, or perhaps indifferent is a better word for it. He'd been in a relationship and it had ended badly."

Frieda suddenly felt cold. Had Sandy mentioned her name?

"He hated talking about it. But sometimes I felt he was like someone who had been in a terrible car crash or suffered a terrible loss. Well, he had suffered a terrible loss and he wasn't over it. In fact, I'd say he was stuck in it and didn't even want to move on."

"I'm so sorry," said Frieda, painfully aware that almost for the first time she was saying something truthful. "That must have been hard for you. Being involved with a man who wasn't emotionally available."

Veronica said to Ethan: "You're a lucky boy. Carla's a clever woman, isn't she?"

"No!" Ethan scowled at her.

"He was such an intelligent man," said Veronica to Frieda. "He was intelligent about everything except his own life. He was drinking too much, he didn't look after himself. He needed help and he wouldn't be helped. It's awful what we do to each other, isn't it?"

"Yes. It is." Frieda liked Veronica and felt that they could have been friends in another life.

"And what we can't do. Sometimes it felt like I was standing by a lake watching a man drown and I couldn't do anything about it." Suddenly Veronica Ellison's expression looked vulnerable and touching. "I'm not normally that sort of person—I don't like being helpless. Why am I telling you this?"

"Because I'm a stranger."

"That's probably it. Anyway, he'd just had an affair with someone else before me and he seemed to feel he'd behaved pretty rottenly, although he didn't go into any details. He never went into details. I'm sure he was also seeing another woman while we were together. If you can call it together. And then, sure enough, he moved on. But even when he was doing it, I felt sorry for him, rather than angry. But that's my problem, I suppose."

"I don't think so," said Frieda. "Unless having insight and being compassionate is a problem. Which, of course, it can be."

Veronica raised her eyes and studied Frieda's face. "Hmm," she said thoughtfully. "You really didn't sleep with him?"

"No." Frieda didn't lower her gaze. "As I said, it wasn't the right time. And I wasn't the right person for him." That, at least, had turned out to be true.

"I think you would have been good for him. Someone not in his intellectual world. Someone grounded, sensible." She met Frieda's gaze. "That sounds rude. It wasn't meant to be."

Frieda shook her head. "So at the end, when you last saw him, Sandy was sad, distressed."

"There was something else."

"What?"

"I think he was scared."

"Oh. Why?"

"I don't know."

"Why do you think he was scared?"

"I just knew. I can't explain."

"He didn't actually tell you?"

Veronica frowned. "This is turning into an interrogation," she said.

"Sorry. But had someone threatened him?" Frieda persisted.

"The police have asked me all of this already. I don't know why I should go through it again with a nanny. Why does it matter so much? Sandy's dead."

"It matters because someone killed him. Perhaps he knew he was in danger."

"Perhaps. But I've told you everything I know—though I don't understand what you're looking for. Now I need to go."

Frieda lifted Ethan onto the floor. His hand was sticky and hot in hers.

"Thank you," she said. "I appreciate it." Although in truth, apart from discovering that Sandy had perhaps been scared, she hadn't got much further. All Veronica could tell her was what she had already known: that Sandy had been unhappy and his life had become in some ways dysfunctional.

"It's been such a shock," said Veronica. "For all of us."

"Yes."

"As a matter of fact—" Veronica stopped, biting her lip.

"What?"

"I was going to say that a group of us are having a little memorial for Sandy this evening. We felt we had to do something. There can't be a funeral yet because of the investigation."

"That sounds like a good thing."

"It's nothing formal. It's at the home of his head of department. People will speak of their own particular memories of Sandy, perhaps one or two people will read things. I wondered if you might like to come."

Frieda thought about Sandy's sister, Lizzie, and of those friends of his she'd met and who would recognize her at once, no matter what she was wearing.

"I'm not sure," she said. "Who'll be there exactly?"

"A small group of us from the university and then a few other people who knew him and whom we knew how to get in touch with. Not his family, not that he had much family, and nothing intimidating." She smiled encouragingly at Frieda. "You wouldn't need to say anything. But it might be good for you to hear other people remembering Sandy as well."

"Sandy," said Ethan, suddenly and loudly. "Where's Sandy?"

Frieda leaned across and wiped his mouth comprehensively.

"It's kind of you," she said to Veronica. "I think that I'd like to come."

Back at Sasha's house, Frieda made Ethan a lentil salad, which he didn't eat, and then played a game of hide-and-seek with him. It was true what she had said to Veronica: children really do view things differently. Ethan thought that if he couldn't see her, then she couldn't see him. He stood in the corner of the room with his hands over his eyes and she loudly tried to discover his whereabouts. Then he slithered under the table with his wooden animals and she could hear him talking to them, a bit bossy but confiding. When his voice stopped she peered under the tablecloth and saw he had fallen asleep, his hands clutching his miniature toys and his mouth half open. She gently pulled him out of his den and laid him on the sofa, pushing a cushion under his hot head and closing the curtains so his face wasn't in the sunlight. She sat and watched him for a while, the breath puffing his lips and the flickering of his eyes in dreams. What was he dreaming of, she wondered, this mysterious little creature? What did he see when his eyes were closed?

When Sasha returned, Frieda was reading a book to Ethan. It was about lots of animals sitting on a broomstick and he knew it almost by heart and joined in with the words.

"This is the sixth time I've read it," said Frieda, standing up. "If I try to read anything else, he holds his breath so that his face goes bright red. I was afraid he would pop. It's amazing how much power a small child can have."

"But has he been all right?" She bent to kiss Ethan but he wriggled free of her and disappeared under the table, where they could hear him banging things.

"He's been good."

"You saved me."

"Hardly."

"I've taken tomorrow off—they think I'm going to a conference in Birmingham—so I can sort out child care. I can hardly bear the thought of it. Beginning all over again with some stranger. I'd almost rather give up my job, but I don't know if I'd cope with that—just being a mother, losing that structure and identity in the outside world. That's what I'm really scared of: collapsing, going mad like I did before. I never want to go back to those days. I never want Ethan to see me like that. He must not."

"Perhaps you don't have to bear it," Frieda said, after a pause.

"What do you mean?"

"I can cover for a while. A week or two. Especially if you take some of the holiday you're owed."

"Are you serious?"

"Of course."

"Why?"

"Because you need someone to look after Ethan, someone you can trust." Frieda forced herself to smile reassuringly. "People don't really look at a woman with a child and that's what I want."

"Tell me about it." Sasha's tone was rueful.

"So we would be helping each other out, until you find a replacement."

"I can't tell you how wonderful that would be."

"Wait," said Frieda, with a sterner expression. "You need to think about this. By not reporting me, you're committing a crime."

"That doesn't matter."

"It might."

Sasha shook her head decisively. "Nobody will know."

"Except Ethan."

"Ethan won't tell anyone. He's not old enough—he doesn't make connections. If something's not there it doesn't exist any longer."

Frieda thought of Ethan standing with his hands covering his eyes, thinking he had made himself invisible. "Right," she said. "Let's see how it goes."

"I don't know what I would have done without you, Frieda. Seeing you this morning was like a kind of dream—well, it still is. I half expected Christine to be standing at the door with her jacket on, looking disapproving. She was an awful woman, wasn't she?"

"She was."

"I don't know why I put up with her."

"She's a bully."

"Perhaps I attract bullies."

"Perhaps you do," Frieda said. "You should think about that."

"What about you?"

"What about me?"

"What's going to happen to you?"

"I don't know."

"Where are you living?" Frieda didn't answer. "You can't be in hiding forever."

"I don't intend to be. I just need to ask some questions. And answer them as well."

"It's like a nightmare."

"It seems real enough to me."

"Do they really think you did it?"

"Yes. With some reason," she added. "The evidence does point to me. I thought I knew who killed him, I was certain, but I don't."

"You have no idea?"

"No."

"And if you don't find out, then what will happen to you?"

"I'm thinking about you, just now," said Frieda. "What if the police come in a few days and ask about things?"

"I'll deny everything."

"What if they ask about your child care arrangements?"

"Why would they?"

"But what if they do?"

Sasha thought for a moment. "I don't know what I could say."

"No," said Frieda. "But I do."

The gathering for Sandy was at seven, near Tower Bridge. Frieda went back to her rooms first. She needed to wash—though washing wasn't very satisfactory when the shower was feeble and the water cold—and to change into something less brightly loud.

When she approached her door, she stopped in her tracks. She had seen something, a shape. Then the shape moved, and Frieda saw it was a figure sitting hunched up, matted dark hair, a baggy shirt, bare feet.

"Hana," she said, going forward and bending down to the woman.

Hana lifted her head. Her face was barely recognizable: the left cheek was mashed and swollen and the left eye closed. The nose looked broken.

"Come with me," said Frieda, taking the woman and heaving her to her feet. She smelled of tobacco and fried onions and old sweat; there were damp patches under her arms and a dark V down her back. There was blood on her collar and down the front of her skirt and splashes of it on her bare, grubby feet.

"Carla." Her voice was thick. "I was going to—"

"Don't talk yet. Here."

She led her inside and sat her on the stained sofa, then ran water into a bowl and carefully washed Hana's face; the water turned red and cloudy. The woman made small moaning noises.

"I think you need stitches. You should go to the hospital."

Hana shook her head wildly. "He'd kill me."

"He's already nearly killed you."

"You don't understand."

"Who is he?"

Again Hana shook her head, although the movement obviously hurt her.

"Is he your husband? Your partner?"

"Do you still have whisky?"

"Yes." Frieda rose and poured some into the tumbler. Hana drank it as if she were thirsty, though much of it dribbled down her chin. Frieda could see blood in her mouth. "Have you thought of going to the police?"

"No!"

"Or a women's refuge."

"I have no money. Not a penny. He has everything. My papers, all of it."

"You can still leave him. You have a choice."

"You don't understand," the woman said again. "It's different for people like you. I have nothing. Nothing," she repeated. "He has even taken my shoes away. I said I was leaving, I was going to stay at my cousin's, and he cut my shoes up and did this." She touched her mangled face very gently with the tips of her fingers. "This is my life," she said. "I was stupid to think it could be different."

Frieda looked at the woman's softly hunched shoulders, her battered face, her dirty feet and her bloodstained, tatty shirt. "I can help you," she said.

"How? You're here as well, aren't you? What can you do?"

"Wait."

Frieda stood up and went to the bedroom. She pulled her holdall from under the bed. Tucked inside her walking boots was the cash she had withdrawn from her bank on the day she had left her life behind. She counted it out: she had six thousand two hundred pounds left. She counted out three thousand one hundred pounds and pushed the other half back into her boot.

"Here," she said, holding the money out to Hana as she returned to the living room. "Take this."

Hana's eyes widened and she shrank back as if she were scared. "Why?"

"So that you can leave."

"No. *Why?*"

Frieda looked at the money in her outstretched hand. "That's not important," she said. "It's for you."

Hana took it and stared at it dazedly. She licked her dry lips and gave a huge sigh that turned into a kind of snort. "Is this a trick?"

"No."

"You're a strange woman."

"Maybe. Who isn't? Take my flip-flops as well," said Frieda.

"What?"

"You have no shoes. I don't need these. I have others. They'll fit well enough."

She slid off the flip-flops and passed them over. Hana stared at them as if they might blow up.

"I've got to go out in a minute," said Frieda. "I just need to wash and change."

"Can I have some more whisky?"

Frieda slid the bottle along the table and left Hana on the sofa. She went back into her bedroom and looked through the clothes she had bought, none of which she liked or felt comfortable in. She selected the dark gray trousers she had got for the funeral, and then a blue T-shirt to go over the top. It had a large green star on the chest. Her top half looked like a cheerleader's; her bottom half like a frump's. Carla Morris would probably wear some makeup but Frieda Klein was tired of Carla Morris and left her face bare, though she put on her fake glasses.

"I need to go now," she said to Hana.

"Yeah." Hana's eyes had a glazed look. She knocked against her chest as if she were a door she could open. "Me too. My new life's waiting."

"You can do this."

"You think so?"

16

Frieda thought at first she must be in the wrong area. She was on a busy road just south of Tower Bridge. Buses and lorries were thundering past warehouses and housing estates, but she turned onto a side street and found herself in a Georgian terrace. Each house was painted a different color—light blue, yellow, pink—and there were blue tubs of flowers in the front gardens.

She reached number seven and knocked at the door. It was opened by a woman in her late sixties, tiny and wiry, with a shock of gray hair and small eyes gleaming behind her glasses. She looked surprised.

"I'm Carla Morris," said Frieda. "Veronica Ellison invited me. I hope that's all right."

The woman took Frieda's hand in a firm grip. "I'm Ruth Lender," she said. "Come in."

Frieda stepped inside and felt a sudden burn of memory. It came from the smell: books, beeswax furniture polish, herbs; it was the dry, clean smell of her own home. For a moment she was standing in the hall of her narrow mews house and a cat was at her ankles.

"You were a friend of Sandy's?"

Frieda nodded. She at once liked this woman, as she had liked Veronica. She was glad that Sandy had found friends and at the same time had an acute sense of what she had rejected. She had had several clients over the years who had fallen desperately in love with partners or spouses after they had died: death is a great seducer. She was in no danger of that with Sandy, but there was the feeling that the wretched and angry man of the last eighteen months had receded and the other Sandy, the one of quick intelligence and kindness, was clear to her again. She was glad of that.

"Carla, you say? I don't think he mentioned you to me."

"It was a long time ago."

"It's sad, isn't it, how we want to get back in touch with people once they have died?"

The house was spacious, and shabby in a way that Frieda liked: the kitchen had a rickety wooden dresser in it, and unmatching chairs around the wooden table, on which were dozens of glasses, tumblers, side plates and a wooden board on which were several oozing cheeses. The large living room was lined with books; piles of papers and periodicals were stacked up by the wall, evidently pushed there to clear a space for the gathering. There were about twenty-five people already in the room, perhaps more. She scanned the faces quickly, waiting for the shock of recognition, but none came. All these people were strangers to her. Some of them obviously knew each other and stood in small groups, holding wineglasses and talking; others stood at the edges of the room, unsure. She saw Veronica with two men, one spindly and fair, the other squat, barrel-chested, with a rumbling voice that carried across to her. A young man pressed a glass into her hand and moved away. The woman next to her caught her eye and smiled shyly, hopefully.

"My name is Elsie," she offered. She had an accent that Frieda couldn't place.

"I'm Carla. It's good to meet you. How did you know Sandy?"

"I was his cleaner. He was a very nice man."

"He was."

"Very polite."

"Yes."

"And tidy too. My work was easy. Although sometimes"—she lowered her voice—"sometimes he broke things."

"Broke things?"

"Yes. Plates. Glasses."

"Oh." Frieda was nonplussed. "You mean, deliberately?"

"He put them in the bin, but I always knew."

"Really?"

"One woman I worked for used to put all her chocolate wrappers into a tied-up plastic bag in the bin. She was very thin." The woman held her hands close together to indicate her employer's extreme narrowness. "But she ate many chocolate bars each day."

Frieda spoke neutrally, looking away from the woman: "So what did Sandy want hidden?"

"No wrappers. But he was worrying."

"How could you tell?"

"More drink. More cigarettes. More lines in his face. More broken plates. Worry."

"I see. Do you know why?"

"No. We all have worries, after all."

"That's true."

"I know there was a woman who left him and he missed her. He told me once, when he had drunk some wine."

"Really."

"I saw her photo on his desk, before he put it away."

Frieda tried to maintain her expression of mild interest.

"Dark and not smiling. Not so beautiful, in my opinion."

There was a ping of sound as Ruth Lender rang a spoon against the rim of her glass; the room fell unevenly into silence. She was standing at the end of the room, by an upright piano that Frieda now saw had a large framed photo of Sandy on it: a head-and-shoulders portrait of him, in a suit with a white shirt. He was half smiling. His eyes were looking straight at her.

"It's good to see you all here," Ruth said, as the faces turned to her, solemnly anticipatory. "And although none of us wants this to be formal or constrained, it is nevertheless a time for us to talk about Sandy and remember him, each in our own way. Because he died so young, and so shockingly, because there's a horrible mystery about his death, because there won't be a funeral yet, it seems important to find ways of talking about our feelings and of saying good-bye to him."

"Hear, hear." This from the barrel-chested man beside Veronica.

"In about an hour we will have snacks—most of them inspired by food that Sandy loved—and we know how he loved good food, good wine. Not-so-good wine." A ripple of laughter ran through the room.

"But, first, let's see if we can express some of the things we feel." She paused, took a sip of her wine. Frieda recognized a woman who was used to speaking in public, giving lectures.

"Some of you have come prepared, I know, but everyone should feel free to have their say—or to remain silent, of course. It's always hard to break the ice, so I thought I'd begin." She reached across to the top of the piano and pulled a small pile of cards from it. "But I don't want to give you my purely personal memories of Sandy—who, by the way, I was responsible for bringing to the university, because I considered him smart and imaginative and forward thinking, and I never for an instant regretted it. I've spoken to colleagues and some of his students, people who can't be here today, and they've given me sentences or phrases or single words that they thought summed him up."

She took another sip of her wine, then put it on the piano, and pushed her glasses more firmly into place.

"So, here goes. Terrifyingly clever . . . Didn't suffer fools gladly . . . Intellectual in the best sense of the word . . . Better than me at poker. Handsome . . . Cool . . . A dab hand at the cutting remark . . . Someone you wanted on your side . . . He had a nice laugh . . . A man whose good opinion I valued . . . He was the best teacher I ever had and I wish I'd told him that . . . I will miss him . . . I was a bit scared of him, to be honest . . . Very competitive . . . He had a fearsome backhand spin . . . He loved blue cheese and red wine . . . Complicated . . . Mysterious . . ."

Frieda listened as the words continued. She was remembering Sandy as she had seen him outside the Warehouse, his face contorted in anger, and then suddenly she saw him the first time they had gone back to his flat, his face smoothed out with happiness so that he looked younger and more innocent. She would hold on to that.

Someone else was standing up now, a tall, gangly man with angular features and quick gestures, who introduced himself as Sandy's close colleague; he was talking about a conference he and Sandy had been to, an argument about the artificial notion of self that continued through the night with Sandy fresh and vigorous, drinking whisky. At times, the man's voice became husky and he had to stop, clear his throat. When he was done, Veronica came forward.

"I just want to say a couple of things." Her cheeks were flushed and Frieda could tell that she was nervous. "As some of you in the room know, Sandy and I had our ups and downs. I saw him when he was vulnerable and I saw him when he was harsh, even cruel at times, though I think he was really a very kind man. One of the words used about him earlier was 'complicated,' and he certainly was. But he was the real deal. He'd lived, he'd loved, he'd suffered. None of us here knows why he died, but the person who killed him killed someone who is irreplaceable and will be missed by all of us."

Her voice trembled and her eyes filled with tears. The gangly man who had spoken before her put his arm around her shoulders and led her back to her place in the corner. Frieda saw a tall woman with black hair and extraordinary blue eyes put out a hand in comfort.

There were more stories. A man who had played squash with Sandy described his ferocity on court to laughter from the room. An old woman read a poem by John Donne in a voice so quiet people had to strain to hear it. Someone else read out a favorite recipe of Sandy's in a thick Scottish accent and said he would e-mail it to anyone who wanted it. A woman with tattoos running down both her bare arms said how good he was with kids and a voice called out: "Ask Bridget about that. She'll have stories to tell."

The black-haired, blue-eyed woman Frieda had noticed before glared. "None that I want to share, thank you," she said in a clear voice. "Sandy was a private man."

The atmosphere chilled for a moment. People exchanged awkward glances, but Frieda looked at the woman with interest. She had turned her back and was looking out of the large French windows onto the garden, which was lush and overgrown, with roses in blowsy flower.

A woman came forward holding a violin and introduced herself as Gina. Frieda knew about her, although they had never met. Gina said she and Sandy had been involved a long time ago, and although they hadn't met for many years, she had wanted to be here to play something for him. She said she had chosen a Bach piece that he had loved. She played it with sinuous skill, apparently in a world of her own. Frieda saw a couple of people pressing their fingers into the corners of their eyes or pulling tissues from their pockets.

Refreshments followed. Young people, whom Frieda guessed to be Sandy's students, carried trays around with snacks on them. She took a blini with smoked salmon on it and made her way across the room toward the woman who had refused to speak about Sandy. She was talking to Veronica; the gangly man stood beside them. He had a thin, clever face and almost colorless eyes. As she approached, Veronica saw her and beckoned.

"Hi, Carla," she said. "These are my good friends Bridget and Al. Al worked closely with Sandy," she added.

"Hello," said Frieda. She shook their hands. Bridget was almost as tall as Al, and her strong, vivid appearance contrasted with his pale thinness. She was all color and form, while he was made up of planes and angles.

"Carla knew Sandy a long time ago," explained Veronica.

Bridget looked at her, taking in her stupid T-shirt and dowdy slacks, her roughly cut hair.

"You were right, he *was* a private man," Frieda said to her. "I always felt he was hard to properly know."

Bridget frowned and looked away; she wasn't going to be drawn into reminiscences.

"In fact," said Veronica, after a pause, "Carla might be just the person you were looking for."

"I'm sorry?" said Frieda.

"Carla's a nanny," continued Veronica. "Aren't you, Carla?"

"Oh, yes."

"Bridget and Al have been let down by theirs and are looking for someone to step into the breach."

"That's right," said Al. "We have a girl of three and a boy of just one. Are you available?"

"No." She remembered she was Carla here, not Frieda, and added in a more conciliatory tone: "Not really."

"Not really?" Bridget raised her thick eyebrows and smirked. She seemed in a jangled and impatient mood. "What does that mean?"

"It means I'm not really available."

"Well, if you change your mind, give us a call." Al pulled a wallet out of his jacket pocket and extracted a card.

Frieda turned away but Veronica followed her to say: "Don't mind Bridget. She's upset."

"Because of Sandy?"

"They were close. She and Al were the nearest thing Sandy had to a family."

"I thought he had a sister."

"Well, yes. But Sandy spent a lot of time at Al's house and the kids were very attached to him too."

"I see."

"She doesn't do sad. So she does angry instead. Poor Al," she added fondly.

"Complicated?" said Frieda. "What did you mean by that?"

"Complicated?"

"You said Sandy was complicated."

Veronica seemed discomposed. "Nothing in particular. But don't you feel that events like this don't really show people the way they were? It's always 'they liked this' or 'they were good at that.' We're all messier than that."

"In what way was Sandy messy?" said Frieda.

"He could be difficult," Veronica said awkwardly, and Frieda felt she couldn't push any further.

A large man was seated on the spindly piano stool, his dimpled hands rippling delicately over the keys. In the corner Frieda thought she glimpsed Lucy Hall, who had been Sandy's PA several years ago, but Lucy showed no sign of noticing or recognizing her. Sandy's cleaner was talking to Ruth Lender; she towered over the tiny professor, and tears were running down her cheeks. Gina was putting her violin back in its case. Frieda considered talking to her but decided against it: what was the point of hearing an old flame's fond memories?

Then, out of the corner of her eye, she glimpsed a figure with red hair and turned away sharply, staring fixedly out at the garden with her back to the room, not daring to move. She heard Ruth greet him, and Veronica's voice joined them.

"Lawn needs cutting," said a voice beside her. It was Al.

"I suppose so. I like it a bit wild."

Very cautiously she adjusted her position and glanced to her left. The man with red hair was standing near the piano. He was holding a glass of wine and talking to Veronica and Ruth; he seemed hot and a bit agitated. He dabbed a handkerchief against his freckled forehead. She had been right: it was Tom Rasson, married to Sandy's sister, and someone she had met many dozens of times. The room was emptying and she felt exposed, standing there in her shallow disguise. He had only to look her way to see Dr. Frieda Klein, the woman who had thrown over his brother-in-law, who had identified his body, who had run from the police, suspected of his murder, who had turned up with a shorn head to snoop on the people who had become his friends.

"Let's have a look at it," she said to Al.

She bent down and tugged the lock at the base of the French windows. It came up reluctantly. She yanked at the handles and the doors swung open with an audible snap; warm air gusted into the room. She stepped out into the garden, the grass long around her ankles. It was twilight and she could smell the flowers and the moist earth. Al stepped out after her politely.

"Do you like gardening?" he asked her.

"Not really," she said. "But I like being in gardens." She gave him a smile. "I ought to be going. Perhaps I can leave this way."

She went swiftly round the back of the house and through the side gate she'd seen when she arrived, drawing back the stiff bolts to release it, raising her hand in a wave to Al, stepping out onto the pavement, walking away.

17

When Frieda got back to her flat, she sat on the sofa for several minutes. There was no radio to turn on, no music to listen to, no book to
take down from the shelf. It was almost restful, except that there were
always noises from outside, shouts, the banging of doors, car horns. She
really didn't want to transform this dingy space into anything that
resembled a home, and had no impulse to make it into her own territory. But she needed to buy some more things, cleaning stuff, basic
supplies. She would do some shopping in the late-night store, fix a meal
and make a plan.

She got up and walked into her bedroom, pulled the bag out and
took out her walking boots. She pushed her hand into one boot, then
into the other. She repeated the action to make sure, although she was
already sure. All of the money was gone.

Frieda felt quite calm: it was as if she had been expecting this to
happen. She was neither fearful nor distressed, but was conscious of a
sense of steely resolve. She went out of the bedroom, out of the front
door and along the balcony. She counted the flats until she found the
right one, then knocked on the door. Nothing. She knocked hard again.
She heard movement and the door opened. The man was so large that
he filled the doorframe. He was wearing jeans and a shiny blue football
shirt and had long dark hair, really long, down to his shoulders. He was
holding a TV control.

"Is Hana here?" said Frieda.

The man just stared at her. His gaze was heavy, like something
being laid on top of her to hold her in place. Frieda couldn't tell if he
had heard her or if he even understood English, but she could sense the
weight of his hostility. She knew that she was putting herself in danger,
yet she didn't feel scared because she was so angry.

"Hana," she repeated. "I think she's got something of mine. I need to talk to her."

Still no answer.

"I would like you to answer me," she said. "Because I know you understand what I'm saying to you."

It had happened even before she knew it was happening. She was pushed, across the balcony, hard against the railing. His right hand was on her neck, pushing her back. She noticed the oddity that his feet were bare and that his breath smelled meaty as she teetered backward and wondered almost abstractly whether this was it, whether he was going to push her over the railing. He shifted his grip, grasping the top of her shirt.

"I never even want to *see* you again," he said. "You hear me?"

Frieda didn't think an answer was required.

"I said, you hear me?"

"I hear you," said Frieda.

The man held on to her shirt for a few more seconds, then released her and gave her cheek a light slap. He walked back inside and shut the door.

Frieda went back to her own flat. She felt in her jacket pocket. She found a twenty-pound note and a five-pound note. She had four pound coins and some change. She considered for a moment, gathering her thoughts, then she went out and down the stairs and into the street. She needed to walk, as if it were a way of converting her anger into something purposeful. She passed through streets, through a park, along the side of a graveyard, along the side of a railway bridge with car-repair shops under the arches. Suddenly she stopped and looked around. She had been seeing nothing, hearing nothing. She hadn't even been thinking in any coherent way. She tried to orient herself. For a moment she thought she was lost but, with difficulty and a few wrong turnings, she was able to find her way back.

She remembered that she hadn't eaten but she wasn't hungry anymore. She half undressed and got into bed, but as hour after hour passed, the idea of sleeping seemed impossible. A few feet from her was that man: she could still feel his hand on her neck and his breath on her face. At one point she reached for her watch and saw that it was half past two, and she thought of getting up, leaving the flat and walking through the streets again, as she often did at times like this. Instead she lay in the dark and thought about the process of going to sleep, of letting yourself drift into unconsciousness, and wondered how people did it, how she had ever managed it before. And she thought of everyone in London, everyone in the world, who needed—once every day— somewhere to go to sleep.

And then she must have been asleep herself because she woke with a start. She looked at her watch. She needed to hurry. She got up and undressed and washed in the trickling shower and pulled on more clothes and ran out the front door and took the train up to Sasha's. It cost her three pounds, which left her with just over twenty-six. She thought about people who made calculations like this every day—each pound mattering, each bus or train journey adding up, every cup of coffee in a café something to be budgeted for. The world felt a very different place if you didn't know how you were going to get to the end of the week, much more precarious, much scarier. She had always known this, but now she felt it—and all of a sudden she remembered herself at sixteen, without money and alone in the world, and it was as if she'd come in a circle back to that time when she had had nothing.

But, of course, she didn't have nothing, because she had friends.

"I need to borrow a small amount of money."

"Of course. Is something wrong?"

"I just need some cash."

Sasha looked through her purse. She had fifty pounds and gave Frieda forty.

"Can I use your phone?" asked Frieda. "I'll be very quick."

Sasha handed her the phone and Frieda stepped out into the hallway. She took the card from her pocket, the one she'd been given the previous day. It felt as if Fate had pushed her into this.

When she had finished, she was about to rejoin Sasha and then hesitated. She felt that she had no choice but, at the same time, as if she were violating a promise she had made to herself.

She dialed Reuben's number: no reply. She swore softly to herself.

"Is everything all right?" said Sasha.

"I didn't know I was saying that aloud." Frieda thought for a moment, then tapped in another number. There was a click on the line.

"Is Sasha? I have been—"

"No, Josef. It's me."

"Frieda. What happen? Where are you?"

"I need your help."

"Of course. Tell me."

"I can't get through to Reuben. I need you to go to him and borrow some money. Say, five hundred pounds, which I will of course repay as soon as I'm able."

"Frieda," said Josef. "Your money. What happen?"

Frieda felt the question like a punch on a bruise. Her immediate impulse was to say nothing, to deflect him. But then she surprised herself and, simply and fully, told Josef everything, about Hana, about the money, about the man. When she was finished, she waited for Josef's anger, his surprise. But there was nothing.

"OK," he said calmly. "I see Reuben. I bring the money."

"Is this safe for you?" said Frieda. "Have the police been bothering you?"

"No. Nothing now. Reuben say loud noise in newspapers. Some journalists poking. No problem."

"I can't say how sorry I am to be asking you this."

"Then don't say."

She ended the call and turned to Ethan, who had come into the hallway.

"Are you ready?" she asked him, and he stared solemnly at her. "We're going to have an exciting day."

Bridget Bellucci lived in a terraced house in Stockwell, polished wooden floors, paneling, abstract paintings, French windows leading out onto a long garden. She introduced Frieda and Ethan to three-year-old Tam and one-year-old Rudi. Then she spread out Tam's collection of fluffy toy animals on the carpet in the living room.

"Why don't you show them to Ethan?" she said.

Tam did not seem especially enthusiastic about this. She picked up one of the animals and hugged it defensively, turning her back on the rest of them. Ethan sat down heavily on the floor and took out his own little pile of wooden animals, which he carefully arranged in front of them, his lower lip jutting out. Bridget gestured to the sofa. She was dark under the eyes; her hair was unwashed.

"I thought you weren't available," she said to Frieda. "What changed your mind?" She didn't seem especially grateful.

"I've got Ethan. But I could help out for a few days until you find someone. If that's what you want."

"It is what I want. I'm about to call work and say I'm sick." She gave a snort. "That's what we do—it's OK to be ill yourself, but woe betide you if you take time off for your children. But I can't pretend to be sick for too many more days."

There was a shriek from Rudi. Bridget looked at Frieda and Frieda bent down and scooped the little boy into her lap. He was hot and heavy and slightly damp.

"What do you do?"

"I teach Italian at the language school. Usually I have mornings free and work in the afternoons, then several evenings a week." She was still curt. "I'm half Italian."

"You look half Italian."

"Yes, well." She scrutinized Frieda. "You're not my idea of a nanny."

"What is your idea of a nanny?"

"Young, for a start."

Frieda shrugged. "What happened to your child care?"

"She suddenly decided she was homesick. I suppose I should ask some questions. Do you have any references?"

"No."

"Oh?"

"I'm not a real nanny. I'm just doing this for a friend."

"I must have misunderstood. Could I talk to this friend?"

"Of course," said Frieda. "She's at work at the moment. But I can get her to call you."

Bridget looked at Ethan, who was clopping two of his horses along the wooden floor. "I suppose he's a sort of reference. He looks happy enough." She bent down and put her face close to Ethan. "Are you happy with Carla?"

"No," said Ethan. "Not Carla. She—"

"He's fine," said Frieda. "Here." She passed Ethan a few more of his wooden animals. Tam took one from him and put it into her mouth, where it bulged in her cheek. Ethan was so astonished he couldn't even roar. His eyes and mouth grew round.

"Give that to me now," said Frieda to Tam, holding out her hand.

Tam stared at her, mutinous. Bridget looked on, waiting to see what would happen.

"Now, Tam," repeated Frieda.

"Are you going to count to ten?" Her voice was muffled because of the toy in her mouth.

"Certainly not."

There was a silence. Then Tam spat the animal into her hand.

"Thank you," Frieda said. "Now, Ethan, show Tam your animals."

"Why?"

"Because you're in her house and sometimes it's more fun to play with another person."

"Is there anything you'd like to ask *me*?" Bridget said. Her voice had become marginally friendlier.

"I'd like to be paid in cash."

Bridget gave a laugh. "It all feels a bit under the counter."

"It's how I work."

"How much do you charge?"

Frieda was blank for a moment. What was a plausible amount?

"Eighty pounds a day?"

"Great. Fine. I'll pay you at the end of the week. When can you start?"

"Now."

"Really?"

"Yes."

"OK. Today it is. I don't have to leave for another hour. Shall we have coffee and I can tell you any practical details you need to know?"

"I'd like that."

"You keep an eye on them. I'll bring it through."

Frieda did keep an eye on them. Rudi remained placidly on her lap while she watched the two older children with curiosity. Most of the time, they ignored each other; occasionally there were brief moments when they seemed to notice the other's presence. At one point, Ethan put out a hand and touched Tam's hair, which was vivid orange and curly, like a fire on her scalp. She was nothing like her mother.

Bridget came back into the room and handed Frieda her coffee. "What will you do with them today?" she asked.

"I thought perhaps we'd go to a cemetery."

"A cemetery!"

"It's sunny and warm and I think there's one near here that's good for exploring. We can take a picnic. What time will you be back?"

"Late. But Al will get home at about five thirty or six. Is that all right?"

"Fine." Frieda took a sip of her coffee, which was rich and strong. "Did Sandy come here a lot?"

"Yes, he did. But why do you want to know?" Bridget's voice became cold once more.

"Because the thing we have in common," said Frieda, "is Sandy. We both knew him."

"He's dead."

"He's dead, but—"

"Murdered. Luridly famous. And people who haven't seen him for ages—"

"Like me."

"—like you, like countless others, are all of a sudden fascinated by him. They should mind their own business."

"You're angry."

"Yes, I'm angry—angry that everyone's suddenly wanting to be his best friend, now that he's gone."

"And angry simply because he's dead."

"What?"

"You're angry because he's dead," repeated Frieda; she told herself that she was Carla, the nanny, but she didn't feel like Carla. She could feel Bridget's anger, coming off her like hot steam, and noticed how her cheeks were flushed. She watched Tam pull a series of ribbons out of a red cardboard case and hand them to Ethan, who held them between his fingers, his face intent. "Because he's no longer here."

"Do you want this job?"

"Looking after your children, you mean?"

"Because if you want it, don't keep on asking about Sandy. I've had enough. Leave him in peace. And me."

The day was hot, almost sultry, but inside the cemetery it was cool and dim. Light filtered through the leaves, falling in trickles on the grave-stones, many of which were covered with moss, their inscriptions inde-cipherable. The place was overgrown, full of brambles—it would be a good place for blackberries in the autumn—and birdsong. London felt far off, although they could hear the rumble of traffic in the distance. Frieda pushed Rudi in the buggy and Tam and Ethan played a chaotic and increasingly quarrelsome game of hide-and-seek, before sitting on a fallen log to eat their picnic.

Frieda thought about Bridget. Whenever Sandy was mentioned, she became tense and enraged, and she wondered why. If they had been sim-ply friends, would Bridget be so passionately defensive about him? Had they been lovers? Bridget was beautiful and strong, and Frieda could see why Sandy might fall for her, but she was married to one of his close colleagues and she was the mother of two tiny children. But Veronica Ellison had said that Sandy had had a relationship he felt bad about. Perhaps Bridget was also consumed by grief and guilt, and the terrible effort of keeping such a thing secret now that Sandy had been killed. Or perhaps there was something more—

"Frieda." Ethan tugged at her hand.

"She's Carla," said Tam. "Mummy said so."

"No." Ethan was firm but his face was troubled. "Frieda."

"Carla." Tam's voice was a chant, jeering. "Carla, Carla, Carla."

"Let's go," said Frieda, piling the remains of the picnic into the bag and picking up Rudi, laying a consoling hand on Ethan's hot head. "We can buy ice creams on the way home."

Rudi was asleep by the time they reached Bridget and Al's house and she lifted him into his crib. Then she put Tam and Ethan in front of a DVD that Tam chose. It was four o'clock and Al wouldn't be back until half past five.

She started in the living room, acting on the assumption that even if Tam and Ethan looked up from the cartoon they wouldn't think it odd that she was pulling open drawers and cupboards, riffling through papers. She didn't know what she was in search of, just that she was looking for something that would explain Bridget's angry distress over Sandy. She found bills, she found bank statements, she found an architect's drawings and brochures about houses to rent in Greece and Croatia. There were playing cards, board games, a ball of rubber bands, sketch pads with no sketches in them, simple sheet music for the violin, with pencil notations on it, stacks of publications about neuroscience going back several years, a whole drawer of postcards and birthday cards to both Al and Bridget, none of which were from Sandy. The two children didn't look up; both had their mouths open in an identical expression of befuddled attention.

In the hall, she looked at the photos on the walls, but none of them was of Sandy—there were several of Tam and Rudi and a couple of Al and Bridget when they were younger. Al was even thinner than he was now, narrow-shouldered, narrow-hipped, freckled, pale-skinned. Bridget was lustrous, like a dark fruit. Dangerous, thought Frieda, walking into the kitchen, where she found only kitchen things. At least one of them was obviously a serious cook. Like Sandy had been: she imagined him in there, among the sharp-bladed knives and copper pans, the complicated array of spices, rolling up his sleeves. She glanced at the recipe books, half expecting to see one of his among them.

She went up to the mezzanine floor and found a small study that looked out over the garden. She knew at once it was Bridget's, although she couldn't have said why. It was lined with books and there was a violin with a broken string propped on the windowsill. The desk was scattered with papers. There was a laptop but when Frieda opened its lid, it asked for a password. She pulled open the first drawer, which was full of pens, pencils, scissors, staples and paperclips. The next drawer contained a sheaf of photographs that she flicked through. Faces she didn't know, obviously from many years ago; probably Bridget's family and, yes, there was Bridget herself as a girl, immediately identifiable, even to the slightly defiant expression on her face as she looked at the camera. At the back of the drawer was a metal box that was fastened with a flimsy lock. Frieda picked it up and shook it, hearing the soft rustle of papers. She twisted at the lock but it didn't give. On the wall to the side of the desk was a painting of a woman under an umbrella. She looked at Frieda with a disappointed expression.

"I don't have time to explain," Frieda said to her and, taking the scissors from the drawer she had first opened, she inserted the point into the lock and twisted it sharply. The lock gave at once and she opened the lid and looked inside. There were dozens of letters. Why would someone keep letters locked away at the back of a drawer? Frieda lifted the first one out; it was written in blue ink in a bold, slap-dash hand that wasn't Sandy's. What was more, the ink was faded and the date at the top of the letter was twelve years previously—for, of course, few people wrote letters nowadays. Frieda looked at it and saw it was a love letter, written to Bridget before she was a mother, before she knew Al probably. It seemed like a letter written late at night, in an intoxication of sexual passion, and a feeling of shame gripped her. She lifted her head and met the eyes of the woman under her umbrella.

The rest were also love letters, all written by the same person, whose name was Miguel. She didn't read them, but she did look at the few small photos at the bottom of the box, which were of Bridget young and naked. This box that she had broken into, while the children watched a cartoon downstairs and Rudi slept, was simply the treasure trove of a lost affair that was nobody's business but Bridget's. It was her secret younger self, the self she had once been.

Then she heard the front door open and shut and a voice call out: "Hello!" She heard Al say: "Where's our savior Carla, then?" and Tam mumble an inattentive reply.

The footsteps were coming lightly up the stairs. She had no time to leave the room and the study door was open so that he couldn't fail to see her, standing in his wife's study. There were letters all over the surface of the desk and the drawers were open. She gathered up the letters and put them into the box, pushing it back into the drawer, but as Al entered the room she realized she hadn't put away the photographs, so she laid one hand over the top of them. She picked up the small pair of scissors in the other hand.

"Carla," he said. It was neither a greeting nor an accusation; he simply said her name. His pale eyes moved over her, then around the room.

"Hello, Al," said Frieda. She heard her voice, calm and friendly, and felt the photographs under her spread hand. "How was your day? I didn't expect you home yet."

"I got away earlier than usual." His voice was perfectly amiable. "But my day was fine, thank you. Meetings. Timetables. Budgets. All the stuff of an academic life. How was yours?"

"Good. We had a picnic in the cemetery."

"Bridget told me you were going there. I was intrigued." He smiled at her. "What are you doing in here?"

"I needed these." She lifted the scissors. "I tore my nail to the quick. The ones in the kitchen were too big."

"I see. Can I help?"

"No, it's fine. I've done it."

"Good. Shall we have a cup of tea? The children seem happy enough. Is Rudi asleep?"

"Yes. But I'll be on my way, if that's OK with you. I should get Ethan home."

Her hand was still laid across the photographs of Bridget, naked. With a smooth movement, she slid them over the desk and held them by her side, still covered by her hand, then followed him out of the room. She went into the bathroom and slid them into her pocket—she could return them tomorrow—then checked on Rudi, who was stirring now, his face creased by the pillow, his eyes cloudy with sleep. She changed his nappy and took him downstairs. Ethan was half asleep on the sofa and she sat down beside him and took his hand. She saw a small, faint bite mark on the wrist.

"We'll go home soon," she said softly.

He nodded. So she gathered together his wooden animals, lifted him into the buggy and said good-bye to Al, who told her how grateful he was and who didn't know that she had pictures of his naked wife tucked into her back pocket.

"I'm sorry about Sandy," she said, as she was leaving. "I know you were close to him."

"Thank you. Yes, he spent a lot of time with us. I think we were like the family he didn't have. The kids liked him. He and Bridget used to cook huge Sunday lunches together most weeks. They were quite competitive about their cooking." He looked at Frieda, but it was as though he were looking through her. "He used to say that in some ways Bridget reminded him of someone he once knew."

"Who was that?"

"He never said. Just someone. I gathered there was a woman he had been with. She sounded like a bitch." The word seemed odd coming from polite, freckle-faced Al. "But Sandy was incredibly private, as you probably know. I could spend all night drinking and talking with him— and did, quite a few times, especially when we were away at conferences together—but he was like a clam about some things. His love life, for instance." He sighed then added, "You should be on your way. Your little fellow's falling asleep."

It was true. Ethan's head was lolling and his eyelids drooping.

"I'll be back tomorrow," said Frieda.

Al looked distracted. He smiled at her. "Splendid."

At the end of the day, Frieda stopped off at the mini-supermarket a few streets away from the flats. Lunchtime salads were being sold off at half price. She bought a rice salad and a roasted vegetable salad and took them back to the flat. She was very tired, but she sat at the table to eat, then made herself tea before climbing into bed. She went straight to sleep, as if a trap door had been opened under her. She was woken suddenly out of a vivid, violent dream by a sound she couldn't identify. Had it been part of the dream? No, it was continuing. Someone was knocking at her door. She stayed in bed. It must be a mistake; they would realize it and go away. But the knocking continued. She got out of the bed and pulled on her trousers and a sweater. She went to the door.

"Who is it?" she said.

"Is me."

She opened the door, and Josef and Lev stepped into the room, pushing the door shut behind them. Josef was holding two large gray canvas bags; he looked stern, but he gave her a small bow in greeting and, for a moment, his brown eyes softened.

"Your things," he said. "Clothes, books, everything in bag now."

"What's going on?"

"Three minutes," said Lev.

"Why are we doing this?"

"Later," said Josef, and the two men walked around the flat, picking up clothes, pulling the sheets from the bed, tipping kitchen implements into the bag. Josef poured the milk down the sink.

"Has something happened?" Frieda asked, but neither of the men paid her any attention.

"All done," said Josef. "Last look."

Frieda picked up a pair of socks, a hairbrush, her notebook and some pencils. All were tossed into the bag.

"Key?" said Lev.

Frieda took the key from her pocket and handed it to him.

"We go now." He steered Frieda out of the front door and in the direction away from Hana's flat. They went down some narrow stairs that Frieda hadn't previously noticed, through an alleyway between two of the buildings, past industrial-size bins and through a gateway that brought them onto the street. A car gave a little beep and the lights flashed. Lev helped her—it was almost like a push—into the backseat and the two men sat in the front. Lev started the car and drove away, turning this way and that, until Frieda felt entirely lost.

"Here," said Josef, and Lev pulled to the side of the street by a junction with a larger road. Josef took a bundle from his jacket pocket and handed it to Frieda. She saw that it was money.

"Is this from Reuben?" she said. "That's far too much."

"Reuben is away. This is your money. Some of it. Three thousand. A bit more. That was all we get."

"Josef, what have you done?"

"We get your money back."

"What about Hana?"

The men exchanged glances.

"He not a problem for her," said Lev. "For a while."

Frieda leaned forward, took Josef's right hand in hers and turned it over. The only light came from a streetlamp, but she could see it was bruised. "What have you done?"

Josef's expression hardened and there was a light in his eyes that she had never seen before. It made her uncomfortable.

"Frieda. Two things. You don't go back there. Not near there, not ever. OK?"

"No, not OK."

"And the other thing. This not game, Frieda. Not showing your money. This man push you a little. Next man have a knife or two friends."

"Josef, what did you do?"

Josef opened the car door and moved one foot onto the pavement. "I get money back. End. What you want?"

"Not that."

"I go now. Remember, I still don't know where you live."

He slammed the door, put his large hand flat against the window near her face in a gesture of farewell, and was quickly gone.

"I don't know where I live either," Frieda said.

Lev's expression was curious. "I take you," he said.

Lev drove quickly, turning left and right, like he was trying to avoid being followed. Frieda just looked out the window.

"Where are we going?"

"Different part," he said. "Elephant and Castle. You know Elephant and Castle?"

"A bit."

"Near Elephant and Castle."

After a mile or so, Frieda saw that they were on the New Kent Road.

Then Lev turned off onto a smaller road, drove under a railway bridge and into a street lined on both sides by apartment buildings much like the one she had left, but less abandoned-looking. Under the streetlights she could see areas of grass behind railings, lines of parked cars. Lev turned again and parked. They got out and Frieda looked around. On one side was the building. She saw the name on a sign, Thaxted House. The railway ran along the other side of the street and, beyond that, Frieda could see two tall tower blocks, speckled with lights.

Lev took the bags from the car and gestured her toward a door on the ground floor. He unlocked it and led her inside into a dark hallway. He pushed the light switch on with his elbow and led her through into the kitchen. Frieda saw the torn lino on the floor, the mismatching chairs, a battered and stained old gas cooker. But the kitchen was clean and there were bowls and several oven dishes washed up by the sink.

"Someone lives here," said Frieda.

"I show you your room," said Lev.

"But will they mind?"

"Not their business."

"Who are they?"

Lev only shrugged and led her back into the hall, past two rooms with closed doors. He put a finger to his lips. He pushed open a door.

"OK?" he said.

Frieda looked in. There was a bed, a bedside table, a rug, nothing else. Again, it was clean and tidy. She walked to the window and pulled the net curtain aside. It was barred, but through the glass she could see pools of light in the darkness. There was a square expanse of grass, bounded on all sides by the flats.

"You've done too much," she said.

He gave a small nod in acknowledgment. He handed her his key. "Take more of the care," he said. "And I will now say good-bye."

He held out his hand. Frieda shook it, but then, without releasing it, examined Lev's hand more carefully. The knuckles were raw, like Josef's had been, the skin stripped off them. "What did you do to him?"

Lev took Frieda's right hand in his hands. It seemed tiny and lost in his grasp. He let it go. "You been in fight ever?" he said.

Frieda didn't answer. She had, once or twice.

"I hate the fighting," said Lev. "The fear, the blood. The people who think the fighting is a joke, that is . . ." He seemed as if he would spit to demonstrate his contempt. "You cannot have a piece of a fight, a half of a fight, a little of a fight. Then you are hurt. I don't fight." He looked down at his hand with a rueful expression. "But when I do fight it is everything. No limit, no stop. It is like love."

"Like love," said Frieda slowly, repeating his words rather than asking a question.

"You get up close, you feel the smell, you feel the touch, you feel the breath, and you do not stop. Most of the people cannot do that. I talk to Josef. You, Frieda, I think you can." Almost absentmindedly, he took something from his pocket. At first she couldn't see what it was. Then she could. He was holding a knife by the blade. The handle was polished dark brown wood.

"What's that for?" said Frieda.

"For you. Keep by you always."

"I can't have a knife."

"Ach. You never use probably." He snapped it shut, then leaned forward and slid it into the pocket of her jacket. "Careful. Is sharp. Very."

"But—"

He shook his head.

"None of the way," he said. "Or all of the way. If you have the . . ." He searched for the word. He tapped his belly.

"Stomach," said Frieda. "The stomach for it."

"Yes. You have, I think."

He left the room and Frieda heard the outside door open and close. She rummaged in her bags and found her toothbrush and toothpaste, soap and a towel. She walked out and found the bathroom. As she brushed, she noticed a pink plastic razor on the side of the bath and a shelf with shampoo, conditioner, a packet of tampons, jars of cream, a black eye pencil, a bag of cotton wool. There was nothing that looked as if it belonged to a man.

She got into the bed and switched off the light, then lay and stared up at the ceiling. A jagged crack, like a coastline, crossed the ceiling, all the way from one side of the room to the other. She heard the rumble of a train passing, a goods train. It seemed to take forever.

She was woken by voices. She pulled her clothes on, and as she left her bedroom, the voices became louder and then there was a crash and a shattering and then another bang. She walked through to the kitchen. At first she had difficulty working out what was going on. A woman was kneeling on the ground, picking up fragments of a plate. Frieda could make out her shock of blond hair and her dark clothes, but she couldn't see her face. Another woman was standing beside the sink. She had brown hair and dark, almost black eyes, and she was banging a wooden spoon on the edge of the sink's metal rim, to reinforce the point she was making. Both women were speaking at the same time in raised voices and Frieda couldn't even make out whether they were speaking English or not.

"Hello?" she said, but there was no sign that they had even heard her. She rapped hard on the table and the two women stopped.

"How you get in?" said the dark woman.

"I slept here last night," said Frieda. "Lev brought me."

"Lev?"

The blond woman said something, maybe in explanation, and the two women started shouting at each other again.

"Please," said Frieda, and then she said it once more, almost shouting herself. The two women looked at her, almost in puzzlement. "Is there a problem?"

The two women were panting, as if they'd been in a fight.

"No problem," said the dark woman.

"I'm Carla," said Frieda.

The blond woman frowned. "I am called Mira," she said.

"I am Ileana," said the dark woman.

"Hello," said Frieda, holding out her hand.

Mira hesitated for a moment. Then she wiped her hand on her trousers and took Frieda's.

"You're bleeding," said Frieda. There was a bubble of blood on Mira's index finger.

"Is nothing."

Frieda knelt down and picked up a couple of the fragments. "You've had an accident."

"That was not the fucking accident," said Ileana.

"Oh," said Frieda. "Shall I make us some tea?"

"There is no fucking milk," said Ileana.

"That's all right."

"No fucking tea."

"I'll go and get some."

When Frieda got back with tea and milk, Mira was in the bathroom. Frieda made the tea.

"Shall I pour a tea for Mira?"

"No," said Ileana. "She long time there. The hair. The nails. The skin." She made a sound expressing contempt.

Frieda poured two mugs. Ileana looked at her suspiciously. "What you do?"

"Different things," said Frieda. "I'm a nanny at the moment. Mainly."

"Children," said Ileana, as if that was all that needed to be said.

"It's not that bad," said Frieda. "What do you do?"

"In a market. The Camden Market."

"On a stall?"

"The Spanish food. The paella."

"Are you from Spain?"

"Braşov."

"That doesn't sound Spanish."

"Romania."

"Do you work with Mira?"

Ileana pulled a face. "Never. She is hairdresser."

"I've got to go in a few minutes," said Frieda. "Is there anything I need to know?"

Ileana thought for a moment. "No rules. Buy own food probably. Help clean. Pay for the heat with us. Careful with bringing people."

"I will be."

"Mira has the boyfriend. English." Ileana pulled the face again.

"Not nice?"

"He just see the face and the body and the sex."

"All right."

"If lights go, there is box by front door."

Frieda stood up. Ileana looked at her with a puzzled expression. "You are English?"

"Yes."

"And you are here?"

"Just for a bit."

"Strange."

Frieda tried to think of something to say that would make it seem less strange, but she couldn't think of anything.

18

Reuben gave a dinner. Josef was there, of course, since he lived with Reuben, paying no rent but fixing the house, buying the vodka and cooking most of their meals, and so were Sasha, Jack Dargan, Frieda's sister-in-law Olivia and Chloë. Chloë was just back from college, where she was taking a course in joinery and carpentry.

"It's just a phase," said Olivia, who had dreamed of having a doctor for a daughter.

"I'm learning how to make chairs," said Chloë. "Tables. That's more than you've ever done."

She and Jack sat as far away from each other as possible: they had gone out, split up, got together again, and now they had once more separated. Jack ignored her, his cheeks flushed and his tawny hair standing up where he had pushed his hands nervously through it. Chloë glared at him and sometimes made loud, sarcastic remarks. Olivia had got dressed up for the occasion: she wore a purple skirt and lots of beads, and had tied her hair up in a complicated arrangement, with what looked like chopsticks sticking out of it. Her eye shadow was green and her lipstick red and she was already on the way to being drunk and slightly tearful. She sat next to Reuben and told him how she had recently let herself into Frieda's house and sat in the living room and howled. "Like a baby," she said. Reuben patted her hand and refilled her glass. Only Sasha was silent.

Josef had cooked far too much food. He had spent most of the afternoon preparing summer borscht with cucumber and lemon added, wheat soup, his familiar pierogis—savory and sweet.

"And *holopchi*," he said, putting the steaming dish on the table. "And *pyrizhky*."

"You know I'm a vegetarian?" asked Chloë. "What can I eat?"

Josef sighed in heavy disappointment. "There is much cabbage," he said. "Cabbage rolls, cabbage buns. And soup with no meat."

"Fish? Because I don't eat fish either."

"We all drink a toast to Frieda now."

He filled six shot glasses to the brim with vodka and passed them around. "To our dear friend," he said. His brown eyes glowed.

"To Frieda," said Reuben.

"Who's an idiot," added Jack.

"To Frieda," said Sasha, softly, as if to herself, raising her glass but taking only a delicate sip.

"Now that we've done that . . ." said Reuben. He turned to Josef. "Well?"

"What?"

"I'm not blind and I'm not stupid."

"What is this?" said Josef.

"About Frieda."

"I know nothing," Josef said. "Nothing."

"Creeping round the house, leaving in the middle of the night, whispered conversations. And I can always tell when you're lying. And you won't meet my eyes."

Josef bent across the table and stared into Reuben's eyes. The two men stayed like that for several moments, the room around them quite silent. Then Olivia began to giggle and they sat back. Josef knocked back another glass of vodka and wiped his forehead with a large handkerchief. Reuben sipped thoughtfully at his glass of wine.

"We're her friends too," Reuben said.

"Sacred promise," said Josef.

"Where is she?"

"No. That is secret to her."

"But you've seen her?"

"I cannot say."

Sasha spoke, so quietly they had to lean forward to hear her. "If Josef's made a promise, he should be allowed to keep it," she said. "Frieda has good reasons for wanting to remain hidden." She tossed the rest of her vodka down her throat and spluttered.

"Whose side are you on?" asked Reuben.

"I didn't know it was a question of sides."

"I help her find place," said Josef.

"To live?"

"My friend sort it."

"Where?"

"Gone from there now."

"Gone? So where was she?"

Josef made a vague helpless gesture.

"Where *is* she now?"

"I do not know."

"You're lying."

"I am not."

"Is she all right?" This from Chloë, who spoke in a fierce whisper as if someone might be listening in.

"Hair all gone and odd clothes."

"Hair gone?" Olivia gasped. "All of it?"

"Why doesn't she come to us?" said Chloë. Her eyes had suddenly filled with tears and she blinked them away.

"She doesn't want to get us into trouble," said Reuben. "She's protecting us."

"Fuck that," said Olivia ferociously, and one of the chopsticks fell out of her hair. "If she'd killed ten men I would still be on her side."

"She hasn't killed anyone," said Sasha. Her face was white and her cheeks very pink. Her fingers plucked at the tablecloth. "That's the point. If the police think it's her, they won't find who really did it."

"How do you know?" asked Jack.

"I just do."

"She's told you, has she?"

"No!"

"Why have you gone all red?" Olivia was examining her. "You look slightly feverish."

"I'm just tired."

"Yes, I know," said Olivia. "I'm sorry."

"I keep thinking," said Jack, "that we should ask ourselves what Frieda would do."

"We know what Frieda would do because she's gone and done it."

"I mean, in our position. Would she just sit and wait, like we've been doing? Except Josef, of course."

"Is there anything else you know, Josef?" asked Chloë. "Is she OK for money?"

"I think," he said.

"What can we do?" Reuben asked moodily. "We don't know where she is. We don't know what she's up to. We can't contact her."

"We'll have to follow Josef," said Olivia. "Put a trail on him."

"I? No!"

"But what would she do?" repeated Jack, tugging at his disordered hair. "She'd do something, I know she would. And so should we."

"Has anyone talked to Karlsson?" asked Chloë.

"Poor sod." Reuben poured himself another glass of wine. "He's in trouble as it is. It's complicated, being Frieda's friend."

Detective Constable Yvette Long had to pull Karlsson out of an interview.

"It's the commissioner," she said.

"All right."

"Your car's outside. You need to go in a minute." She looked at her watch. "In fact, now."

"Where to?"

"The Altham station."

"Altham?" Karlsson frowned. That was where Hussein was based. "Have they found Frieda?"

"Not that I've heard. Shall I come along?"

"If you like. You might draw some of the fire away from me."

They didn't speak again until they were in the back of the unmarked police car.

"Did he say anything?"

"Who?" said Karlsson. "The commissioner?"

"The cabbie. I'm talking about our case. Did he confess?"

"He didn't say a single word. He didn't even look me in the eye."

"But we've got the DNA. And the girl's statement. That should be enough."

"It'll just take longer. And she'll have to give evidence."

Karlsson didn't seem interested in talking. He just stared out of the window.

"Any idea what this is about?" Yvette asked.

Karlsson didn't answer.

"She shouldn't have done this," Yvette continued. "She's just causing trouble. She . . ."

Karlsson looked round at her and something in his expression made her stop.

"Coffee?" said Commissioner Crawford.

An office at Altham police station had apparently been cleared and prepared for him, almost like a royal visit. On a conference table there was a flask of coffee, a jug of water, a plate of biscuits and a bowl with apples and tangerines and a bunch of grapes. Detective Chief Inspector Hussein was sitting on the other side of the table. In front of her was a glass of water, a file and her phone. Karlsson and Long helped themselves to coffee and sat down. The commissioner took his own coffee, added two lumps of sugar and stirred them in. "How's your rape case going?"

"We'll charge him later."

"Excellent." The commissioner smiled. Yvette found his affability more alarming than the briskness and impatience she was used to. "See? It looks like you can manage well enough without your friend."

Yvette looked at Karlsson. She saw his jaw flex slightly. She recognized the signs and felt a sudden lurch. Was Karlsson going to say something? But he didn't speak immediately. He picked up his coffee cup with great care and took a sip.

"I was pulled out of the interview," he said at last. "Is something up?"

"I suppose this is a bit painful for you."

"In what way?"

The commissioner's expression changed from warmth to one of concern. "Your special adviser going on the run like this."

"It's unfortunate," said Karlsson.

"Don't you want to know how the search is proceeding?"

"How is it proceeding?"

"It's not," said Hussein.

There was a pause.

"At this point," said the commissioner, "you're supposed to say something like 'What a pity' or maybe make a suggestion."

"All right. I'll make a suggestion. As well as looking for Dr. Klein, I think you should be exploring other angles."

The commissioner's face reddened. Yvette knew what was coming.

"There are no other angles. Frieda Klein absconding was a clear admission that she did it." He paused. Karlsson's failure to answer made him even angrier. "Well?"

"Frieda didn't commit the murder," said Karlsson. "But if she had done something like that, she would own up to it. She wouldn't go on the run."

"As you bloody well know, she already did kill someone and she didn't own up to it."

"She didn't kill that person either."

"Of course she did."

"If she had done it, there was no reason to deny it. It was a clear case of self-defense."

Crawford pushed his cup away. "Coffee break's over," he said. "DCI Hussein and I have some questions for you."

"What questions?"

"Have you had any contact with Frieda Klein?" Hussein asked.

"No."

"If she contacted you, what would you say?"

"I don't normally answer hypothetical questions. But I'll answer that one: if Frieda contacted me, I would ask her to give herself up."

"Why?" said Crawford, with what was nearly a sneer. "Haven't you read the file? Your friend is almost certain to be convicted."

"Because it's the law."

"It's a pity you didn't manage to persuade Klein before she disappeared."

"I've never managed to persuade her of very much."

"You know her," said Hussein. "Have you got any suggestions?"

"Not really."

"That's not much help," said the commissioner.

"I guess she'll be avoiding anywhere she normally goes."

"We missed her at that hospital. Why do you think she went there?"

"To see her patient, wasn't it?"

"Yes, but why?" asked Hussein.

"Didn't you interview him?"

"He wasn't very coherent. He'd been horribly beaten up and injured. His fingers had been smashed and some of them chopped off. But, as far as I can tell, she asked questions about how he was, where he'd been, who had hurt him, that sort of thing."

"So she was concerned about him."

"Mm. But it's an odd thing to do, isn't it, go somewhere she knew she might be recognized in order to show her concern?"

"I don't know. It's the kind of thing Frieda might do."

"What about her friends?"

"What about them?"

"Do you think they're helping her?"

"You need to ask them."

"It's not just a matter of asking them. I'm also asking you. What do you suspect?"

Karlsson thought for a moment. "I think her friends would help her if she asked them. And I don't think she would ask them."

"You're her friend," said Hussein.

"She hasn't asked me."

"If she did, how would you respond?"

Commissioner Crawford looked at his watch. "Fun as this is, we don't have time for a discussion about hypothetical situations," he said. "I'm confident that DCI Karlsson will contact us about anything we need to know. Meanwhile we have an appointment."

Karlsson and Yvette stood up and began to leave, but the commissioner smiled and shook his head. "You're coming too, Mal," he said.

"Where?"

"You know the old saying: when all else fails in an investigation, hold a press conference."

"I didn't know that saying."

"It starts in five minutes and it's a chance for you to show that you're a part of the team."

"Is it something I need to show?"

"And *you*," said the commissioner, pointing at Yvette, "you can stand at the back and learn something." He gestured to Karlsson to follow him, and as he turned away, Yvette mouthed something at his back.

"By the way," said Hussein, as Crawford led them through the corridors, "another friend of yours will be joining us onstage."

"Who's that?" said Karlsson, and as he said the words he had a sudden sick feeling as he realized what the answer would be.

The Pauline Bishop Suite was named after a policewoman who had fallen in the line of duty and today it was almost full. Lights were being set up and there was an expectant, bustling murmur. Yvette edged her way along the back. She felt a sense of apprehension as if she were about to watch a play that she knew hadn't been properly rehearsed. There was a flash of lights and they filed up onto the platform: the commissioner, Hussein, a tense-looking Karlsson, and Professor Hal Bradshaw, in a somber gray suit, white shirt and dark tie that made it seem as if he were in charge of the whole operation. They sat down and his expression was serious and thoughtful.

Hussein gave a brief précis of the case, of Frieda Klein's role as chief suspect and of her disappearance. Yvette barely listened. She knew that conferences like this were partly a charade. She had seen parents asking tearfully for a child to be returned, a husband asking for a witness to the murder of his wife. If a witness came forward, that was good but it wasn't the only point of the exercise. Almost always the parents or the husband or the boyfriend were suspects and it gave an opportunity to see their demeanor under the spotlight. Was that what this was? Did Hussein think that Karlsson was holding something back?

Hussein finished her statement, then Commissioner Crawford leaned forward toward the microphone and said a few words.

"I want to take this opportunity to apologize to the public. This woman, Frieda Klein, was at one time employed by us. Her record has been checkered, to say the least, but we could never have anticipated anything like this. All I can say is that we are going to make every effort to bring her to justice. I'll now hand you over to the very distinguished psychiatrist Professor Hal Bradshaw, who can speak with more authority about Klein's bizarre behavior. Professor Bradshaw?"

Bradshaw waited several seconds before speaking, as if in the deepest of thought.

"I need to be careful," he said, "because I understand that Dr. Klein"—he said the word "doctor" as if holding it between tongs—"is facing a serious criminal charge and I don't want to prejudice any proceedings. I just want to comment that, based on my long experience in this field, it is all too common that unstable, disordered people are attracted to the field of crime. They try to get involved in investigations. They try to help." He put his fingers together into a lattice. "The reasons are many and complex and it is hard to say exactly what it was about Dr. Klein that caused this behavior: it could be a narcissistic personality disorder, it could be a need for attention, it could be vanity, it could be greed, it could be neediness, it could be—"

"But will such things help *catch* her?" interrupted Hussein, unable to contain herself.

"If I may say, that's your job," said Bradshaw, and Hussein's expression became almost as frosty as Karlsson's. "All I will say is that she is in a disordered state, unrooted, homeless. She will probably draw attention to herself before too long." The commissioner started to speak but Bradshaw raised a hand to stop him so that he could continue. "I just want to say that I must add that Klein has a history of violence when provoked. Or when she feels she is provoked. If people see her, they should be wary of approaching her. By the way, if anyone has further questions, I'll be available afterward."

"Thank you," said the commissioner. "Wise words. And now I'd like to bring in Detective Chief Inspector Karlsson. He is not involved in the inquiry but he has worked with Klein and he wants to make a personal appeal. Just in case she happens to see a broadcast of this conference."

Karlsson hadn't known that this was how his contribution was going to be framed. Anger flared through him and he set his jaw, then took a deep breath and looked at the bank of cameras. Which direction was he meant to look in? He chose a TV camera.

"Frieda," he said. "If you see this, I want you to come back. I know you have your own views about this case." He thought for a second. "Just as you have your own views about everything. You have to come back and to trust us." He paused again. "You've done valuable work with us and we owe you a lot. The best way——"

"All right, all right," said the commissioner. "That's enough of an appeal. Any questions?"

There was a flurry of questions, mainly directed at Hussein. As they began, Karlsson, whose face was as expressionless as a stone statue, turned very slightly and caught Yvette Long's eye. After a few questions, the commissioner wound up the proceedings. As they filed off the stage, he leaned close to Karlsson's ear and whispered: "'Valuable work.' What the fuck was that?"

Karlsson didn't reply. He edged his way through the dispersing crowd of journalists and met Yvette at the back of the room. He gave her the slightest hint of a wink.

"One day," said Yvette, "Bradshaw's going to offend the wrong person and something bad will happen."

"Oh, he's already done that," said Karlsson.

"But you did mean what you said earlier? That Frieda didn't do this."

Karlsson turned to her but he didn't reply. He just looked tired.

19

The following day, as they returned from the park where Ethan and Tam had been paddling in the pool and Rudi and Frieda had sat on the grass with a basket of strawberries watching them, it started to rain heavily, as if the swollen sky had split. They ran, the two children holding on to either side of the buggy, splashing through puddles that seemed to appear in seconds, but were drenched to the skin when they reached the house. It made all but Rudi, who was kept dry by the hood of the buggy, strangely happy. Ethan stood in the hallway and dripped rivulets onto the bare boards, a wide smile on his normally solemn face. Frieda collected towels from the bathroom. She stripped their clothes off and dried each child vigorously until they squealed and wriggled. She sat them on a sofa and covered them with a quilt, then made them hot chocolate that they drank with noisy slurps. Outside the summer rain clattered against the windowpanes and bounced off the road.

Rudi kept tipping forward on the sofa, so she put him in the high chair and gave him some wooden spoons to bang. She regarded him curiously: he was a mystery to her, with his darting eyes, his clutching hands, and the sudden piercing sounds he made. Sometimes she could make out emergent words from the jumble of syllables. What did one-year-olds think about? What did they dream about? How did they make sense of the world, when it came at them with so many sights and sounds and smells and clutching hands and peering faces? She picked up the spoon he flung across the room and handed it back to him and he glared at her.

Frieda had a spare set of clothes for Ethan in case of accidents, so now she went up to Tam's bedroom, where she rummaged through drawers, pulling out some trousers and a green-and-white striped top. On her way upstairs she took the opportunity to replace the photos in the box in Bridget's desk drawer, though she could do nothing about the broken lock, and on her way downstairs she paused by Bridget and Al's room, hesitating. She could hear Tam's and Ethan's voices, and the bang of Rudi's spoons. After the last time, when all she had found had been old love letters that nobody should see except Bridget herself, she had told herself she shouldn't pry anymore. But if that was the case, what was she doing, the counterfeit nanny, towing three tiny children around parks and wiping their faces? The only reason she was here was because something about Bridget's reaction to Sandy's death had alerted her. So she pushed open the door and stepped into the room.

The large double bed was unmade, and there were clothes tossed onto chairs and lying on the floor. There was a pile of laundry in the corner. There was no wardrobe in here, and dresses and shirts hung instead from the long clothes rack. Most of them were Bridget's—colorful garments in cotton and silk and velvet. There was an astonishing number of shoes along the floor. The room felt very female, as if Bridget had taken up most of the space, leaving Al just one side of the rumpled bed, and a small table on which sat a pile of books.

She gazed around her. She didn't know what she was looking for, or where she should look for it. There were tubs of face cream and tubes of body lotion on Bridget's bedside table, as well as a novel she had never heard of and a dial of birth-control pills; underwear and T-shirts in the chest; makeup and jewelery on the small dressing table by the window. She pulled open its small drawers, seeing tangled necklaces, hairbrushes, face wipes, several bottles of perfume. She ran her hand along the clothes hanging from the rack, feeling the soft brush of their different textures. Something jangled in the pocket of a scarlet velvet jacket and Frieda put her hand in and pulled out a set of keys. She held them in her hand. Two Chubb keys, two Yale keys, their metal cold against her palm. She heard the bang of Rudi's spoon and the hammer of rain outside. She put the keys into her pocket and went downstairs again, making sure to close the bedroom door behind her.

Rudi fell asleep and Tam and Ethan played with some wooden bricks and soft toys and mostly Frieda just sat and half watched them. She intervened from time to time—when Tam tried to wrestle a doll from Ethan's grasp, or when Ethan reached for an exotic and fragile vase on a bookshelf—but mainly her thoughts were elsewhere and the children were just a slightly agitating noise in the background.

Sasha came home very late, when Ethan was already in bed. She had had a tiring day and her face was drawn. Frieda saw how sharp her cheekbones were, how thin her wrists.

"I'm so sorry," Sasha said. "I just couldn't get away. We had an after-work meeting that went on and on, and all I could think of was that I was—"

"It doesn't matter." Frieda put a hand on Sasha's arm. "Really. That's why I'm here, so that you don't have to be anxious all the time. I'll make you some tea and then I'll go."

"Tea? Wine. Frank's coming round in about an hour to talk about child care arrangements."

"Just a very quick drink."

But as they went into the kitchen, the doorbell rang, and then the door knocker was rapped hard and Sasha's hand flew to her mouth. "It's Frank," she whispered. "He's the only one who does that."

"I thought you said he was coming in an hour."

"He's early."

The bell and the knocker sounded again.

"I don't really want to see him," said Frieda.

"No. I know. Oh, dear."

"I'll wait upstairs."

"He might be ages."

"Then I'll read a book."

She went swiftly upstairs and into the little room that served as a spare room and study. The front door opened and she could hear Frank's voice greeting Sasha and Sasha replying. There was a book of photographs by a German prewar photographer on the shelves. She pulled it down and turned the pages slowly, looking at the faces of people who were long dead. She thought about what they must have lived through, those who were posing so calmly for the camera. She had a sudden longing, so sharp it was like a physical blow, for her garret room at home, the sketchpad and soft-leaded pencils, the silence of the rooms and London lying outside, vast and glittering in the night.

Their voices came from the front room but mainly she couldn't make them out. She heard some of Frank's phrases: "We can't go on like this"; "We have to make arrangements." Sasha's replies, such as they were, were just a murmur through the wall. The voices were raised slightly: "I know you've been having a hard time, Sasha. You look thin and tired. But it doesn't need to be like this."

Frieda tried not to listen. She was used to hearing people's secrets. It was her job. But now she thought of what she was doing in Bridget and Al's house, ferreting through drawers, knowing what she shouldn't know; listening to Frank and Sasha as they talked about their future. She went on looking at the photographs, but still she heard the voices, and she thought about Sandy, his bitterness when they had parted. They, too, had loved each other once, and for her the ending had been like the tide going out, the gradual withdrawing of passion and a sense of a shared future. For him it had been like a blow falling, leaving him wounded, humiliated and confused. For a while, he had become like a stranger to her but now that he was dead she felt close to him again, and full of a terrible sadness for him.

She heard Frank's voice again, the scraping of a chair. He must be standing up.

"Yes." Sasha's voice was subdued. "I will."

Then the front door opened and shut, and after a few moments, Sasha called up to her that Frank was gone.

They sat at the kitchen table and drank a glass of wine. Sasha was visibly agitated. She told Frieda that Frank thought they should try again.

"And what did you reply?"

"I told him I would think about it."

"Is it what you want?"

"I'm just tired out, Frieda. Just tired out."

"I know you are."

"I feel all wrong."

"In what way?"

"I can't say." She shook her head from side to side. "I can't explain."

"You could try."

"You've got enough going on in your life as it is. You've already done so much to help me." She took a large mouthful of her wine. "Actually, there's something I should tell you."

"What's that?"

"I met up with everyone last night. Reuben and Josef and Jack, Chloë and Olivia."

"Oh."

"Everyone wants to help you, Frieda. That's why we met—it was like a meeting that Reuben convened. With great quantities of Ukrainian food, of course, and vodka."

"That's kind," said Frieda, neutrally, imagining them all there without her. "You didn't say anything?"

"No, of course not, although it felt impossible to behave naturally. Jack kept saying: 'What would Frieda do?'"

Frieda smiled. "Did he? And what *would* Frieda do?"

"No one knew."

"Good."

It was after ten when Frieda left Sasha. The rain had stopped and the night was cool and clear, with a moon showing above the rooftops. Puddles glistened on the streets and the plane trees dripped. She walked at a steady pace and before long she was on such familiar ground that she scarcely had to think about where she was going. Her feet took her along streets she knew well, whose names spoke to her of their history, past an ancient church, rows of houses and shops, and then Number 9, the café her friends ran and where she always took her Sunday breakfast. Down into the little cobbled mews. And at last she was there, standing at the dark blue door.

Was this stupid? Yes, almost certainly it was. It was the most stupid thing she could do, but while her head told her to stay away, her heart ordered her to go on, and her heart was stronger. The longing in her was great, so she took the keys that she'd found in Bridget's jacket from her pocket. There were two Chubbs and two Yales. She took the smaller Chubb and inserted it into the locks, then one of the Yales, and as she had known as soon as she had seen them, they fitted, turned. The door swung open and she was home.

For a moment, she stood in the hallway and allowed the house to settle around her. It still smelled familiar—of beeswax polish and wooden floorboards and many books, and also of the herbs that she had on her kitchen windowsill. Josef must be watering them for her, as he had promised. A shape slid against her legs and she bent down to stroke the cat that was purring softly, unsurprised by her return. She knew she mustn't turn on the light, so she made her way into the kitchen to find the torch that she kept there.

Switching it on, she moved from room to room, the cat at her heels like a shadow, taking in everything the torchlight fell on. The chess table, the pieces still there in the pattern of the last game she had played through; the empty hearth and the chair beside it, waiting for her; the large map of London in the hallway; the narrow stairs taking her up to her room, where the bed was made up with fresh sheets, just as she had left it, and the bathroom where Josef's splendid bath sat. Up the next, even narrower, flight of stairs and into her garret study. She sat down at the desk, under the skylight, and picked up a pencil. On the blank page of the sketchbook she drew a single line. When she returned, she would make that line into part of a drawing.

She went downstairs once more and shook a small amount of cat food into the bowl and put it on the floor. When the cat had finished eating, it left through the cat flap without a backward glance. She washed the bowl and placed it on the rack where she had found it. Then she turned off the torch, put it back into the drawer and then, just as she was opening her front door, she saw something that, for a moment, stopped her in her tracks, her skin prickling. There was a table just inside the door where she put mail and keys. On it was a small metal box she didn't recognize, about the size of a thick book. A red light flashed intermittently. It wasn't hers. It was obviously a sort of camera or sensor and, of course, the police had put it there, as she should have known, if she had thought about it, that they would. Put it there just in case she was stupid enough to come back. She had been stupid enough. She had been so careful and now, with one stroke, she was visible again. She quickly left the house, double-locking it behind her.

But she hadn't finished yet. She walked through Holborn and then along Rosebery Avenue and left, up smaller streets, until she came to Sandy's flat. This, too, she knew to be recklessly foolish. She had learned her lesson and she didn't even try to go inside, simply put the Chubb key into the front door and felt it fit and turn. She pulled it out again and put it back into her pocket, then turned away and left. So Bridget had Sandy's keys, and she had Frieda's keys as well.

From Islington to Elephant and Castle was a walk she knew well, the first part at least, following the course of the buried, lost, forgotten Fleet River down Farringdon Road to the Thames, then across Black-friars Bridge. She stopped to lean over the bridge, as she always did, to see the swirling currents of the great river, as if it were fighting against its own flow. Then she turned south and, though it was the middle of the night, there were still people around and taxis and buses and vans. There was never an escape from all of that. It was nearly dawn before she lay down on the narrow bed and closed her eyes and did not sleep.

20

Frieda was woken by her phone. For a moment, she was disconcerted because so very few people had her phone number. She lifted it up and saw it was Bridget.

"Sorry to ring so early."

"That's all right."

"I wanted to catch you. We've got the morning off, so we thought we'd take the children to the zoo. So you needn't come in until about one, or half past. Sorry about the late notice."

"That's fine."

"We'll pay you anyway."

"It doesn't matter."

"Well, we can argue about that when we meet."

Frieda looked at her watch. Ethan was with Sasha today and she had four clear hours. It was a chance she might never get again. Within five minutes, she was washed and dressed. As she was opening the front door, she heard a hiss behind her. She turned round. It was Mira.

"You take the potato?" she said. "The salad."

"What?" said Frieda. "No, I wasn't here."

"Ileana," said Mira darkly.

"I'll buy some food while I'm out," said Frieda. "I'll make a meal."

"Thieves," said Mira.

"What?"

"Thieves and gypsies. All of them."

"All of what?"

"The Romanians."

"Where are you from?"

"Ruse."

"I don't know where that is."

"It is Bulgaria."

Frieda felt in her pocket and took out a twenty-pound note. She handed it to Mira. "That can go toward food and whatever. And you don't mean that about Gypsies and thieves."

"Lock your door," said Mira.

"There isn't a lock on it."

"That is your problem."

"Later," said Frieda, opening the door.

In another five minutes she was on the bus with a black coffee. She sat upstairs looking at people heading to work or to the shops. More and more she felt different from all that, all the people in the real world of jobs and houses and attachments, people with places to go, appointments to keep. She felt the same estrangement when she opened the door of the house. It felt as if the family had been snatched away in an instant, leaving toys scattered where they had fallen, mugs and plates on the kitchen table. The house still smelled of the people who had left, the coffee, the perfume, soap, skin cream, talcum powder.

She thought for a moment, and then began to walk from room to room, the kitchen and the living room and upstairs to Bridget's den and the bedroom. The house felt familiar to her now and she had already searched these rooms. She had opened the drawers and the cupboards. She paused in the bedroom and looked out of one of the large windows that faced the street. An idea had occurred to her: it was somewhere in her mind but she couldn't quite grasp it. What was it? Let it go. Her rummaging and searching had produced nothing so far. Nothing except the keys. They had the keys to Sandy's flat and they had the keys to her house. Suddenly the idea came to her. She ran down the stairs two at a time. The device at her house, inside the door. How could she be so careless a second time? She looked at the alarm inside the front door. It was switched off. Frieda felt a sudden jolt of alarm. Was it possible that someone was still in the house? Could Al be on the top floor? No, she told herself. They'd just forgotten to turn on the alarm.

But the idea of Al stayed with her. Frieda had mainly been thinking about Bridget, that she might have had an affair with Sandy. Somehow she seemed like Sandy's type, maybe more his type than Frieda had been. But Al was his colleague and his friend. Had he suspected something, known something? The rooms she had looked at so far had felt like Bridget's territory, even the shared bedroom. But she had never been to the top of the house. She walked back up the stairs, past the bedroom, up to the next floor. She knew better, but even so she walked as quietly as she could. The stairs ended in an attic room that had been converted into an office. On the side away from the street there were two large skylights. Frieda walked across and looked out. She could see the Shard and the Gherkin and the Cheese Grater, those big buildings with silly names, as if London were slightly ashamed of them.

She turned to the room. In the center was a large pine desk, with a computer surrounded by piles of papers and cards and CDs. There was a mug full of pens and a cup containing paper clips. There was a wooden pencil box, two toothbrushes, a flash drive, a compass, a watch, an energy bill, two pairs of headphones and a small framed photograph of the children. There were books everywhere, on makeshift wooden shelves on two of the walls, stacked on the floor. There were also piles of different scientific journals. On another table there was a CD player and more piles of CDs, a shredder, an empty magnum-size bottle of wine and a tangle of cables and chargers. On one space of bare wall there was a messy watercolor, presumably painted by Tam, and a photograph of Al crossing the line in the London Marathon. Frieda leaned in close and looked at the time: 04.12.45. Was that good?

Frieda pulled open the drawers of the desk one by one. There was nothing unexpected: checkbooks, blank postcards, a stapler, Sellotape. Another drawer contained a pile of credit-card statements. Frieda scanned them quickly: petrol, railway tickets, a supermarket, coffee, a couple of cinema visits, names that were probably restaurants. Frieda put them back. She didn't even know what she was looking for. Another drawer contained cardboard files. Frieda took them out and riffled through them. They looked like lectures, presentations, chapters of a book. Frieda replaced them in the order she'd taken them out and turned her attention to the computer.

FRIDAY ON MY MIND 175

She touched the keyboard and the screen lit up, no password required. There were dozens of files and documents on his desktop, professional-looking, counterparts of what she had seen in the files. She clicked on his browser and looked at his history. It was a mixture of news, buying a book, weather, the London Zoo website, Twitter, a long article on a university website, a blog article, and that was just today. She didn't have time to make any kind of thorough search.

She clicked on his e-mail. The inbox contained 16,732 messages, but this was easier. She typed in Sandy's name and the screen filled with messages from him. She clicked on one of them and suddenly it was as if a window had been opened, bringing a familiar smell and a memory of long ago. Sandy was in the room with her. The message was nothing special, just a line saying they should get together before some departmental meeting or other and grab a coffee. The sheer casualness of it, the spelling mistakes: Frieda could almost see him sitting there typing it. It was like she was looking over his shoulder. She had to pause a moment, gather herself, stop thinking about the wrong things.

She clicked on message after message and she quickly became frustrated. Sandy had never been one for treating e-mails like old-fashioned letters. They were for saying "Yes" or "Maybe" or "Make it 11:30" or, on occasion, "We need to talk." He'd never even been very comfortable talking on the phone. He'd told her that if there was anything important to say, you needed to say it to someone's face so you could see their eyes, their expression. Otherwise it wasn't real communication. She clicked on the last message he had sent:

If you really want to talk about this (again), I'm in my office tomorrow.

S

Frieda thought for a moment. That seemed like something. She looked at the previous message from him. It was from a week earlier, a routine message telling Al about a change of room for a seminar. She read the last message again. Talk about what? She clicked on Al's "sent"

messages and scrolled down to the most recent, just an hour earlier
than Sandy's message:

Dear Sandy,

I've taken the weekend and you're wrong, I'm still angry. If you
think I'm just going to roll over about this, then you don't
understand me.

Yours, Alan

The previous message to this was from a week earlier and enclosed the
CV of a Ph.D. student; the one before and the one before that contained nothing significant.

And then Frieda heard a sound from downstairs. Or thought she
did—just a faint scraping. She stood quite still and listened but all she
could hear was the thump of her heart and in the far distance a radio
playing, a door slamming. A bead of sweat trickled down the side of her
face. She should quickly finish what she was doing and leave. She turned
back to her task, but then she heard another sound, definite this time,
louder. It was the front door opening and then closing. She took a step
back from the computer and tried to breathe steadily.

Frieda tried to remember something she might have been told. Did
they have a cleaner? Was someone coming to stay? Perhaps that was
why the alarm hadn't been turned on. She thought of staying where
she was in the hope that the person would leave—but what if they
didn't leave? Or if they came upstairs? If they came into this room and
found her standing there? She waited, scarcely daring to breathe, and
could hear nothing from downstairs. Whoever it was who had come in
must be standing in the hall, not moving—unless they were moving
silently, on their toes, coming up the stairs toward her. She turned her
head toward the door, half expecting to see someone standing there,
but who?

Then she did hear footsteps. Not fast but purposeful. Perhaps they
would go toward the kitchen and she could dash into the hall and

through the front door. But the footsteps paused at the foot of the stairs and then there was no doubt: they were coming toward her. She took a deep breath. There was no choice, really. She restored Al's computer to the way it had been and walked down the stairs, which curled round themselves, so that as she approached the main flight she had a clear view: Bridget was standing a few steps up the stairs, hand on the banisters and face gazing at her with an expression of fierce contempt. For a moment the two women stared at each other, neither of them moving, and it seemed to Frieda that everything she said now would be a charade. Nevertheless she adopted a light tone as she walked down toward Bridget.

"Hi," she said. "I came over because I thought I'd left my watch here. I took it off when I was playing with the children."

The words sounded so lame as she spoke them that Frieda could anticipate Bridget's questions: why couldn't you just collect the watch later? Why were you looking for it upstairs? Frieda was composing plausible answers in her head but Bridget simply said: "And did you?"

In answer Frieda held up her left hand, showing her watch on her wrist.

Bridget barely glanced at it, but kept her gaze fixed on Frieda's face. Her eyes glowed. She had a very faint smile on her face now, not a happy one.

"I thought you were at the zoo," Frieda said. She could feel the pulse in her neck and she put out a hand to touch the wall's reassuring solidity.

"Yes. I know you did."

"Is something wrong?"

Bridget looked at Frieda as if she were assessing her and then seemed to make up her mind.

"Follow me," she said. "Carla."

The two women walked through to the kitchen. Bridget pulled open a drawer in the kitchen table.

"I've got my watch," said Frieda, her voice sounding tinny in her ears. "I can leave now and come back for the children later."

"Oh, stop it, for goodness' sake. Just stop." Bridget's voice rang out clear and sharp, and Frieda felt a tingle of shame spreading through her.

"All right," she said. "I'll stop."

Bridget took out a newspaper and threw it down on the table. Frieda barely needed to look. She saw the headline: "Police Psych Goes on Run." And there was a picture of her, one that had been used before. It had been taken of her without her knowledge.

"It looks like you've made some attempt to disguise yourself. It wasn't enough."

"Obviously not."

"Well? *Well?*" Bridget slammed her fist on the table so hard that the mugs on it jumped. "Is that all you have to say? Sitting there so cool and proper. My *nanny*. Fuck. The woman who screwed up Sandy's life, finding your way into *my* house, looking after *my* children, snooping through *my possessions*."

"Have you called the police?"

As Frieda asked the question, she was making calculations in her head, asking herself questions. What was Bridget planning? Was Al really with the children or was he in the house as well? Or perhaps he would be waiting outside. She pictured the network of roads and tried to think of which way she would run.

"Ha! Not yet." She slid her hand into her jacket pocket and pulled out a mobile, held it up. "But my fingers are itching."

"Where's Al?"

"Out. With the children. Where you can't get at them. How could you?" Bridget's voice was suddenly loud. "This isn't some kind of game. Those are our fucking children. Clearly you don't mind what happens to yourself, but what about them? You're a fugitive, you're wanted for murder, you probably are a murderer. A murderer of my dear friend."

"I looked after them well," said Frieda. She glanced at the back door. The key was in the lock. She could feel her muscles tensing in readiness.

Bridget raised her hands and Frieda stepped back. She let her hands fall.

"I've never hit anybody in my life. But I could punch you and grab you and kick you."

"I understand."

"No, you don't. You've been in this house, this house where you would never have been welcome, and you've lied and you've lied. How can you do that? How are you so good at that?"

"I'm sorry I lied. But I was looking after your children like anyone would look after them."

Bridget gave a bitter shout of laughter. "Are you insane? Is that your line of defense? I've never met anyone like you. You're off my scale." She took a few deep breaths, as if she were trying to calm herself down. "Let's go out into the garden. I feel trapped in here, as if I'm going to explode with something."

Bridget and Al's home was just a medium-sized terraced house, but when they stepped into the garden, Frieda felt as if they were stepping into a park. The garden was narrow but quite long and there were gardens on either side and another row of gardens at the far end. There were huge plane trees and a birch and fruit trees, all hidden from the streets that surrounded them. Bridget led them along a path to a paved area with a wooden table surrounded by metal chairs.

Frieda sat on one. It felt cold even on this sunny morning. "Why haven't you called the police?" she asked.

"I'm asking the questions, not you."

"All right."

"I wasn't asking for permission. And I'm on the brink of calling the police. But I wanted to talk to you myself first. You've been going through our stuff. At first I couldn't believe it. Things had been moved around—at least, I thought they had. But nothing was gone. I just had to be sure. Now I am. You're the woman Sandy's friends hated. You're the woman who's wanted for his murder. And you're in my house, looking after my children."

"Yes."

"It's your turn. Did you kill Sandy?"

"No."

"Why should I believe you? The police obviously don't."

"If I'd killed him, I wouldn't be here trying to find his murderer."

"So that's what you're doing, is it?"

"Yes."

"You would say that."

Frieda shrugged. "Perhaps. But it's true. That's all I can say. I did not kill Sandy."

"And why here, in our house? What are you doing? What the *fuck* are you doing, Frieda fucking snoop Klein?"

"You and your husband weren't just friends with Sandy."

"Oh, weren't we?" Bridget folded her arms across her chest and glowered.

"What was the problem that Al had with Sandy? The one he was complaining about."

An expression of distaste appeared on Bridget's face "Go on," she said.

"What do you mean?"

"I'll answer your question, but only after you tell me—truthfully—how you know that Al was having a problem with Sandy."

"Because I read his e-mails."

"Do you never think about people's privacy?"

"Not when somebody has been murdered. Not when I've been accused of killing him."

"So you read through Al's e-mails. And?"

"Is it true that Al was angry with Sandy?"

"Disappointed."

"He seemed extremely disappointed in the message I read."

"Sandy was shaking up the department. One thing he did was to shut down a research project that some of Al's Ph.D. students were working on."

"Was he being unfair?"

Bridget shrugged. "Who knows? I suppose it was Sandy's job to make decisions like that and it was Al's job to feel a bit aggrieved about it. He was pissed off, he probably slammed a few doors, but he wasn't going to kill Sandy because of it."

"You'd be surprised at the little things that would make someone kill someone else."

"You learned that as a therapist?"

"Partly."

"Al couldn't do something like that."

Frieda didn't reply.

"I know that you're going to say that anyone could do it. But he didn't." Bridget paused, then began again in an angry tone: "Anyway, why am I defending myself to you? I just need to pick up the phone and the police will be here in two minutes and they'll lock you up. Or are you going to stop me somehow?"

"I'm not going to stop you," said Frieda. "If you want to call them, I'll just sit here."

Bridget glared at her. "Before I call them, is there anything you want to tell me or ask me?"

"The police searched my house. They found Sandy's wallet hidden in a drawer. Somebody must have put it there. Someone with a key to my house. Not many people have a key to my house. But you do."

"Do I? I didn't know that."

"Do you want me to show you?"

"You probably know more about what's in my house than I do. I suppose you mean the keys I got from Sandy."

"Yes."

"And you want me to explain why I've got them."

"Yes."

Suddenly Bridget laughed. "Let me get this straight. At the time you were wandering around South London with our tiny children while the police were hunting for you, you thought that Al, or maybe even Al and I together, like some kind of Bonnie and Clyde, murdered Sandy because of an argument in the office. And then, having killed him and disposed of the body, we decided to plant evidence in the house of his ex-lover, someone we'd never met and knew almost nothing about. Is that right?"

"That was one possibility."

Bridget looked around the garden as if she were only noticing it for the first time. "About three months ago, it was around one o'clock in the morning and I was sitting here. I was wearing a sweater, a thick jacket and woolly hat. And Sandy was sitting where you're sitting now."

"At one in the morning?"

"We talked here for a bit and then we started to feel cold. We felt we needed to move around. So we walked out of the house and down to Clapham Road and then we walked around the Common for an hour, I think, maybe more."

"Were you having an affair?"

Bridget flinched. "That's the sort of moment when someone would slap you round the face. I was going to say 'Carla.' It's hard to shed an old habit. Frieda Klein. Frieda fucking Klein."

"Were you?"

"He knocked on the door after midnight and woke me up. Al is a heavy sleeper. He was apologizing. He knew about the children and how little sleep we were getting. He said he was thinking of doing something stupid and he needed to talk to someone and I was the only person he could think of."

"You mean . . ."

"You know what I mean."

"Yes. He was contemplating suicide."

"So we talked. He said a lot and I said a bit. Mainly I listened. Then he went home. But he gave me a set of keys, just in case. The ones you found."

"What did he tell you?"

"That he'd come back from the States for a relationship that had fallen apart and he didn't think he was managing his life properly and he couldn't see a way forward." She gave Frieda a look that had a flash of anger in it. "But I suppose you're used to people lying on your couch and saying things like that to you."

"I don't have a couch. What did you reply?"

"Nothing clever. I said that it was hard to believe but it would pass. He just had to wait and trust in his friends."

Frieda felt a pang. She should have been the one telling Sandy that. It was good advice and, in the end, that was what a lot of therapy for troubled people came down to. Just wait: gradually the pain will change and become more bearable. But she had been the cause of the pain.

"Was it just once?"

"It was only that extreme just the once. But we talked from time to time. Sometimes he would phone late at night."

"After all that, after all you did for him, wasn't it a bit strange that he damaged Al's career?"

"Are you serious?" said Bridget, in a tone of contempt that made Frieda wince. "You think we're like that: I help you out when you're in distress and, in return, you do my husband some kind of favor at work."

"He may have been trying to prove something."

"Like what?"

"It can be difficult to be helped, to feel that someone has rescued you."

"You sound like you've got quite a low opinion of humanity."

Frieda stood up. "You never know how people will react," she said. "Are you going to call the police now?"

"Al didn't do it. I didn't do it." There was a long pause. "And I don't think you did it."

"But someone did," said Frieda.

"I know."

"And I need to find out who."

"*We* need to," said Bridget. "He was my friend. I won't call the police."

"Have you told Al about me?"

"No." She hesitated. "Not yet. I don't think he'd be very understanding, though."

She hadn't told her husband about Sandy's despair either, thought Frieda. There was a silence. Frieda looked at Bridget, her broad, sculpted face and her strong arms, and Bridget looked straight ahead, her hands clasped together. She seemed to be waiting.

"Can you help me?" Frieda said at last, softly.

Bridget looked round then, eyebrows raised. Her anger seemed to have evaporated. She was sad instead; sad and weary. "I've got young children. I can't do the sort of things you do."

"There only needs to be one of me," said Frieda.

"I can't believe I'm doing this. Next time I'm going to insist on proper references."

21

Josef was very hot. He was up in the loft of the Belsize Park house, inserting insulation foam between the wall cavities. Although there were skylights in the roof, through which the sun poured, there was also an extra-bright Anglepoise light rigged up to shine into the corners. Josef felt that he was trapped between its heat and the sun's. There was grit in his eyes, a sheen of sweat and dust on his skin. His hair was damp and his feet itched.

Near him, another man was hammering the wall partitions back into place. He struck each nail with a loud, precise first blow, then followed it with a series of brisk taps that reminded Josef of a woodpecker. The man was solid, with muscles that rippled in his arms, and a shaven head that every so often he would wipe with a large cloth.

For the most part, they worked in silence, except to grunt a few words to each other—about the heat, the dust, the wealth of the owners who were ripping apart a perfectly good house in order to erect another inside its shell. Yesterday the man—his name was Marty—had had a radio with him but today he was empty-handed. They could hear the sounds of other builders beneath them: music, curses, the ugly shriek of a saw on metal.

At eleven Marty laid down his hammer. "I'm going for a smoke. Coming?"

Josef nodded and gratefully straightened up. They went down the several flights of stairs, through rooms, most of which were like their own mini building sites, and out into the garden. It was long for a London garden and sloped upward toward the back wall between high trellises, and it, too, was evidently a work in progress. The two men sat on a step beside what would one day be the paved barbecue area but which was now piled with bricks and lengths of pipe. Josef pulled out his packet of cigarettes and offered one to Marty, but he shook his head and proceeded to roll his own, his stubby fingers deft.

Josef smoked his cigarette slowly, between swigs from his water bottle, and half closed his eyes against the bright shafts of sunlight. He was thinking about what he would cook tonight—perhaps something Ukrainian. And thinking about his homeland made him think of his two sons, whom he hadn't seen for so long now, although his wife—ex-wife—had sent him photographs recently. Taller, more solid, their hair darker and cut shorter, they looked strange to him although not like strangers, familiar yet far off. And thinking of his sons and the pain in his chest that their absence caused him made him think of Frieda, for only Frieda knew something of what he felt about this—and it was at this moment that the back door swung open and two people, a man and a woman, walked into the garden.

At first Josef thought they must be surveyors or architects. The man, who looked like a rugby player, was wearing a light gray suit, and the woman, who was small and moved with a purposeful air, a biscuit-colored skirt with a white blouse and flat shoes. He narrowed his eyes, then let out a groan.

"What?" asked Marty.

"I know that woman. She is police."

"Police?"

"They come for me, I know."

"You? What have you done wrong, mate?"

"I? Nothing. They do wrong." But he was uneasy. He remembered the state Frieda's temporary neighbor and robber had been in when they had left him. But how could the police know anything? He told himself it was impossible.

Hussein and Bryant picked their way through the debris in the garden.

"Mr. Morozov," said Hussein. "DCI Hussein."

She held out her identification but Josef, still sitting on the step, waved it away. "I know. We met. You are hunting Frieda."

"Looking for her. We'd like a word with you."

"All right."

"In private."

"You want me to go?" said Marty. He stood and moved to the end of the garden, his back to them, where he started to roll another cigarette.

"Do you know why we're here?" asked Hussein.

Josef shrugged.

"I think you know where Frieda is."

"I know nothing."

"You know we have a camera rigged up at her house."

"I notice it, of course."

"So we know you go to her house every day."

"It is not a crime."

"You stay there quite a long time."

Josef flushed. "So?" he said.

"What do you do?"

"Feed cat. Water plants. Make sure things are nice." He scowled at the two officers. "For when she can come home again."

"Sometimes you stay there an hour."

"Not a crime," Josef said again. He wasn't going to tell them that he wandered round the house, sat in Frieda's chair, stood in her study, feeling her presence.

"When did you last have contact with her?"

He waved his hand in the air. "When she left."

"I don't believe you."

Josef gave his shrug.

"You understand that we could have you deported," said Bryant, suddenly.

"You know nothing," said Josef. "So you try to scare me. But I am not scared."

"Did you know she was there?"

"What?" Josef squinted at her. "Frieda?"

"Yes."

"In her house?"

"Yes."

"Ah," he said. It was like a sigh.

"Did you know?"

"No."

"Did you leave anything for her?"

"No."

"Why was she there?"

"Is her home." He stood up and took a swig from his water bottle. "Perhaps homesick. I left everything clean and good for her."

"You think she went simply because she was homesick?"

"Do you know the homesick feeling?"

Hussein made an impatient gesture. "She is in serious trouble. If you are a true friend, you will tell us how to find her before things get any worse."

"I am a true friend," said Josef. "I will say nothing. Except you will see."

"What will we see, Josef?"

"My name is Mr. Morozov."

"Yes, Mr. Morozov. We are not your enemy."

"Frieda's enemy is my enemy."

"We are not Frieda's enemy. But we need to find her. And we think you can help us."

"No."

"Perverting the course of justice is a serious crime."

Josef didn't reply. He took his cigarettes out of his back pocket, tapped one out and lit it.

"You have our card," said Hussein. "If you think of anything."

They left, and Josef sat down on the step once more. Marty joined him.

"Fuck," he said. "I couldn't help catching a bit of that. You're a friend of that woman who's on the run?"

Josef nodded. "She is my friend."

"And you know where she is?" Marty sounded admiring.

"Maybe. Maybe not."

"Will they find her, do you reckon?"

"No."

"But she can't stay hidden forever."

"Is true." The expression on Josef's face became somber. He ground his cigarette into the brickwork and stood up. "We should work."

"I want another biscuit."

"No. Three is enough."

"I want one." Tam's voice rose higher. Her face became redder. "I want a biscuit."

"No."

"I'll scream."

"That won't help."

Tam opened her mouth so wide it seemed to take up most of her face and emitted a piercing shriek. Frieda picked up Rudi, who was trying to haul himself up on her legs, and put him on her lap. His weight felt comforting and his hair was clean and smelled of shampoo. The screaming went on, with little hiccups in between.

Bridget appeared in the doorway carrying two mugs of tea. "What's happened?"

"Nothing."

"Did she fall over?"

"No."

"I want another biscuit," roared Tam. "Carla said no."

"Oh, is that all?"

"It's not fair."

"Fair?" Bridget's eyebrows went up and she looked down at her daughter skeptically. "Here's your tea." She handed a mug with a picture of a puffin on it across to Frieda. "I've found a nanny, by the way," she said, almost casually.

"That's probably for the best."

"Yes."

They sat and drank their tea. At last Tam was winding down. She put her thumb in her mouth and within a few seconds had fallen asleep, her legs stretched out in front of her.

"Welcome to the world of motherhood," said Bridget. "Nappies and tantrums and grazed knees and stained clothes and broken nights.

Time's never your own." She smiled at Frieda. "As you might have gathered, I'm not a particularly patient person."

"Going to work must make it easier."

"I'd go mad if I was with them all the time."

"Perhaps because you love them so much," said Frieda. "Perhaps that's what makes it so overpowering."

Bridget shot her a glance. "You're being Frieda Klein now, aren't you, not Carla? The Frieda Klein Sandy loved."

Frieda rested her chin on Rudi's head. He, too, was beginning to fall asleep. She could feel the rise and fall of his breath through his body. "It's not enough," she said thoughtfully.

"What? Love?"

"I mean, it still doesn't make sense that Sandy should become so desperate because I had left him and his life had gone awry."

"You don't think losing someone can make you desperate?"

"I'm a psychotherapist, remember? It's what the loss uncovers in you that brings on despair, not the loss itself. Sandy was a deep-feeling man but he was also strong and quite good at protecting himself."

"You think?"

"I do. Don't you?"

"He didn't protect himself from you."

"But that's not why he should have felt on the edge. You say that he wasn't managing his life properly."

"That's right."

"What did he mean by that?"

Bridget hesitated; she was still clearly reluctant to betray his confidences. "He felt guilty."

"Guilty about relationships with women?"

"Mostly, I think."

"Can you say anything more about that?"

"Do you think this has anything to do with his death?"

"I don't know."

"He had a series of flings," said Bridget. "And he didn't always end them very well."

"I met Veronica Ellison," said Frieda, thinking of the words Veronica had used to describe how Sandy had been with her at the end—cruel and indifferent, because he himself was wretched.

"Yes." Bridget smiled. "Carla was very resourceful, wasn't she?"

"Do you know who the other women were?"

"I know a few. There was a research assistant at the university—Bella. Bella Fisk. She was smitten, I think."

"But he wasn't?"

"No."

"And then there was someone called Kim. Or Kimberley. I can't remember her last name."

Frieda frowned. A memory wormed through her. "Was she a nanny?"

"Another?" said Bridget. "She might have been."

"His sister had a nanny called Kimberley."

"That's the kind of thing he was doing."

"Anyone else?"

"There were other women but I've no idea who. They were the ones he talked about to me."

"Is there anything else you can think of?"

"Well." Bridget looked out of the window for a moment. "He was scared."

"Scared?" This was what Veronica Ellison had also believed. "But you knew that, didn't you?"

"Why would I know that? We hadn't really spoken for a long time." Frieda remembered her last sight of Sandy, outside the Warehouse, flinging a black bin bag of possessions at her, his face contorted.

"He said he was trying to call you about it. He thought you'd be the one who would know what to do. Didn't he talk to you about it?"

She looked into Bridget's face. "I deleted all his messages."

"And you didn't listen to them first?"

"No."

They sat in silence for a while, Rudi on Frieda's lap, like a squashy warm parcel, and Tam between them, husky whimpers coming from between her parted lips.

"You have no idea why he was scared?" Frieda asked at last.

"No. But he was right to be, wasn't he?"

• • •

Frieda walked back to Elephant and Castle. It took her almost an hour. The day had turned to early evening, softly bright, and the streets were full of people in their summer clothes. Teenagers on skateboards rattled past. Couples lingered, their arms entwined. The pavements outside pubs overflowed with drinkers.

She walked under the railway bridge and along the side of Thaxted House. She thought of her own little house, which in the summer was cool and clean and dim, as if it were under water. The longing she felt for it was so sharp it made her breath shallow. She unlocked the front door and stepped inside. She heard voices from the kitchen, talking, laughing. She went on to her own room and pushed open her door.

"Frieda," said a voice, as she closed it.

She spun round.

"Josef! What are you doing here?"

"Nice woman let me in."

Josef made shapes in front of his chest.

"Ileana," said Frieda. "And you shouldn't do that. You should say, 'the brown-haired woman.' And you should go."

"I must help."

"No! You must not help. Go away."

"Frieda, I cannot bear."

Frieda stepped forward and touched him on the shoulder, looking into his sad brown eyes. She could smell the vodka on his breath. "It's all right. Who else knows I'm here?"

"Nobody. I tell nobody. I ask Lev and he show me the place. I dodge and duck so nobody can follow. Not the police." He sniffed contemptuously. "Not anyone. I keep your secret." He laid his large hand over his heart. "I help you."

"Josef, listen. You more than anyone have too much to lose. They could deport you."

"Threat." He waved his hand dismissively. Then he bent down and took a bottle of vodka out of his canvas bag. "This is horrible place. Shall we have a drink?"

Frieda looked at the bottle in his outstretched hand, then around her at the dismal little room, the low sun glinting in through the smeary windows, the thin orange curtains hanging limply. She smiled suddenly. "Why not?"

Josef's face brightened. He bent down once more and took out two shot glasses. "Always prepared," he said.

"To homecomings," said Frieda.

They clinked glasses and drank.

About five seconds after Josef had left, there was a knock at Frieda's door.

"What?"

The door opened and Mira's grinning face appeared in the gap.

"He's gone?" she said.

"Yes, he's gone."

"He can stay," said Mira. "He can stay all the night."

"He's just a friend."

"Yes, yes," said Mira, laughing. She came into the room and looked around for somewhere to sit. There wasn't anywhere.

"We talk about you, Ileana and me."

"I wish you wouldn't."

"Ileana say you running away from husband."

"And what do *you* say?"

"I not sure. But now we meet Josef. Interesting man."

Frieda stood up and started to edge Mira toward the door.

"You wouldn't like him," she said. "He's Ukrainian."

Mira looked puzzled. "Ukrainian not so bad. Romanian bad. Russian a bit. Not Ukrainian."

Frieda pushed the door shut.

22

A homeless man had been found kicked to death and left behind a Dumpster near King's Cross. Karlsson thought it was one of the most depressing cases he had ever dealt with: not just that the man, whose name he didn't know, had been so mutilated and then discarded like a piece of rubbish, but that there was no one who claimed his body, knew his identity or anything of his life, or cared that he was dead. The victim looked old but the pathologist said he was only about fifty. His possessions, which he had pushed about in a rusty old supermarket trolley, had been scattered nearby and had been found near his body; they consisted of a sleeping bag, some pieces of quilting, a few cans of white cider, a plastic bag of cigarette butts, six used-up cigarette lighters and some dog food, although he hadn't owned a dog. Nobody had seen anything; nobody knew anything; nobody cared.

He looked at the photographs of his two children, Bella and Mikey, that were on his desk: that man had been a little kid once; a baby who had squirmed and cried and smiled. How did a life go so off the rails? "Poor sod," he muttered.

There was a knock and Yvette put her head round the door. "Sorry to disturb you."

"I needed disturbing. What is it? Any new leads from the lads?"

"No. But it's not about that. There's someone who wants to see you."

"Who?"

"A woman called Elizabeth Rasson. I asked her what it was about but she said she wanted to talk to only you. She's very insistent."

"Elizabeth Rasson?" Karlsson frowned. "But that's—" He stopped. "Never mind. Send her in."

Lizzie Rasson came through the door in a rush and stopped, looking around her as if unsure of where she was or how she had got there. She was very thin, with a sharp collarbone, and her face wore a dazed expression that Karlsson was familiar with.

"Mrs. Rasson," he said, offering his hand. "Won't you sit down?"

"Lizzie," she said. "We met once. Or were in the same room. You won't remember."

"I think I do."

"It was a long time ago. I remember you because I don't usually meet police officers, and also because Sandy really didn't like you."

"Right."

"Sandy's my brother."

"I know."

"Was. Was my brother. I keep doing that. How long does it take?"

"To use the past tense, you mean?"

"Yes."

"It'll probably feel strange for a long time."

"I'm talking so that I don't have to say anything, if you see what I mean."

"I do. Please." He pulled out a chair and she sat down in it abruptly, her long legs folding under her. He saw how bony her shins were.

"We were very close when we were children—there's only fourteen months' difference between us. We drifted apart a bit when we were adults but then this time, when he came back from America, I saw a lot of him. He wasn't in a good way and he came to our house a lot and, well, we're family. I was the only family he had, after . . ." She bit down on her words, rubbed her face.

"What can I do for you?"

"You're a good friend of Frieda's, aren't you?" Lizzie continued, as if he hadn't spoken.

"She's my friend, yes."

"Yes." The single syllable was heavy with bitterness. "That's why Sandy didn't like you. He thought the two of you were too friendly. He was jealous. Especially after it all ended. She treated him very badly, don't you think?"

"The ends of relationships are always painful," Karlsson said guardedly. "And Frieda—"

"Yes, yes, Frieda's a special case. Even now. Do you think she killed my brother?"

The directness of the question took Karlsson by surprise. "No."

"You mean, you don't think she did."

"I mean that she didn't."

"Why? Because she's your friend?"

Karlsson blinked and pinched the top of his nose between his thumb and forefinger. "I suppose it comes down to that," he said at last.

"Lucky Frieda, to have such friends. But you don't sound very much like a detective."

"That's because I'm not a detective in this case. You do understand that I have nothing to do with the inquiry? If you need to know anything, or if you have anything to say, you should speak to DCI Hussein. I can give you her number."

"That's not why I'm here."

"Why are you here, then?"

"I've been thinking."

Karlsson waited.

Lizzie wrinkled her nose and looked into the distance. "About the last few weeks of Sandy's life."

"Go on."

"He was all over the place. You know Sandy—*knew*. He was quite controlled, reserved. But not in the time before he died. He kind of unraveled, if that makes sense."

Karlsson nodded but didn't speak. The light was flashing on his phone but he made no move to answer it.

"He'd done something bad," said Lizzie.

"What had he done?"

"I don't know."

"You should speak to Sarah Hussein. It might be important."

Lizzie made an impatient gesture with her hand. "I'm speaking to you. He wasn't just troubled, he was scared."

Karlsson leaned forward in his chair. "What was he scared of, Lizzie?" he said softly. "Who was he scared of?"

"No. Not like that. You don't understand."

"Then tell me."

"He kept trying to call Frieda."

"Yes, I knew that."

"But she wouldn't answer. He called and he e-mailed and she never replied."

"I think she believed that there was nothing to be said."

"No. He wasn't pursuing her—not at the end, anyway."

"What do you mean?"

"I don't think he ever stopped loving her, so when he was scared he was frantic to get in touch with her." Tears filled Lizzie's eyes. "Frantic," she repeated.

"He was calling Frieda for help?" asked Karlsson.

"No."

"Then what?"

"I thought she killed him, so it didn't matter. But if she didn't, then I have to warn her, however cruel she was."

"Please. You have to be clearer. What are you saying?"

"He wasn't scared for himself. He was scared for her. He thought she was in danger."

Karlsson stared at Lizzie Rasson. He felt a bead of sweat work its way down his temple. "Your brother believed Frieda was in danger."

"Yes."

"He told you that himself?"

"Yes. But he was drunk when he told me, and when he died and Frieda was OK, I didn't think it meant anything. Just a wild notion. But now you have to warn her. It's the last thing I can do for Sandy."

"I don't know where she is. But we need to tell Sarah Hussein."

"You have to warn her," she said again. "Before something terrible happens to her as well."

After Lizzie Rasson had left, Karlsson picked up the phone and called Hussein, who listened to what he had to say in a silence so complete that he kept having to check that she was still there.

"What do you think?" he said when he had finished, although he had left out the part about the need to warn Frieda.

"I think this is probably a red herring and that Frieda Klein killed her ex and that's why she's disappeared. If she was innocent, why would she do that?"

"Because she was being framed."

"That's a theory," Hussein said. "But it's not one we can usefully pursue until Dr. Klein is in custody."

"Sandy was scared Frieda was in danger. Then Sandy was killed. Doesn't that suggest you're looking in the wrong place for the murderer?"

"No. It suggests that we need to find Frieda Klein and question her."

"But—"

"I appreciate your concern," Hussein said. "And I hope that *you* appreciate I'm not trying to stitch up your friend but to get to the truth. That's my job. That's what I intend to do. And that's what is in everybody's best interests, including Frieda's."

"Of course," said Karlsson.

"So are you going to help?"

"What do you mean?"

"Where is she? I assume that's why Mrs. Rasson came to you, not me—because she thought you could let Frieda know she was in danger. I'm not entirely stupid."

"I never thought you were."

"So?"

"I don't know where she is."

"You had better be telling me the truth."

"I am. I don't know."

Karlsson didn't know, but after he had spoken to Hussein he told Yvette he was going out for a while. Thirty-five minutes later, he was sitting in Reuben McGill's office in the Warehouse. Reuben, his shirt-sleeves rolled up, sat on the sill of the open window and smoked.

"Is this going to be awkward?" he asked.

"I'm concerned for Frieda's safety. I need your help."

Reuben threw his cigarette stub out of the window and turned toward Karlsson. "Is this a way of getting me to talk?"

"Frieda's in danger."

"Yeah, yeah."

"I'm here as Frieda's friend. I'm not on the inquiry."

Reuben looked at him through narrowed eyes. "What kind of danger?"

"I don't know. But Sandy was trying to warn her before he died."

Reuben came away from the window and sat at his desk, his chin propped on his hands. "I don't know what I can do," he said.

"You don't need to tell me where she is, but you need to tell her what I've told you."

"I don't know where she is." He met Karlsson's skeptical gaze. "It's the truth. She's disappeared."

"You have no way of getting in contact with her?"

"No." He unfolded his hands so that they covered most of his face and closed his eyes. Karlsson waited. "You swear you're not tricking me?"

"I'm not tricking you."

Reuben spoke slowly, reluctantly. "I don't know why I'm saying this. But if anyone knows anything, Josef does. I may have done a terrible thing telling you that."

"I won't get him into trouble."

"Frieda would never forgive you."

"Where is he now?"

"He's working at a house in Belsize Park. He's stubborn. As you know."

"We'll see."

Reuben nodded and wrote down the address on a piece of paper that he tore from the pad and handed across the desk. "If this goes wrong," he said, "I'll come for you with all the weapons in my psychotherapeutic arsenal."

"I'll remember that," said Karlsson. He took the paper and left.

He found Josef in the back garden of the house. He was with a group of men, drinking tea, smoking. Josef saw him and rose to his feet, looking wary. "Nothing to say."

Karlsson took him by the arm and led him away from the group of men, who were watching them curiously. "There's something you should know."

"You think you scare me?"

"I'm not going to threaten you." He held up a hand to stop Josef interrupting. "I'm not going to ask if you know where she is. I'm just giving you this." He thrust his hand into the inside pocket of his jacket and pulled out the letter he had written in the café down the road.

Josef stepped away from it as though it were a bomb that might explode in his face. "This is trick."

"What trick could it be? I am giving you a letter. It would be good for Frieda if she read it, but that's up to you."

"I know nothing."

"Then I'm wasting my time." He waited a moment. "I'm Frieda's friend and I have reason to believe that she's in danger."

"You are police."

"That too. But you can still trust me."

Josef wrinkled his face, which was grimy. There was dust in his hair and Karlsson saw that his hands were blistered.

"You say danger," he said.

"Yes."

Josef glowered at him. "If I take it, then it means nothing."

"OK."

He held out the letter once more and this time Josef took it. As soon as Karlsson had gone, Josef pulled out his phone. Frieda had given him her new number. He dialed it. No answer.

Frieda felt that she was on the verge of saying good-bye to Ethan, for the moment anyway. This couldn't go on. They got onto a bus and went upstairs to the front. Ethan stood up on the seat and stared out of the window and gave a running commentary on what he could see: people and pets and cars and bikes and houses and shops. The bus went through Elephant and Castle and down the Old Kent Road. They got out and Ethan said he was tired and that he was hungry.

"Wait," said Frieda.

She took him by the hand and led him off the main road and to the right and there, improbably, as if by magic, was something Ethan had never seen before. She led him through the gate, across the cobblestones, into the stables. Two horses peered out of their stalls, looking curiously at them. Frieda lifted Ethan up.

"You can touch," she said. She put out her free hand and stroked the soft, salmon-pink skin between one of the horses' nostrils. Ethan shook his head and leaned away. He didn't dare touch the horses but he didn't want to leave. Even when Frieda led him back out onto the pavement, he stared back behind him, as if he thought the stables might vanish when he stopped looking at them. Then they walked past the forge. Frieda tried to explain what a horseshoe was. Ethan just frowned. Frieda couldn't tell whether he didn't understand what she was saying or whether he did understand but didn't believe it.

They continued following the telltale slopes and banks. Frieda noticed a broad pipe crossing the railway line. A few minutes later, she led him off into a little side-street. On the ground there were two manhole covers.

"Do this," she said, and knelt on the ground and put her ear to one of them. He copied her. "Can you hear it?" she said.

He sat up and nodded.

"Do you know what it is?" she said.

He shook his head.

"Long, long ago there was a river," she said, "a little river. It ran through the streets and there were boats in it. And the horses—like the horses we saw—the horses drank from it. But then they hid the river. They covered it and built houses and roads on top of it. And people forgot about it. But the river is still there." She rapped on the metal cover. "That's it, down there. It's called the Earl's Sluice."

"Sluice," he said solemnly.

"That's it. Only you and me know that it's there and we won't forget it, will we?"

"No," he said obediently.

She stood up and held out her hand.

When they reached the Thames, Ethan put his head against the railings, as if he were trying to get at it. He seemed hypnotized.

"This way," said Frieda, leading him westward along the riverside path. After a few hundred yards, when Ethan was starting to weigh on her, dragging on her arm to signal his tiredness, she bent down and spoke to him in a whisper. "I've got a surprise for you," she said.

"What?"

She led him through the little gate into the city farm. When Ethan saw the goats and the cockerels and the rabbits, he stood still, with his mouth open. Then he started to run around, pointing at this animal, then that one and then another. After a while, Frieda took him to the café and bought him an ice cream, but he was restless, then started to cry and say he wanted to go back to the animals. So Frieda took her coffee, walked out and watched him as he went back into the enclosure.

A school party arrived, a crocodile of six-year-olds, all wearing high-visibility yellow vests, like a team of miniature construction workers. After a time, Ethan went and stood next to two little girls. One was holding a rabbit while the other stroked it. A young female teacher came across and said something to Ethan that Frieda couldn't hear. Ethan looked round and pointed at Frieda. The teacher took him by the hand and led him across to her. "I'm sorry," she said. "He can't be with our children. Something might happen."

"Not while I'm here," said Frieda.

"It's the rules," said the teacher. "It's not my decision."

"It never is," said Frieda.

The teacher looked puzzled, but Frieda just led Ethan away, tired, complaining, overexcited, shouting that he wanted to stroke the goat.

23

The site manager was called Gavin and he wasn't pleased.

"What kind of emergency?" he said.

"Back in an hour," said Josef. "Two maybe."

"Two hours? What is this? A hobby?"

"I'll cover for him," said a voice.

The two men looked round. It was Marty.

"What are you talking about?" said Gavin. "If you can do his job and your job, then what do we need him for?"

"Joe is the best man on this job. And if he says it's an emergency, then it's an emergency."

Josef looked at the two men with some apprehension. Things were either going to get better or they were going to get worse. Gavin's face reddened, but something in Marty's expression changed his mind. "Two hours," he said. "And don't make a habit of it."

As he left, Josef gave a nod of thanks to Marty.

"Is there a problem?"

"Just a friend."

"This Frieda?"

Josef shrugged. "Maybe."

"She's lucky to have you as a mate."

"No. I am the lucky one."

Every part of the journey seemed to take longer than it should have. Josef had to wait for the lift at Chalk Farm station. The train stopped in a tunnel for ten minutes, with repeated apologies to passengers over the loudspeaker. As he emerged from Elephant and Castle, he got a signal and rang Frieda again. Nothing. He ran to the flat where Frieda lived, knocked at the door and rang the bell. Nothing. He knocked again and heard sounds inside. Finally the door opened. It was the blonde, the one without the breasts.

"Carla, is she here?"

"I don't know. In bedroom, maybe."

Josef walked past her and pushed open the door of Frieda's room. The bed was made as if for an army inspection. He looked round. Mira was at his shoulder.

"She not here much. Work with the children, I think."

"Where?"

"I don't know."

He took out the letter and looked at it. Should he give it to this woman? He thought of Frieda and then he thought of Karlsson. Karlsson was breaking the law. It felt like too much of a risk. He put the letter back in his pocket.

"Tell Frieda to call me," he said. "If she ring or come back, say to call me. Important."

"You can wait," said Mira. "Have coffee."

"No," said Josef. "Just to call me."

Frieda sat in the Watched Pot coffee shop and waited. Bella Fisk had been very reluctant to meet her but had eventually agreed to give her ten minutes of her time. Frieda wondered how she would identify her. But the door swung open, a woman walked in and Frieda was sure. She was starting to recognize Sandy's type. Bella was tall, in a dark dress, with blue leather boots that were only half laced up. She had brown frizzy hair and looked fierce and clever. She noticed Frieda's glance and came over to the table.

"What's this about?" she said.

"Thank you for agreeing to see me."

"Yeah, but why are you so keen to dig around in the past?"

"I knew Sandy. Some time ago. Can I buy you a coffee? We'll just be a few minutes."

She sat down. Frieda went over to the counter and ordered two coffees.

"Nice place," she said when she returned.

"It's not too bad," said Bella. "It's my local. A friend of mine is coming in a few minutes. We're going out."

"Fine," said Frieda.

"What do you mean, 'fine'? Of course it's fine. I said ten minutes. So, tell me what this is all about."

"Everybody's shocked about what happened to Sandy. I've been trying to talk to people who knew him."

"Why?"

"I want to know how he was. In those last days."

"Old lover, was he?"

"A friend," said Frieda.

A faintly ironic smile appeared on Bella's face. "If you say so." She paused as a middle-aged woman arrived with two vast coffee cups on a tray. After the woman had gone, Bella stared at Frieda with a challenging expression.

"So . . . what was your name?"

"Carla."

"Carla. Funny. He never mentioned that name. So, Carla, you want to know about Sandy's work life?" Frieda didn't reply. She just sipped slowly at her coffee and waited. "All right," said Bella. "Who have you been talking to?"

"I just want to hear how Sandy was."

There was a pause. Bella's demeanor had changed. She was thinking hard and seemed restless.

"I don't know what this is about. Are you some kind of stalker?"

"No. Sandy's dead. You can't stalk a dead person."

"I'm not so sure about that," said Bella. "By the way, if—when—my friend turns up, maybe we can stick to the work bit with Sandy. I mean, it's not a big thing—Tom and I aren't anything all that much—but you know how it is when you've just met someone."

"Of course. How was it with Sandy?"

Bella narrowed her eyes. "You know, I'm still trying to make you out. I'm trying to imagine going round to one of my ex-boyfriends' ex-girlfriends and asking how things were with him."

"I know it must seem odd. But meanings change when someone is killed. Old rules don't apply. For complicated and painful reasons, I feel I need to find out about Sandy's life before he died."

"To lay him to rest, you mean?"

"If you like," said Frieda.

"Did he hurt you?"

Frieda gritted her teeth. "Perhaps."

"OK, then. But I don't think I can help you much with whatever it is you're after. He never mentioned you, if that's what you want to hear. Sorry. And I wasn't that close to him. We worked together, we had a couple of meals, we hooked up a few times. That was all."

"You make it sound like nothing."

"It wasn't nothing," said Bella, looking down into her coffee. She hadn't touched it. "But it wasn't that much more than nothing."

"Why did it end?"

"I don't know. How do these things work anyway? You meet someone, you get on, you sleep together a few times and then it just stops happening."

"Did you mind?"

Bella's smile was graver now, less mocking. "You're persistent, I'll give you that. I haven't said this to my real-life actual friends. I should be better at this than I am. Sandy was good to work with and he seemed to be in some kind of distress and I thought he needed me. Well, maybe he did, but not in the way I expected. It wasn't his fault."

"Someone said that he was behaving badly to the women he was with."

"Oh, *someone*." Bella Fisk sounded derisive.

"That perhaps he hurt people and then felt guilty."

"Is that what happened to you?"

Frieda didn't reply.

"He didn't hurt me. There were no promises on either side. The woman he was kind of with before me, or maybe alongside me, she was a bit upset, I think—but not for long. She soon found comfort elsewhere."

"Who was that?"

Bella Fisk's eyes narrowed. "I don't see why you'd want to know."

"Was it Veronica Ellison?" asked Frieda.

"You know already, so why ask me?"

"She was upset."

"Only until she hooked up with Al."

"Al."

"It doesn't matter."

"You mean Al Williams?"

"You're beginning to spook me a bit. What are you looking for? Why does it matter anymore? Nothing's going to bring him back."

"Just some answers," said Frieda. Her brain was working furiously. Veronica had been with Sandy, then with Al. Al was married to Bridget, who had been one of Sandy's closest friends and the person he turned to when in difficulty. What did it mean? And did Bridget know? She remembered when she'd first seen both Bridget and Al, at the party in memory of Sandy, and how they had both comforted Veronica after her little speech. But Bella was talking and she forced her attention back toward her. She was saying something about the small world of academia and how incestuous it could feel: her with Sandy, Veronica with Sandy, Veronica with Al . . .

And then she stopped because the door had opened. A man walked in, wearing black jeans and a leather jacket. He nodded at Bella and came over and sat at the table. Bella introduced him.

"This is Carla," she said. "She used to be a friend of Sandy's. I told you about Sandy."

He shook Frieda's hand. It was almost enclosed by his. "It's the first time I've known anyone who was murdered."

"Did you know Sandy?"

"Well, I know someone who knew him."

"You make it sound like it's funny," said Bella, and she got up and walked through a door at the back of the room.

"Sensitive subject," said Tom, watching her go. He turned back and looked at Frieda with interest. "Bella mentioned Sandy, but she never mentioned you."

"This is the first time we've met."

"I don't understand."

"I'd lost touch with Sandy. I wanted to meet someone who'd worked with him."

"So what do *you* do, Carla?"

"I've been working as a nanny."

"Is that fulfilling?"

"It's a temporary thing."

"Interesting," said Tom. "Now then, Carla, would you like to meet for a drink some time?" He asked her as though he were offering her a bag of crisps.

Frieda couldn't stop herself turning in the direction Bella had gone. Did it make sense to feel hurt and protective on behalf of someone she didn't know? "Er, we're having a coffee now," she said carefully.

"You know. A drink."

"I don't think so."

"It never hurts to ask," said Tom cheerfully. "Win some, lose some."

"Bella left the room about thirty seconds ago."

"Oh, Bella?" Tom looked as if he had entirely forgotten her. "That's just a thing."

There didn't seem anything left to say. Tom went over to the counter and bought a large cappuccino. He and Bella returned to the table together. Tom sat back, drank his coffee and gazed benignly at Bella and Frieda as if they were two old friends. Frieda just wanted to get away, but there was one more question she needed to ask.

"Did Sandy seem at all nervous? Scared, even?"

"Why would he be scared?" said Tom.

"He was murdered," said Frieda. "And I was asking Bella."

"But why are you asking?"

"He was a friend. I'm concerned."

"Bit late for that," said Tom.

"I know," said Frieda, getting up.

"He seemed fine," said Bella quickly. "He was working hard. But he was all right."

"I'll pay for this," said Frieda.

"I already paid," said Tom. "You can pay the next time."

• • •

Frieda was getting used to hanging around playgrounds. This one was in Parliament Hill Fields, by the running track. Frieda could see her, pushing a toddler on the swing. There were too many people around and this time there was no hiding her identity. They moved to the roundabout. Frieda looked at her phone. There was another message from Josef. She'd deal with that later. How long were they going to be? Finally the pair emerged from the playground and made their way along the railings, then to the left, across the railway bridge. Frieda shadowed them and when they reached the street she saw that there was nobody around. She walked quickly up and touched the woman on the shoulder. She looked round.

"Kim," she said.

Kim's expression moved from shock to bafflement. "Frieda?" she said. "What on earth . . ." And then the bafflement turned to outrage. "How did you even find me here?"

"Lizzie told me where you'd be," said Frieda.

"She wouldn't talk to you."

"I didn't say it was me."

"Are you crazy? Are you completely fucking crazy?" She took her phone from her pocket. "I'm calling the fucking police."

"Wait," said Frieda.

"Why?"

Kim was holding the little boy by the hand. He wore a blue T-shirt with a space rocket on it. Frieda knelt down so that they were face to face. "What's your name?" she said softly.

"Robbie," he said.

"Hello, Robbie. I'm just going to talk to Kim for one minute, OK?" She stood back up. "Did Lizzie know about you?"

Kim's eyes flickered. "What do you mean, about me?"

"About you and Sandy, when you were working for her."

"You bitch."

"Put the phone away, Kim. I want to talk to you for one minute and then I'll go. But if you won't talk to me, I'll have to talk to someone." Frieda put her hand on Kim's shoulder. "Look at me, Kim. I'm someone who has nothing to lose. You need to believe that. But if you answer my questions, I'll go. Do you understand?"

"It didn't mean anything."

"I don't care."

"It just happened."

"It doesn't matter."

"It was after you'd split up."

"How long did it last?"

Kim looked surprised. "Last? We only did it twice. Well, once, really. The first time he couldn't properly—"

"I don't need to hear that. How did it end?"

Kim's face had gone very red. "It was stupid. I had a crush on him and we both knew it was a mistake. He wasn't in a good place."

"Was he frightened?"

"Frightened? No. He was just a bit down. He was nice in a way. He apologized. But you don't really want to be apologized to when you're both, you know . . ."

"Who knew?"

"Why would anyone know? I just felt I'd been stupid." Kim looked down at Robbie, who was weighing on her arm. "I didn't think he would talk about it, but he must have told you."

"Sandy didn't tell me."

"You mean he told someone else?"

"What about friends?" said Frieda. "Boyfriends?"

"It wasn't something I wanted to talk about."

"All right," said Frieda. "That's all."

She turned to go, but Kim put a hand on her arm. "Wait, can I ask you something?"

"What?"

"What are you up to?"

"I don't know," said Frieda. "One thing led to another."

It wasn't until the evening that Frieda got the letter that Karlsson had written to her. She called Josef and he said—in a loud whisper—that he would meet her at her place as soon as he could get away. She could hear loud bangs and people shouting.

When she got back to the house, Mira was cutting Ileana's hair. Dark wet locks lay over the kitchen floor. There were two mugs of tea on the table, and the atmosphere was peaceable. Frieda put the milk she had bought in the fridge and then unpacked supplies: tea bags, coffee, cleaning stuff. "That looks good."

Mira snipped her scissors in the air beside Ileana's ear. "You next."

"I don't think so. My hair is short enough."

"Not shorter. Just more style. Layers." She pointed the blades at Frieda. "Choppy."

"It's very kind of you but—"

"You buy food for us. We would like to make a return. It makes us feel better."

Frieda was about to refuse once more, but what Mira said stopped her. Reuben always told her how bad she was at accepting gifts, asking for help, and it was true. Everyone wants reciprocity.

"All right," she said reluctantly. "Just a trim, though. Nothing drastic."

So it was that Josef found her with a towel draped over her shoulders and her wet hair being busily snipped at by Mira.

"Cut again?" said Josef in dismay. "But Fr—" He remembered in time. "Is already short. Why more so?"

"I think Mira feels I could be more stylish. What is it you want to give me?"

Josef reached inside his jacket and drew out the envelope, creased now with smudges of dirt across it.

"I told nothing," he said. "Not even that I give it to you."

"All right." She took the envelope, which was blank, and laid it on her lap. Little tendrils of her hair fell to the floor. Mira's hands were oddly comforting on her scalp.

"Go ahead," said Mira. "Don't mind me."

Frieda slid her finger under the gummed flap, then drew out the piece of paper, which she unfolded. She saw the first words—"Dear Frieda"—and at once folded the paper and laid it back on her lap, under her hand. Karlsson. She had recognized the writing at once. Why was Karlsson writing to her and how had he known Josef would be able to find her? She closed her eyes for a few seconds. The scissors were cold against the nape of her neck.

"All done," said Mira. "You want to look in mirror?"

"I'm sure it's fine."

"Very chic."

"That sounds good." She stood up and removed the towel. "Thank you so much."

"I just dry it."

"No. It's fine. I can do that."

"Really?"

"Really." She looked across at Josef, who had made himself a cup of tea and found the biscuits in the cupboard. "I'm going to read this. Stay there and I'll come back shortly."

"You want me to come?"

"No." She took the letter and, instead of going to her room, went outside with it. There was an area of scrubland near Thaxted House, where a house had been demolished, that was like an alternative garden, with butterflies among the buddleia, and weeds and nettles pushing their way out of the cracks in the concrete. She sat with her back against the wall at the far end and opened the letter.

Dear Frieda,

I am going to give this to Josef on the off-chance that he will know how to get it to you. You may be in danger. Sandy's sister, Lizzie Rasson, came to see me. She told me that in the last few weeks of his life, Sandy had been urgently trying to contact you because he wanted to warn you. This is all I know. She had no idea why. I think you should take this seriously. Hussein doesn't know I'm writing this letter or that Josef knows where you are.

Frieda—please give yourself up. They'll find you and things can only get worse. If you go to the police, you'll be safe. The investigation will continue. I promise.

Please take this seriously.

Yours, Karlsson

Frieda read the letter slowly, carefully. She noticed how formal it was—how he didn't once make any reference to their shared past and their friendship or draw her attention to what he was risking for her. And he was risking a lot, she knew—his entire career. She put the letter into her pocket and leaned back against the wall, feeling its rough brickwork through her thin shirt. Just as when she had seen him on television, pale and strained beside the commissioner, she felt the impulse to go to the nearest police station and give herself up. Have done with this.

Then she thought of Sandy's body in the morgue, her name tag on his wrist. She thought of how she had erased all those texts and voice-mail messages and e-mails, not reading them first. If what Karlsson was telling her was true, then she was looking in the wrong direction, or at least thinking in the wrong way about his death. Bridget had said he was scared, but now it seemed that he had been scared for *her*, rather than for himself—or as well as himself, perhaps. Which meant that his murder was linked to her life as well as his own. Of course she had always known this, because his wallet had been planted in her house and she had been framed. But she had assumed she was a convenient red herring. Now she had to assume that she was a target. She made herself think clearly, sorting through the fragments in her mind. Sandy had been murdered by someone who had tried to frame her. The murderer was not Dean Reeve, as she had at first assumed, because Dean had been far away, punishing Miles Thornton. Sandy had been in a dysfunctional state in the months leading up to his death—missing her and angry with her, treating women badly, feeling guilty, thinking of ending his life, scared by something or someone, sure that Frieda was in danger. Why would she be in danger, if it weren't Dean? Why would they both be in danger from the same source—or had Sandy been killed simply as a way of getting to Frieda? That thought was so terrible that, for a moment, she stopped thinking and simply sat in the warmth of the dusk, staring at the fading blueness of the sky.

Sandy had been filled with guilt; with guilt and with fear. Why? She forced her mind against the question, as if the pressure of thought would give her an answer. She remembered him outside the Warehouse, shouting something—what?—and flinging the bag of her possessions at her. An idea came to her and she held on to it because she had nothing else, no solid ground.

Josef was still there when she returned. He and Mira and Ileana and another woman, who introduced herself as Fatima, were drinking vodka and he was teaching them a game that involved lots of slapping down of playing cards and shouting. But when he saw Frieda, he stood up at once and crossed the room to her.

"It's fine," she said.

"What can I do now?"

"Nothing."

"Shall I take answer?"

"No." She hesitated. "If you see him, say thank you."

24

Frank was looking after Ethan the following morning so Frieda didn't have to collect him until after midday. She went instead to Bridget and Al's street and, standing a few hundred yards away, called their number. Bridget answered.

"It's me, Frieda. I wondered if I could have a quick word with Al. It's just about things at King George's that he might be able to help me with."

"All right," said Bridget. "But, Frieda"—her voice dropped so that Frieda could scarcely make out her words—"he still doesn't know."

"Doesn't know what?"

"Doesn't know who you are."

"You haven't told him?"

"Not yet."

"That's extremely discreet of you. I'd assumed you would tell him."

"It's complicated," said Bridget. "I don't know how he'd take it. A nanny who's wanted for murder."

"I can see that."

"And he doesn't know about Sandy's darkest moments either."

"You're good at keeping secrets," said Frieda.

"I'm good at knowing whose secret it is to tell. Remember that when you talk to Al."

Al came onto the phone. "What can I do for you?"

"It's a bit awkward," said Frieda. "I'm actually outside the house but there's something I need to ask you and I'd prefer to do it in private."

"What? You're outside right now?"

"Yes."

"But you don't want to come in?"

"That's right."

"I don't understand this at all, but I was about to go for a run. I'll be with you in five minutes."

He came jogging toward her with his white shins and knobbly elbows and knees.

"Bridget says you wanted to know something about Sandy's job. But why are you interested in that? And why do you want to talk about it out here?"

Al didn't know who she was and she was at a loss to explain herself to him. "I've been thinking about Sandy's murder and some things have come up." She was conscious of Al's nearly colorless eyes on her face as she spoke, and of the tameness of her words.

"I'm confused," said Al pleasantly. "You're a nanny, right? *Our* nanny. At least, you were."

"Yes."

"And, for some reason, you want to ask me something about Sandy because you've been thinking about his death."

"I know about you and Veronica Ellison," said Frieda suddenly. She'd had enough of this charade.

"I beg your pardon?"

"I said, I know about you and Veronica Ellison."

He stared at her and she stared back.

"I'm not even going to answer that," he said at last.

"Sandy had some kind of an affair with Veronica, and then you did."

"Your point being?" he asked. His voice was still perfectly polite.

"I wondered if Sandy knew about it. Or Bridget."

"Did you now?"

"I can't ask Veronica. She's on holiday and not answering her phone. I thought you could tell me."

"Are you quite mad?" he asked. He didn't say it rudely, more in a tone of amazement. "Why on earth should I tell you anything at all about my private life?"

"Because it might help me understand why Sandy died."

Al reached into the pocket of his running shorts and drew out a miniature iPod wrapped in its headphones. He started painstakingly untangling it.

"Does Bridget know?" repeated Frieda.

He looked up, resting his eyes on her with an expression of disdain. "No, she does not. And I hope she never will—unless, for some reason that I don't pretend to understand, you think it fit to tell her." He gave her a curious little smile. "Of course, you will have to do what you think is right."

Frieda thought of the passionate love letters from long ago that she had found in the locked tin in Bridget's study. But it wasn't the beautiful Bridget who had the secret to hide, it was her studious, gangly husband. She felt sick with herself but nevertheless asked the next question.

"Did Sandy know?"

"I've no idea. I assume not. Who would have told him? And what makes you think you have the right to ask me these questions? And now I'm done. And you, my friend, are likely to get into trouble if you go around asking questions like that. Everyone isn't as understanding as me." He put the little buttons into his ears, shutting her off, gave her a nod, turned his back on her and broke into a slow trot.

That afternoon, Frieda took Ethan to the park. He was in high spirits: he hurled bread at the ducks, and at the playground tumbled from slide to seesaw to swing, where she pushed him high into the air and he screamed in joyous fear. As she lifted him again and he collapsed into the buggy, she looked at the little boy's face, in which she could see both Sasha and Frank. She would miss him, she realized. She had got used to the way he slid his hand into hers or fell asleep on her lap with a suddenness that always surprised her.

She gave him his cup of juice and a biscuit and pushed the buggy out of the park onto the road that led toward Sasha's house. It was a muggy, overcast day and she was thinking about Karlsson's letter. She wondered about his children, Bella and Mikey, who had lived in Spain for a long time with their mother and stepfather. She remembered how painfully Karlsson had missed them. He had described it to her as a sharp pain, like something gnawing at him. As she was thinking this, a few drops of rain fell from the sky and there was a low rumble in the distance. She quickened her pace, hoping to get back to the house before the storm. And then she saw the group of young men—boys, really—a few yards ahead of her down the hill, shouting and jostling. It took her a few moments to realize that a figure was lying on the ground in their midst, a man with a thick beard, matted gray hair, grubby clothes. They were taunting him, laughing. One of them picked up an empty beer can and threw it at his head, and from where she stood Frieda heard him cry out in a high, wavering voice. She saw that other people were looking as well, furtively, not wanting to be involved. Rage, which felt pure and clean after the shameful encounter with Al, rose up in her. She bent down and fastened the safety straps around Ethan, who looked at her with his bright eyes.

"Ethan, I'm going to run as fast as I can and you're going to shout as loudly as you can. Your biggest scream. OK?"

"Now?"

"Now."

He opened his mouth very wide and emitted a howl that hurt her ears. She took a deep breath and sprinted down the hill toward the group of youths, the buggy bumping wildly as she went. Ethan's roar became a shriek. The buggy smashed into the first figure and Frieda caught a glimpse of a pimply, startled face. She veered into the next, lifting a fist and aiming it at him. She felt flesh against her knuckles, heard a grunt of pain. The figure on the ground was huddled into a fetus shape, all his pitiful things scattered around him. She swung round again and drove the buggy into a boy in a hoodie, who was staring at her with his mouth open slackly, in an expression of comic surprise.

The group was breaking up. People were arriving from across the street. The man stirred, lifted his head. She saw that he was crying.

"Christ," said a voice excitedly. "You were terrific. Just terrific. How did you do that?"

"I've called the police," said another voice. A man came toward her, his mobile in his hand. "Someone will be here any minute. I got some of it on my phone."

"You can stop screaming," Frieda said to Ethan, although the sounds he was making were hoarse and intermittent now.

"They just ran," the man said to Frieda. "I should have helped you. But it happened before I had time."

"Time to film it," a woman said.

"It's OK," said Frieda. "I'll be on my way now."

"But the police will want to talk to you."

"You can tell them what happened. You saw it." She looked toward the man on the ground, homeless and now beaten up. "Make sure he's OK. Buy him a drink, talk to him."

"But—"

Frieda left, pushing the buggy rapidly back up the hill. By the time she reached the top, Ethan had already fallen asleep.

"I think my child-minding days are coming to an end," she said to Sasha later that evening.

"You've done too much already. I'm interviewing several nannies this week. I'm sure one of them will be fine. I've got several days' leave I can take."

"I can do a few more days."

"You've done enough. I don't know how I would have managed without you. Ethan will miss you. And so will I."

"Right," said Frieda. "Let's talk about your story, if anyone asks questions about this."

Walking away from Sasha's house, Frieda saw Frank coming toward her. It was too late to cross the road or turn aside, so she just kept moving steadily forward, keeping her expression unconcerned. He seemed tired and sad, his dark brow furrowed. And he stared right through her without seeing her, as though she didn't exist. Which was sometimes what she felt herself.

"Look at this," said Yvette Long, flinging a newspaper onto Karlsson's desk.

He picked it up. "All right," he said. "An active citizen. Good for her."

"You're not looking closely enough."

He glanced at the headline—"Have-a-Go Heroine"—and then read the story about a woman with a buggy charging at a group of young men who were assaulting a homeless man. And then at the blurred photograph that showed a woman with very short dark hair, wearing bright clothes, running with a buggy.

"Fuck," he said.

"That's what I thought," said Yvette. "And somebody filmed it with their phone. It's on the website."

"Show me."

Yvette went to her desk and tapped on a keyboard. "Here," she said.

He clicked the "play" button. Things jerked and blurred and then came into focus. There was a youth with his mouth open wide throwing something and then a figure shot into the frame: a woman running and some unearthly noise coming from the buggy she was pushing in front of her, like a battering ram. For a moment she disappeared as another shape passed in front of her, the face out of focus, and then there she was again, her back to the camera. Then the video stopped. It had lasted about twenty seconds.

"It could be her," he said.

"It is her."

He looked again. Yes. And he had a pretty good idea of who had been in that buggy. "Bloody Frieda," he said, but he felt oddly elated.

A few miles away, there was a call for Commissioner Crawford.

"It's from Professor Bradshaw," his assistant told him. "It's something to do with Frieda Klein."

When Sasha opened the door, she didn't just look nervous, she looked distraught.

"I'm Detective Chief Inspector Sarah Hussein. This is Detective Constable Glen Bryant. Can we come in?"

Sasha didn't reply. She flicked her hair away from her face.

"Are you all right?" said Hussein.

"Things are difficult," said Sasha. "I've got a little boy."

"We know."

"And I've just lost my child care, which is irritating."

Hussein and Bryant looked at each other.

"Can we come in?" said Hussein.

Ethan was sitting at a miniature red plastic table drawing with crayons in broad strokes, red and black and brown.

"What is it?" said Hussein, but Sasha picked him up before he could answer and sat on the sofa with him on her lap. He started to wriggle and to grab at her hair.

"I need to put him in his room," said Sasha. "It's time for his sleep."

"We can wait," said Hussein.

Bryant walked around the room, looking at the bookshelves as Ethan's protesting cries receded upstairs. He ran his finger along the mantelpiece and inspected it. "The house needs a bit of a clean," he said.

Sasha came into the room and sat back down on the sofa. Faintly, from upstairs, there was the sound of wailing.

"So he's not quite asleep," said Hussein.

"He doesn't like sleeping," said Sasha. "Even when he's tired out of his skull."

"What's he like at night?"

"The same. I haven't had a proper night's sleep for what seems like my whole life."

"I've been through that," said Hussein. "You need to leave him to cry and he'll go to sleep."

"I've never been able to do that."

Hussein nodded at Bryant. He took a photograph from the folder he was carrying and handed it to Sasha.

"That was taken the day before yesterday near Clissold Park," he said. "A woman intervened in an assault."

"That sounds like a good thing to do," said Sasha.

"She left the scene before the police arrived," said Bryant. "The media are calling her a have-a-go heroine. They're looking for her. So are we."

"Why are you showing it to me?"

"Look more closely."

"Why?"

"Do you think she looks like Frieda Klein?" said Hussein.

"It's a bit blurry."

"People who know her think she does."

"But why are you asking *me*?"

"This mysterious heroine was pushing a buggy."

"Well, then," said Sasha.

"What do you mean, 'Well, then'?"

"It can't be Frieda."

"Unless she was looking after someone else's child," said Hussein. "And, after all, it's quite good cover, isn't it? London's full of people pushing buggies around. People don't notice them."

Sasha didn't reply. She was scratching the back of her left hand as if she had an itch on it. This was the moment that Frieda had talked about. It seemed like years ago. They had rehearsed what she would say.

"We've talked to people who know Frieda or work with her," said Hussein. "And you're the only one with a young child. Why aren't you at work?"

"I told you. I've got a problem with my child care."

"Who was looking after your child the day before yesterday?"

"He's called Ethan."

"Who was looking after Ethan?"

"The nanny."

"Can we talk to her?"

"She's gone."

"Gone where?"

"Back home. To Poland."

"To Poland. What's her name?"

"Maria."

"Maria what?"

"I don't know."

"You had a woman looking after your child and you don't know her second name?"

"I was in a crisis, my other nanny had suddenly left. I'd met her in the park. She said she'd stand in for a while. But now she's gone as well."

"Maria from Poland. Was she connected with an agency? Do you have her bank details?"

"I paid her in cash. I know you're not supposed to, but everyone does it."

"Do you have a phone number for her?"

Sasha took a piece of paper from her trouser pocket and handed it over. Hussein looked at it. "She probably used a pay-as-you-go phone?"

"Probably," said Sasha.

"Would Ethan's father confirm your child care arrangements?"

"We're separated. He leaves it to me mainly. He doesn't really know what's going on day-to-day."

"He's a barrister, is that right? Frank Manning."

"That's right."

"Has he talked to you about your friend, Frieda? About the legal implications?"

"No, he hasn't."

"Many people don't realize how serious it is to interfere with a police inquiry. A person who is caught and convicted will go to prison. Do you understand that?"

"Yes."

Hussein leaned in more closely and put her hand on Sasha's elbow. "I know about you and Frieda. I know that she has helped you in the past and that you owe her a debt of gratitude."

She saw that tears were running down Sasha's cheeks. Sasha took a tissue from her pocket and blew her nose. Hussein felt so close. Just another push.

"This insane behavior cannot continue," she said. "The best thing you can do for your friend is to help us to find her."

Sasha shook her head. "No," she said. Her voice was surprisingly firm. "I don't know. I can't help you."

"Do you understand what you're risking?" said Hussein. "You could go to prison. You'd lose everything. You'd be separated from your son."

"He'd probably be better off without me."

"Ms. Wells. Do you expect us to believe this story? We can check it."

Sasha wiped her face with her tissue. "I've told you everything I know. Check all you want."

"All right," said Hussein. "We'll go through it one more time. And in more detail. And after that, we'll go through it again. We have plenty of time."

After Hussein and Bryant had gone, Sasha walked upstairs to Ethan's room. He was asleep. She leaned down as she always did to check that he was still breathing. Sometimes she was so anxious that she woke him up to make absolutely sure, but this time he shifted slightly and gave a small whimper. Then she walked downstairs, picked up a phone and went out onto the little patio at the back of the house. She dialed a number and heard the click of it being answered.

"Frieda?"

"I'm here, Sasha."

"The police came to my house."

"I'm so sorry."

"It's all right. I repeated what you told me to say."

"I don't mean that. I put you at risk. I put Ethan at risk."

"You saved me and you saved him as well."

"This will be over soon," said Frieda. "For you as well as for me."

"That's what I was ringing about. In a way. I need to tell you something."

"What?"

"I can't tell you over the phone. This needs to be face-to-face."

"That's a bit awkward at the moment."

"I have to see you."

Frieda paused for a moment. "All right. Where?"

"There's a place on Stoke Newington Church Street. It's called Black Coffee. Can we meet there at half past ten tomorrow?"

"Have you got anyone to look after Ethan?"

"Frank's coming round this afternoon. He might be able to take him. Or I'll bring him along. He'll be glad to see you."

"So things are better with Frank."

"I'm trying to get him to do more."

• • •

The next morning Frieda took the train up to Dalston early and she was in Stoke Newington Church Street at half past nine, an hour before her meeting with Sasha. The road was dotted with cafés. She walked past Black Coffee, then crossed the road to another café, about thirty yards farther on. She sat near the window and ordered a black coffee. The café had a pile of newspapers for customers and she took one and opened it on the table in front of her. But she didn't read it. Instead she gazed out at the street. Once, in what seemed a previous lifetime, she and Sandy had sat in restaurants and, as an amusement or an exercise, they had tried to guess the stories and problems of the people at other tables, what they were doing there. Now, looking at the passersby on Stoke Newington Church Street, Frieda did it in earnest. She saw the mothers, in groups, some of them pushing buggies, on their way back from dropping the older children at school. An old woman with a walker made her way with agonizing slowness along the pavement. At one point her walker got stuck where a driveway crossed the pavement. Over and over again she pushed the wheels against the edge of the driveway, and over and over again they wouldn't quite get over. Frieda could hardly bear just to sit there watching. Finally two boys, who probably should have been in school, helped her over the tiny obstacle.

There was a bus stop right next to Black Coffee and a queue of people waiting. Two old women, one with a shopping bag on wheels. A young woman glancing anxiously at her watch, late for work. A young man, early thirties, bomber jacket, jeans, with earphones. Three teenagers, two boys and a girl. The girl looked like she was the sister of one of the boys. A middle-aged couple, together, but not speaking. He was doing something on his phone; she appeared irritated.

The bus arrived, obscuring the queue. When it left, the two old women had gone. The other woman was still looking at her watch. An old man and an old woman separately joined the queue, alongside two teenage girls. Another bus pulled up and then left. The young woman was gone. Frieda felt absurdly relieved. The two boys and the girl and the two teenage girls were gone. But the man with the earphones was still there. Another bus came and then another and another. Frieda came to see the queue as a kind of organism, permanent and permanently changing its constituent parts, mutating, shedding, accumulating. But the man with the earphones was still there.

Frieda ordered another coffee. On the other side of the road, a car was parked on a yellow line. The light was shining on the windows, so she couldn't tell whether anyone was inside. She looked at her watch. It was a quarter past ten. She saw the familiar green uniform of a traffic warden. She watched as he approached the car hopefully. Traffic wardens were paid by results, weren't they? He leaned down toward the car. He seemed to be talking to someone. He moved on without taking action. Across the road, a bus came and went. The man with the earphones was still standing there. If the two of them had been in uniform it couldn't have been any more obvious.

A young woman brought Frieda's coffee.

"Is there a loo here?" Frieda asked.

"Through the door at the back," said the woman, gesturing.

Frieda turned and walked through the door. Straight ahead of her was the loo door. To the right was a doorway that led to a storeroom, with cardboard boxes and canisters. On the left was a fire door. She pushed at it and found herself in a small side street. She walked up it, away from Stoke Newington Church Street. After a couple of turns she found herself walking along railings, then went through an opening and into a park. She just hoped that people weren't still looking for the have-a-go heroine.

Almost without thinking, she headed across the park, then out through the gate on the other side, southward toward the river. For a time she felt her mind was in a fog that only slowly started to clear. So they had got to Sasha. She tried not to think about it and then she realized it was her responsibility, all of it, so she made herself think about it. She imagined the police interviewing Sasha, threatening her with prosecution and with losing Ethan. Losing her son after having lost her partner. Then she imagined Sasha ringing her, what it must have cost her to lure her friend into a trap. Friend. Even saying the word silently to herself made her feel a pang of guilt. Was this what she did to her friends?

Suddenly she found herself on Blackfriars Bridge, staring at the water. A long open-topped boat passed under her. There was a party on board; some revelers at the back waved up at her and one shouted something she couldn't make out. Next to them a dark-haired woman was standing alone, without a drink, both hands on the guardrail. Suddenly she looked up and saw Frieda and they seemed to recognize something in each other and then, almost instantly, the boat was too far away and the moment had gone.

Frieda took out her phone. It was tainted now; it would lead people to her. She leaned her hand over the railing and released it. It hit the water with a small splash she saw but couldn't hear. She stared at the water and suddenly thought of Sandy. This was the river that had taken him and then had given him up. For the first time she thought of the sheer physicality of those days his body had been in the water, carried up and down with the tide, as if he were being breathed in and out.

When she arrived back in the flat she heard voices. She looked through the kitchen door. Ileana and Mira were sitting at the kitchen table. Although it was still early, they were drinking red wine from tumblers and there were the remains of a pizza in a box on the table.

"There is left for you," said Mira. "And some of the wine."

Ileana poured the last of it into a tumbler. It fizzed and bubbled like Coca-Cola. Frieda took a sip. It tasted a bit like Coca-Cola as well. Mira looked at her appraisingly.

"Hair good," she said. "Tired also."

"Thanks," said Frieda.

"No, no," said Ileana. "Eat pizza, drink wine, then sleep."

"I'll just make myself some tea."

"There is no tea. And there is milk but not good." Ileana gave a sniff.

"I'll go and get some," said Frieda. "Do you need anything else?"

It turned out that they did need other things, so many that Frieda had to find an old envelope and write a list.

It took longer than she expected. The list was surprisingly complicated. She twice had to ask the man behind the counter where something was. Each time he sighed, took his headphones off and walked laboriously round the shop. Once he had to climb on a chair, once he went back into a storeroom. Finally Frieda emerged from the shop. It was late afternoon, sunny, warm. But she just wanted to get into bed with a mug of tea. Not to sleep. There was no prospect of that. She just needed silence to process the events of the day.

Almost immediately she felt a nudge and looked round. It was Mira. Frieda was so startled that she didn't know what to say.

"Is no good," said Mira. "Police there."

"Where?"

"In flat."

Frieda still had difficulty speaking.

"But how are you here, then?"

Mira seemed out of breath. Frieda couldn't tell whether it was from physical effort or just the stress of it all.

"Ileana open door. I hear, go into room, out window. I grab some of your things for you. Not much, I have no time."

She held out a plastic shopping bag. Frieda took it. It didn't feel like it had a great deal in it.

"And this." Mira put her hand in her pocket and pulled out a wad of banknotes. "Is yours," she said.

"Thank you. But how did you know where it was?"

"Carla. You put money behind the mirror."

"Yes."

"So I find it."

"Oh." Frieda looked down at the notes, then back again at Mira. "Thank you," she said. "Very much."

Mira glanced at the bag Frieda was carrying.

"You keep food? Is OK."

Frieda just shook her head and handed her the bag.

"Flat no good now," said Mira. "You must go."

"Yes."

Mira took Frieda's free hand, not as though she were shaking it, more like she was restraining her. She pushed Frieda's sleeve up. Then she took a pen from her pocket, clicked it on her chest and started writing on Frieda's lower arm. Frieda saw it was a number.

"You call us," said Mira.

"Some time."

"Good luck from us," said Mira.

"Yes. Will you be all right? With the police?"

Mira held up the bag. "Fine. I have been shopping."

25

Frieda walked swiftly, her sunglasses on and her head held high, but she didn't know where she was going. The police had been waiting for her at the café and they had also tracked her to her new place; everything was closing in on her, all the doors shutting. She briefly thought of calling Josef again, but she no longer had a phone and, anyway, he had done enough, and she couldn't go to yet another strange and lonely room.

She walked until she had no idea of where she was, in a labyrinth of side streets and shabby houses. There she stopped and looked inside the bag that Mira had given her. Inside she found her cafetière, the new red skirt that she hated, two shirts, the dark trousers she had bought for June Reeve's funeral, all the contents of her underwear drawer, the bottle of whisky, which was nearly empty, and a pack of playing cards that didn't belong to her. And, of course, she still had her money, though it wouldn't last her long. She let her thoughts rest for a few seconds on what she did not have: her beloved walking boots, a scarf that had been a present from Sandy, her sketchbook and pencils, her toothbrush, her keys . . . She stood quite still for a moment, with the flat blue sky above her and the hot tarmac under her thin shoes, feeling almost dizzy with the lightness of her life. It was as if she were suspended in space, in time. Then she made up her mind and continued.

An hour and a half later she knocked at the gray door and stood back to wait. When she heard footsteps she removed her sunglasses. The door swung open and Chloë stood in front of her.

"Yes?" she said politely. Her hair was cut very short, almost to a bristle, and she had new piercings and a tattoo on her shoulder. "Can I help?" Then she frowned and her mouth slightly opened. "Fuck."

"Can I come in?"

Chloë reached forward, seized her by the forearm and dragged her across the threshold, slamming the door shut on them both.

Frieda was trying to smile but her mouth felt an odd shape. "I didn't know where else to go."

The words seemed to take both of them by surprise so that they stared at each other for a few seconds before Chloë threw her arms around Frieda's neck and hugged her so hard that she could scarcely breathe.

"I am so happy you're here," said Chloë. There were tears in her eyes.

"It's not for long. Just for the night."

"Fuck that."

"The police are looking for me."

"I know that. But they're not going to find you."

Frieda felt she had arrived somewhere utterly familiar but that it had become strange and dreamlike: to be here, in this house where she had so often sorted out the chaos of Olivia's life or cared for Chloë, and where now she was the outcast, the one in need of help.

"You've cut your hair."

"I know."

"It's not exactly a foolproof disguise."

They went into the kitchen, which was in a spectacular state of disorder, but for once Frieda had no impulse to clean it up. She lifted a straw hat and an apple from one of the chairs and sat down in it. "Where's Olivia?"

"Out for a drink with a new date." Chloë gave a snort. "She said she'd be back for supper."

"I can't meet the date."

"Leave it to me. Let's have a whisky."

"It's not six yet."

"Let me make you something. Scrambled egg? Or a toasted cheese sandwich? I bought one of those toasting machines. I can do it with tomatoes and pickles added, if you want. Or maybe a bath first—would

you like a bath? I can run it for you and you just sit here. Just tell me
what I can do and I'll do it."

"Just tea. I need to make plans."

"Tea. And then you can tell me what's going on—or maybe you
don't want to. Of course, if you don't want to, I won't put pressure on
you but I want to say this. I know you didn't kill Sandy, because you
wouldn't kill anyone and especially not a man you had loved so much—
except, of course, I do know that people often kill the ones they love the
most. Anyway, I know that if you had killed him, you wouldn't have
gone on the run. I know what you're like—I know you believe in facing up to things. But if you had killed Sandy . . ." She saw the look on
Frieda's face and stopped abruptly. "Tea," she said.

"Thank you."

"Biscuit?"

"Just tea."

"Right."

"And then I think I need to borrow some clothes."

"That might be complicated. There's my grubby black goth clothes
or Mum's drunk ballerina or despairing diva ones."

"Something unobtrusive."

"I'll see what I can do. I keep wanting to touch you to see if you're
real."

Frieda held out a hand and Chloë grasped it. "I am real," she said,
as though she were telling herself.

She drank her tea very slowly, then poured herself another mug. The
sun came through the large, smeared windows and lay across the tiled
floor. She could hear Chloë running up and down the stairs, and doors
slamming. Eventually her niece returned to the kitchen.

"I've put a pile of clothes in the spare room," she said. "Take your
pick. They might not be quite the thing. I'm afraid the room's not very
tidy. Mum's been sorting things in there."

"It's fine."

"Have you made your plans?"

"I'll have a shower, if that's OK, then go out. I'll be back later."

"You've only just arrived. What if you don't come back?"

"I will."

"What if someone sees you?"

"I'll make sure they don't."

"I want to come with you."

"No, I've put enough people at risk."

"I don't care."

"I do."

Chloë stared at her, chewing her lower lip. "Can I ask you a question?"

"Yes."

"And you'll answer honestly?"

Frieda hesitated. "Yes," she said eventually.

"If I was in your position and you were in mine, what would you do?"

"I really, really hope that could never happen."

"But you'd do something, wouldn't you? Do you believe you can help other people, but no one can help you?"

"I don't think I believe that." Frieda thought of Mira and Ileana risking themselves to help her, a stranger about whom they knew nothing. She would be in a police cell now were it not for them.

"So. I'm going to help you. If you say no, I'll follow you anyway. Don't look at me like that. I will! I'm not going to let you go off on your own again."

Frieda put a hand across her eyes for a moment, thinking. Then she said, "OK. I'll have a quick shower and put on different clothes and then we'll go."

"Where?"

"I need to fetch something."

"That sounds easy."

"Unfortunately there's a problem."

Frieda pulled off her clothes but as she was about to step into the shower she saw the phone number Mira had scrawled on her forearm. For an instant she thought she should just scrub it off, but something stopped her. She wrapped a towel round her, went back into the spare room, found a pen and some paper, then wrote it down.

After she'd showered, she pulled from the pile of clothes Chloë had left some high-waisted black trousers with wide legs, Chloë's old Dr. Martens and a white blouse that had see-through sleeves and lots of tiny buttons, with a faint perfume still caught in its folds. Better than Carla's clothes, anyway. She ran her fingers through her wet, spiky hair, then tied a patterned scarf round it, put on her sunglasses and went downstairs to find Chloë waiting, hot with excitement, by the door.

"So where are we going?"

"To the Warehouse. I need to find something there."

"Won't someone report you?"

"They'll have gone by the time we get there."

"Do you have keys?"

"No."

"But . . ." And then Chloë stopped. "Oh. Right. That's amazing. How does that work?"

"When I was last there, there was a window with a broken latch. It's been like that for a year."

"So we just climb in."

"I just climb in. You keep a watch out for anyone coming."

"That's a bit boring."

"Good."

They took the Overground to Kentish Town West, almost entirely in silence.

"Is this about Sandy?" Chloë asked.

"Of course."

"What?"

"I'm not exactly sure."

"But you will know," Chloë insisted, both confident and in need of reassurance. "You'll find out."

"I hope so."

"And then you'll be able to come home properly."

"That's the plan."

They left the station and walked along Prince of Wales Road toward Chalk Farm.

"Where have you been, though?" Chloë asked.

"Oh. Places where people go when they don't want to be found."

Chloë took her arm and squeezed it. "I'm so very happy you're not there any longer, wherever it was."

"Tell me how you've been."

"Me? Well, compared with you, not much has happened. It's not been so long since you disappeared." She made Frieda sound like some magic trick. "You know—same old. I like my course, though Mum is disgusted."

"Still?"

"She's going to be disappointed in me for the rest of her life. Instead of having her daughter the doctor, I'm going to be her daughter the joiner."

"Sounds good to me."

"As for Dad . . ." She rolled her eyes.

Chloë talked on: about carpentry, college, the apprenticeship she was now doing at the run-down workshop in Walthamstow, full of men who didn't really know how to treat her, about Jack and how very glad she was to be no longer in a relationship with him—her voice rose and wobbled as she said it—and Frieda led them on a circuitous route toward the Warehouse, half listening to her niece but alert for anything that seemed out of place.

At last they were at the entrance to the building, which was set back from the road. It looked imposing, impregnable. Frieda led Chloë along the small side alley where the bins were kept, and round to the back. Looking up at the houses that the Warehouse backed onto, she saw how many windows there were. For an instant, she thought she saw a face at one; then she blinked and it became an earthenware pot on the windowsill. But there really was a figure in the house to the left. A woman was watering the plants in the conservatory, moving tranquilly through the glassy space. Frieda wondered if she should come back later—but then there would be other people to worry about. Best to get it over with.

"This is the window here." She stepped forward and gave it a sharp tug upward, but it didn't budge. She put the palms of her hands on the frame and pushed hard. Nothing. Through the glass she saw the corridor and, beyond that, the door to her room. "Paz must have got it mended," she said.

"Is there an alarm?"

"I know the code so I should be able to disarm it. And, anyway, if Reuben is the last to leave he often forgets to turn it on."

"Josef should be here. He'd know how to get in."

"We need a crowbar."

"I'm not exactly carrying one with me. I should have brought my tool bag. What about that loose paving stone?"

"I'm not sure we should—"

She didn't have time to finish her sentence, for Chloë had bent down, picked it up and in a single movement hurled it against the window. For an instant, a crazed network of lines appeared in the glass; then, as if in slow motion, everything disintegrated and they were staring at a jagged hole.

Frieda couldn't think of anything to say and, anyway, there wasn't time to say it. She picked out some of the glass, then untied the scarf from her hair, using it to clear away the fragments sticking to the bottom of the frame. Now they both could hear the beeps of the alarm, ready to break into full sound.

She stepped in through the window and looked down at Chloë's scared, excited face framed by the bristle of her hair, her glowing eyes.

"Wait near the front entrance, but out of sight. You've done your bit. More than your bit."

The woman was still watering her plants in the conservatory. A light went on in the upstairs window of the house next door, though the sky was still silver blue. Frieda walked swiftly up the corridor to where the alarm box was, under the stairwell. She punched in the number. The beeping continued. She tried again, slowly, making sure she had it right. Still the red light didn't change to green. The security code must have been changed, or she was remembering it wrong. And, sure enough, after a rapid warning stutter of beeps the great scream of alarms started up, almost ripping her eardrums and rolling around her skull like pain.

She went back down the corridor, still not running and oddly calm, her heartbeat quite steady, and went into her room. It was as if she had never been away. Everything was in its proper place. The books on the shelves, the tissue box on the low table, the pens in the mug above the Moleskine notebook. She pulled open the deep bottom drawer of her desk and, sure enough, the bin bag was there, loosely knotted. She picked it up, feeling the objects inside slide and clink, pushed the drawer shut and left, closing the door behind her. She stepped out of the window. More lights had gone on in the houses. There was someone standing in his garden, his hand shading his eyes, trying to see what the commotion was about.

She walked down the side alley and to the front entrance, where Chloë was pressed against the wall behind a rhododendron bush thick with dying purple flowers. Her face was pinched with fear.

"They changed the code. Come on." She took Chloë's arm and led her onto the road, turning away from the direction they had come in, weaving through side streets. Behind them, the alarm. Her feet were uncomfortable in the heavy boots. Her neck stung, and when she put a hand up it came away smeared with blood.

"What about the police?" Chloë asked.

"The alarm isn't connected to the police station. It kept going off by mistake."

"Did you get what you wanted?" Chloë asked after a few minutes. Her voice was hoarse.

"Yes."

"So it will be all right now?"

"We'll see."

Chloë went into the house first, to check whether Olivia was alone. Then Frieda followed. The instant Olivia saw her she burst into noisy and ecstatic sobs, as though someone had pressed a button on the back of her neck. She wept, exclaimed, waved her hands in the air. Mascara ran down her cheeks. She yanked the fridge open and pulled out a bottle of sparkling wine, even though there was already wine open on the table.

Frieda sat at the kitchen table. She still felt oddly calm, distant from what was going on around her. Chloë made them all scrambled eggs. Olivia drank—from her own glass and Frieda's and Chloë's as well—and talked and asked questions that Frieda didn't answer. The bin bag was at her feet. She thought of the last time she had seen Sandy. He had hurled it at her, his handsome face wild, and shouted. But what had he said? She couldn't remember. She should have paid more attention, before it was all too late.

Frieda lifted piles of clothes, books, photo albums off the bed and put on clean sheets. She had a second shower and pulled on the nightdress Olivia had lent her—white, with a ruffled neck, it made her look like a character out of a Victorian melodrama. Then she slid the contents of the bin bag onto the bedroom floor. A bottle of shampoo rolled across the carpet. There was only an inch left in it.

She picked up items, one by one, starting with the clothes. There was some underwear, a thin blue shirt, a pair of gray trousers, a very old jersey in flecked colors. A copper bangle. A small travel chess set. A sketchbook—she opened its pages and saw drawings she had made all that time ago: an ancient fig tree that grew out of the cracked paving near her house, a bridge across the canal, Sandy's face, unfinished . . . Body lotion. Two books. Lip balm. A green bowl that she had given to him and he was now giving back, wrapped in newspaper—she was surprised it hadn't broken. An apron he had bought for her. A hairbrush. A toothbrush. A spiral-bound pad full of notes she had made for a lecture on self-harm. A photograph of herself that he had taken, and used to keep in his wallet. She turned it so that it lay facedown. A phone charger. A packet of wildflower seeds. Hand gel. A slim box of charcoals, broken into fragments. Five postcards from the Tate Modern. She stared at them: there was one in dusty colors of a woman standing looking out an open window; stillness and silence. She shook the bag and heard something clink. Pushing her hand inside, she found a pair of earrings and a laminated name tag that she must have worn to some conference.

Frieda sat back on her heels and considered the objects. As far as she could tell, there was absolutely nothing here that was suspicious. Just the remnants of a relationship that had ended: all the happy memories that had become sad.

26

"So what did Sophie and Chris tell us about this place?" asked Hussein. They were driving up the New Kent Road in the early-morning cool. Shops were opening their metal shutters, delivery vans unloading boxes.

Bryant shrugged. "They were tipped off anonymously that she was there. But it seemed to be a dead end. Two women—Eastern Europeans—live there and no sign of Klein. That's all."

He turned the car up a smaller road and parked outside Thaxted House. They got out; Bryant spat out his chewing gum and adjusted his trousers, then looked around.

"That's the one," he said, pointing to a door on the ground floor.

"OK."

Hussein walked up to it, pressed the bell, which didn't seem to make a sound, then knocked hard. The door opened on a chain and a segment of face appeared. "Yes?"

"I'm Detective Chief Inspector Hussein." She held up her ID. "And this is my colleague Detective Constable Bryant. Can we please come in?"

"Why?"

"There are some questions we would like to ask you."

"We have already answered questions."

"They were preliminary enquiries. We'd like you to answer them again."

The face disappeared. They heard another voice in the background, then the door shut again, the chain was dragged across, and the door reopened to show two women standing before them. One was tall, with brown hair and eyes that were almost black under a heavy brow; the other was smaller, with a shock of peroxide-blond hair and blue eye makeup. They both had their arms folded across their chests in an almost identical gesture of resistance.

"What questions?" asked the darker woman.

"As you were told by our colleagues previously, we are looking for a woman." Hussein paused for a beat; neither face showed anything at all. "We have reason to believe she has been staying here. Her name is Frieda Klein."

Neither woman said anything.

"She wouldn't have been using that name," continued Hussein.

"Like we said, no woman," said the darker of the two.

"Can we have a look?" asked Bryant.

"No woman," the darker one repeated.

"Who lives here?"

"We live here."

"And your names are?"

"Why you want to know?"

"We're conducting an investigation," said Bryant. "We ask the questions and you answer them."

"I am Ileana. She"—she jerked her thumb—"is Mira. Enough?"

"For the time being," said Hussein. "Are you the only people living here?"

"Yes."

"How many bedrooms do you have?" asked Bryant.

"Ah, this is the bedroom-tax question."

"No." Hussein took another step into the hall.

"Is because our neighbors don't like people like us."

"It's because we are looking for a woman called Frieda Klein." She took the picture of Frieda from her briefcase and held it in front of them. Neither made a move to take it, just glanced at it without expression. "Do you recognize her?"

"No."

"So you've never seen her?"

"Not that I know."

"She is wanted by the police for questioning on a very serious charge and we have been told that she is or was staying here."

"You have the wrong information."

The blonde unfolded her arms. "Look and see if you don't believe."

Hussein and Bryant went into the kitchen first, where they found nothing except pans on the draining board, a well-stocked fridge and half a bottle of vodka on the side, with some playing cards. Then they went into each room. There was a third bedroom, but it was quite empty: just a bed with no sheets on it, a bedside table and a threadbare rug. There was nothing else there at all.

"Thank you for your help," Hussein said politely.

"If you're withholding information . . ." began Bryant, and Hussein put a hand on his arm.

"Let's go," she said. "We've taken up enough of their time."

"It was just another wild-goose chase," Hussein said to Karlsson later. "First that bloody farce at the café and now this."

"There was nothing at all?"

"Nothing. Unless you think that wearing makeup at seven in the morning and drinking vodka and washing your dishes is suspicious."

"Who did the tip-off come from?"

"No idea. Maybe it's like the women said: someone who doesn't like living next door to women from Bulgaria and Romania. How can someone just disappear?"

"It's hard."

"Unless she's getting help." And she looked levelly at Karlsson.

He lifted a hand in repudiation. "I don't know where she is, Sarah."

"And if you did? If you had an idea?"

"I believe she should come back and give herself up."

She rose to go and then at the door stopped. "Do you really believe she didn't do it?"

"Yes."

"Are you speaking as a police officer or a friend?"

"Is there a difference?"

But it was as a friend, not a police officer, that he went in the early evening to Thaxted House, parking several streets away and walking there slowly through the evening warmth. When he knocked at the door, there was no reply. He tried to lift up the letterbox, but it was impossible to see anything. There were no lights on and he could hear no sound.

"What do you want?" a voice asked behind him. Two women stood there, one dark and one blond. They were carrying bags, and from where he stood, Karlsson could smell Chinese food.

"My name's Malcolm Karlsson and I was hoping you could help me."

"We speak already to the police. They find nothing."

"I'm a friend of Frieda."

"We know no Frieda." The dark woman fished a key from her back pocket and inserted it into the lock. The door opened onto a dark hallway. "Leave."

"Fuck this, I know Frieda was here. Whatever name she was using. And I know Josef was also here."

Neither said anything, but he saw the startled look they exchanged. "I sent Josef here with a letter for Frieda. I wanted to warn her."

"You?"

"Yes. Please, can I come in for a few minutes?"

"Mira?" said the dark one. Mira gave a minute nod. They stood aside and he passed into the flat.

They sat at the kitchen table on rickety mismatched chairs and the two women took lids off their steaming cartons of food. Karlsson saw the vodka on the side and recognized it as Josef's brand.

"Hungry?" asked Ileana.

"No, thank you," said Karlsson, although he suddenly was, his mouth watering at the smell billowing from the cartons. "I don't want to get you into any trouble and I understand that you don't trust me. You're right to be cautious. I don't expect you to tell me if Frieda was here. But do you know where she is now? Do you know if she's all right?"

"We know no Frieda."

"Whatever she called herself."

Mira took a huge mouthful of rice covered with a red gloop of sauce, then said thickly, "Everyone asking about this person."

"What do you mean? Sarah Hussein?"

"Her. The man with her. The two who came before. But then this other one too."

"Someone else came here?"

"Look." Ileana rolled up her sleeve and Karlsson saw a red weal across the lower arm, deepening into a bruise. "He do this."

"Who did?"

"Man."

"You're saying someone came here who wasn't a police officer, asking after Frieda, and he hurt you?"

"First all nice and charming. Then he hurt and threaten. Always the same threats that people give, that we be thrown out."

"I'm sorry. But you don't know who he was?"

"Just man," Ileana repeated, as if all men were one and the same to her.

"What did he look like?"

She shrugged. "Nothing."

"Nothing?"

Mira leaned across the table and said: "She mean ordinary."

"I mean, *nothing*." Ileana glared at Mira.

"Not tall and not short," said Mira. "Not fat and not thin. Not ugly and not handsome. Ordinary."

"White?"

"Not not-white."

"I see," said Karlsson, although he didn't. "What about the color of his hair, the clothes he was wearing?"

"Nice jacket," said Mira, wistfully.

"What was his voice like?"

"Just normal."

"Did he have an accent?"

Mira looked at him pityingly. "Everyone has an accent, just not the same one."

Karlsson put the bottle of vodka on the table. Josef filled two shot glasses to the brim. Both men lifted them and tipped the contents down their throats. Josef filled them again.

This time Karlsson only sipped at the vodka. "I met Mira and Ileana."

Josef drained his glass and set it back on the table with a little click. "So?"

"I know that she was there and now she's gone."

Josef said nothing. He regarded Karlsson with his soft brown eyes.

"I need to speak to her, Josef," said Karlsson. "I think she's in trouble. Someone's after her."

"Everyone is after her."

"Do you know where she is?"

Josef poured a third glass for himself and picked it up, turning it in his calloused hands. "No," he said eventually.

"Really?"

"This is the truth." He placed his free hand on his chest. "I do not know."

"All right. If you find her, or if she finds you, tell her I must speak to her. As her friend."

Josef looked troubled. He nodded at Karlsson.

"Thanks. Well, I should be going—is Reuben not here?"

"He's at the Warehouse still. Clearing all up."

"Clearing what up?"

"Trouble. Someone broke in. I have mended the window and he stay there late to make sure all safe again."

"I'm sorry to hear this. Has he called the police?"

"No."

Karlsson didn't go straight home but drove to the Warehouse instead. He rang at the front door and Paz opened it. Her sleeves were rolled up and she wore her hair tied back from her face. Karlsson thought she looked jangled.

"I heard you had a break-in."

"It was nothing."

"Who is it?" a voice called. Then Reuben came into view. "Karlsson. What's up?"

"Josef said someone had broken into the Warehouse."

"Someone threw a brick through the window. You know, kids today."

"Have you called the police?"

He waved his hand airily.

Then Jack Dargan appeared, skidding along the corridor with a cloth in one hand and some cleaning spray in the other. There was a brief silence as he pulled up alongside Reuben and Paz.

"You might as well tell me," said Karlsson.

An almost identical expression of exaggerated bafflement appeared on all three faces.

"What?" asked Reuben.

"It was Frieda, wasn't it?"

"I'm sorry?"

"It was Frieda."

"That's insane. I don't know what you're on about."

Jack pushed his hands through his hair in the familiar gesture, so that it stood up in peaks. "Nor do I." And he gave a small, wild laugh.

"This is me," Karlsson said.

Reuben raised his eyebrows. "I know. DCI Karlsson of the Met."

"A friend."

Reuben gave a soundless whistle. "What would your boss make of it?"

Karlsson shrugged. "I'm hoping he never has to know."

"Oh, for goodness' sake," said Paz crossly. "This is stupid. Yes, it was Frieda. Do you want to see?"

"See?"

"Come with me."

She gestured him to the reception desk and clicked on the computer. And there she suddenly was, grainy but unmistakable: Frieda, striding along the corridor toward them. Her head was held up and she seemed quite composed. It was as if she were looking straight at him, through him.

"Her hair's very short," he said.

"A disguise, I guess," said Reuben. "Of sorts."

"So why was she here?"

"See that bag she's carrying?"

"Yes."

"We're pretty sure that's what Sandy flung at her when he came round to the Warehouse," said Jack. "You know about that. He was angry. I'd never seen him like it."

"What's in it?"

"I looked inside." Paz sounded defensive. "After she disappeared and the police were everywhere and there was the media attention, I went through her room to make sure there was nothing—" She broke off and gave an elaborate shrug, rolling her eyes. "You know."

"That could incriminate her?"

"Yes. But it was just odds and ends, things that she had left at Sandy's. A few clothes, books. Nothing out of the ordinary."

"Do you know where she is now?"

All three shook their heads.

"She's getting reckless, though," said Jack.

Karlsson nodded. "Perhaps she knows that time is running out."

And—maybe because he had spoken those words out loud, confirming his fears to himself—he still didn't go home, although he'd been up since six and hadn't eaten anything since a stale croissant in the canteen. Instead, he drove through the fading light to Sasha's house in Stoke Newington.

27

She was pale, her hair lank, her eyes large in her thin face. He saw that she kept twisting her hands together, that her nails were bitten, that she had a cold sore on the corner of her mouth. He knew that Frieda always worried about Sasha and remembered that after Ethan had been born she'd gone through an episode of post-natal depression that had never entirely passed.

"I just want her to be all right," she said now, wiping the back of her hand against her cheeks.

"That's what we all want."

"I've made things worse for her. But it was so nice for me when she came back. Even when she's in trouble herself, she makes the world seem safer."

"Do you know where she is now?"

"No. I told that policewoman and it's true. She wouldn't say. I've tried calling her but she doesn't answer."

"No idea at all?"

"I don't know if I'd tell you if I had. But I haven't."

"How did she seem?"

"All right. Not scared. Calm. Purposeful. You know what she can be like." Karlsson nodded: he did. "She was good with Ethan as well, in a stern kind of way." She smiled, remembering. "If he cried because he wanted something, it was as if she didn't hear him. He keeps asking about her and the other kids."

"What others?"

"She looked after two other young children as well."

"Frieda looked after *three* children?"

"I know—it's hard to imagine. The parents were good friends of Sandy's—I think Al worked with him."

"I see," said Karlsson. A smile twisted his lips. "That was rather sneaky of her. Do you know their names?"

"Al and Bridget. Hang on. Let me think." She furrowed her brow. "She had an Italian name. Bellucci? I think that's right. I don't know his last name. Why?"

"They might know something."

"Is she going to be all right?"

Karlsson looked at her tightly plaited hands. Then the doorbell rang.

"That'll be Frank," said Sasha. "He's come to return some of Ethan's clothes." She pushed her hair behind her ears.

Karlsson stood up as Frank came into the room. They hadn't known each other well, and hadn't seen each other since the breakup, but Frank shook his hand warmly and asked after his children, even remembering their names. They left the house together.

"Drink?" asked Frank, as they stepped onto the pavement.

Karlsson looked at his watch. It was still not nine o'clock.

"Two men with nothing to go home to," said Frank.

"You make it sound sad."

"There's a place at the end of the road."

Karlsson couldn't think of a reason to say no. That seemed sad as well.

Frank came across to the table, carrying two glasses of beer and two packets of crisps. "You're looking at me with your detective's eye," he said.

Karlsson shook his head. "I feel like I'm seeing myself in a mirror. Except that the person in the mirror is a bit younger and is wearing a much nicer suit."

Frank glanced down at his pinstriped suit, his open-necked white shirt, as if it had taken him by surprise. "I've been in court. It's really just a uniform."

"Did you win?"

"It wasn't much of a victory. The prosecution mislaid some evidence and their key witness didn't turn up. The judge directed the jury to acquit."

"You're good," said Karlsson. "That's what I've heard."

"I can sense a 'but' coming."

"It's an 'and,' not a 'but.'"

Frank ripped open the two packets of crisps. "You've completely lost me."

"It's about Frieda. I wanted to ask you something."

"Oh." Frank held Karlsson's gaze. "Before you go on, I expect you know I was angry with her for a while."

"I had heard."

"I blamed her for the breakup with Sasha." He gave a rueful shrug. "Easier than blaming myself, I suppose."

"I suppose it is. Are you still angry?"

"Not so much. She was always Sasha's friend, first and foremost—and she's someone you want as a friend, isn't she? Someone you want on your side."

"She is that," said Karlsson.

"So I understand now that she was being Sasha's friend. She thought Sasha needed to leave me. Perhaps she was right. Though—" He stopped and rubbed his face with both hands. "What were you wanting to ask about Frieda?"

"I've never quite known what to think about the things she does. I've visited her in a police cell and I've visited her in intensive care, but this is something else. I can't believe it can end well. But however it ends, she's going to need help."

"She's got friends," said Frank.

"Good friends. But what she'll really need is a good lawyer."

"She's got a lawyer, hasn't she?"

"She's got a solicitor, Tanya Hopkins. She and Frieda didn't see eye to eye."

Frank nodded. "It's the job of a solicitor to tell the truth. Often it's the truth that the client doesn't want to hear."

"That's not true of Frieda."

"No, I guess not."

"That's part of Frieda's problem. She doesn't want to get off. She wants the truth."

Frank smiled. "The courtroom isn't like therapy. It's about winning and losing."

"So, what do you think?"

Frank took a gulp of beer. "I don't know. As you know, the police don't like being made fools of. Bear in mind that I knew the murder victim and I'm the ex-partner of one of the accused's best friends. But I'll do anything I can. Just keep me in touch. Here." He took a business card out of his wallet and handed it across. "If she breaks cover, I'll be happy to talk to her. Though she might not want to talk to me."

There was a pause while the two men drank their beer and helped themselves to the crisps.

"She was looking after Ethan for a while, you know," said Frank.

"Yes. Did you know about it?"

"What? At the time? Of course not. Sasha only told me afterward, when the police were suspicious. Frieda had left, and Sasha was in pieces. Thank God—I would have reported it at once. I'm a barrister, for God's sake. I would have been struck off if I'd known and kept silent. But then Sasha would never have talked to me again. Though I think she was quite wrong to do what she did. And so was Frieda."

"Are you on good terms with Sasha now?" asked Karlsson, awkwardly.

Frank stared at him, through him, at something else. "Good terms?" he said eventually. "Doesn't that sound businesslike? How did we get to such a pass? To be on good terms with the woman I loved and who is the mother of my son. I couldn't believe my luck when I met Sasha." He sounded dreamy and spoke as if he were really talking to himself. "She's so beautiful, and I thought I could rescue her. She's someone you feel needs rescuing, isn't she? Sometimes, being with her, I've felt like I've been in a nightmare. It's like I've been watching a very slow accident taking place and I can't do anything to stop it. I feel like I tried everything and none of it worked."

They walked out onto the pavement together. Frank held out his hand and Karlsson shook it.

"So what's your plan now?" Frank asked.

"I don't know. Waiting. Doing what I can to help."

"And what's Frieda's plan, do you think?"

Karlsson made a gesture of helplessness. "Do you know? In all the years I've known Frieda, I've never known what she was going to do. And after she's done it, I often don't understand that either. She broke into the Warehouse. That's the clinic she's connected to."

"What for?"

"I don't know. It was something to do with Sandy, but I don't know what."

Frank wrinkled his brow. "Breaking and entering," he said. "And child endangerment. It's not going to look good in court."

Karlsson turned to go. "I don't think it'll ever get to court," he said. "Something will happen."

"What kind of thing?"

"Aren't you breaking the barrister's first rule?"

Frank looked puzzled. "And what's that?"

"Never ask a question you don't already know the answer to. Thanks for the drink, Frank."

He was very tired now, his eyes sore, but he knew he was far from sleep. He didn't want to go back to his empty flat to lie awake and wonder where Frieda could be and how he could find her. He thought of what Sasha had said and pulled his phone out of his pocket as he walked away from the pub toward his car; he Googled Bridget Bellucci, and in less than a minute had her e-mail address. He wrote a message, explaining he was a friend of Frieda's and would be grateful for the opportunity to talk to her and Al, as soon as possible and in strict confidence. Almost as soon as he'd sent it a reply pinged onto his screen. "Why not now?" it said, and included an address.

Karlsson looked at his watch. It was ten past ten and Bridget and Al lived in Stockwell. But he climbed into his car, put the address in the satnav and drove off.

He thought he had rarely met a couple as dissimilar as Bridget and Al: she vivid and dark-haired, with an olive complexion and Italian gestures; he gangly, sandy-haired, drily self-deprecating, the quintessence of a certain kind of Englishness. Karlsson sat in their kitchen and drank tea. He longed for a whisky but he had to drive later and knew, anyway, that he was in the dangerous mood of alert and heady tiredness, which alcohol would only increase.

He explained once again that he was a detective but that he wasn't there as a detective. He knew that when this was all over—whatever "over" might mean—he would have to think about what he was doing. Not yet.

"Karlsson, you say?" Bridget was looking at him speculatively.

"Yes."

"Is that why she called herself Carla?"

"What?"

"Karlsson. Carla."

"I don't know about that. I'm sure it was just . . ." He found he couldn't reach the end of his sentence. He lifted his tea in both hands and carried it to his mouth.

"How can we help you?" asked Al politely, as though he were there to ask for directions.

"I need to find Frieda."

"She no longer works for us."

"Do you have any idea of where she might be?"

"No," Bridget said. "I never knew where she went back to each evening. I knew very little about her, even after I discovered who she was."

"I see."

"She worked for us," said Al, "because we knew Sandy. God help us, we let her look after our kids, thinking she was a nanny, when all the time she was conducting her own investigation while being wanted by the police."

"She was quite a good nanny, in fact," said Bridget. "Unorthodox."

"I didn't know what she was up to until yesterday." Al cast a glance at Bridget, both rueful and accusing. "For a while, I believe she suspected me of being the murderer."

"Us," corrected Bridget. "Yes, she did."

"Of killing Sandy?"

"Yes."

"Why?"

"I had his keys," said Bridget. "And hers as well."

"Why?"

"He gave me a set of his keys and hers were attached. It was as meaningless as that."

"And I had a motive," added Al. Karlsson couldn't tell if he was angry or amused. "He'd rather shafted me. Professionally, I mean."

"Frieda discovered that?"

"Yes. She found out a lot of things," said Al.

"I liked her," said Bridget. "Why are you so eager to find her?"

"Because I think she's in danger."

"Why?"

"I think that whoever killed Sandy is also after her."

"We can't do anything for you," said Bridget. "We don't know where she is. I tried to help her—I gave her names of women Sandy had been involved with. I told her everything about him I thought might be helpful."

"Like what?"

Bridget sat very still at the table for a few moments. She didn't look at Al when she told Karlsson that Sandy used to confide in her, that he had been in a bad way before he died, that she had been scared he would do something foolish.

Al looked shocked. "You mean, that he might kill himself?"

"Yes."

"And you never thought to tell me."

"It wasn't my secret to tell."

"Even after he'd been murdered."

"Especially."

"Why was he in such a bad way?" asked Karlsson.

"He felt he had made a mess of everything. I think he felt guilty about the way he'd treated various women—hurting them the way he thought he'd been hurt."

"By Frieda?"

"I suppose so."

"And Frieda visited these women?"

"Yes."

"Who were they?"

"I know she spoke to Veronica Ellison and Bella Fisk, who both work at King George's. And then there was the old nanny of Sandy's sister."

"I see. But she didn't find anything?"

"By that time, she'd stopped being our nanny. I don't know what she found."

"Thanks."

"It's Sandy's funeral tomorrow."

"I know."

"I'm speaking and Al's doing a reading. 'Fear No More the Heat of the Sun.' Do you know it?"

"I think I heard it at a funeral."

"Sandy was scared. Did you know that?"

"Did he tell you?"

"He was trying to contact Frieda about it."

"You should have told me, Bridget," said Al. His face was sharp and pale.

"Maybe, but I couldn't. I'm sorry." She didn't sound sorry. She looked at Karlsson. "And I wish we could help. I hope she's going to be all right; I hope you find her before someone else does."

He couldn't sleep and wondered if this was how Frieda felt when she went on her night walks. Perhaps she was on one right now—he tried to imagine where that would be, what she would be thinking, planning.

Tomorrow Sandy would at last be cremated. Frieda would know that, of course. What would she be doing when at eleven o'clock in the morning the mourners gathered and his coffin was carried into the chapel? His family and friends and colleagues would all be there; the police would be there. Where would Frieda be?

28

"I'll be at the service," said Hussein. "You stay in the grounds. We have three other officers on the perimeters."

"She won't be there." Bryant lit a cigarette and inhaled deeply.

"We have to see."

"She'll know we'll be there and looking for her. It's the very last place she'll be."

"The more I know about Frieda Klein, the more I think that the last place might be the first place."

"That sounds a bit biblical."

"What? Oh, never mind."

"Are you going?" said Frieda to Olivia, as they drank coffee in the kitchen.

Olivia put her mug down and leaned across the table. "Chloë says we shouldn't, but I think we must, or at least I must. In spite of everything."

"Good."

"I thought you'd hate the idea."

"It's important to say good-bye."

"Chloë," said Olivia to her daughter, who came into the kitchen at that moment. "Frieda says we *should* go to the funeral."

Chloë looked across at Frieda. "Don't you want me to stay with you?"

"No. But listen, Olivia, there'll be lots of people there."

"I know. The press will come, won't they? What do you think I should wear? Black? Or is that a bit much?"

"The police will be there as well."

"Why? Oh, right, I understand why."

"Will you really be all right?" asked Chloë. She looked troubled.

"I will."

. . .

Reuben put on his summer suit and a bright blue shirt. He lent Josef a jacket that was a bit too small for him, and Josef put a rose in its buttonhole, a small bottle of vodka and a packet of cigarettes in its pocket. He polished his boots vigorously and shaved with extra care.

"She will not come?" he said to Reuben.

"Even Frieda wouldn't be so stupid."

Olivia and Chloë left at half past nine. Olivia wanted to get a good seat. She wore her long gray skirt, a sleeveless white shirt and lots of silver jewelry; her hair was tied up in a complicated knot that was already unraveling and her nails and lips were painted red. At the last minute she remembered to stuff handfuls of tissues into her bag.

"I always cry at funerals. Even if I don't know the person very well—*especially* if I don't know them very well—because then you think about your own life, don't you? God, I could start weeping right now." She allowed Chloë to pull her out through the door.

Frieda washed up the breakfast things, then went upstairs to take a shower and dress. She barely had any clothes but Chloë and Olivia had given her several pairs of trousers and a variety of shirts. She picked out the plainest and coolest of them, for the day was going to be warm. She put on her dark glasses and left the house. It was just before ten o'clock. She had plenty of time.

By twenty to eleven, Hussein had taken up her position at the back of the chapel, and was watching mourners come in. Some of them she recognized: Sandy's sister, of course, Lizzie Rasson, with her husband and small child; several people from the university that they'd interviewed during the course of their investigation. Then she saw Reuben McGill come in with Josef and also the young man from the Warehouse—she couldn't remember his name—with wild orange hair. He was wearing striped jeans and a purple shirt. A woman seated near the front turned round and waved them over with extravagant gestures and Hussein recognized her too: Frieda's sister-in-law, or ex-sister-in-law, there with her daughter.

Gradually the chapel filled up. It was going to be full: soon there would be standing room only. A slender woman and a solid-looking man took a seat across the aisle from her. She recognized Sasha, but not the man.

Frieda walked up Primrose Hill. It was a clear, warm day and she looked down at the zoo and the city beyond, spread out in the sunlight. People lay on the grass, which was already bleached from the summer—it had started early this year. She slid off her shoes and took off her dark glasses. It was eleven o'clock. They would be carrying Sandy's coffin into the chapel now. What music would be playing? Who would pay tributes? She imagined the rows of mourners and she, who had known him so well, wasn't among them. Instead she had come here, where they had so often come together, in all seasons. This was her own private ceremony, but how should she say good-bye to someone she had loved so dearly, left so abruptly, seen descend into a self-destructive and wretched anger?

". . . This is an occasion for people of all faiths and none to say good-bye to Sandy Holland . . ."

Hussein looked round at the solemn faces. The coffin lay on the catafalque and Lizzie Rasson and her husband sat at the front; she was already sobbing silently. Hussein glanced down at the order of service: Lizzie was supposed to be speaking later; how would she manage to do that?

". . . and to remember him, each in their own way . . ."

Frieda let herself remember Sandy as he had been when they first met. She summoned him into her mind, image by image: Sandy laughing, Sandy lying in bed, Sandy cooking for her, Sandy as he had been when she had sought him out after their long separation, at his sister's wedding reception, and the way he had looked at her then. Sandy sitting by her hospital bed, with a stricken face. Sandy standing at her door, returned from the States because she had finally told him about something that had happened to her in her past. And then Sandy angry, baffled, hurt, humiliated, full of jealousy. All of these were him. Only once someone is dead can their many different selves come together.

A striking woman came to the front.

"My name is Bridget," she said in a clear voice. "Sandy was my friend and I loved him. No. I love him. Just because he's dead it doesn't mean he has gone from our hearts. I loved him, but he wasn't easy, as most of you here will know. I want to tell you all a little story about the first time I met him . . ."

Hussein half listened to the words, the appreciative ripples of laughter. Frieda wasn't going to show up. She felt a stab of disappointment because, although she knew it was irrational, she had half believed that Frieda would find a way to say good-bye.

A few people were crying, most of them quietly, but at the front there was a snorting, choking noise that she worked out came from Olivia. Across from Hussein, Sasha had her head on the man's shoulder and he was patting her tenderly on the back.

She wondered where Karlsson was. She had expected him to be there.

In her head, Frieda said good-bye to Sandy. She told him that she was sorry for all that had happened and that she wouldn't forget him. She closed her eyes and felt the soft breeze on her face.

"Hello, Frieda."

The voice came from behind her. For a moment, she didn't move but went on looking at the skyline. Then she turned. "Karlsson," she said.

"I've been looking for you."

"How did they know where I was?"

"They didn't. I did."

"How?"

"I know that you and Sandy used to come here a lot together."

"So now you're a mind reader as well as a detective."

"May I join you?"

"Do I have any choice?"

"Of course. If you tell me to go, I'll go. But please don't do that."

"You're not here in"—she gave a wry smile—"an official capacity."

"I'm not."

"You're crossing a boundary, Karlsson."

"I crossed it some time ago."

"It's what you used to get so angry with me for."

"Don't think I won't again."

"All right, you can join me."

He sat beside her on the grass, took off his jacket and rolled up his shirtsleeves. "You brought me up here once, many years ago. I asked you to tell me something interesting about what we were looking at and you pointed to the zoo and said that, not so long ago, foxes had got into the penguin enclosure and killed about twenty of them."

"About a dozen, I think."

"Right. Your hair's not so bad. I was a bit shocked when I first saw it on the video."

"What video would that be?"

"The one of you breaking into the Warehouse."

"Oh."

"Which, of course, Reuben kept from the police."

"I'm sorry anyone else has to get involved in this."

"They'll catch you soon, you know."

"I know."

"When they do, it won't be pretty."

"No."

"And in the meantime, I think you're in danger."

"I think perhaps I am. I feel that someone is always one step ahead of me."

"How can you be so calm?"

"Am I calm?"

"The question is, Frieda: what are we going to do?"

She turned her face to him and he felt the brightness of her gaze. Then she touched him very lightly on his arm with the tips of her fingers. "I appreciate that 'we.'"

They both sat in silence, gazing at the horizon of tower blocks against the blue sky.

"Will you give yourself up?" he said at last. "It would be better than being caught and we could get you the best legal team there is. I've already started making enquiries."

"Not yet."

"Sarah Hussein is very fair."

"I'm sure that's true."

"Where are you living?"

She just shook her head at him.

"Tell me what to do, Frieda. Now that I've found you, you can't just melt away again."

"Just a few more days."

Karlsson stared straight ahead, at the haze over the city. "Promise me something."

"What?"

"Contact me, day or night, if you need my help."

"That's kind of you."

"I notice you're not promising. Do you have a mobile?"

"I threw it away."

"Here." He took his jacket from the grass beside him and took his wallet out of its breast pocket, opened it to find a card. "Keep this with you. It's got all my different numbers on it. And this is my home land-line." He wrote the number on the back of the card.

Frieda took it. "I should go now. I feel a bit exposed here and the funeral must be nearly over."

Karlsson looked at his watch. "Yes. About now."

Frieda slid her feet into her shoes and put on her dark glasses. She stood and smiled down at him. "Good-bye," she said, raising her hand in a farewell salute. "Thank you, my friend."

29

When Karlsson arrived back at his office, Yvette Long was waiting for him. She looked anxious.

"Glen Bryant called. Hussein wants to see you."

"I'll get back to her."

"He said it was urgent."

"All right."

"Where were you?"

"I was meeting a contact."

"Is there something I should know?"

"Better not."

"Also, a man called Walter Levin came to see you."

"Who's he?"

"He was a bit vague. I think he was something to do with the Home Office. Gray hair, glasses. Said 'super' rather a lot."

"I've no idea what that would be about."

"He left a card." Yvette pointed to his desk.

"I don't have time for that now."

Karlsson called Hussein. It was very brief and Yvette watched him until he was finished. "I'm going straight over," he said, and then he noticed her expression. "What?"

"You've cut me out," she said.

"Only for your own good."

"She'll be all right," said Yvette. "However this turns out."

"Are we still talking about Hussein?"

"This is me," said Yvette. "Don't make it into a joke."

"I'm not sure she'll be all right."

"What about you?"

"We'll see."

On the car journey over, Karlsson's head was full of thoughts of what he ought to say, questions he needed to ask. But when he arrived at the station, he wasn't taken to Hussein's normal office. Instead, without explanation, the young female officer knocked on the door of a conference room. Then she opened it and stepped aside to allow Karlsson past. There were only two people inside. At the far end of the room, at the end of the long table, were DCI Hussein and Commissioner Crawford. So this was what it was all about. As Karlsson closed the door behind him, he felt strangely calm. He walked along the table and sat opposite the two of them. There were a jug of water and glasses on the table. He took one and filled it with water. He looked across the table.

"No, thank you," said Hussein.

The commissioner didn't reply. Karlsson noticed he was flexing a muscle in his jaw, as if he were forcing himself to remain silent.

Karlsson took a sip from the glass, then placed it carefully on a coaster decorated with the insignia of the Metropolitan Police. A crown on top of a star. A star that looked more like a snowflake. It was like he'd never noticed it before.

"I've just been at the funeral," said Hussein. "As you know."

"Yes."

There was a pause.

"I'm expecting you to say something," said Hussein.

"What?"

"Something like: was Frieda there?"

"Of course she wasn't there. I've got another question, though."

"All right."

"Do you seriously believe all of this?"

"I don't understand," said Hussein.

"Do you still, having lived with this investigation, believe that Dr. Frieda Klein, a qualified doctor, a practicing therapist, and a one-time consultant to this police force, murdered her ex-partner, dumped his body in the Thames—oh, and having done that, left a wristband with her own name on it on the body? Do you believe that?"

Karlsson looked at the commissioner. He expected something, a sigh, a snort of derision, but there was nothing. There was a tinge of pink in his cheeks, but that was all. The commissioner looked like a man who had already made up his mind and thought that this meeting was just noises, something he had to sit through.

"It's not what I believe," said Hussein.

"Of course it's what you believe. We're not machines."

Hussein shook her head. "This feels like my first week at Hendon." She banged her fist on the table. "You build evidence, you construct a case. If the case isn't strong enough, then Frieda Klein can defeat it in court. What you don't do is go on the run. You follow the rules, you obey the law. I've been to countries where the police act on their hunches or their personal beliefs and bend the law to fit them. I wouldn't want to live there. Would you?"

"This case against Frieda Klein is being pursued by people with a grudge against her."

"This isn't a case against Frieda Klein. When I was put in charge, I'd barely heard of her. And at every stage of the inquiry, if you—or anyone else—had relevant evidence, then I was willing to hear it. You never gave any."

"It's not just that," said Karlsson. "The inquiry got too focused on Frieda from the beginning."

"That's the thing. All this talk about 'Frieda this' and 'Frieda that.' It sounds like you're defending a friend. That's not the way policing is meant to work."

"She didn't do it. That's the simple fact."

"This is the Frieda Klein you saw in a police cell after an assault in a restaurant. The Frieda Klein who cut a woman's throat."

"Even Hal Bradshaw never said that was anything but self-defense."

"Except that Frieda Klein never admitted to it at all. And even now, while on the run from the police, she has become involved in another brawl."

"You mean intervening to prevent a crime?"

"That's enough," said the commissioner. Karlsson knew Crawford as a man with a temper, but now he was speaking quietly. "None of this is relevant. Just for the record, I would like to say that DCI Hussein has conducted this investigation in an exemplary manner."

"Shall we wait until it's over before we say that?"

Now Crawford's eyes did flash with anger but he didn't speak for a few seconds. He looked down at a piece of paper on the table in front of him. With one hand, he adjusted it slightly. When he began to speak, it was slowly and distinctly, like a solicitor reading from a legal document.

"We have heard that you have been interviewing people concerned with the case. Is that true?"

"Who have you heard from?"

"Is it true?"

"I've talked to some people I thought might provide information."

"Did you receive authority from DCI Hussein?"

"No."

"Did you file a report?"

"No."

Crawford picked up a pen and scratched something on his piece of paper. Karlsson could see that he wasn't making notes but doodling.

"Just one more question," said Crawford. "Have you had any contact with Frieda Klein?"

Karlsson took a deep breath. He had been waiting for this moment. After this, there would be no going back.

"Yes, I have."

Both Hussein and Crawford started visibly. But when Crawford spoke, it was in the same restrained tone.

"Have you seen her?"

"Yes."

"Can we get this clear?" said Crawford. "Have you been in touch with a fugitive during a police hunt for her?"

"No, I saw her today."

"Did you inform Hussein?"

"I'm informing her now."

"I'm assuming you didn't take her into custody."

Karlsson thought for a moment. "I didn't agree with her decision to . . ." He paused, searching for the right words. "To go it alone."

"Go it alone?" said the commissioner, raising his voice slightly.

"And I think she's now in danger from whoever actually did this murder."

"Oh, you do, do you?"

"Yes, I do."

"You're suspended, of course. Clearly you'll be facing disciplinary charges. Now that I've heard the full extent of your behavior, I'll be consulting on the possibility of criminal charges. I don't need to tell you the consequences of perverting the course of justice."

Karlsson stood up.

"I can't believe you've done this, Mal," said the commissioner. "To yourself. To your colleagues."

Karlsson reached into his pocket, took out his police badge and tossed it onto the table. "I should have done it before," he said, and he turned and left the room.

30

Chloë had gone straight to the workshop from the funeral; Olivia had gone to the wake and she would probably be the last to leave, outstaying all of Sandy's closest friends, sitting into the evening. Frieda was alone in the house in the late afternoon. She made herself a mug of tea and took it out into the overgrown garden to drink it. She knew she was becoming careless about keeping herself hidden, even reckless. Perhaps she almost wanted to be caught: to give herself up, to give up, to yield control. The sun came through the branches of the trees and fell in patterns on her skin. She drank her tea and wondered what she should do next. She felt that she had reached an impasse, in this search and in herself. She had said to Karlsson she needed a bit more time—but time for what? She did not know.

At last she went indoors, washed up her mug and went to her bedroom. She looked at her tiny pile of possessions and imagined her house, all the rooms empty, the cat stepping in and out of the cat flap that Josef had fitted. On the floor was the bin bag that Sandy had thrown at her, and she pulled the objects out again one by one, folding the blue shirt, the gray trousers and the jersey and adding them to her other clothes, putting the books by the side of her bed, flicking through the sketchbook once more, taking the photo of herself that he used to carry in his wallet and crumpling it in her hand. She picked up the apron that he'd given her, thinking she would pass it on to Chloë to use, then heard something rattle faintly in the oversized pocket. She put her hand in to draw out what was there. She looked into the palm of her hand and for a while was absolutely still.

Had she known all the time? Had all her labor, all her searching and running, been so that she wouldn't have to know what she had always really known?. She couldn't tell. The understanding settled in her, like something cold and heavy. Outside, all the sounds of the summer day continued, the cars and voices and laughter and music playing through open windows, and inside it was silent.

Karlsson went home. He went from room to room. In the children's room, he adjusted the covers on the beds as if they were about to arrive. He went into his garden where the sun was now low in the clear sky and smoked a cigarette, with his eyes closed, listening to the blackbird that had built its nest in the tangle of bushes near the back wall. He was no longer a police officer. So what was he? Who was he?

He pulled on his running things, put a key into his pocket and set off, running hard, wanting to tire himself out and to empty his mind of thoughts. But a thought came to him and he couldn't let it go or it wouldn't let him go. He stopped in the park and made himself concentrate. The person who had been to see Mira and Ileana, who had threatened them, had been a man. They hadn't been able to describe him, but this man must have been the one who had tipped off the commissioner or Hussein. Who would have done that? Who would have known enough about Frieda and about him to have gone to the top to shaft him and further isolate her? Who hated them enough to do that, with a personal and intimate hatred? An image came into his mind and he didn't understand why he had never thought of it before. That was who it must have been.

He ran back to his house so hard it left a pain in his side. After a brief cold shower he pulled on a pair of jeans and an old shirt—clothes that in no way resembled the ones he had worn as a detective chief inspector. He turned on his laptop and went to Google Images, then printed out a sympathetically smiling photograph. Forty minutes later he was knocking at the door of Mira and Ileana's flat.

"They're not here," said a voice behind him, and he turned to see an old man in a wheelchair, folded and neatly pinned trousers where his legs used to be, and a small dog sitting on his lap. "They both went out."

Why had he assumed they would be there, waiting for him? "Do you have any idea of when they'll be back?"

"No."

"Thanks anyway."

"The blond one sometimes works in the salon on the high street. It stays open until seven or eight. She might be there."

"Salon?" asked Karlsson stupidly.

"Hairdresser," said the man, making a snipping movement with his fingers. "Just a few minutes away. Next to the flower shop."

"Thank you."

He half ran there, not knowing why it seemed so urgent to him. Through the window he could see Mira standing over a middle-aged woman, scissors in hand, so he pushed the door open and went in. It was a tiny place, with just two sinks, and an old-fashioned dryer standing like a beehive in the corner.

"Sorry to bother you," he said to Mira.

"What are you doing here?"

"I needed to ask you something."

"I'll be done in ten minutes."

"It's important."

Mira patted the woman on her shoulder apologetically and turned toward Karlsson. He pulled out the photograph of Hal Bradshaw and said, "Was this him?"

"What?"

"The man who asked after Frieda and threatened you. Was it him?"

Mira took the photo and looked at it, frowning. "No."

"No?"

"No."

"Are you sure?"

"Yes."

"Look one more time."

"It wasn't him."

"Can you perhaps tell me where I can find your friend so she can confirm that?"

"It wasn't him," repeated Mira. She looked at him in a kindly manner and added, "I'm sorry. I want to help you. It just wasn't."

Karlsson nodded. He put the photo back in his pocket. "Just a thought." The words sounded meaningless. He realized he was very tired. "Thank you," he said, and went out into the street. He walked aimlessly along for a few minutes, then stopped by a plane tree and lit another cigarette. Why did he feel so disappointed when it had just been a notion he had seized on? He finished his cigarette and dropped it to the ground. Thoughts and ideas flitted through his brain and it was almost as if he were watching them pass. Frieda had said to him that morning that someone always seemed to be one step ahead. The same person who had told Crawford or Hussein about his attempts to help her. He put a hand to his forehead as if to keep his thoughts from flying away from him. Then he took his phone from his pocket and Googled a different name. He pulled up an image. Yes.

Frieda walked there. She didn't put her dark glasses on because she didn't really care who saw or knew her. She had set out on a journey to find the truth and now she had found it and couldn't lose it again, however much she might wish to. She took a deep breath and knocked at the door.

Karlsson walked back to the salon, cradling his mobile in his hand as if the picture might escape. He held it out to Mira, who was drying her customer's hair now, and in the large mirror he saw her nod slowly and certainly.

"Yes," she said. "Yes. It was him. Yes. I am sure. Yes."

Sasha opened the door. "I'm so glad. Come in."

In the hall, Frieda opened her fist. "I found these."

Sasha smiled. "Ethan's wooden animals. He loses them everywhere. He'll be happy to get some back. He's upstairs in his room now—I was reading to him. He doesn't seem to want to go to sleep. Will you come and say good night to him? He'll be excited to see you again. He talks of you all the time."

"Not just now."

"But you didn't come here just to give me a few little animals."

"I did."

"What is it?" She looked into Frieda's face. "You're scaring me."

"I found them in the pocket of an apron I left at Sandy's." Sasha's face was blank. Frieda continued: "He had packed all the things I'd left at his flat and he flung the bin bag at me when I was coming out of the Warehouse. It was my last sight of him."

"Frieda, what are you on about?" Sasha gave a small laugh, but her face had changed. It was gray.

"You should have told me."

"What? What should I have told you? I don't understand this."

"Why did Sandy have Ethan's animals? Because he was visiting you? Or because you were visiting him?"

Tears were running down her cheeks. "Frieda, don't look like that."

"You and Sandy."

Sasha put her face into her hands and through her fingers said, in a muffled voice, "I wanted to tell you. Every time I saw you, I wanted to. I nearly did so many times. And then when I arranged to meet you in the café—I had made up my mind at last, but you didn't come."

"I wish you had told me, Sasha."

"It was only after you weren't with him. I would never have . . . Not ever. You have to believe that. And only a few times. Because everything was so awful and he needed comfort and so did I and we both felt terrible after. Terrible. It made everything worse, not better."

"When was it?"

"Why does that matter?" She was sobbing now. "I didn't do anything to hurt you. He was lonely and in a state and so was I. Don't be angry with me."

"I'm not angry, Sasha. Please tell me when it was."

"Months ago. When everything was going wrong with Frank. And then Sandy was almost mad with guilt because he thought he'd betrayed everybody, you, me, Frank, himself, the whole world. He said he had ruined everything he most cared about."

"Who knew?"

"Nobody knew. Not a single person. I swear. Nobody knew."

"Somebody knew."

"What are you saying?"

"Nothing. I'm not angry." Frieda put a hand on Sasha's shoulder. "You didn't do anything to hurt me. It's not your fault."

"What isn't? Where are you going?"

But Frieda kissed her on one cheek, then the other, and left.

Five minutes later, Sasha heard her doorbell ring again and then a violent knocking.

"Karlsson!" she said, as she opened the door. "What's the matter?"

"Have you seen Frieda?" he asked. He put a hand on her shoulder, gripping it tightly. "Tell me the truth now. I need to know."

"Yes. She's only just left."

"Where did she go to?"

"I don't know. I promise I don't know."

"Do you have a way of contacting her?"

"No."

"Why was she here?"

"Is it important?"

"Yes."

"All right." Sasha lifted her head and met his gaze. "She found out I had an affair with Sandy."

"With Sandy? How could you?"

"If was after they split up. But I feel so terrible about it."

"Where's Frank now?"

"Frank? I don't know. Maybe at work. He sometimes stays until midnight, working. Or at his place. It's not his day for Ethan and—"

"What's his address?"

"Ten Rayland Gardens. It's only a few minutes from here."

Karlsson was turning to go but Sasha put out a hand and stopped him.

"Why? What's happening?" Her voice had a sob in it. "What have I done? He didn't know. Nobody knew. Karlsson, what's going on?"

"I need to go, Sasha. If Frieda comes, tell her to contact me at once, and you call me as well. Even if it's three in the morning." He pulled his card out of his wallet and handed it to her. "And if you see Frank, call me directly. Do you hear?"

Sasha started to speak but Karlsson was gone, running down the street, talking into his mobile as he went.

"Sarah," he said. "It's me, Karlsson."

"I don't think there's anything more to say." Her voice was cool. He could hear children's voices in the background: she must be at home, with her family.

"You have to listen. This is of vital importance. The man who killed Sandy is called Frank Manning."

"Frank Manning?"

Karlsson had to force himself to be calm, to explain to Hussein about Frank's relationship to Sasha, his knowledge of her affair with Sandy and his grievance against Frieda, how he had threatened Mira and Ileana. Then he gave her Frank's various addresses and told her he would forward her Frank's phone number.

"Where are you going to be?"

"I need to find Frieda."

"Just don't do anything to fuck this investigation. Anything more."

He took the card that Frank had given him out of his wallet and texted the number to Hussein. Then he called the number himself, but it went to voice mail and he didn't leave a message. He looked up Rayland Gardens on his phone. It was just a few minutes' walk from there. And what else was he going to do?

The pubs were overflowing onto the streets, people standing in groups on the pavements in the evening sun. Karlsson strode rapidly through them. He thought of Frieda that morning, sitting on the hill, her shorn head turned toward him, her bright glance upon him, with London spread out in front of them. Where was she now?

He came to Rayland Gardens and stopped in front of number ten. There was no way of knowing if anyone was in: the curtains were open and there were no lights visible, but it was still quite bright outside. He went to the front door and tried to peer through the mailbox but could see nothing except a small strip of floorboard. At that moment, two cars drew up a few yards up the street and, turning, he saw Glen Bryant get out of the first one. He stood back and watched. Bryant knocked on the door and waited. Nothing. He knocked again, more loudly and for longer. Again, nothing. He saw Bryant take out his mobile and knew he would be calling Hussein. Karlsson was sure that Frank wasn't there.

He turned and walked back down the road with no idea of where he was going or what he should do.

"'Can't you sleep, little bear?'" read Sasha. It was the fourth time she had read the book that evening. It was one of Ethan's favorites; he liked the words and he loved the pictures, and often he would fall asleep while she was reading it, like the little bear in the book, who is carried out to look at the bright yellow moon. But that evening, Ethan was wide awake. His eyes glittered and there were excited pink spots on his cheeks.

"Again," he said, as Sasha reached the final page.

"It's very late. Why don't you try closing your eyes and I'll stroke your hair?"

"Where's Daddy?"

"You'll see him very soon."

"Now."

"Not now, Ethan. Now it's nighttime. Time for you to go to sleep."

"Now!" repeated Ethan. "I see Daddy now."

"No, you don't."

"Yes. Yes, I do!"

"OK. I'll read you one more story, and then I'm going to turn out the light."

"The window."

"I'll leave the curtains a bit open so some light comes in, all right?" For Ethan hated true darkness.

"Will he come again?"

"Who?"

"Daddy."

"Of course. Very soon. Just a day or two."

"Not now?"

"No. Please go to sleep. I'm very tired."

"I wanted him to say good night to me."

"Ethan—"

"He stood and stood."

"Who—Daddy?"

Ethan nodded. "I waved. He didn't see me."

Sasha sat very still on the bed. Then she took one of Ethan's hands and said in a low voice: "Do you mean you saw Daddy tonight?"

Ethan nodded and snuggled against her. "In the window."

"What was he doing?"

"Waiting."

"Why was he waiting, darling?"

"For Frieda," said Ethan, as if it were obvious. "Frieda walked away and then Daddy walked too. I waved but Daddy didn't wave back. Was it a game?"

But Sasha had gone from the room and she hadn't even turned out his light.

Karlsson had gone toward Hackney with a miserable feeling of having nowhere to go and nothing to do. He bought a coffee and drank it as he walked south along Kingsland Road, lighting another cigarette. Then his phone rang. It was Hussein. Frank wasn't at his chambers and he wasn't at his house. They were widening the search and also getting a warrant. She would let him know what they found.

"What can I do?"

"Nothing," she replied firmly, but not unkindly. "You can do nothing."

As she spoke, a message came up on his screen: there was an incoming call from Sasha. Without saying good-bye, he cut Hussein off and answered. "Yes?"

"Frank was here." Her voice was a wail.

"Now?"

"No. When Frieda came."

"What?"

"Ethan's just told me. He saw Frank from the window, outside the house. When Frieda left here, Frank followed her."

He called Hussein and told her. His voice seemed to come from far off; he heard his words as if they were a stranger's and he heard her answer.

"All right," said Hussein. "Where would Frieda have gone, given that she clearly hasn't gone to the police?"

"Perhaps she would go to her own house. In fact, that's the first place to try."

"We're sending officers there now."

"Or even her consulting rooms."

"Good. Yes. Right. Anywhere else?"

"I don't know. You could try Reuben and Josef. Olivia, perhaps. Jack, though that's not so likely."

"Right."

"She might want to go to people who knew Sandy best—his sister, or his friends."

"OK," said Hussein doubtfully.

"Otherwise—I don't know. She walks," he added uselessly.

"Walks?"

"When things are on her mind, when she's troubled and needs to think, she walks and walks. Through the night."

"Where does she walk?"

"All over."

"That's not much good."

31

Karlsson tried to think it through clearly, but it was like he was in a storm. Where would she go? She knew now, so the sensible thing would be just to call the police. Wouldn't it? But she didn't have a phone. All right. Get in a cab. Straight to the police. But Frieda never seemed to do the sensible thing and Hussein had said she hadn't. And was this really the sensible thing? Did she actually have evidence that would convince the police? Did she realize the danger she was in? He knew that if he did nothing, or didn't think of the right thing, something would happen. Something that he would hear about on the news.

He took out his phone and stared at it helplessly. It felt like that terrible phase where you had lost something and you were looking in the places you had already looked in. He dialed Reuben's number. Reuben answered immediately as if he had been waiting for the call.

"I know, I know," Reuben said. "The police called me."

"What did you say?"

"Nothing much. A couple of names. Obviously I mentioned that she was most likely to go home or to her consulting room."

"I've been through that with them. They're already on to it. I thought maybe she'd turn to you. You're her old friend, her therapist."

"No, I'm not."

"She's known you longer than anyone. I thought she might turn to you."

"I don't mean that," said Reuben. "I mean, I'm not her therapist. Not anymore. That was long ago, when she was training. In the last couple of years, she was seeing someone else, someone she really rated."

"What's their name?"

"It was . . ." There was a long pause. Karlsson wanted to shout at Reuben to fucking remember. "Thelma something."

"Do you think she might go to her at a time like this?"

"It's not likely but I suppose it's possible."

"Then I need a name. A proper name. And a number."

"Wait. I think I know where I can find it. I'll call you back."

Karlsson felt so agitated that he couldn't stay still. He was shifting from foot to foot. He could hear a rushing sound in his ears. He stared at his phone, willing it to ring. He started to count. He promised himself that it would ring before he got to ten. It rang at fourteen.

"Thelma Scott," said Reuben.

Karlsson got her number and dialed it instantly, praying that she wasn't with a client or abroad or asleep. He was almost taken aback when a woman's voice answered.

"Dr. Thelma Scott?"

"Yes."

"My name's Malcolm Karlsson. I'm a police detective and I'm a friend of Frieda Klein's and this is very urgent. Have you seen her?"

There was a pause. He tried to imagine how he himself would react to a call like this. Did it sound trustworthy?

"Not for a while," said Scott. "I know that she's been in some sort of trouble."

"She's in trouble now. I mean, not trouble, but danger. I need to find her urgently."

"I don't know where she is. I haven't seen or spoken to her for several weeks."

"I need to find her. This moment." He made himself stop and think. "If things were really urgent, where would she turn? The police are trying all her friends, but I thought she might contact you."

"I haven't heard from her. I'm truly sorry."

"All right," said Karlsson in a dull voice. None of this was working. He was about to say good-bye when Scott spoke again.

"Did you say you were called Karlsson?"

"Yes."

"Are you the detective?"

"I'm *a* detective."

"She mentioned you. Have you considered that she might turn to you?"

"Me?"

"Yes."

"But"—he was bewildered—"she doesn't know where I am."

"Doesn't she know where you live?"

Karlsson stared at his phone. "Oh, for fuck's sake," he said.

He looked up and down the road. Taxi after taxi passed him, coming up from the City, but they were all taken. He called Hussein on his phone.

"I'm at Manning's flat," she said.

"And?"

"It's clean."

"I can imagine."

"No, really clean. It smells of bleach, like a laboratory. This place has been scoured."

"He's a lawyer. He knows about evidence. So you've got nothing."

"I didn't say that. Even lawyers can't clean in the cracks between floorboards. We've got hair from the pipe under his sink. There are stains behind the radiator in the living room. Something happened here. I'm sure of it."

"Have you got him?"

"Once we've got this back to the lab."

"No, I mean got him. Arrested him."

"There's no sign of him or of Frieda."

"I think she might be at my place. You're nearer than me, only a few minutes away."

He managed to flag down a taxi and gave the address. He settled down in the back.

"Stupid stupid stupid," he muttered to himself.

Frieda rang the bell. There was no answer. She knocked at the door. No answer. But she knew where Karlsson kept a spare key. Next to the door there was a pot with a plant that didn't look very well.

"People will look under the pot," Karlsson had told her, "because that's where people keep keys. And they won't find one. And they'll give up. So they won't notice that there's a loose brick next to the path and that there's a key hidden under that."

Frieda had suspected that quite a lot of people hid their keys under loose bricks, but she hadn't said anything. Fortunately, because she lifted up the brick and there was the key. She let herself into the house. Inside she could smell something, like food that had been left out. She could make herself coffee, but what she should probably do first was clear up. And she would start with throwing away whatever it was that she could smell. But before that, she would phone Karlsson. As she looked around for the phone, there was a gentle knock on the front door.

Frieda felt a moment of relief. But at the very moment she pulled the door open, she suddenly wondered why Karlsson would knock at his own front door and she knew that, of course, he wouldn't, and then the door was pushed hard against her and Frank was inside and the door was slammed shut. She turned and ran toward the back of the house. He was nearly on her—she could hear him breathing and feel the heat of his body. She felt him behind her, hands on her shoulders, and she was slammed forward into the wall, and everything went sparkly yellow, then slammed again in another direction, through a door. She saw other colors, a clown mobile hanging from the ceiling, a poster of a football. Something from deep inside her mind told her she was in a child's bedroom. Karlsson's children's bedroom. She pushed back but it was hopeless. Frank towered above her. She felt a blow on the side of her head and staggered back against the wall.

Now everything happened very, very slowly, as if she were watching it through frosted glass and with muffled ears. Frank had his left hand on her neck, pinning her against the wall. She felt something uncomfortable against her back. Probably the corner of a picture frame, she thought, and it seemed that she had a lot of time to think, that she could just let this happen, sink quietly into blackness and rest. Frank's face, his fierce eyes, were close to hers now. She saw the whiteness of his cotton shirt. He was breathing heavily. The feel of it, the smell of it reminded her of something. What was it? And then she remembered Lev, talking to her as he delivered her to that flat in Elephant and

Castle. What was it he had said? All or nothing? Was it something like that? She didn't look away from Frank. She mustn't distract him. Her eyes stared straight into his eyes. What strange things eyes were.

She felt in her pocket. Yes. And, yes, she remembered his words. None of the way or all of the way.

Frank raised his right hand and she saw a glint, the blade of a knife. He moved his face closer now, so that when he spoke it was in little more than a whisper.

"You can't speak. There's nothing to say. I cut Sandy's throat with this. But he was unconscious. You won't be. I want to watch."

As he was talking, Frieda was remembering her first year at medical school, anatomy. What were they? Subclavian and carotid. She gripped on it in her pocket. She delicately pulled her hand from her pocket. One chance. Only one chance. Then her hand pulled up and the blade snapped open. Up and in. Lev had said it was sharp. Very sharp. It must have been, because Frieda felt no resistance, almost as if the handle pressed against the white cotton had no blade. But within a second a rosette of the deepest scarlet spread around it.

Frank looked down in puzzlement and mild irritation, as if he had noticed an untied shoelace or an open fly. He stepped back and Frieda held on to the handle of the knife and pulled it back. There was a gur-gling sound and she felt something warm and wet on her face and her jacket. She looked down at the sticky redness. Had she been stabbed as well? She looked back at Frank.

"You fucker," he said. "You've . . ."

He couldn't say any more. The knife fell from his grasp. He tore at his shirt. The blood was coming out of him, not like a hose but in spurts. He looked down at his chest with a kind of interest. Spurt, nothing, spurt, nothing. He made a few staggering steps. Everything seemed to be turning red. The rug, bedspread, even a picture on the wall. Then his legs gave way and he fell heavily, out of control, half propped up against a low child's bed. His eyes already looked blurry, unfocused.

Frieda took a few steps toward him, still clutching the knife, but she immediately saw that he was no kind of threat. She remembered her training again. Arterial bleeding. What was it her prof had said? Arteries pump, veins dump. How long did he have? A minute? Two? She thought of Sandy, the man beside her in bed, walking beside her, dead on that stainless steel. Was she going to watch him die, just as Frank had been about to watch her die? The thought instantly made up her mind. She sprawled across Frank, sitting on his thighs. He was looking straight toward her but Frieda wasn't even sure if he was aware of her. She ripped at his shirt, tore a rag off, and pushed it against the wound, as hard as she could manage, with almost her whole weight on it. She could hear herself panting. Had the blood flow stopped? There was so much of it, on him, on her, everywhere around, that it was hard to tell.

Some sort of spark appeared in Frank's eyes. Was it anger? Frieda leaned closer to him. There was a strange intimacy. She could smell his breath. It was sweet.

"If you try anything," she said, "anything at all, I let go and you die. Got that?"

Frank gave a kind of a groan but whether it was a response or a moan of pain or just nothing at all, she couldn't tell. She managed to free her right hand and move toward his neck. Another groan.

"I need to check your pulse," she said.

It was slow. His blood pressure was falling. Now there was the sound of sirens and a car pulling up and ringing and banging on the door. Frieda's face was almost against Frank's and she saw a flicker.

"I can't answer the door," she said. "If I get up, you'll bleed out by the time I'm back. We'd better hope that they can break it down."

It seemed that they couldn't. There was more ringing on the door and banging and then finally, the sound of the door opening. Frieda shouted something and there was a sound of steps. She looked round and saw a young police officer step into the room, the shocked expression on his face, then actually step back out. Almost immediately the room seemed full. She saw uniforms and faces she couldn't make out.

"Jesus, Frieda, what's happened?"

She saw Karlsson's appalled face. Hussein was beside him.

"I can't move," she said. "If I move he'll die."

Karlsson was looking around his children's room. Frieda could see that there was even blood on the mobile above the bed. Her whole body felt stiff and sticky with it.

"I'm so sorry," she said. "So sorry."

Different people were staring at Frieda and at Frank and some of them went pale. She heard the sound of someone vomiting. Then there were men and women in green overalls lugging bags. One of them, a young man, red-haired, leaned over and stared at Frieda's hands on Frank's chest.

"Fuck," he said. He turned to Frieda, then looked at her hands, at the blood. "Are you a doctor?"

"Yes. Of a kind."

"What did this?"

"I did," said Frieda. "With a knife."

"All right," said the man slowly. "Keep your hands there." He glanced around. "Jen, get on the other side. Gauze."

A young woman rummaged through a bag and produced what looked like a toilet roll. She unraveled it and ripped off a sheet.

"What's your name?" said the man.

"Frieda Klein."

"OK, Frieda. On the count of three, you're going to remove your hands and get them out of the way. One, two, three."

Frieda raised her hands and at the same moment felt herself lifted up and away from Frank. She was laid down, almost forced down, on a stretcher.

"Are you injured?" a voice said.

"No," said Frieda.

"She's bleeding," another voice said.

"I'm not bleeding. It's not my blood."

But it all felt too tiring and she just lay back and felt hands on her and the stretcher was being carried down the hall and the sun was in her eyes and the flashing lights and then she was inside the ambulance and the doors were slammed and there was the sound of the siren and then the doors were opened again and Frieda just saw the blue sky briefly, then strip lights. The stretcher became a gurney. To one side she saw a police uniform, the officer struggling to keep up. There was still all that to deal with. The gurney stopped in a corridor. There was a murmured conference, that endless search in every hospital for space, for a room or a bed. She heard a man shouting and swearing. Something was thrown. Men in uniform ran past her, down the corridor. The shouts continued, then became muffled. Finally her gurney was pushed into a cubicle and she was lifted onto a bed.

A doctor leaned over her. She was young, the age of one of Frieda's own students. Frieda slowly gave her name and age and address. Her mind was clearing and she felt a dull ache of tiredness.

"So where does it hurt?" asked the doctor.

"It doesn't hurt anywhere."

The doctor looked down at Frieda with an expression of dismay. Frieda followed her gaze.

"This blood isn't mine," she said. "I just need to get home and wash it off."

"I don't . . ." The doctor started to speak, then stopped. "I need to see someone."

There was a blue curtain at the end of the cubicle. The doctor pulled it aside and disappeared. Within a couple of minutes she was back.

"Apparently you need someone to look at your head," said the doctor.

"I'm fine."

"Someone's on their way down from Neurology to assess you."

Frieda looked at her watch. "I'm leaving in five minutes," she said.

The doctor's eyes widened in dismay. "You can't," she said.

"You'll find that I can."

"I'll need to check." The young doctor rushed back out through the curtain. Frieda sat up on the bed. She held up her hands and looked at them. She wiggled the fingers. It all seemed fine. Time to go. The curtain was pushed aside and a man stepped inside. He was dressed in jeans and white tennis shoes and a short-sleeved checked shirt. He had curly dark hair and he was unshaven.

"This cubicle's taken," said Frieda.

With a frown, the man picked up the clipboard that was on a hook at the end of the bed. "I'm meant to have a look at you." He put the clipboard down and saw Frieda properly for the first time.

"Goodness," he said.

"It's not mine," Frieda said.

"Yes, but still. What happened?"

"I was attacked."

"Looks like you fought back."

"I had to."

"And you hit something big."

"The subclavian artery."

"Are they dead?"

"I managed to stem the bleeding."

"Not all of it. From what—" And then he stopped and looked at Frieda with a new interest. "I know you," he said.

"Yes."

"Don't tell me."

"All right."

A slow smile spread across his face. "You need to take off your shoes and your socks."

Frieda slipped them off.

"Can you flex your toes?" he said. She did so. "That's fine. Do you know what day it is?"

"Friday."

"Splendid."

"It began on a Friday and it ended on one."

"You've lost me there."

"Never mind."

"You came to my flat and took me to see a woman with a really interesting psychological condition."

"That's right."

"Weren't you working with the police?"

"I was."

"How did that work out for you?"

"It was mixed."

"Did you find out who did it?"

"Yes. But I ended up in hospital that time as well. And it wasn't just someone else's blood."

He took a penlight from his pocket. "Look up at the corner." He aimed the light at one eye and then the other. "I'm Andrew Berryman."

"I remember," said Frieda. "You were playing the piano. As an experiment into the ten-thousand-hours theory, where many hours each day of hard work trump innate ability."

"The experiment didn't work," he said. "I gave up."

"Neurological abnormalities. That was your field, wasn't it?"

"It still is."

"I thought of getting in touch with you once or twice. For your professional opinion."

He put his penlight back in his pocket. "You should have done," he said. "And you're fine. Except . . ." He rubbed the side of his face. "You say that the last time we met, it ended up with you in hospital. And now you're here again. I don't like blood. That's why I went into neurology."

"I didn't want this to happen."

"You're a therapist, aren't you?"

"That's right."

"Don't therapists believe that everything happens for a reason?"

"No, they don't."

"My mistake."

"So, have you finished?"

"You're probably in shock, after what you've gone through. So you should be kept under observation."

Frieda stood up. "No. I'm done here."

"Are you planning on just leaving?"

"That's right. I live only a few minutes from here."

"You can't walk the streets looking like that."

"I'll be fine."

Berryman shook his head disapprovingly. "I'll get you a lab coat. And I'll walk you back."

"I don't need that."

"I'll walk you back, which will allow me to assess your psychological state. You can agree to that or I'll have you forcibly restrained."

"You can't do that."

"You're covered in blood. You've been brought by ambulance from a crime scene. You wanna bet?"

"All right," said Frieda. "Anything. So long as I can leave."

32

Josef had kept the plants watered and fed the cat, but a fine layer of dust lay over everything and there was a slightly musty smell in the rooms, whose windows had remained closed through the hot summer weeks of Frieda's absence.

She worked slowly and methodically throughout the morning, vacuuming, wiping surfaces, pulling weeds from the pots on her patio. She took all of the clothes that she had worn as Carla to the charity shop a few streets away and put out clean towels. The fridge was empty, apart from a jar of olive paste and eggs long past their sell-by date that she dropped into the bin. She went to the shops and bought herself enough for the next few days: milk, bread and butter, some bags of salad and Sicilian tomatoes, salty blue cheese, smoked salmon that she thought she would eat that evening, raspberries and a little carton of cream. She let herself imagine the evening ahead of her, alone in her clean and orderly house, with the cat at her feet.

Then she went up into her study at the top of the house and wrote e-mails to her patients, saying that she was ready to start work again next week, and if they wanted to return they should let her know. Before she had sent them all an answer came back from Joe Franklin, simply saying: "Yes!" She wrote his name in her diary on the days she had always seen him.

At three o'clock that afternoon she went out and took the Underground from Warren Street to Highbury and Islington, then walked the remainder of the way. She walked more slowly than usual, aware that she was putting off the moment when she would knock at Sasha's door.

The door swung open and Reuben was standing in front of her, holding out his arms in welcome. She stepped into his embrace and he hugged her and ruffled her short hair, told her what she knew already—that she was back at last. Then there were quick light footsteps and Ethan flew into view. He was wearing red shorts and a blue T-shirt and holding an ice cream that was melting over his hand as he ran.

"Frieda!" he yelled. "I'm going to make a frog box with Josef and Marty."

"A frog box?"

"For frogs to be in." Some ice cream plopped to the floor. He took a violent lick at the cone.

"Who's Marty?"

"He works with Josef," said Reuben. "Ethan's taken a shine to him."

"I see. Where is Josef?"

"Here." And there he was, coming down the stairs. He stopped in front of her and, for a moment, couldn't seem to find the words. His brown eyes gazed at her. "And glad," he said. "Very glad for this sight."

"Thank you, Josef." Frieda took one of his large calloused hands between hers and pressed it. "How's Sasha?"

Josef glanced at Ethan, whose face was now covered with ice cream, then back at Frieda. He shook his head from side to side. "In bed," he said.

"Mummy's ill," said Ethan brightly. "But only a little ill."

Who was going to tell him about Frank? wondered Frieda, and when and how? It was going to be hard. "I'll go and see her."

She mounted the stairs. At the door to Sasha's room she paused, listening. She could hear faint rasping sounds, like a muffled saw. Sasha was weeping. Reuben had told her on the phone that Sasha had been crying steadily since she had found out the truth. "Almost like a machine made for crying," he'd said. "With no variation, no diminution or increase."

Frieda pushed the door and entered. The curtains were closed against the bright day; Sasha lay under her covers, a humped shape from which came the sound of sobbing that was like a distressed, strangulated breathing. In and out, in and out.

Frieda sat on the side of the bed and put out a hand to comfort the shape that rose and fell with the weeping. "Sasha," she said. "It's me.

Frieda." She waited but there was no response. "I'm here, Josef and Reuben are here. Ethan is here, and we're all going to look after him. We're going to look after you. You will come through this. Can you hear me? Nothing will be the same again, of course, and you won't be the same, but you will come through."

She sat on the bed for a while longer, then rose and opened the window so that the warm air came into the room. "I'm going to make a pot of tea," she said. "I'll be back in a few minutes. OK?"

There was a sudden sound and she stopped. "What are you saying?" Frieda asked.

"It was me." The words were barely discernible but, once said, they seemed to replace the sobbing in their repetitive lament. "It was me it was me it was me it was me."

Frieda sat down on the bed again. "No. It wasn't you. We don't get to say that. Frank was a jealous and controlling man. He couldn't bear to feel humiliated. Would something else have set him off? Maybe." She stroked Sasha's hair. "We do things, some of them foolish or wrong, but we don't know what the consequences will be. You slept with Sandy when you were feeling abandoned. I didn't listen to what he was trying to tell me. We just have to live with that. A terrible thing has been done, but not by you. And you're not going to be destroyed by it."

Sasha was still murmuring the words but they had merged into a wretched trickle of sound. Frieda stood up once more and left the room. Josef and Reuben were in the small garden with Ethan, who was hammering a nail into a plank of wood, blissfully absorbed and supervised by Josef. Reuben was smoking a cigarette and talking on his mobile.

"OK?" he asked, when he ended the call.

She nodded. She felt she had no more words left inside her; the thought of talking, explaining, exhausted her. "I think I had better stay here for a bit," she said at last.

"No," said Reuben.

"What?"

"No. You are going to stay in your own home, the home I know you've been homesick for."

"Someone has to be here."

"Indeed. Paz is arriving in about half an hour, with provisions."

"Thank you," she said.

"It's nothing," he said.

"It's not nothing, Reuben. It's a lot. Everything you've all done."

"One day you'll have to learn that you can't do everything all by yourself."

"Yes."

"And one day we will talk about all of this."

"One day."

"But for now, for God's sake, go home."

She went home. She had a long bath, then roamed through each room, making doubly sure everything was in its proper place. She ate smoked salmon on rye bread and drank a single glass of white wine. She played through a game of chess, with the cat on her lap, and she promised herself that tomorrow she would sit in the garret room and draw. She felt peaceful and immeasurably sad. She thought over these last weeks when she had stepped out of her life, living in strange, unlovely places and among marginalized people, free and unanchored and alone. Now she was back here in her beloved house, her possessions about her, schedules being reassembled and order reestablished. She thought of Karlsson's face as he had bent over her in his children's bedroom, which was now daubed and sprayed with blood. Where was he now? Then she thought of Sasha, lying in her bed weeping, as if the weeping would never stop. Of Frank in his hospital bed, flanked by police officers. Of Ethan, who didn't understand how his life had changed. Of Sandy, now just ash and memory, and the future he would not have.

33

Tanya Hopkins arrived in a taxi to pick up Frieda from her house. For several minutes after the taxi had set off again, she didn't speak. Frieda didn't mind long silences. She was used to them. Sometimes a patient would sit facing her for a whole session without speaking. Usually therapy was about talk but it could also be an escape from the press of words, and that could be good too.

But although Tanya Hopkins wasn't speaking, it didn't feel like silence. She was staring out the window, away from Frieda, yet it was clear that she was thinking hard. Frieda could even see her lips moving, as if she were silently talking to herself. Finally she turned to Frieda. "I suppose you know where we're going."

"To see the police."

"To see the police," said Hopkins, like an echo. "They haven't told me what it's about, but it's not hard to guess. They will be informing us whether they are planning to proceed with any charges." She paused, but Frieda showed no sign of speaking. "Perverting the course of justice is an obvious possibility."

Frieda looked round. "Did I pervert it?"

Hopkins shook her head. "I don't know. You perverted something. I'm not exactly sure what." She looked at Frieda with a resigned expression. "At this point, I would usually tell my client to leave the talking to me, but I don't suppose it would do any good."

"I'm sorry I put you in a bad position," said Frieda.

"No, you're not," said Hopkins.

Frieda thought for a moment. "I'm not exactly sorry. If the same thing happened, I'd do it all again."

"Which means you're not sorry at all."

"But what I'm really sorry about is that, as a by-product of what I did, you had to go through all that trouble."

"That is the most pathetic apology I've ever heard in my life."

"It's not an apology. It's a description of my state of mind."

"I don't even know how to respond to that."

"You didn't have to keep me on as a client."

Hopkins managed something of a smile at that. "I wouldn't foist you on anyone else," she said. "But there are consequences, you know."

"Consequences? If I'd followed your advice, I would have pleaded guilty to a crime I didn't do."

"It wasn't advice. It was an option. But I wasn't just talking about consequences for you. What about your friend DCI Karlsson?"

"What about him?"

"He's been suspended."

Frieda felt that someone had punched her very hard in the solar plexus. She gave a small moan. "Oh, the idiot."

"It wasn't just yourself you were risking. You must have known that."

Frieda looked out the window of the taxi, looked without seeing. She felt overcome by rage and nausea and shame. Suddenly, through all of that inner fog, she saw that the taxi was driving up Pentonville Road. "This isn't the way to the police station," she said.

"I got a call this morning changing the location."

The taxi pulled to the curb and the driver turned round.

"The road's blocked off to traffic," he said. "You'll have to walk from here."

The two of them got out and walked along Chapel Market, past the stalls. There was a smell of cooking meat that made Frieda feel queasy. Hopkins checked the piece of paper in her hand.

"This can't be right," she said.

They were standing beside a doorway between a bookie's and an optician's. She pressed the bell. A scratchy, unintelligible voice came from a little speaker next to the door. Hopkins leaned in close and gave her name and Frieda's. There was a buzzing sound and she pressed the door but it didn't open. She pressed the bell again. They heard a sound inside and then the door was opened by a young, spiky-haired woman wearing a blue T-shirt and dark jeans.

"I'm sorry," said Hopkins. "I think we must have the wrong address."

"Tanya Hopkins and Frieda Klein?" said the woman cheerfully. "Come on in."

They followed her up a set of dingy stairs and through a door into what looked like an abandoned office. It was a large space with only a desk and several unmatching chairs.

"You're to wait here," the woman said to Hopkins. "I'm to take Dr. Klein upstairs."

"That's not possible," said Hopkins. "If there's any meeting with DCI Hussein, then I have to be there throughout."

"DCI Hussein won't be coming," said a voice, and Hopkins and Frieda looked round. A man had come through a door at the far side of the office.

Hopkins started to say something, then stopped. "I know you," she said.

"But you can't remember where from," said the man.

"At the police station," said Frieda. "The meeting before . . ."

"Before you absconded. Yes, that one. My name's Walter Levin."

"What's this about?" said Hopkins suspiciously.

"I need five minutes with Dr. Klein."

"That's not possible. We have an important meeting with the police."

"Please," said Levin.

Hopkins looked at Frieda. "I don't like this. Not one bit."

"All right," said Frieda. "Five minutes."

"This way," he said.

She followed him up a set of stairs, then another. There was a metal door in front of him.

"These premises don't have much to recommend them. But they do have this." With that, he pushed open the door and Frieda stepped through and found herself out on a roof terrace.

"Come and look," he said.

He led her to a set of railings at the front façade of the building.

They looked down at the market. He pointed across at the cranes at the back of King's Cross and St. Pancras.

"You forget that you're up on a hill here," he said.

"I'm sorry," said Frieda. "I'm not really in the mood for small talk. What's this about?"

"What were you expecting it to be about?"

"About whether I'm going to jail or not."

"Yes, well, Commissioner Crawford is rather keen on your going to jail."

"What about DCI Hussein?"

"She's more agnostic on the matter."

"So why am I talking to you?"

"There's a big fat file on you. About your brief career as a Metropolitan Police consultant."

"That didn't work out too well."

Levin smiled. "That's a matter of interpretation."

"Well, it almost got me killed and the commissioner wants me in prison, so you'll excuse me if I have a slightly glass-half-empty view of the situation."

"What about working for me?"

Frieda had been looking down at the market stalls but now she turned to Levin. There was a casualness about his demeanor, as if he were never quite serious. But there was a coldness about his gray eyes that made him difficult to read. "Who exactly are you?"

"What did I say when we met before?"

"You said you'd been assigned from the Home Office."

"That sounds about right."

"I've no idea what it means."

"What it means is that I can put a stop to any possibility of your being prosecuted."

"In exchange for what?"

"In exchange for your availability."

"Availability for what?"

"To do the sort of thing you do."

"Can you be more specific?"

"Not as yet."

In the street a cyclist was wobbling precariously between the stalls, with shopping bags hanging from the handlebars.

"No," said Frieda. "I can't do anything like that. Sorry."

Levin took off his glasses and polished them on his rather shabby striped tie. "There's one other thing."

"What's that?"

"Your friend Karlsson."

"What about him?"

"He interfered with a criminal inquiry. He's facing jail time as well. And his case is more serious than yours. He's a police detective. It's the sort of case where judges talk about the foundations on which justice depends."

Frieda looked round sharply. "If you can help Karlsson out of this, then . . ." She thought for a moment. Then what? "Then I owe you a favor."

"A favor," said Levin. He put his glasses back on. "Jolly good. I like that." He beamed at her and his eyes remained sharp. "Of course you know that a favor's a dangerous thing."

He held out his hand and she took it but then let it go.

"How do I know you're a good person?" she asked.

"I'm keeping you out of prison. I'm keeping DCI Karlsson out of prison and returning him to the Met. Doesn't that make me a good person?"

"Some people wouldn't think so."

34

Karlsson saw Frieda before she saw him. That was unusual. Normally she was alert to her surroundings, wary of being looked at, or being caught. But for the second time in just a few days, she was unaware of his approach. She was leaning on the railing, looking out at the river. Behind him the lorries and buses were rushing along Chelsea Embankment. The noise and the stench of the fumes seemed to be trapped by the summer heat, and he could feel the rumble of the vehicles in his feet.

"This is a strange place to choose," he said, and Frieda, turning, gave him a nod of recognition. He leaned on the railing beside her. A tourist boat was passing. They could hear the tinny sound of the guide's commentary. A voice on a loudspeaker said that the River Thames was a pageant of history. It was from here that Francis Drake set off to circle the globe. And it was here that he returned with a ship full of treasure and became Sir Francis Drake.

"I hate the Embankment," Frieda said.

"That's a strong word."

"There used to be huts here on the shore. Boatyards and wharves and jetties. Then they destroyed them and replaced them with this highway. It was like London was turning its back on the river, pretending it didn't exist."

"It was quite a long time ago."

"One day they'll demolish the Embankment, all the way from Chelsea to Blackfriars, and we'll have a riverbank again."

"Which doesn't explain why you arranged to meet here."

"I wanted to be by the river. But I didn't want to be in the middle of a market or a riverside pub."

"A riverside pub," said Karlsson. "Now that sounds tempting."

"Some other time."

"This is about Sandy?"

"You know, we'll probably never know where he entered the water."

"Has Frank said anything?"

"From what I've heard, he's made no statement at all."

"Does it matter?"

"Legally? Probably not. But it matters to Sasha. It matters to his sister."

"And to you?"

"Nothing Frank could say could make it any better, or make it less awful. The thought of his body floating in the river during those days and nights is a horrible one. But what's really painful is what he went through when he was alive."

"And yet you came down here."

"Yes. To say a sort of good-bye, another good-bye. Strange, isn't it?"

"Then what am *I* doing here?"

"I wanted to say a sort of good-bye to Sandy and a sort of sorry to you."

"You don't need to say sorry."

Karlsson saw Frieda come closer to laughing than he had seen for a very long time.

"Really?" she said. "I got you suspended and almost fired. And also I'm sorry about Bella and Mikey's room."

"I don't think I'm ever going to tell them why it has been redecorated. I guess I owe you a debt of thanks for my reinstatement."

"You don't look especially happy about it."

There was a pause. "When I got the news," he said finally, "it was like being woken out of a sleep and getting up and feeling your muscles ache and wondering whether you can really face the day."

"It sounds like I owe you another apology."

"No," said Karlsson. "We have to face the day in the end. We can't sleep all the time. But I tried to check up on your Mr. Levin."

"What did you find?"

"Nothing. Nothing at all."

"What does that mean?"

"I'm not sure. Did anybody ever warn you about owing favors to someone you don't know?"

"Probably."

They both looked at the river in silence.

"I'd like to live by a river," Karlsson said.

"I'm not sure that I would."

"Why not?"

"I don't know," said Frieda. "I like walking by rivers, following them where they lead. But to live beside one would be like living next to a dark abyss. You'd always wonder what lay beneath the surface. And it's worse than an abyss. It's moving, always trying to pull you down and away."

Karlsson shook his head, laughing. "Frieda. It's just a river."

Several miles away, Josef and Marty were sitting in a pub not far from the house in Belsize Park on which they had been working for so many months but which was now finished.

"It was a good job," said Josef, drinking his second pint of beer. Surreptitiously he drew his vodka bottle out of his pocket and took a swig before offering it to Marty. "Big."

"Yeah," Marty agreed. He put the bottle to his mouth and tipped it back. A tattoo rippled along the muscles of his forearm. "Took care of the summer at any rate."

"Summer is not over," said Josef. "In Ukraine now is hot, very hot, with storms."

"Ukraine. That's where you come from?"

"Is my home. Kiev."

"It's a long way off," said Marty vaguely.

"Much trouble there. Fighting and death. But is very beautiful. Many forests."

They were both silent for a while, drinking.

"I have sons there," said Josef eventually. "Two sons who grow tall without me."

"That's tough."

"Do you have sons?"

"A boy called Matt. Little red-headed kid. But I don't see him now."

"No? Is hard."

"Yeah. But it's better to be free."

"You think? Free is to be alone."

"I don't mind that. I can do what I want. Go where I want. Just pack up my bag and leave."

"Where do you go now?"

"I dunno. I'll leave London. I've done what I wanted here."

"Soon?"

"Maybe even tonight."

"Just like that, you leave?"

"Just like that." Marty snapped his fingers.

Josef nodded. "No homesickness?"

"How can you feel homesick if you don't have a home?"

"I don't know." Josef frowned: he knew it was possible but didn't have the words. He finished his beer and wiped the back of his hand across his mouth, then looked at the clock on the wall. "I must go," he said. "I am meeting my friend Frieda."

"Ah, that Frieda. Is she OK now?"

"Yes, all OK. But like a soldier after battle."

Marty gave a slow smile. "I read about it. It was in all the papers and on the telly."

Josef hesitated, then said: "Do you want to come along?"

"To meet your Frieda? No, mate, I should be getting on. I've things to do before I go. But thanks for the offer." He stood up and held out his hand. "Bye then, Joe," he said. "You take care."

Josef stood as well and the two men shook hands slightly awkwardly.

"You helped me out," said Josef.

"It was nothing."

Marty slapped Josef on the back and left the pub. Light rain was speckling the dusty pavements and the air was thick, promising a downpour. He took two buses and then walked up Seven Sisters Road, whistling under his breath, his tool bag slung over his shoulder. At the Taj Mahal

Hotel—on the sign the "J" had slipped, which had always annoyed him—he pushed open the frosted-glass door and leaned on the bell until a very small and whiskery woman appeared from the back, wiping her hands on a stained apron.

"What?" she said suspiciously.

"I'm Marty, from three B. I'm leaving tonight."

"Leaving?"

"Yeah. I'm paid till the end of the week."

"No refunds."

"That's OK."

He went up the stairs two at a time and unlocked the door to his room. It was small and barely furnished, but there was a microwave and a kettle and a small fridge and he didn't need much. He poured the last of the milk down the sink and unplugged the kettle. His bags were already packed. Just a few more things to put in.

He took the newspaper clippings off the wall. The ones about Frieda Klein absconding, most of which carried the same photo of her, a photograph that had been used in previous stories. The ones about the have-a-go heroine charging at the group of youths with her buggy in order to rescue the homeless man. It made him smile: he'd known at once it was her. The ones about the arrest of Frank Manning on suspicion of murder. The article in which Malcolm Karlsson's picture appeared. He slid them all into the top of his case and zipped it shut. There were two keys on the bedside table, a Chubb and a Yale, and he put them in the inner pocket of his jacket. He'd managed to go through Josef's bag one day and filch the set of keys Josef had for her house—just for an hour or so, enough time to go to the locksmith and get copies made.

He looked round the room to make sure there was nothing he had missed, then slung his tool bag over one shoulder, his duffel bag over the other and picked up his case.

Then Dean Reeve left, shutting the door behind him, whistling as he went.

Nicci French's first Frieda Klein mystery is also available from Penguin Books.

Read on for the first chapter of . . .

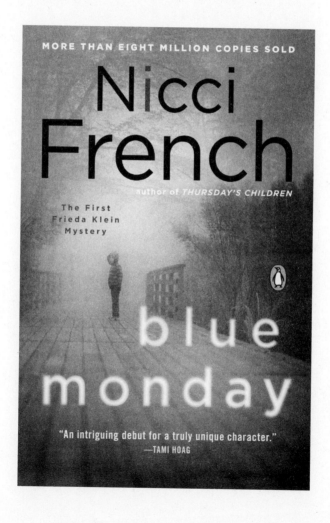

MORE THAN EIGHT MILLION COPIES SOLD

Nicci French

author of *THURSDAY'S CHILDREN*

The First Frieda Klein Mystery

blue monday

"An intriguing debut for a truly unique character."
—TAMI HOAG

1987

In this city there were many ghosts. She had to take care. She avoided the cracks between the paving stones, skipping and jumping, her feet in their scuffed lace-up shoes landing in the blank spaces. She was nimble at this hopscotch by now. She had done it every day on the way to school and back ever since she could remember, first holding on to her mother's hand, dragging and jerking her as she leaped from one safe place to the next; then on her own. Don't step on the cracks. Or what? She was probably too old for such a game now, already nine, and in a few weeks' time she would be ten, just before the summer holidays began. Still she played it, mostly out of habit but also nervous about what might happen if she stopped.

This bit was tricky—the paving was broken up into a jagged mosaic. She got across it, one toe pressing into the little island between the lines. Her plaits swung against her hot cheek, her school bag bumped against her hip, heavy with books and her half-eaten packed lunch. Behind her, she could hear Joanna's feet following in her steps. She didn't turn. Her little sister was always trailing after her, always getting in her way. Now she heard her whimpering, "Rosie! Rosie, wait for me!"

"Hurry up, then," she called over her shoulder. There were several people between them now, but she caught a glimpse of Joanna's face, hot and red under her dark fringe. She looked anxious. The tip of her tongue was on her lip in concentration. Her foot landed on a crack and she wobbled, hitting another. She always did that. She was a clumsy child who spilled food and stubbed her toes and stepped in dog poo. "Hurry!" Rosie repeated crossly, weaving her way past people.

It was four o'clock in the afternoon and the sky was a flat blue; the light flared on the pavement, hurting her eyes. She rounded the corner toward the shop and was suddenly in the shade where she slowed to a walk, for the danger was over. The paving stones were replaced by tarmac. She passed the man with the pockmarked face who sat in the doorway with a tin beside him. There weren't any laces in his boots. She tried not to look at him. She didn't like the way he smiled without really smiling, like her father sometimes, when he was saying good-bye on a Sunday. Today was Monday: Monday was when she missed him most, waking up to the week and knowing he wasn't there again. Where was Joanna? She waited, watching the other people flow past her—a flurry of youths, a woman with a scarf round her head and a large bag, a man with a stick—and then her sister emerged from the dazzle of light into the shadows, a skinny figure with an oversized bag, knobbly knees, and grubby white ankle socks. Her hair was sticking to her forehead.

Rosie turned again and walked toward the sweetshop, considering what she would buy. Perhaps the Opal Fruits . . . or perhaps Maltesers, though it was so hot they would melt on the way home. Joanna would buy the strawberry laces, and her mouth would be pink and smudged. Hayley from her class was already in there, and they stood together at the counter, picking out sweets. The Opal Fruits, she decided, but she had to wait to pay until Joanna arrived. She glanced toward the door and for a moment she thought she saw something—a blur, a trick of the light, something different, like a shimmer in the hot air. But then it was gone. The doorway was empty. Nobody was there.

She tutted loudly, over a screech of brakes.

"I always have to wait for my little sister."

"Poor you," said Hayley.

"She's such a crybaby. It's boring." She said this because it was something she felt she ought to say. You had to look down on your younger siblings, roll your eyes, and sneer.

"I bet," said Hayley, companionably.

"Where is she?" With a theatrical sigh, Rosie put down her packet of sweets and went to the entrance to look outside. Cars drove by. A woman wearing a sari walked past, all gold and pink and sweet-smelling, and then three boys from the secondary school up the road, jostling against each other with their sharp elbows.

"Joanna! Joanna, where are you?"

She heard her voice, high and cross, and thought, I sound like my mom in one of her moods.

Hayley stood beside her, chewing noisily on her bubble gum. "Where's she gone, then?" A pink bubble appeared out of her mouth, and she sucked it back in again.

"She knows she's supposed to stay with me."

Rosie ran to the corner where she had last seen Joanna and stared around, squinting. She called again, though her voice was drowned by a lorry. Maybe she had crossed the road, had seen a friend on the other side. It wasn't likely. She was an obedient little girl. Biddable, their mother called her.

"Can't find her?" Hayley appeared at her side.

"She's probably gone home without me," said Rosie, aiming at nonchalance, hearing the panic in her tone.

"See you, then."

"See you."

She tried to walk normally, but it didn't work. Her body wouldn't let her be calm. She broke into a ragged run, her heart bumping in her chest and a nasty taste in her mouth. "Stupid idiot," she kept saying. And "I'll kill her. When I see her, I'll . . ." Her legs felt unsteady. She imagined herself getting hold of Joanna by the bony shoulders and shaking her until her head wobbled.

Home. A blue front door and a hedge that hadn't been cut since her father had left. She stopped, feeling a bit sick, the nausea she had when she was going to get into trouble for something. She banged the knocker hard because the bell didn't work anymore. Waited. Let her be there, let her be there, let her be there. The door opened and her mother appeared, still in her coat from work. Her eyes took in Rosie and then dropped to the space beside her.

"Where's Joanna?" The words hung in the air between them. Rosie saw her mother's face tighten. "Rosie? Where's Joanna?"

She heard her own voice saying, "She was there. It's not my fault. I thought she'd gone home on her own."

She felt her hand grabbed, and she and her mother were running back down the road the way she had come, along the street where they lived and up past the sweetshop where children hung around the door, past the man with the pockmarked face and the empty smile, and round the corner out of the shade and into the dazzle. Feet slamming and a stitch in her ribs, over the cracks without pausing.

All the while she could hear, above the banging of her heart and the asthmatic wheezing of her breath, her mother calling, "Joanna? Joanna? Where are you, Joanna?"

Deborah Vine pushed a tissue against her mouth as if to stop the words streaming out of her. Outside the back window, the police officer could see a slender, dark-haired girl standing in the small garden quite still, her hands by her side and a school bag still hanging off her shoulder. Deborah Vine looked at him. He was waiting for her answer.

"I'm not sure," she said. "About four o'clock. On her way home from school, Audley Road Primary. I would have collected her myself except it's hard to get there on time from work—and anyway she was with Rosie and there are no roads to cross and I thought it was safe. Other mothers leave their children to go home alone and they have to learn, don't they, learn to look after themselves, and Rosie promised to keep an eye on her."

She drew a long, unsteady breath.

He made a note in his book. He rechecked Joanna's age. Five and three months. Where she was last seen. Outside the sweetshop. Deborah couldn't remember the name. She could take them there.

The officer closed his notebook. "She's probably at a friend's house," he said. "But have you got a photograph? A recent one."

"She's little for her age," said Deborah. She could hardly get the words out. The officer had to lean forward to hear her. "A skinny little thing.

She's a good girl. Shy as anything when you first meet her. She wouldn't go off with a stranger."

"A photo," he said.

She went to look. The officer glanced again at the girl in the garden with her blank white face. He'd have to talk to her, or one of his colleagues perhaps. A woman would be better. But maybe Joanna would turn up before it was necessary, tumble in. She had probably wandered off with a friend and was playing with whatever five-year-old girls play with—dolls and crayons and tea sets and tiaras. He stared at the photograph Deborah Vine passed him, of a girl with dark hair like her sister's and a thin face. One chipped tooth, a severe fringe, a smile that looked as if she had turned up her mouth when the photographer told her to say "cheese."

"Have you got hold of your husband?"

Her face twisted.

"Richard—my . . . I mean, their father—doesn't live with us." Then as if she couldn't stop herself, she added: "He left us for someone younger."

"You should let him know."

"Does that mean you think this is really serious?" She wanted him to say no, it didn't really matter, but she knew it was serious. She was damp with fear. He could almost feel it rising off her.

"We'll keep in touch. A female officer is on her way here."

"What shall I do? There must be something I can do. I can't just sit here waiting. Tell me what to do. Anything."

"You could phone people," he said. "Anywhere she might have gone."

She clutched at his sleeve. "Tell me she'll be all right," she insisted. "Tell me you'll get her back."

The officer looked awkward. He couldn't say that, and he couldn't think of what else to say.

Every time the phone rang it was a little bit worse. People knocking at the door. They'd heard. What a terrible thing, but of course it would be all right. Everything would be all right. The nightmare would end. Was there anything they could do, anything at all? Only ask. Say the word. Now the sun was low in the sky and shadows lay over streets and houses and parks. It was getting cold. All over London, people were sitting in front of TV sets or standing at stoves, stirring the pot, or gathering in smoke-fogged groups in bars, talking about Saturday's results and holiday plans, moaning about little aches and pains.

Rosie crouched in the chair, her eyes wide. One of her plaits had come undone. The female police officer squatted beside her, large and plump and kind, patted her hand. But she couldn't remember, didn't know, mustn't speak: words were dangerous. Nobody had told her. She wanted her father to come home and make everything all right, but they didn't know where he was. They couldn't find him. Her mother said he was probably on the road. She pictured him on a road that stretched away from him and dwindled into the distance under a dark sky.

She squeezed her eyes tightly shut. When she opened them, Joanna would be there. She held her breath until her chest ached and her blood hammered in her ears. She could make things happen. But when she opened her eyes to the police officer's nice concerned face, her mother was still crying and nothing had changed.

At nine thirty the following morning, there was a meeting in what had been designated the operations room at Camford Hill police station. It was the moment when what had been a frantic search was turned into a co-ordinated operation. It was given a case number. Detective Chief Inspector Frank Tanner assumed command and made a speech. People were introduced to each other. Desks were assigned and argued over. An engineer installed phone lines. Corkboards were nailed to walls. There was a special sort of urgency in the room. But there was something else that nobody said out loud but everybody felt: a sickness somewhere in the stomach. This wasn't a teenager or a husband who had disappeared after an argument. If it had been, they wouldn't have been here. This was about a five-year-old girl. Seventeen and a half hours had passed since she had last been seen. It was too long. There had been an entire night. It had been a cool night; this was June and not November, and that was something. Still. A whole night.

DCI Tanner was just giving details of the press conference that was taking place later that morning when he was interrupted. A uniformed officer had come into the room. He pushed his way through and said something to Tanner that nobody else could hear.

"Is he downstairs?" said Tanner. The officer said that he was. "I'll see him now."

Tanner nodded at another detective, and the two of them left the room together.

"Is it the father?" said the detective, who was called Langan.

"He's only just arrived."

"Are they on bad terms?" Detective Langan said. "Him and his ex."

"I reckon," said Tanner.

"It's usually someone they know," said Langan.

"That's good to hear."

"I was just saying."

They arrived outside the door of the interview room.

"How are you going to play it?" said Langan.

"He's a worried father," said Tanner, and pushed the door open.

Richard Vine was on his feet. He was dressed in a gray suit with no tie. "Is there any news?" he said.

"We're doing everything we can," said Tanner.

"No news at all?"

"It's early days," said Tanner, knowing as he said it that it wasn't true. That it was the reverse of the truth. He gestured to Richard Vine to sit down.

Langan moved to one side so that he could observe the father as he talked. Vine was tall, with the stoop of a man who feels uncomfortable with his height, and had dark hair that was already turning gray at the temples, though he couldn't have been more than in his mid-thirties. He had dark, beetling brows and was unshaven; there was a bruised look to his pale, slightly puffy face. His brown eyes were red-rimmed and looked sore. He seemed dazed.

"I was on the road," said Vine, without being asked. "I didn't know. I didn't hear until early this morning."

"Can you tell me where you were, Mr. Vine?"

"I was on the road," he repeated. "My work . . ." He stopped and pushed a flap of hair back from his face. "I'm a salesman. I spend a lot of time on the road. What's that got to do with my daughter?"

"We just need to establish your whereabouts."

"I was in Saint Albans. There's a new sports center. Do you want to know the times? Do you need proof?" His voice sharpened. "I wasn't anywhere near here if that's what you're thinking. What's Debbie been saying about me?"

"I'd like to know times." Tanner kept his voice neutral. "And anyone who can corroborate what you're telling us."

"What do you think? That I've abducted her and hidden her away somewhere, because Debbie won't let me have the kids overnight, that she turns them against me? That I've . . ." He wasn't able to say the words.

"These are just routine questions."

"Not to me! My little girl's gone missing, my baby." He sagged. "Of course I'll bloody tell you times. You can check them. But you're wasting your time on me and all the while you're not looking for her."

"We're looking," said Langan. He thought: Seventeen and a half hours. Eighteen, now. She's five years old and she's been gone eighteen hours. He stared at the father. You could never tell.

Later, Richard Vine squatted on the floor beside the sofa where Rosie huddled, still in her pajamas and her hair still in yesterday's plaits.

"Daddy?" she said. It was almost the first thing she'd said since her mother had called the police yesterday afternoon. "Daddy?"

He opened his arms and gathered her in. "Don't worry," he said. "She'll come home soon. You'll see."

"Promise?" she whispered against his neck.

"Promise."

But she could feel his tears on the top of her head, where the parting was.

They asked her what she could remember, but she couldn't remember anything. Just the cracks in the pavement, just choosing sweets, just Jo-anna calling her to wait. And her swell of anger against her little sister, her desire for her to be somewhere else. They said it was very important that she should tell them everyone she saw on that walk home from school. People she knew and people she didn't know. It didn't matter if she didn't think it was important: that was for them to decide. But she hadn't seen anyone, just Hayley in the sweetshop and that man with the pockmarked face. Shadows flitted through her mind. She was very cold, though it was summer outside the window. She put one end of her unraveling plait into her mouth and sucked it violently.

"Still not saying anything?"
  "Not a word."
  "She thinks it was her fault."
  "Poor kid, what a thing to grow up with."
  "Sssh. Don't talk as if it's over."
  "Do you really think she's still alive?"

They made lines and walked across the wasteland near the house, very slowly, stooping occasionally to pick things up from the ground and put them into plastic bags. They went from door to door, holding a photograph of Joanna, the one the mother had passed over on that Monday afternoon, with a block fringe and an obedient smile on her thin face. It was a famous photo now. The papers had got hold of it. There were journalists outside the house, photographers, a television crew. Joanna became "Jo" or, even worse, "Little Jo," like a saintly child heroine from a Victorian novel. There were rumors. It was impossible to know where they started, but they spread quickly round the neighborhood. It was the tramp. It was a man in a blue estate car. It was her father. Her clothes had been found in a Dumpster. She'd been seen in Scotland, in France. She was definitely dead and she was definitely alive.

Rosie's granny came to stay with them, and Rosie went back to school. She didn't want to go. She dreaded the way people would look at her and whisper about it behind her back and suck up to her, trying to be her friend because this big thing had happened to her. She sat at her desk and tried to concentrate on what the teacher was saying, but she could feel them behind her. *She let her little sister get snatched.*

She didn't want to go to school but she didn't want to stay at home either. Her mother wasn't like her mother anymore. She was like someone pretending to be a mother, but all the time she was somewhere else. Her eyes flickered about. She kept putting her hands over her mouth as if she was keeping something in, some truth that would otherwise burst free. Her face became thin and pinched and old. At night, when Rosie lay in bed and watched the car lights from the road outside move across her ceiling, she could hear her mother moving around downstairs. Even when it was dark and everyone else in the world was asleep, her mother was awake. And her father was different, too. He lived alone again now. He hugged her too tightly. He smelt funny—sweet and sour at the same time.

Deborah and Richard Vine sat in front of the TV cameras together. They still shared a surname, but they didn't look at each other. Tanner had told them to keep it simple: tell the world how they missed Joanna and appeal to whoever it was who had taken her to let her come home. Don't worry about showing emotion. The media would like that. Just so long as it didn't stop them speaking.

"Let my daughter come home," said Deborah Vine. Her voice broke; she covered her newly haggard face with one hand. "Just let her come back home."

Richard Vine added, more violently, "Please give us our daughter back. Whoever knows anything, please help." His face was pale and blotched with red.

"What do you think?" Langan asked Tanner.

Tanner shrugged. "You mean, are they sincere? I've got no idea. How can a kid disappear like that, into thin air?"

There wasn't a summer holiday that year. They had been going to go to Cornwall, to stay on a farm. Rosie remembered them planning it, how there would be cows in the fields and hens in the yard and even an old fat pony the owners might let them ride. And they would go to the nearby beaches. Joanna was scared of the sea—she shrieked when waves went over her ankles—but she loved building sand castles and looking for shells, eating ice-cream cones with chocolate Flakes stuck into the top.

Instead, Rosie went to her grandmother's house for a few weeks. She didn't want to go. She needed to be at home, for when Joanna was found. She thought Joanna might be upset if she wasn't there; it would be as if she didn't care enough to wait.

There were meetings in which detectives leafed through statements by fantasists, previous offenders, eyewitnesses who had seen nothing.

"I still think it's the father."

"He has an alibi."

"We've been through this. He could have driven back to the area. Just."

"No one saw him. His own daughter didn't see him."

"Maybe she did. Maybe that's why she won't say anything."

"Anyway, anything she saw she won't remember now. It will just be memories of memories of suggestions. Everything's covered over."

"What are you saying?"

"I'm saying she's gone."

"Dead?"

"Dead."

"You're giving up on her?"

"No." He paused. "But I am taking some of the men off the case."

"That's what I said. You're giving up."

One year later, a photograph enhanced by a new computer program, which even its inventor warned was speculative and unreliable, showed how Joanna might have changed. Her face was slightly filled out, her dark hair a little bit darker. Her tooth was still chipped and her smile was still anxious. Some newspapers carried it, but only on an inside page.

There had been a murder of a particularly photogenic thirteen-year-old girl, and this had dominated the headlines for weeks. Joanna was an old story now, a tingle in the public memory. Rosie stared at the picture until it blurred. She was scared she wouldn't recognize her sister when she saw her, that she would be a stranger. And she was scared that Joanna wouldn't recognize her either—or would know her but turn away from her. Sometimes she went and sat in Joanna's room, a room that hadn't been altered since the day she disappeared. Her teddy was on her pillow, her toys stacked in the under-bed boxes, her clothes—which would be too small for her—neatly folded in drawers or hanging in the wardrobe.

Rosie was ten now. Next year, she would go to secondary school. She had begged to go to the one a mile and a half away in the next borough, two bus journeys, because there she would no longer be the girl who had lost her little sister. She would just be Rosie Vine, year seven, shy and quite small for her age, who did all right in every subject but wasn't the best at anything except, perhaps, biology. She was old enough to know that her father drank more than he should. Sometimes her mother had to come and fetch her home because he couldn't look after her properly. She was old enough to feel that she was an older sister without a younger sister, and sometimes she felt Joanna's presence like a ghost—a ghost with a chipped tooth and a plaintive voice, asking her to wait. Sometimes she would see her on the street and her heart would miss a beat and then the face would resolve into the face of a stranger.

Three years after Joanna disappeared, they moved to a smaller house a mile or so away, nearer to Rosie's school. It had three bedrooms, but the third one was tiny, like a box room. Deborah Vine waited until Rosie had left in the morning before she packed away Joanna's things. She did it methodically, lifting soft piles of vests and shirts into boxes, folding up dresses and skirts and tying them into bin bags, trying not to look at the pink plastic dolls with their long manes of nylon hair and their fixed, staring eyes. In the new computer-enhanced image, Joanna looked quite composed, as if her childish anxiety had slipped away from her. Her chipped tooth had been replaced with an undamaged one.

• • •

Rosie started her periods. She shaved her legs. She fell in love for the first time, with a boy who barely knew she existed. She wrote her diary under her bedcovers and locked it with a silver key. She watched her mother dating a stranger with a bristly brown beard and pretended she didn't mind. She poured her father's drink down the sink, though she knew it would do no good. She went to her grandmother's funeral and read a poem by Tennyson in a quiet voice no one could really hear. She cut her hair short and started going out with the boy she had been so smitten with when she was younger, but he couldn't live up to her idea of him. She kept a small pile of printouts in her underwear drawer: Joanna at six, seven, eight, nine. Joanna at thirteen. She thought her sister looked exactly like *she* did, and for some reason this made her feel worse.

"She's dead." Deborah's voice was flat, quite calm.

"Have you come all this way to tell me that?"

"I thought we owed each other at least that much, Richard. Let her go."

"You don't know she's dead. You're just abandoning her."

"No."

"Because you've found a new husband and now . . ." His glance at her pregnant belly was full of disgust. "Now you're going to have another happy family."

"Richard."

"And forget all about her."

"That's not fair. It's been eight years. Life has to go on, for all of us."

"*Life has to go on.* Are you going to tell me that this is what Joanna would have wanted?"

"Joanna was five when we lost her."

"When *you* lost her."

Deborah stood up, thin legs on high heels and a round stomach pushing at her shirt. He could see her belly button. Her mouth was a thin, trembling line. "You bastard," she said.

"And now you're deserting her."

"You want me to destroy myself as well?"

"Why not? Anything rather than *life has to go on*. But don't worry. I'm still waiting."

When Rosie went to university she called herself Rosalind Teale, taking her stepfather's name. She didn't tell her father. She still loved him, though she was scared by his chaotic, unchanging grief. She didn't want anyone to say, "Rosie Vine? Why does that ring a bell?" Even though there was less and less chance of that. Joanna had melted into the past, was a wisp of memory now, a forgotten celebrity, a one-hit wonder. Sometimes, Rosie wondered if her sister was just a dream.

Deborah Teale—Vine, as was—prayed secretly, fiercely, for a son, not a daughter. But first Abbie and then Lauren arrived. She crouched over their baskets at nights to hear them breathe; she clutched at their hands. She wouldn't let them out of her sight. They reached Joanna, they overtook her and they left her behind. In the attic, the boxes of Joanna's clothes stood unopened.

The case was never actually closed. Nobody made a decision. But there was less and less to report. Officers were reassigned. Meetings became more sporadic, then merged into other meetings, and then the case wasn't mentioned at all.

Rosie, Rosie. Wait for me!

AVAILABLE FROM PENGUIN BOOKS

The Frieda Klein Mysteries

Blue Monday

When five-year-old Matthew Farraday is abducted,
psychotherapist Frieda Klein finds herself serving as the reluctant
sidekick of Detective Chief Inspector Karlsson at the center of a
desperate race to find the kidnapper.

Tuesday's Gone

In *Tuesday's Gone,* the solitary London psychotherapist returns
in a page-turning thriller even more twisted than the first in the
series, *Blue Monday.* Frieda can't help but feel that her victim was
killed to involve her in the investigation and that her past isn't
done with her yet. Is Frieda the next victim?

Waiting for Wednesday

In the third volume of the bestselling Frieda Klein series, the
brilliant but troubled London psychotherapist returns—only to
journey into a darkness from which there may be no return.

Thursday's Children

In *Thursday's Children,* Frieda faces her most personal case yet
when a former classmate appears at Frieda's door, begging for her
help. But confronting the ghosts of the past turns out to be more
dangerous than she ever expected.

**PENGUIN
BOOKS**